The Termination Clause

The Termination Clause
A Novel

Tom LaMarr

Owl Canyon Press

© 2020 by Tom LaMarr

First Edition, 2020
All Rights Reserved
Library of Congress Cataloging-in-Publication Data

LaMarr, Tom
The Termination Clause — 1st ed.
p. cm.

ISBN: 978-1-952085-02-4
Library of Congress Control Number: 2020946564

Owl Canyon Press
Boulder, Colorado

Disclaimer

According to unnamed sources, a certain Black Lab is seeking legal counsel. Other than that, all characters and situations herein are creative inventions. Mr. LaMarr's real-life writer friends are quite likable folks with more discipline and talent than any ten characters in *The Termination Clause*, and his favorite high school English teacher is much cooler than the one depicted in these pages. Regarding the Black Lab, the author offers no comment.

For Anne

Chapter 1
⌘

WHAT GOES UP

The assassin seemed strangely closed minded for someone who, in killing people for a living, clearly rejected conventional morality. Yet logic rolled off the hulking stranger much as the rain was doing. The man had a job; he planned to complete it. Clay would be wise to stop wasting his fucking breath, considering, as the killer maintained, there was so little of it remaining.

"But this, this is crazy." The words came out anyway, hurriedly escaping, a bit high in pitch, a recording sped up. "I didn't do anything."

The two men shared a metal grid platform some 200 feet above the ground, placing them near the top of Duchaine's tallest communications tower—and much too close to the punishing storm clouds. Maybe eight feet across, the square platform stopped at an ice-cold handrail that didn't seem high enough to prevent a sudden slip on wet iron from morphing into a 200-foot plunge. Decking the tower above and below, cell antennae had been slapped on in no apparent order, with some clustered together and others very much alone, giving the overall feel of a grade schooler's art project.

"Whatever you're getting, I'll triple it." Clay spoke loudly too, to counter the freight train pounding in his head, steel on steel, wheels hitting rail joints. "You know I've got the money."

The assassin stared through him as if he were already a ghost.

"Fifty, no, one-hundred thousand. That's pretty good pay for walking away."

Hard to believe it was still afternoon. The dense gray drizzle blocked out sun and sky, much as it concealed the streets of his hometown, spreading outward from the base of the tower so far below. Take away the rain and he would see his old high school, a quasi-castle with gray stone spires defending its four corners. He'd see the rolling green ridge that hid the downtown and

Mississippi River. He might even see Jacques Duchaine's Grave, an oversized rook chess piece crowning a bluff to watch over the mouth of Crayfish Creek. The weathered limestone monument honored the city's namesake, a French-Canadian trapper responsible for discovering the area a mere 98 centuries after the Native Americans had. Clay's hometown, Clay's favorite place.

Absorbing another body-wide shiver, he doubted he'd ever felt this cold, even as measured against 34 Wisconsin winters. His clothing and hair were soaked like laundry pulled out mid-cycle, same for the killer's dark gray trench coat. Off in the distance, a faint ball of lightning expanded and faded. He waited for the rumble of thunder, two seconds, three.

"Referrals are key to my business." The assassin spoke slowly in a deep, crushed-gravel voice. "You might say they're the butter on my bread." Clay thought he detected a slight southern accent although this could have just been the leisurely pace of his delivery. The killer seemed to value preciseness, which didn't bode well for his target. "If I don't produce each and every time," the man said, "I don't get called." His head was disproportionately wide like a slumping, post-Halloween Jack o' Lantern, even if Clay couldn't remember seeing one quite this scary. The eyes were dark, the eyebrows bushy and wild as if making up for the lack of hair on the glistening dome above them. A purple scar bisected the left cheek. "Shoot or scoot. It's not unlike being an actor."

"Actors are permitted an occasional flop." Leaning back on the handrail, Clay shuddered as the cold metal pressed against his wet shirt back. "You know it makes no sense to kill me. Not in the slightest." He shook a small inland sea from his hair. "Who gets killed for not finishing a novel?"

"I have to assume that's a rhetorical question," the assassin said, "because we both know I'm looking at the answer."

"You know I don't deserve this."

"I hear that a lot." The assassin paused to wipe his face with a sleeve. "What matters here," he resumed, "is someone thinks you do. It's not like I selected your name at random on Facebook."

Here, the assassin had a point: this perilous crossing of paths had not simply happened by chance. Hundreds of seemingly inconsequential inter-sections had, by necessity, preceded this big one. Clay's life, in the fashion of most other lives, had revealed itself like an intricate online map scrolling into view with obstinate slowness. Ever so gradually, blind turns replaced crossroads, which in turn gave way to poorly marked exit ramps, pointless detours, and crushing dead ends that falsely advertised themselves as short-cuts. If the choices had seemed overwhelming at times, with even the smallest of these inviting almost infinite permutations, this made it even more remarkable that Clay had selected the only possible combination of routes that could have placed him on this iron-mesh tower platform trembling before a man who intended to end his life while pummeled by winds as cruel as the rain, especially when those winds turned the rain on its side.

The waterlogged trench coat bulged at sharp angles. Weapons, but what? This guy liked having options at hand. Clay knew this from seeing a truncheon and automatic rifle—and from being tased when the killer first reached the tower's top platform. In the ogre's defense, Clay had been kicking his head at the time, trying to prevent him from climbing out of the ladder's narrow casing. The jolt burned like fire for more than a minute. When it eased up, the man was standing over Clay whose body had reflexively curled up in a fetal position. He still felt pain in his back and legs where the killer's boot had administered karma, along with several bonus kicks.

A fresh, frigid gust cut straight through Clay's skull. Thoughts broke loose, collided, collapsed. He needed to say something. One more distraction. One last delay. Anything.

"You, you speak well for a professional killer."

"Because?" The stranger seemed to consider his words. "I'm supposed to be your stereotypical movie villain?"

"I didn't say that." The tower groaned, producing a loud, creaking metallic sound. "Still—"

"Philosophy major," the killer said. "What was I supposed to do?" The man's right hand disappeared beneath the lapel of his coat. "I really hate to kill and run but you and I have got something to finish."

Which almost struck Clay as funny given that he was facing his imminent demise precisely because he was not good at finishing things. "Someone could have told me this was the penalty for failing to deliver," he protested. "That might have provided incentive."

"I'm going to need one thing from you." The assassin was lighting a cigarette, or trying, sabotaged by rain. He had not retrieved a weapon. Clay no longer detected a southern accent. "One simple act."

"Like?"

"For you to fall down this ladder. All the way down, make it look like an accident. I can knock you unconscious first if you like, make it pain free. I'm not a monster."

Clay slid a few inches left on the handrail, away from the killer. "I'll give you all the money that's left. My Gold Wing, yours. The Volvo, too."

The stranger smirked. "Volvo's are for college professors, hardly my choice of wheels. Liberals, too. Liberals with bumper stickers—"

"We're talking almost $140,000. You won't have to keep the Volvo."

"Liberals with bumper stickers who drive three miles under the speed limit."

Clay spoke even faster than before. "All I need would be, say, twenty thousand. To help me disappear and start a new life in Mexico. The rest I withdraw and give straight to you. We place my empty wallet and bloody clothes on the river bank down by the dog track, leaving the cops something to play with."

"You've given this some thought. I'll grant you that." The man gave up on lighting his wet cigarette. He threw it past Clay's head where it would fall through the darkness until hitting the ground with much more gentleness than a human body. "But here's a thought. How 'bout you shut the fuck up and let me whack you good just once over the head? Swift and efficient. Everyone happy."

"*All* the money. Every last cent."

"Your other choice is for me to demonstrate the tools of my trade, slowly, one at a time. It's more work for me but ends the same way, with you taking a tumble. That was a biggie for my client, making it look like an accident."

"No one will believe it."

The killer shook his head. "We both know what the coroners and insurance inspectors are going to say, I mean besides 'He looks like a squirrel squished by a car.' They're going to conclude, 'He must have been crazy to climb that big thing in a storm. But he was a writer. They're not exactly known for common sense.'"

Fresh cranial pounding dropped Clay to his knees. "I'm sorry I fucked up so badly," he whispered, his eyes tightly closed. "Forgive me, Marta. I wanted to grow old with you."

"Get back on your feet. Go out with some dignity."

"I made so many mistakes."

"We all make mistakes," the assassin said. "It's part of being human."

"That may be true," said Clay, his voice cracking, "but I wish I'd made better ones."

***

It had been warm and cloudless two years before when Clay met Randolph J. Simper for lunch at the most expensive restaurant in Duchaine. Overlooking the Mississippi River valley, Jacques D's Supper Club was named for the French-Canadian trapper turned mining magnate who paddled there by canoe in 1782 to outfox the Fox Indians. The story Clay had grown up with had Jacques introducing himself as a deity, then supporting his claim by pouring kerosene on Crayfish Creek and setting fire to the water. His divinity established, he demanded the Fox dig mines in the limestone bluffs to excavate lead on his behalf. During the centuries that followed, a lot of things got named after Jacques Duchaine, starting of course with the city of Duchaine and including Clay's high school and college. The list also laid claim to the much smaller town of West Duchaine across the river in Iowa as well as the distinctive gray steel-truss Jacques Duchaine Bridge that connected West Duchaine to real Duchaine. Locals on both sides of the river still referred to the manmade caves that pocked the bluffs as foxholes.

Sitting across from Randolph at a round table set for two, Clay had been trying to not seem *too* impressed but this required work on his part. Not only did their table boast the restaurant's best view—they sat only feet from the wall of tall windows opening onto a postcard-perfect panorama—it was also separated from the nearest tables by at least eight yards in any direction. From his comfortably padded seat, Clay could see the river valley stretching north to Lock and Dam #8. He saw the marina and City Island dog track.

"How's writing?" asked Randolph as he folded his cloth napkin and tucked it into his sky-blue jacket collar as a well-behaved five-year-old might do at Thanksgiving dinner. The image fit Randolph, who looked considerably younger than his 32 years. His complexion was every bit as pale as it had been in high school and his finely curled auburn hair still bushed out on both sides. His puffy cheeks remained a wind-chafed red, creating the extremely misleading impression of chubbiness.

"It gives me something to do," Clay said. "How's being a quasi-retired zillionaire software genius?"

"Fulfilling for the most part." As known to everyone in Duchaine, Randolph had invented the hugely successful StripOff App for smart phones that allowed users to take photos of fully clothed human beings and create highly detailed nude approximations. Although body size was non-negotiable—Randolph, it was said, took pride in the app's "realism"—users could adjust for nipple width and pigmentation, color and proliferation of pubic hair, and penis length. These customizations, it was assumed, revealed whether users despised or desired the subject being StripOffed. Users were also known to employ these to upgrade their own appendages. The customizations did one more thing, and that was to make Randolph what Duchainers call a shitload of money. The initial download apparently didn't cost much but the resulting addiction demanded an expensive series of must-have upgrades. Clay had read several articles about Randolph's "monster" and how it enabled its handlers to take sexual fantasies to new, invasive extremes. And while he didn't understand the facial and body morphing technology of Randolph's 3D animation technology, he did understand that his old classmate had reset the bar for sexual objectification.

"Is it true," Clay asked, "you really moved back here to stay?"

Randolph said, "I wanted to be close to friends," which struck Clay as funny, because apart from himself Clay couldn't remember Randolph having friends at Duchaine Senior High. What he did remember was a tribesman assigned to a very wrong tribe: nervous, withdrawn, quick to back down from any threat.

An eagle swooped down just beyond the wall of glass to snatch a rabbit and carry it off. This prompted a collective "Whoa" from the other diners with tables close to windows. Shooting straight up, the bird and its prey disappeared completely from sight. Seconds later, a misshapen furry meteor fell to Earth. The eagle had dropped the rabbit, letting go in midair to deliberately kill or maim its victim, or more perversely, to play with its food. The drama struck Clay as both impressive and awful, reflective of a planet where intelligent life emerged and evolved yet never got past eating itself. It was the ultimate expression of power. *I am going to devour you... after I fuck you up.*

The raptor swooped down to reclaim its prize. "Daddy, you've got to help," a young girl cried from behind Clay. "He's hurting the bunny." Good thing, thought Clay, these windows are thick. She can't hear the rabbit screaming, which is what rabbits do when they realize they were right to fear carnivores all along. Good thing, he amended the thought, I can't hear it either.

Neither captor nor critter returned after this, and the tables nearby stayed silent. Randolph, strangely, had shown no reaction to the food-chain demo, yet had seemed to cringe, if ever so slightly, at hearing the sound of a child's voice inside a restaurant. He followed this by forcefully placing his fork on his plate, producing a loud deliberate clink.

"You didn't really answer my first question," he resumed now while jerkily adjusting his shirt's collar with pale, slender fingers. "What are you working on? Is it funny like *Give Me a Second While I Execute the Dog?*" This was Clay's first and so-far only book, his collection of *Musings, Essays, and Actual Stories* published two summers before by Wisconsin's prestigious Small Packages Press. The book had been a regional success: Number One in Madison; Eighteen in Chicago. Good reviews popped up in Tampa, Fresno, and several other cities outside the Midwest. A few ended with great predictions for Clay's first novel, the one promised in the brief author bio on the book's paper jacket. Clay's publisher helped negotiate the sale of television-serial rights for the title story. The future looked good, or had at the time.

The main course arrived, six plates of it, and Randolph fought an impulse to sneeze, scrunching his nose as that rabbit may well have been doing before his day went south, while daintily retrieving the matching sky-blue handkerchief Clay had not noticed before from a breast pocket. Resurveying Randolph's overall appearance, Clay mused that were he the multi-millionaire engineer-inventor trading California for Wisconsin he wouldn't have bothered packing the yacht club attire.

Clay was equally perplexed by the cologne overkill. Which wasn't to say it smelled bad; obscenely rich app inventors didn't send their personal shoppers out for Old Spice. But smell it did, more than holding its own against the many competing aromas of a bustling restaurant. Was Clay getting a whiff of the insecurity no amount of money could purchase away: the last, lingering scent of high school? Clay even thought he detected a touch of makeup beneath Randolph's eyes. His extremely pale skin, now fully recovered from acne, seemed almost to shine, the way Marta's did right after she applied moisturizing lotion.

"Allergies," Randolph apologized before blowing his nose—daintily again. He folded the handkerchief and tucked it neatly away. "I have a proposal," he said. "I want to invest in your novel."

Clay started to laugh but Randolph stopped him with an outstretched palm. "Hear me out, old friend. Hear me out."

Chapter 2

⌘

A LA HORA DE LA CENA DESPEDIDA
(DISMISSED AT DINNER)

What Randolph J. Simper proposed was to give Clay an advance in exchange for a percentage of the profits from the novel once published. It would be a sizable investment by most standards—the number Randolph had in mind contained six digits. Upon hearing the offer, Clay nearly spouted, "Where do I sign?" but held himself back, knowing he should talk with Marta first. He took a deep breath, and doing his best to project an aura of calm, told Randolph he would consider the proposal. Randolph suggested he do just that. They would meet again at that very table "in exactly one week."

Unable to believe his luck, Clay turned his focus toward not grinning like an idiot who had just been voted Chief Idiot. Having time to write; it was all he craved. Having the time to come up with a plot compelling enough to carry an entire novel, money would buy this. His teaching job at Duchaine University had turned out to be real work. Students expected him to read and grade their work, no matter how unreadable or appropriated. And here sat Randolph J. Simper, multi-multi-millionaire, offering to rectify this grave injustice.

With business out of the way, Randolph seemed to relax, if only slightly. He ordered an iced tea and vodka—"Grey Goose, of course"—and asked Clay questions about other Duchaine Senior alumni. "What was that I read about Peanut Booth's parachuting accident?" "Is it true Hound Dog got married again?" Then, between carefully measured bites of Herb Braised Rainbow Trout with Orange-Saffron Sauce, he asked one pertaining to Clay.

"So, you and Martha? Children?"

Looking up from his own Buttery Lobster Tuesday Lunch Special, Clay explained they were waiting for Marta to finish her MBA at the University of Wisconsin's Duchaine Annex. Randolph smiled when Clay added, "She says she'll need to be making more money when she has *two* children to feed."

"So... *Marta*, what's that?"

"Same wife, new name. She dropped the *h* on her birthday last year, stopped going by Martha. It's part of reclaiming her Latino heritage. She was adopted, you know. Honduras."

"I did know that, of course." Randolph placed his emphasis on the last two words. "We dated briefly in high school. I'm sure you knew that."

Clay kept his comment, "Twice... you went out with her *twice*, as part of a *group*, the year before I got to know her," to himself, but should have said something to prevent Randolph from making the conversation even more awkward, which Randolph did by saying, "That was a long time ago and as we both know it never went anywhere. I've known lots of girls since then, of course." Which made him sound like anything but someone who'd known lots of women. "Randolph likes the ladies, and the ladies like Randolph."

He stopped to sip his vodka and iced tea, and Clay used the break to dilute the discomfort. "People with kids can be strange," he said, prefacing an anecdote from *Give Me a Second While I Execute the Dog*. "We were at a Christmas party for Marta's work a few years back. When the host held out a plate of holiday treats, I selected what seemed like an ordinary frosted Christmas cookie. It was a choice I immediately regretted. 'This cookie!' I sputtered. 'What is it?' The host replied, 'My daughter baked those.' This left me to ask, 'Out of what?' The answer to my seemingly innocent question was soy-based wheat substitute—in a Christmas cookie, for Christ's sake."

Randolph smiled, an expression that made him look uncomfortable.

"Wait, it gets worse. She told me the frosting was a fine, imported Brie. Dyed with all-natural food color."

Randolph laughed, almost too enthusiastically. "That's rich, my friend. That's rich."

The now beaming author ordered his own vodka and iced tea to be sociable—"Grey Goose, of course"—and shared a second anecdotal excerpt. His lobster grew cold.

The first thing Clay did after getting home was hang his suit jacket neatly in the bedroom closet while retaining his dress shirt and pants. He enjoyed wearing decent clothes even at home, just as he enjoyed shopping for them, especially when Marta drove with him to Madison's upscale Waterside Mall. Dressing well made him feel organized and efficient even if that efficiency was often wasted on grading papers.

He walked back downstairs to his office where he intended to work on his novel, the very novel Randolph wanted to make part of his portfolio. As of that mild spring Tuesday afternoon, Clay had compiled sixteen pages of notes, most having to do with character development. His primary creations, Jared Purvis and Pita Wishart, had been together five years. She was finishing college while he struggled as a surrealist painter who used "reclaimed objects" as his canvas. Jared wanted to start a family but something kept them waiting, something more than Pita's studies, and that something was the missing storyline they desperately needed to become larger than life and worthy of novelization.

Like Marta and everyone else who had ever believed in his talent, Jared and Pita were waiting on Clay. They weren't impressed that six of his discarded plots had recycled into short stories and essays, three of which had been published in respected literary journals like *Prairie Roots* and *Boston Prep.* "Author, author, it's us, your characters. Some marching orders, please." Now, at last, these were coming.

With all the other demands on his time and thought, how could anyone think it fair that freshman PE majors rejected by the University of Wisconsin needed their papers graded so they could grudgingly fulfill their core English requirement? Clay felt like he was spinning his wheels in a snowbank, a trap made slicker and deeper with each attempt to move forward. He needed a great plot, one that would sustain an entire novel, pulling him to dry ground like a friend with a winch on his pickup. Now, thanks to Randolph J. Simper, he could already feel his tires breaking free from the slick, deep ruts.

Sinking back into the ergonomically designed faux-leather chair that invited sleep as much as it did productivity, Clay checked his email and tinkered with Paragraph Six.

Jared couldn't believe his luck in finding a discarded black rotary phone next to a neighbor's garbage bin.

Break time followed: quick trip to the kitchen where Clay enjoyed his hard-earned, once-a-day sweet, on this particular afternoon a three-tablespoon serving of double-dark chocolate gelato. He should have been enjoying his even rarer once-a-week indulgence—Tuesday was the day for it—but Hey Howdy Family Grocers had been out of cream-filled long johns, a problem that had ranked as a major disappointment at 11:15 that morning but now seemed significantly less significant in the buttery aftermath of lunch.

Placing the container back in the freezer, he leaned in over his Black Lab, Argos, who almost completely concealed the small rug meant to catch food that spilled out of the cluttered refrigerator—a duty the dog had assumed. Losing his balance ever so slightly, Clay came close to stepping on a furry fold of flesh. Looking up, the dog clicked its tongue with great force, mimicking the sound of a massive army retreating through slushy snow in boots sticking like plungers. Except for the fact that Argos was louder. He wanted gelato. He wanted gelato straight from the container.

"Enough, dog. Save it for Pavlov."

Back at his desk, Clay yawned, and yawned again. His screen read *3:18*. In need of fresh air, he walked Argos around the block. Three driveways from home, the dog paused to pee on Clay's pant leg and shoe. "Damn, buddy, we need to work on your walk etiquette. Inanimate objects… garbage cans, trees… these are appropriate targets. My leg not so much. You're supposed to aim *away* from your owner."

At 4:15, wearing fresh slacks and socks, he typed an all-new paragraph that showed promise as an essay even if it represented a distraction from the novel he should have been writing. It concerned long john pastries and how the local Hey Howdy supermarket always sold out of the white frosted ones with white cream fillings first thing every morning. Why, Clay's paragraph demanded to know, did the Hey Howdy bakers even bother with the lesser pastries that sat drying in the display case all day when they could increase their profits by simply doubling their cream-filled long john output?

Writing this left him feeling hungry. But he would exercise restraint and wait for dinner. After all, what was a writer without discipline? Proud of himself for shedding the two pounds he'd put on over the winter, Clay knew it would be even easier to exercise discipline once he was no longer required to keep himself awake to read student papers the dog could have written.

May 25th. Last day of the semester. When better to throw off his shackles? Just over a month away, a mere 32 days, and he'd be emancipated from these demands on his time… his *writing time*. He considered one more bonus of sudden success: a loving partner taking breaks from her otherwise endless studies to show how much she appreciated a great American novelist in the making. How could she not be impressed that someone so thoroughly believed in Clay's talent as to invest $200,000? Could there be a more powerful aphrodisiac? Like lighting a match, then dropping it in a swimming pool filled with however much kerosene you can buy for $200,000, it would more than reignite the once mighty inferno that now barely smoldered, his wife having traded her passion for managerial economics, applied statistics, and business law. There he was, a 32-year-old man with fully working parts, the most important of which had been mostly laid off. *To have and to hold*, that was the vow. He did not recall anything about holding off, holding it in, or holding tight.

He reminded himself she would soon have the summer off from her studies, a prospect which, before Randolph's offer, had dominated his thoughts. Three months of animal bliss and going out for Chinese food and walking on the floodwall just below the dam. He and Marta would celebrate the Third of July together, sharing a blanket on Cleveland Park's limestone overlook as skyrockets released their colorful, orgasmic explosions above the river valley. (Duchaine, like other smaller cities, contracted their fireworks displays one day early to avoid competing with Des Moines and Madison and their respective budgets.)

Clay had also booked reservations for a sunset cruise on the Pride of Duchaine to celebrate Marta's birthday in June, their ninth anniversary having been sacrificed on the altar of her advanced degree.

Come fall, however, the oppressive schedule would return, with Marta spending most of her time away from home, even when she was physically present. She faced two additional years of MBA classes, culminating in a collaborative study group project that counted for much of her final grade.

Argos followed Clay to his office and claimed a spot beside the swiveling desk chair, placing his snout in very close proximity—an eighth of an inch or less—to the thigh of his gelato hoarding master. "Wasn't there more in the freezer?" the dog seemed to be asking. "You could go back and get what's left, share it with a friend." Clay sighed, and glancing at the clock in the screen's lower right corner, knew he needed to get back to his teaching work. Even if he didn't have class until early the following morning, he had skimmed only three of the twenty-six essays he was supposed to mark up and grade.

Leaning back in his chair—it really was comfortable—he imagined Marta appearing in his doorway, then leaning against the frame while she assessed the situation through piercing, dark brown eyes. Since he was the one doing the imagining, he dressed her thin shapely body in a sleeveless T-shirt and very short shorts, none of which stopped her from saying, "Aren't you supposed to be working? For someone who complains about not having enough time, you sure do a lot of sitting around."

He examined his surroundings, zooming in on the one suggestion of clutter. He kept his office neat; as with his choice of dress, he saw no value in sloppiness. Yet there stood a stack of unread books rising like a jagged rock formation sculpted by eons of wind. The twenty-some titles and author names visible on the side facing him seemed to beg, "Notice me. Read me." But while Clay did in fact notice these books, he would not likely read them unless he accepted the offer from Randolph, the one that gave him time to catch up on everything that needed catching up, starting with his gifting the rest of humanity a new novel for their stacks.

"If you're going to write," Clay had been telling new students for as long as he'd been teaching creative writing courses, "you need to read. Dickens. Twain. Atwood. Read the classics. Read the shit. Most of all, read." With

Randolph's help, he could now undo years of ignoring his own advice.

Argos whimpered, announcing he wished to be fed one hour ahead of schedule. "Have some dignity," Clay said before finally relenting and returning to the kitchen to give the dog a bowl of Cheerios that were just on the cusp of getting stale. Argos gulped it down with all the speed and finesse of a wood chipper. "Slow down, boy. Slow down," Clay cajoled him. "Food is meant to be tasted." The dog was supposed to be losing weight but sadly lacked the discipline to carry it off. Only the night before, Marta had noted, "He's big as the couch," prompting Clay to add, "and almost as smart."

At five o'clock, Clay began reading his students' essays. At 5:20, after feeding Argos his official dog-food dinner, he turned his attention to human dinner, the making of which he did each Tuesday. Seeing the need for something celebratory—and still savoring the memory of his seafood lunch—he pulled up a favorite online recipe, jalapeño shrimp scampi.

Home from her day at the Wisconsin Workforce Development Center, Marta ran upstairs, which proved a good thing as she soon appeared in pajamas that would have popped up very near the top of Google search results for *sexy negligee*. She gave him a kiss that added to the promise. Was she planning to skip her study group that night? Highly motivated, he prepared dinner quickly.

"Shrimp scampi?" she said, leaning over the pan to take in the aroma. "What's the occasion?"

"My big, mysterious lunch. That was today."

"With Randy Simper? Oh God, you didn't invite him for dinner?"

"Of course not," Clay said. "And he calls himself Randolph now."

"Hmm," said the woman who had reinvented herself by changing her own first name.

"He wants to invest in my writing."

Marta looked confused.

"Randolph's a huge fan of my first book." Clay looked away, spatula in hand, to shovel the shrimp onto a platter. "He's read it five times."

He placed dinner at the center of their small glass table. Next to it, a fat faux candle, molded of plastic and battery-operated, did its best to flicker convincingly.

Marta took her seat. "But investing in your writing? Did you ask why?"

"As a matter of fact, yes. Randolph said he wants to see a Clay Turner novel as much as I do. If he gets a return, so be it, he would consider this a bonus. The bigger reward would come with knowing he played a part in its creation. He plans to give me $200,000."

"Wow," said Marta.

"Wow is correct," said Clay. "This, after all, is everything I've needed, everything I've hoped for. A break from teaching, more time to write."

"You know he went out with me a few times in high school," Marta continued, "back when we were juniors."

"As part of a group," Clay quickly inserted. "Getting pizza with friends."

She seemed to consider her next words with care. "I know it was a lifetime ago but when I told Randy there would be no third time, he told me I was making a big mistake. I know it sounds crazy, but is he showing off his wealth now, showing me I did make that mistake?"

"You would have been—what?—sixteen? That's a long time for him to hold onto something like that. And what reason would he have to think you're unhappy? If we're going to trace his motives back to high school, I was one of the few kids who didn't ignore him or treat him like a jerk. He could just as likely be doing this as a way to say thanks." He paused, realized he should hold onto his next comment, then said it anyway: "A lot of kids thought he was gay. Closeted away for who knew why."

"It's funny. My parents didn't care for him *un poco.*" This, inserting occasional Spanish into her speech (and more-than-occasional Spanish whenever she argued or drank a third Chardonnay) was something Marta had been doing since removing the *h* from her given first name. Adopted as a baby, the woman who would become Clay's wife grew up as Will and Winnie Jewell's only daughter in a comfortable, upper middle class home that lacked even the slightest nod to her Latin heritage. While residing in that house close to Eagle's Nest Park, she became a beautiful woman with dark eyes and darker hair and flesh boasting a smooth, olive-bronze complexion that became even more stunning during long Wisconsin winters when all the other local flesh, or the little that could be seen of it without help from StripOff, turned nearly as pale as the much-too-frequent snow. Now, at thirty-two and in her tenth year of marriage, Marta still looked twenty, unlike the husband who lugged around an increasingly bulging stomach and had started balding near the back of his *muy* pale skull.

Adding to the inequality in their marriage, fitness came easily to Marta, keeping her slender in all the right places without ever once forcing her to drink a diet pop. She also benefitted from a total lack of alcoholism, boasting the superhuman ability to go weeks without wine or beer. She profited, too, from a talent for self-deception in that she sincerely believed healthy foods did not taste awful. She rejected Clay's argument that if Cheetos and Boston Cream Pies turned out to be the healthiest choice for human nourishment no sane person would ever even glance at kale again.

Clay was still handsome enough, he reminded himself, with his closely shaved wisp of a beard, his brown hair falling into slightly disheveled bangs while covering the tops of his ears, and his own dark eyes that, in combination with his drooping eyebrows, had once been described by a drunken older woman in a bar as "bedroom eyes." But he wasn't as handsome as when he got married. He was hardly stunning like Marta.

"My parents wondered what anyone could see in someone like Randy," she said next. "Thinking back, wasn't it their job to protect me from English majors and not future software titans? I suppose it's a good thing for both of us that high school girls don't take things like earning potential into account."

Marta laughed to show she was joking, but Clay couldn't help but feel the sting.

"I know it's all strange," he resumed. "But I think he's doing this for the reason he said: he loves my writing. He's got more money than everyone else in this town put together. If he thinks it would be fun to pour a little bit of that money into something with true, lasting value, who are we to say no?"

"Maybe he's always been attracted to *you*." Marta reprised her just-kidding laugh. Never mind that Clay had entertained this very thought while eating lunch at Jacques D's. "Or maybe he's looking for a tax write-off."

"Randolph's return, if there is one, would be 30% of the advance and 10% of subsequent profits, including sales and movie rights. Money from public appearances would stay in our pockets."

"You've never made any money from public appearances."

"But if I did—"

"He really offered you $200,000?"

"Yes, or to put it more temptingly, four years of earning $20,000 more than I would have made at Douche U."

"I'm not trying to be negative," Marta said. "We all know you have the talent. But my workday went on forever and this just feels weird. Does he know how writing works? Seriously, since when have you expected to get rich your first time out with a novel? Does he know he'll probably lose most of his investment?"

"And maybe he'll make it back. If not, he gets a legacy. Randolph J. Simper, patron of the arts. Randolph J. Simper, lover of lit."

"It still sounds like *mucho* pressure," Marta observed.

"Not compared to writing while having to prepare lessons and grade papers and read whiny emails from students who somehow forgot to write those papers."

"I don't know, it sounds a bit risky, taking $200,000 out of someone else's pocket—"

"*Deep* pocket."

"All the more reason to not fall in."

"What about *your* scholarship?" Clay asked the MBA student who never exhibited any qualms about accepting her La Excelencia Scholarship for Midwestern Hispanic Graduate Students. "I thought that was the MBA motto: Never say no to money."

"What if you can't produce? What if there's no book... *no legacy*? Won't Randy want his advance back? If you're thinking a rich person won't miss a fifth of a million dollars, you're certifiably *loco*. Rich people like their money."

"Freed from distractions, I'll finish the book. Two years tops. Another year to see it in print. In the meantime, we would have paid off my student loan, got rid of your car loan."

Marta was silent for a moment. "What if we both took a few days to think about this? Who knows? Maybe it's a great idea... it's just such a... *extraña sorpresa*. We can talk over the weekend."

"He gave me a week. We're going to meet at Jacques D's next Tuesday. That's when I give him my answer."

Clay took a bite of shrimp, followed by a sip of tea. Exhibiting typical Argos behavior, the dog licked Clay's pant leg in an attempt to extract some scampi flavor from his so-called master's flesh. Were Argos bigger, Clay knew, the dog wouldn't stop at licking. Clay would be missing his shin.

"Argos, Argos," he muttered, "show some restraint. You're better than that."

Marta glanced at the microwave clock. "*Mierda*, seven o'clock. I've got to hit the books." In a few hours, Clay knew, she'd be asking him to bend down under the overhead lamp to help solve indecipherable mathematical equations that could have been created by cats sleeping on laptop keyboards. "You're supposed to be *inteligente*," she would say from the aura that reminded Clay of a streetlight in foggy darkness as it illuminated Marta's hunched over figure at the plain wooden table in the corner of their otherwise dark bedroom. "What am I missing here?"

"A very long series of random numbers, letters, and symbols," he would reply. "How can this matter to anyone?"

Now pushing aside his own plate, Clay said, "I thought you guys had study group tonight."

"Wednesday. Always Wednesday."

Clay pictured his wife sitting at the broad, round Bolivian rosewood table in the Chamber of Commerce meeting room—on loan to the study group from the member who happened also to be Chamber President—while gazing back at six successful men of business who shared her desire to multiply their successes. They all thought Marta was hot; Clay was sure of that one detail. It made him insecure.

"The scampi," Clay said. "I thought it was pretty good."

"Mine could have been spicier," she said. "But it was *muy delicioso*. At least you didn't add sugar. You're such a slave to your sweet tooth; the closer something tastes to a doughnut, the more you enjoy it."

"Long johns," Clay corrected her. "I love those long johns they bake at Hey Howdy. My big, once weekly treat."

"*Sí*," said Marta. "The pure sugar pastry injected with a sugar filling."

"It's the only pure sugar pastry they sell out of by nine each morning. You'd think someone there would realize that long johns, unlike some of their lesser pastries, deserve more shelf space. It would make a good study for your group at school."

Marta smiled and shook her head. "Just don't tell me it's the theme of a new essay." She got up to leave, but stopped first at his side of the table. She bent down to give him a long, garlicky kiss that intensified his desire to see her play truant from her studies. Straightening back up, she said, "Who knows? Maybe Randy is serious about wanting to see you succeed. Everyone knows you're a good writer."

With that, she left him alone with Argos, who at least helped clean up by sucking down the shrimp tails and licking the pan and plates. "Your diet," Clay admonished the dog. "I really don't know what to do with you."

Chapter 3
⌘

THE KNIGHT IN HAND-TAILORED ARMOR

Following his lunch with Clay, Randolph J. Simper made his way home on the soft-leather backseat of a silver stretch limo hand-assembled to order in L'Aquila, Italy. Hidden from the world behind dark tinted windows, he remained silent even as he and his driver passed through the high iron gate of his Victorian-style mansion—a mansion identical in style and design to his $40,000,000 California manor despite his paying only 12.5 to have this one constructed on a high green hill just east of Duchaine. The mansion itself had no lawn, only garden after garden of varied, vibrant flowers. Per research commissioned by Randolph, women liked flowers.

Dropped off at the front door, he took a deep breath and entered the foyer where the air stayed a comfortable 67 degrees and the humidity was permanently set at 34%—the prescription for maintaining a youthful appearance as determined by a team of biologists in Randolph's employ. The mansion's 42 dimly-lit, high-ceilinged rooms that would have passed for auditoriums in a school or city building were filled with Randolph's favorite music choice, which was none. Randolph J. Simper preferred silence.

Two attractive Hispanic women with long dark hair silently welcomed him home by applying an exotic moisturizing lotion to his face. Two men with neatly trimmed brown beards appeared, each bearing a younger, slightly thinner resemblance to the author Randy had just taken to lunch. The men removed Randy's hand-tailored apparel, expanding moisturizing access to his torso, arms, and legs. The lotion came from an endangered vine found only in the Amazon rainforest. Randolph stored hundreds of bottles in an airtight vault in the mansion's basement, not far from the bowling alley that had yet to be used.

Randolph smiled ever so slightly as the men helped him slip into the handmade silk robe lined with "virgin kitten fur" given to him by his Chinese hosts while touring the factory district that ultimately won the contract to manufacture a StripOff spinoff: an electronic game console that went on to become Randolph's first and only failure, even if he had preferred to spread the blame among the 163 engineers and marketing specialists who sacrificed their jobs to the fiasco.

Without thanking his four servants, Randolph retreated to his study and voice-activated a Plasma screen the size of a billboard attached to the room's north wall. (Always face north when possible. Sleep with your head pointed north. He'd read this somewhere as a teen.) Now, the brightest light in Randolph's mansion was provided by a photo from a Duchaine Senior yearbook. Its subject stood near the center of the school courtyard on a bright spring day, smiling a wide, luminescent smile as if greeting someone special, someone who should have been Randolph. It was this photo he had used as his personal test model when perfecting StripOff.

Make that: when perfecting the early StripOff software. Since then, Randolph had come close to achieving virtual perfection through a series of progressively more upscale StripOff add-ons, while his virtual test subject learned to do all kinds of interesting things. The most talented incarnation resided in Randolph's master bedroom dancing slowly, seductively—au natural, of course—as an incredibly lifelike StripOlogram. This fully three-dimensional companion relied upon proprietary software yet to hit the marketplace and representing a huge step forward from anything achieved by anyone before. Yet, amazing as it was, Randolph couldn't deny that his creation, like all his creations before, lacked something essential, something fundamental, causing him to wonder how something so flawlessly beautiful could leave him feeling empty.

But now at last: a solution in hand. "I can't believe you're married to that shallow phony," he whispered to the source of the light. "You need to be rescued."

A crow cawed directly outside a window, its sound mostly muffled by the dark velvet drapes. Randolph reached for the closest phone and pressed 3 for Outdoor Security. "Is no one paying attention today?" he asked. "I want the intruder removed from my property."

Chapter 4
⌘

GRAND VIEWS

Clay's phone buzzed at precisely 12 noon. *Meet me at Grandview Park,* read the text from Unknown Caller.

Come alone and tell no one appeared one minute later.

Finally: *Make certain you are not followed.*

He replied, *This is great. Didn't know you were home.* He still couldn't deny his surprise at this. As one of his oldest and very best friends, Solstice Blume owed him some advance notice. *Unfortunately, I've got classes all afternoon. Wish I could skip but can't. Would tomorrow work? Late morning?*

The response came quickly. *11:30 it is. Henry Dodge Pavilion.*

Perfect, he thought, recalling how many times he and Solstice had driven to that open air rotunda as high school seniors to smoke bud, share deep thoughts and fantastical dreams, and compare notes that revealed their similar tastes in women as girls their own age rode past on bikes. Closing his eyes now, he saw the face described by a *Milwaukee Tribune* interviewer as pixyish and by the *St. Louis Gazette* as cherubic. He saw the short, black bangs and mischievous blue eyes, all supported by a thin, boyish body that made her look even younger.

More than a decade had passed since they last met in the park, a decade that had turned his close friend into the most successful writer he knew. He met up with her whenever she visited Duchaine, whether at the River Valley Bookstore or Cortino's Italian. This time would be different, though. Better, in fact. For once, he would be the one bearing good news. Sure, that news required some editing—he doubted she would be as impressed by his $200,000 advance were it attached to the name Randolph J. Simper—but what kind of person bores a friend with every superfluous detail?

He looked at his phone: *12:41.* Grabbing his car keys, he again wished he could skip classes.

Mentally, he did.

Standing in front of his Creative Writing class, the torrent of memories dragged him along like a tree ripped free by the flooding Mississippi, leaving him every bit as useless as the eight students staring past him at the slow-moving clock on the classroom wall.

"People," he said, retreating to his chair behind the desk, "Here's a flash writing assignment. Tell me about your first pet, or if you didn't have one, why that was so." Turning his feigned attention toward his laptop, he fully surrendered to the current, and why not? The students would never notice his absence, and Solstice represented a substantial chunk of his life, his writing life in particular. Their paths were wound and bound together like helixes of DNA, similar goals, similar talents. And if there existed dissimilarity in levels of success, Clay felt confident the disparity would soon be washed away in a flood of his own making. He pictured bookstore shelves lined with a novel that was Number One for its eighth week running, a reading room filled with fans seeking his autograph, a separate line snaking out the front door. As happy as he had been for Solstice when she got her first contract for a novel, this felt better. He liked being the one with good news.

***

For as long as Clay had known her, Solstice Blume had been more than a good, trusted friend.

She'd been his rival.

That distinction had been inevitable from the first day of eleventh grade when Clay met the girl from Ann Arbor who, as talk had it, "moved here after losing everything."

"She's a writer, too," Ms. Jensen, the fifth-period English teacher, had told Clay. "A good one."

This turned out to be irrefutably true, in part because, to Clay's way of thinking, Solstice held every unfair advantage available to a writer. Like dead parents she could not reach or please. Like her drunken, eccentric guardian, Aunt Ruthie, collecting box cutters and taxidermic saltwater fish. Like her own fashionably non-traditional sexual orientation. The baggage Solstice carried through life was stuffed with the stuff of writing: loss, betrayal, a family of eccentrics, what writers call material. Thank God she was only gay and not transgender or something equally exotic.

Then came all the endearing quirks, starting with the dyslexia that helped make her unique and original while forcing her to triple check her spelling even as she refused to use a laptop, choosing instead an ancient, hand-me-down Selectric typewriter. She imbibed more caffeine than any other living creature ever, mostly in the form of iced tea, even though she seemed to possess an inherent shitload of energy. (Granted, Clay asked himself now, when had he ever seen her without caffeine coursing through her bloodstream?) She could be remarkably childlike, right down to forgetting to tie a shoelace and continually showing unwarranted trust and generosity, especially when it came to paying for meals or books or ganja. She loved non-fiction books about pirates. "I know they weren't the greatest feminists. But heck, they were pirates." She window shopped eBay for the most overpriced eccentric offerings. "Look. An 1892 Alaska gold mining deed. Only 27 mill to Buy It Now." She walked Lucy the Cat on an elastic leash. The pair only made it a block each way, but this took as long as one hour.

Of greatest importance to Clay's personal evolution, Solstice out-weirded his own weird sense of humor—she once wore glasses without lenses for an entire week of high school—and no doubt helped shape his own absurdist take on reality. As writers, they dabbled in what she called "the dark arts," encouraging each other to add increasingly deeper and darker dyes to their cauldrons of humor.

And while, yes, the two quickly became competitors in his eyes, they also became allies at Duchaine Senior where Jenni Jensen religiously called on the pair to read their respective "wonderful creations" in front of Fifth Period English. At lunch, they sat together on the sloping hill that bordered the football field to share teenaged bluster of becoming hugely successful authors with Clay emphasizing the aspects of royalties and fame while Solstice focused on technical perfection. Clay talked, too, of all the places he would live and write: New York; Madrid; Key West. Solstice usually nodded her head in silence, reminding Clay that her ideal writing location was "a room with a desk."

Their bold dreams still registered a pulse the spring they got their BA's in English, hers with a side of Education. The two friends received emails confirming acceptance into the University of Wisconsin's Graduate Writers Collective beginning that fall in Madison.

"This is going to be Paris in the 1920s," Solstice had enthused while they got high from their already high location. Bankston Quarry's limestone ledge commanded a view of the Mississippi rolling south on its way to Mark Twain's birthplace.

Embracing her picture of them as Hemingway and Stein, Clay closed his eyes and smiled broadly. "Paris in the 1920s. The Lost Generation." He felt no desire to risk their high by sharing a new complication.

Following her graduation with honors from nearby North Iowa State, his new girlfriend Martha Jewell had decided to stay in Duchaine to be near her parents. Clay in turn had promised to make the 80-mile drive home each and every weekend. Ernest Hemmingway would not have done this.

Come mid-July, he learned Martha was pregnant, and this forced him to make what should have been a much more difficult choice. With her quick, curious mind, she had far more to admire than simple beauty. She laughed at his jokes and encouraged his writing to the point where she was willing to talk with an adoption agency about the baby's future. Surveying his options, Clay saw only one. Over lunch at Cortino's, he asked Solstice, "What kind of fool walks away from the best fortune he's ever known?"

"She's something special," agreed Solstice. "I'd stay for her."

Eating dinner that evening in the very same restaurant—Cortino's made the best calzones—Clay told his girlfriend, "Anyone can write a classic novel, but not everyone can have a baby."

She laughed. "I want you to write your novel."

"We can do both."

She asked if he was sure.

"Yes," he said, "of two things." He slid off his chair, placed a knee on the floor. "I want to be a great dad. I want to be your husband."

She smiled, and putting the restaurant's weak lighting to shame, seemed to radiate her own.

"Well?" he said.

"I'm going to make you say it."

It was his turn to laugh, and after waiting a few seconds, he looked up into her eyes. "Will you marry me?"

She leaned down to give him an incredibly tight hug. They kissed, only to be interrupted by the waitress asking, "Do you need anything else?" Their food had arrived.

"Absolutely not," Clay said, helping Marta back into her seat. "We're good. Great, in fact."

Ignoring the beautiful panzerotti on his plate—sculpted by loving hands and bronzed by deep frying—he turned to Marta and asked, "That was a yes, right?"

She laughed, even while wiping a tear from her eye.

"You probably need a few minutes to plan your dream wedding," he said. "But what are your thoughts? Thousands of guests? Tropical island?"

"Smaller, sweeter, shorter," she said. "A big wedding has never been high on my list. And as a practical matter, I don't need *thousands of guests* asking why the bride's avoiding Champagne."

Two mornings later, Clay kept an appointment with Duchaine University's president, Arthur C. Peckham, to talk about his own revised future. Sitting in the president's oak-paneled office, furnished in light oak to match, Clay asked if there might be a place for his skills in the D.U. English Department, and if so, could Peckham arrange as part of Clay's compensation for joining that department an invitation to workshop with Fillmore Banks, a retired professor who had published a fairly successful novel as a much younger man?

"You could be a great asset here," Peckham replied, "more than qualified to teach the basic writing courses we offer here. I'm sure we can get Banks on board."

"I won't need a Master's?" Clay asked.

"Oh, you'll have a Master's."

"Since when does D.U. have a graduate program?"

"No, no, nothing like that," Peckham replied. "We're going to advance you the degree, then count your hours here—the time you spend teaching and prepping—toward it. It's not like teaching a class is all that different from taking one."

"You can do that?"

"We can pretty much do as we please," Peckham said. "I know everyone thinks accreditation is some huge badge of honor. Accredited school... good school. But I'll take flexibility over accreditation any day. I've always seen it a straitjacket of sorts."

When Clay got up to leave, the president extended his hand and, while shaking Clay's, said, "What I said about being an asset here. I do more fundraising than anything else. Maybe you could help with the occasional flyer or silent auction catalog. That doesn't seem too much to ask. Who knows? Maybe you'll find it's your real talent."

"I guess," Clay said.

"Outstanding," Peckham said. "Let me email some info on our upcoming summer outreach program. It's our biggest direct mail effort of the year. It'll give you a chance to show off your stuff."

Driving home, Clay muttered, "Seriously? It's not bad enough I'm teaching at Douche U. You're making me a copywriter?" Perhaps he still harbored a few reservations about the changes coming his way.

The wedding took place outdoors on a perfect Sunday afternoon in Eagle's Nest Park. A borrowed video camera recorded the ceremony from a tripod, its short, wide lens facing the bride and groom standing center stage in the Eagle's Nest Park bandstand. Will and Winnie Jewell flanked them on the left, balancing out Clay's parents on the right. Will and Winnie, like Clay and his bride, had dressed formally for the occasion. Vera Turner wore loose-fitting slacks, Archie a short-sleeved, button-up shirt. Clay was pleased to simply see them there.

Fittingly, an eagle circled high overhead in a cloudless sky. From somewhere in the distance, wafting in and out of audibility, an ice cream truck played a jingly "Rubber Dolly." Colorful in their casual outdoor wear, twelve friends sat on the concrete benches that circled the stage. Claiming center of the very front row, Solstice took photos with her phone.

Clay's older brother did not attend, which came as no surprise. Graham had not once returned home after fleeing high school a few weeks shy of graduation. Clay was finishing his sophomore year at the time. Graham did send a wedding present: two pounds of Green Leaf Pain Relief, illegally transported across three state lines by the United States Postal Service. It was a product of Graham's own place of employ, Bud Wiser. A note read, *Sorry, I can't be there but you know I can't be there. I promised to never return and I'm keeping that promise. Come visit.*

While Martha danced with her father to Ed Sheeran, Solstice turned to Clay and said, "You're a lucky man. You have a smart, beautiful partner, you're going to have a smart, beautiful family. As for your writing, we both know it's only a matter of time. Make the world your writers collective. Submit your stories... and please, please, keep me posted."

***

Clay wasn't so sure he needed the outside world, in love as he was with his own. A lucky man indeed, he shared each day with someone who embraced small pleasures with passion, who encouraged him to "Aim high, you can always course correct later," who made him try new things, whether in restaurants, theaters, or bedrooms. They also shared a spacious, three-room apartment where he wrote short stories and read books about teaching. Martha had landed a job she "liked well enough" and looked forward to the time she'd have off with their new baby. On weekends, they drove around looking at houses for sale.

As for embracing the future coming his way, he saw himself making a pretty good dad by following a fairly simple prescription: in any crisis or conflict, he would imagine how his own father might have reacted, then do the exact opposite. More important, Clay saw himself making a pretty good dad because he truly wanted to be one, a family man taking love from people he loved as opposed to book-buying strangers. There was so much demanding his concentration and hope without the distraction of wanting to dazzle mankind with his writing. He could leave this to Solstice; he truly believed this at the time.

Interestingly, Solstice had also fallen in love—with a book. After reading the sci-fi classic *Space Merchants*, her passion for writing became genre-specific. She still had feelings for "every other book ever written," but would now focus exclusively on writing her own funny, intelligent sci-fi. *SF Digest* took her short story about a once-resilient single mom watching doomsday get the upper hand through mass extinction caused by overpopulation and self-fulfilling doomsday myths. "End of an Era" climaxed with a description of a dinosaur dying at the side of a road, revealing the Weaver family to be warm-blooded Mesozoic reptiles.

Clay found the premise clever—and familiar—a remnant of stoned conversations between two high school seniors perched on the limestone cliffs of Bankston Quarry. He suspected the idea had been his, even while accepting that the problem with ideas shared while stoned was their untraceability. But whoever planted the seed, Clay and Solstice had both fertilized its early growth.

Seeing the story in print, he didn't think she had adequately answered the question that lingered in its aftermath: *What happened to all the fossils? As much as I like the premise, which could have been hers or could have been mine, wouldn't human-like reptiles bringing an end to a geological era through their own avariciousness leave zillions of fossils?*

Halfway through October, Martha miscarried. No more sonograms with the funny doctor Clay liked. No more Happy Preggers yoga classes. No more playfully arguing over Adele and Beyoncé as names.

It was pretty much no more anything.

After several eggshell-fragile weeks spent grieving in what had become a cramped apartment as silent as a tomb, Clay reminded his wife they would have other chances, beginning whenever she was ready. "I made you some dinner," he added. "Jalapeño shrimp scampi." She was in bed staring blankly at the TV on the dresser, its sound turned completely down. The clock read six-thirty. Clay stood in the doorway.

"You could still take advantage of your acceptance to the Collective," she surprised him by saying. "The second semester isn't that far away." Clay told her he no longer thought it important, reminding her he was meeting with Fillmore Banks right after Thanksgiving break to begin the "one-on-one mentorship" that would take up four hours each Tuesday. "It's an incredible opportunity."

Clay saw no need to revive the fact that two previously planned summits had fallen through, each at the older writer's bidding and each in the late-night hours preceding the planned meeting.

Like many Duchainers, Clay knew that Fillmore Banks once gained attention with a darkly comic novel disparaging their hometown. Placing himself in a much smaller subgroup, Clay had actually tried reading *Fish Story*. A high school senior at the time, he made it only two chapters, his attention span no match for what Solstice had warned was a challenging read. "Think *Finnegan's Wake*, but more opaque." None of this diluted their general sense of awe. "How often do you hold a real novel by a real writer from your own town?" she said. "It would be cool to meet him."

Fish Story recounted the trials of a failed musician returning home from Greenwich Village to "ceaselessly somnolent southwest Wisconsin." Tiberius Sloane intended to become the proverbial big fish—giving the book its title—in a small pond. The plan met resistance. It didn't matter that the "incomparable finger-picking maestro" had honed his craft on the same stages that launched Bob Dylan. Tiberius faced brutal competition from "two rudimentary songsmiths with one skill between them, promoting their consummate competence in a city the size and sophistication of a modest NASCAR crowd." Wherever the protagonist went, there they were, hawking cassettes or performing new songs.

Ironically, Fillmore Banks returned to live in Duchaine after his decently received literary debut failed to pay his New York rent, and after two unsuccessful attempts at second novels inspired his agent and editor to drop him. Real-life Duchaine proved more welcoming to Banks than his fictionalized version, and he basked in the limelight of local celebrity. The *Duchaine Lamplighter* profiled him often until readers tired of his promise to "show those arrogant idiots out east what a great novel looks like." Fillmore Banks ended up teaching at D.U. where Peckham's predecessor gave the author an honorary Ph.D. and conferred the title of professor.

Banks lived in a two-story brick house that, having fallen into serious disrepair, looked as if it were teetering at the very top of Ninth Street's steep hill. It was the kind of house you couldn't help but notice as you drove by, the kind of house that made kids think, *haunted*, and parents say, "Kids, stay away from that house."

Clay visited on a December afternoon that was, for the upper Midwest, unusually bright and warm, qualities that did not penetrate the walls of this house. Peeking past the curtain that mostly covered the front door's small window, he saw nothing but darkness. It took Fillmore Banks several minutes to answer the ringing and knocking, which had Clay wondering if sound, too, was prohibited from entering the void. When Banks did at last appear, he did so sparingly. The door opened slowly, revealing a tired face that seemed to float on the darkness.

Once inside, Clay couldn't detect a single source of light. He could barely discern the outlines of curtains covering windows. It was he who ultimately turned on an overhead light after feeling for switches as he entered the musty hallway. Almost surprised to find working electricity, he beheld a thin, wrinkled man with wild cotton-tuft hair that brought to mind the elderly Albert Einstein. Tiny tufts of Kleenex fuzz dotted his chin, making Clay wonder if Banks kept the lights off even when shaving.

Clay now sat in a faded blue loveseat that looked Victorian but had to be older as it predated the invention of comfort. His back ached. His eyes burned, reacting most likely to dust that had not been disturbed in ages. Silence settled in its place. Banks said nothing, not even to offer a glass of water. Clay checked his phone; four minutes had passed.

Finally, "So, you're the guy Beckham wants me to teach how to write?"

"Peckham."

"Do I look like a bird? Why would I peck someone? For God's sake, whatever are you talking about?"

"Nothing," Clay said. "Nothing important. I am honored to have this opportunity."

"Well, of course."

Another lull followed. Clay said, "This is a very interesting house. I understand it's been in your family since the early 1900s."

He was relieved to hear Banks say, "I need to run an errand. Your car seems an excellent place to continue this conversation." And so Clay's initial mentoring session segued into a trip to Mulgrew's Affordable Quality Spirits on lower Main. Once back home, Banks poured himself a cup of cheap Scotch which gradually reduced his body-wide shakes. Approximately twenty minutes into this self-medication process, he must have stabilized to his own satisfaction, enabling him to talk about writing, specifically his own writing and how it was unfairly ignored a mere four decades after publication.

This became a weekly routine. Clay didn't mind. Anything to get off the loveseat.

"The passing of time," Banks grumbled more than once. "It's a goddamned bulldozer. Plowing everything under." Fillmore Banks was a bitter man, and had he owned a car and been capable of driving it, he would have taken that bitterness to New York and "shoved it up the asses of those stuck-up know-it-all editors."

Clay's first take-home assignment came five weeks into the sessions. This took the form of *Fish Story*, which he was now eager to read in its entirety, certain he would appreciate the work more as an adult. Unfortunately, his disappointment proved as dense as the prose that had earned Banks these snippy lines, Googled by Clay, in a 39-year-old *Times* review: *Fillmore Banks is never content to use a two syllable word when five will do. At times, the reader may feel as if he picked up a thesaurus and not a novel.*

In Chapter Three, *Gloominess descended like a phosphorescent silver cloud of condensed water vapor encircling dry ice losing a battle with warm water.* There were many other sentences like this one, yet not one single example of genuine humor, which must have been dark to the point of being invisible. *Tiberius Sloane woke coated in perspiration on the vacuous morning following his Acoustic Evening at Greenwich Village's legendary Pisshole Cafe. It had been a debacle, a debacle witnessed by no one, the very thing that ensured its status as debacle.*

Equally egregious, the book downgraded Clay's hometown from great place to live to steaming rural backwater. Real-life Duchaine, for example, boasted a fairly liberal city government, early to stand for gay rights and equal pay for equal work. Fillmore Banks' Dulcene, on the other hand, could have been located in central Kansas. *Forget equality for women and Dulcene's almost non-existent minorities, the town was still grappling with the dread Right Turn on Red. One unfoundedly pompous city council member had been duly ostracized for proposing to socialize the municipality's trash collection, placing it under the city's governance. Folks in Dulcene didn't cotton to communism.*

Clay stayed positive when delivering his verbal book report, of course, praising Banks for his inventive plot, strangely compelling characters, and abundance of wit. Clay followed these lies with a small request: "Would you be willing to read four of my own essays and stories?" Banks smiled and said, "Certainly… once we have reached that place in our journey."

He added, "And please don't call me *Mr.* Banks. I prefer *sir.*"

Clay's second assignment came two months and nine liquor store visits later. He was to read *Cruel Comedown*, Fillmore Banks' unpublished second novel. This was a tale of a brilliant writer at odds with a myopically greedy publishing industry. It was a story of broken promises, followed by very understandable, at least in the protagonist's mind, revenge. In the margins, Clay found notes that looked scrawled by angry chickens—*Fuck you, Jack, you goddamn brain-dead philistine, this scene is both intrinsically powerful and utterly essential to the plot*—and circular amber stains the circumference of Scotch glasses. *I can find another agent.*

It took Banks four months to reach and deliver his verdict on two of Clay's stories, by which time one of them had appeared in the electronic edition of *Plow and Pen*. Clay's twenty-two double-spaced pages were now decorated with their own Scotch stains and nearly illegible chicken scrawls. *An eminently serviceable attempt at humor and rudimentary character development*, the final scratchings noted. *You have learned much in our time together, Cal.*

Clay's job at Duchaine University provided even more opportunities to hone his disingenuousness. In producing flyers for the World Famous Chocolate and Cheese Lovers Festival and the Riverside Alumni Art Walk on the River, he discovered a knack for cutting and pasting language from online Ivy League fundraising pleas. He took his inspiration from grading student papers, having learned early on the only ones worth reading had come to life in this Frankensteinian manner.

Peckham loved each new production, making comments on the order of "By God, Turner, you really did find your true talent."

At times, Clay felt no better than his students.

He needed a break, an open-ended sabbatical from Peckham and Banks and students who should have dropped out years before and parents who called to express indignation over grades that threatened to puncture the otherwise straight-A bubbles of their clueless, coddled prodigies. He needed more time to work on his own stuff, including the novel he saw in his future. This goal had become important again.

Helping him survive these steady assaults on his intelligence, Clay's non-writing, non-academic life tasted as sweet as the long johns he had recently discovered at Hey Howdy. He and Martha had mostly moved past the miscarriage and, silently agreeing to hold off on starting a family, were happy as a couple. If anything, a shared frustration with work strengthened their bond. Seeing her position as File Coordinator for the Wisconsin Workforce Development Center as a "suffocating dead end," she talked about going back to school, telling him she wanted the kind of salary that came with a Master's, "a real one." If she waited too long, the opportunity might just roll past like the Mississippi's waters.

When she and Clay weren't working, they took picnics to the lock-and-dam overlook in Eagle's Nest Park and enjoyed long walks on the floodwall's pedestrian path. Their love life burned with all the passion due a pair of relative newlyweds. He brought home flowers and Champagne; she laughed while reading his stories. They had trouble getting out of bed on weekends, and not because they were sleeping. On Friday and Saturday evenings, they gingerly dipped into the wedding present from his brother. *Green Leaf Pain Relief. Since 2004. A Product of Colorado. Sold For Medicinal Purposes Only.*

On their second-year anniversary, they purchased a two-story house on Cleveland Avenue that seemed fairly modern for the neighborhood with its attached three-car garage. Their move was helped in part by a generous gift from Winnie and Will. This put Clay only seven blocks from the house he grew up in: a single-story wood-frame house too small to comfortably cage a writer of unusual promise, one stoner brother, and two parents who managed to be concurrently present and absent. The new address also placed Clay close to the woods he explored as a child, the steep limestone bluffs, and the jagged outcropping that provided what was indisputably the best view of downtown Duchaine and its river valley setting.

On their fourth anniversary, Clay sat beside Martha on the living room couch while she fired up her iPad and picked out a three-year-old Black Lab from Wisconsin Lab Rescue. The dog came home Tuesday. Clay named it Argos from Homer's *Odyssey*.

Having never owned a pet before—Clay's parents thought it bad enough to have kids—he was surprised to learn how demanding one could be. He loved dogs (of course he loved dogs, everyone loves dogs, everyone says so) but whenever he worked at home, whether grading papers or scribbling lesson plans on the backs of Taco Bell napkins or struggling to shape a short story, Argos wanted attention. And walks. And food. And going outside to chase tennis balls that stopped looking like tennis balls after a few games of fetch. Clay did his best to be a good pack leader; he gave Argos these things. But the second he returned to his work, Argos returned to whimpering. It took six weeks for Clay to give up on going out back to lob tennis balls, choosing instead to keep a box of dog treats on his desk. Argos gained weight and whimpered with greater frequency as if his previous whimpers had not been addressed. Clay began writing essays about their time together. These pieces came easily.

When walking Argos to Cleveland Park, he continued to be amazed at how often strangers—that large subset of the human race that didn't have to bend down and collect the dog's generous outpourings in flimsy plastic bags that sometimes leaked through tiny holes—smiled and said "Beautiful pup" as they passed or stopped to pet the goofy embodiment of carefreeness. Clay got this from children, delivery guys, and women the age of his students, making him realize that no prospective abductor scheming to lure another human being into a windowless Ford E-series van would be fully equipped without a Black Lab.

"He works under the assumption that everyone is his best friend," Clay would say to dog-loving strangers. "Also, that every object is food until proven otherwise."

Clay was also heard to say, "Jesus, Argos, that's goose shit, not a breath mint. You have redefined disgusting."

Back home, he wrote more essays.

On a Tuesday afternoon early in his sixth year of teaching, Clay was lecturing his last class of the day, Writing the Right Résumé, from behind his desk: "And for goodness sake, don't call it Douche U in your résumé; spell it out and spell it correctly, Du-chaine University." One student was staring out a window close to his desk, another was picking his nose, trying to hide the activity behind an open textbook.

Questioning the point of his own attentiveness, Clay peeked at his phone to see he had an email from Small Packages Press. The independent publisher had been recommended to Clay by Solstice after she met its founder at a Writers' Collective conference. During that meeting, Solstice had spoken "glowingly" of Clay's writing. Small Packages, in turn, had contacted Clay without first seeing his work, at which time he agreed to send them everything he had.

Still looking down at his phone, he gave his class a meaningless writing assignment, "Pretend you need a résumé to get into a better school," then opened what turned out to be an acceptance email.

We liked most of the stories and essays, the message began, *but it is Argos, that wonderful, lovable, larger than life Lab, that makes this collection such a joy to read. "Give Me a Second while I Execute the Dog" seems the obvious piece to anchor the collection.* Reading these words, Clay felt bad about shouting, "Dog, I'm going to sell you for parts," that very morning after Argos swiped a great, gross wad of used Kleenex tissue from the downstairs bathroom wastebasket. He also envisioned writing a new essay on how to save money by simply feeding pets trash. "A Dog Owner's Guide to Recycling."

Two months later, Clay saw his page proofs. So did a number of respected authors, assuming they actually received his blurb-seeking letter and three sample chapters, and assuming they bothered to open the envelopes hand-addressed by Clay. The great John Irving sent him an encouraging letter, but refused to violate a pledge made early in his career to never again blurb. An assistant to Margaret Atwood sent a photocopied poem explaining the math that prevented her from doing more: one me, thousands of you, no time. This left Clay to seek a more accessible author, one eager to see his own name on the jacket of a book printed in this millennium. *A promising literary debut,* raved Fillmore Banks, *Give Me a Second While I Execute the Dog takes its hallowed place alongside other outstanding books by eminent Duchaine authors. You'll want to give it multiple seconds of your time.*

Eight months later, Clay's collection appeared in hardcover, announcing to the world his qualifications as an intellectually endowed, witty, and somewhat detached observer of the human condition. Solstice, who had recently moved to Portland for a first teaching job, used her blog, *Solstice Celebrations*, to plug the collection. (Yes, she had purchased a laptop, but only for blogging and messaging, and with spellcheck disabled.)

If you haven't bought Clay Turner's hilarious sampling of wisdom and wit, she encouraged her followers, *I suggest you do so now.*

The University of Wisconsin's *Badger Herald* concurred: *Flashes of brilliance.* The *Des Moines Register* heralded *an original voice with true wit.* The *Denver Post* warned, *Dog lovers beware!*

When *Publishers Weekly* came through, it was also to Clay's delight. Although he did not earn a starred review, the publication declared, *Good things come in Small Packages.* Their review concluded with the question: *When do we see the novel?*

His proud wife threw him a publication party. Solstice talked about flying in for the event, ultimately sending her regrets, saying she had to "meet with someone in New York." Duchaine Senior English Teacher Jenni Jensen drank Chardonnay on ice, beaming with pride and a visible buzz, while Fillmore Banks, who would later ask Clay for a ride home by way of the liquor store, emptied a fifth of Chivas Regal. Arthur C. Peckham handed strangers an all-too-familiar flyer for his upcoming fundraiser, while other Douche U faculty members who had shown little inclination to socialize with Clay in the past now congratulated him on his achievement.

With each new triumph more addictive than the last, with each new peak dwarfing the previous summits that could never be dwarfed, Clay was having fun. Giving his first reading to a standing room only crowd at Madison's Red Letter Bookstore, he felt Mark Twain famous well before the ovation that included everyone present save a woman who had come to make sure his appearance would not pass without drama. The post-excerpt Q and A session began with this pale, gaunt, fiftyish woman, whose T-shirt proclaimed her loyalty to PETA and whose straight black hair with jarring silver streaks was so long it touched the floor on both sides of her chair in the front row, asking, "Why should we reward you for mistreating your dog? If only poor Argos could write a book."

Unfazed, Clay thought, *You'll have to do a lot better than that to take down a writing teacher used to surly, omniscient twenty year olds.* "It's humor," he said. "Nothing more, nothing less. As both dog owner and writer, I do the best I can. I'm sure Argos, were he capable of properly assessing the situation, would be thrilled with the attention he's getting." The audience applauded and rewarded Clay by purchasing the book, guaranteeing it a Number One placing in the *Wisconsin State Journal* Best Selling Fiction chart.

The crowds got bigger. Sales figures, too. Clay drove as far as Chicago and Omaha for readings. In four bookstores, readers brought dogs, a choice that no doubt brought the dogs claustrophobia. Some of these pooches got books signed in their honor. *For Rocky... For Teddy...* Solstice called to say a friend had staked out the Madison reading. "She says you were incredible.

She likes the book, too." Leigh Cooley, the Chief Editor for Small Packages Press, called to thank Clay for her "first major success," adding, "We're close to adding a fifth digit to your totals."

At Clay's most successful reading, hosted by Duchaine's River Valley Bookstore, his students turned out more faithfully than they ever had for actual classes, correctly assuming it would help their grades to be seen waiting in line for the privilege of purchasing a signed copy of their instructor's book. Ninety-six sold, an impressive feat. Clay even had a groupie. The downtown library's acquisitions manager, a woman with a slim equine face leaned in close while Clay signed her copy of *Give Me a Second* to ask, "So, Mr. Turner, just how married are you?"

Providing a blindingly clear answer to the question, Martha promptly snatched the book—from where, Clay wasn't sure, she was talking with the store's owner only seconds before—and explained that the book, like her husband, wasn't available to just anyone. Acquisition denied.

Only two days later, a producer at the Comedy Cluster cable network called to share her interest in basing a television series on the book's title story. "My brother lives in Omaha," said Brenda Vrotsos. "He picked up your book after reading a review and predictably fell in love with Argos. He wants to know if he'll get a finder's fee."

Vrotsos told him Comedy Cluster had originally planned to directly option it. "That would have put a pretty good chunk of change in your pocket. But this deserves bigger. Our cable network includes several premium channels. I see a major Moviemax series. You can't imagine how huge that would be for me. Um, you too, of course."

He called Solstice to share the news. "Clay," she answered. "This is… serendipitous. I was just about to call you."

She let him tell his story, congratulated him effusively. But the moment she had time to share her own news, she delivered it breathlessly. "My first novel. It's under contract." She tried sharing the plot, but kept getting ahead of herself. "Sorry, I just learned this, minutes ago. What I'm feeling is way beyond excitement. You're the first to hear."

She barely let him say, "I'm flattered."

"It's called, *Time As Measured in Cats*. You've got the dog market. I'm taking cats."

With that, she had another call, one she "had" to take. "I'll tell you more. Soon."

She did this the following morning. The email said only, *I should have shared this months ago.* A Google attachment made up for the cover note's brevity. It was 310 pages long.

***

Solstice Blume's novel began in 2292. The good news for humanity existing in that future was that a giant corporation had discovered a means to achieve immortality. The bad news? A giant corporation had discovered a means to achieve immortality. The equivalent of yesteryear's cable TV provider, Ufinity charged subscribers to hook up to an apparatus that was fittingly similar in physical appearance to a cable box. No one outside of Ufinity's upper management knew how these devices circumvented the atrophy that typically came with aging.

Corbin Dykstra stared at the bills spread side by side on his living room carpet. A2Z Coal Power and Gas. ComTel and REcycling. Mostly he stared at a single one, Ufinity Plus. Corbin couldn't believe he was 60 days past due on his monthly payment for the subscription, no more than he could believe Ufinity had jacked up the price three times in twelve months. Eight thousand Arpaio's seemed nothing less than extortion. He needed more money, either that or to do the impossible by cutting back on his outlays for Inst-A-Pleasure and Lotto Swipes. Addictive indulgences, sure. But no one could say these weren't necessary for his survival. He wouldn't last a week without them.

Clay loved the premise and not only because it could well have been his. He felt sure he'd heard it before, at least partly from his own lips while getting high with Solstice in high school. He had, of course, completely forgotten that hazy riffing session until this moment. Solstice must have made notes when she got home. He felt pretty sure she kept a journal.

Corbin leaned back in his hard metal folding chair and hooked himself up to the wide, black Ufinity box. He felt relieved, even glad, to see it still worked, that it was still capable of doing whatever it did to his atoms and molecules and genes and whatever. "They haven't cut me off." He had been late on payments before and knew from experience that the customer reps at Ufinity did not pride themselves on patience. They weren't too big on politesse either.

He had to come up with A8,000. Soon. Or get used to the idea of dying.

It didn't help that his girlfriend, an admittedly odd term to apply to a woman 212 years old, needed help with her own rent and addictions and Ufinity subscription. He spent more money on Constanze Cruz than he did on Inst-A-Pleasure, which while pretty damned expensive itself, always lived up to its name. He could think of only one reason for sticking with Constanze and it was the same reason responsible for his having six ex-wives and thirteen children, beggars the lot. This was his boredom, his infinite boredom, immortality's most serious side effect. With each passing year, and there promised to be many, Corbin's shabby, much too familiar world looked even shabbier. But after 98 years at the same job, 23 now without a raise, he couldn't imagine how anything could ever change.

Corbin lived in the Libertarian Republic of Texas where taxes devoured most of his income. These helped support the Police Guard that employed every fifth Texan. His taxes also helped pay for the military juggernaut that made up another fourth of that population: a standing army charged with defending The Homeland against the Republics of New Mexico and Arizona.

Corbin often wished he had immigrated to the People's Republic of California before the walls went up. He had been more conservative then, however, railing about the "suckers and slaves in La La Land who let their government extract 42% of their wages in taxes." That seemed like a bargain now, seeing that it bought every Californian free job retraining and Universal Immortality and Universal Health, all of which he could use—and seeing that he got very little in return from being in his own Republic's 56% tax bracket. His third wife lived in California; he could have fled with her in 2160. (He'd go now if it didn't mean certain death. Border walls made much more sense when they were built to keep others out.)

Corbin also paid a good chunk of his very stretched income for insurance premiums. Ironically, immortality came with risks because a body resistant to aging and disease could still sustain injury and, yes, die, especially in a world that had many more billions of guns than it had people. Almost as scary, on the streets between his cube-artment and his work and his girlfriend's cube-artment, solar powered Flashwagens drove hundreds of miles per hour while drivers X'ed on their X-Comms (an ear-imbedded speaker coupled with a tiny wrist-imbedded video screen). And who could forget that New Mexico was known for violating the Invisible Laser Drone Treaties of 2136?

Inspiring a rare positive admission, Corbin was grateful to have been 32 when Ufinity hit the market. This was his "virtual age," and would remain so forever—or as long as he kept his subscription current and avoided oncoming traffic. Had Corbin been, say, 72 when the service became available, he would have looked and felt that age forever. (As of now, there was no way to reverse aging, only to suspend it.) Corbin was also grateful to be both thin and relatively sober. For until recently—with the very pricey introduction of Ufinity Gold—alcoholism and obesity still had the power to shut down key internal organs.

By the time he finished reading—and Corbin's band of rebels had brought down Ufinity—Clay was impressed with what Solstice had done with their premise. He was also pleased to know he came first in the Acknowledgements, obviously in recognition of his significant, if stoned contribution.

A few days later, Solstice Blume dominated the Sunday *Lamplighter*'s People Section, starting with a headline that yearned to be as endless as it was clunky: *Every Day Is Summer Solstice for This Amazingly Talented Duchaine Writer Who Used to Be My Student!* This introduced an interview conducted by Jenni Jensen (the call Solstice had to take?) who used her brief bio to announce she had retired from her English teaching position to "write exclusively for the prestigious *Duchaine Lamplighter.*"

Solstice Blume, the author of a delightful debut novel entitled Life As Measured in Cats, *has been writing wickedly dark humor since she was a student in my high school English class. Now, with* Life As Measured in Cats, *she's headed for the big stage. A sure to be science fiction classic,* Life As Measured in Cats *had me laughing until I cried and crying until I laughed just as it will have you laughing until you cry and crying until you laugh.* Life As Measured in Cats *is due this December (just in time for Christmas shopping!) from Krumpf and Sons, New York, Montreal and London.*

Whatever jealousy Clay felt over the novel deal he wisely beat back or simply denied. Solstice Blume, a writer who had never once faltered in her role as Clay's biggest, most generous supporter, had earned her big break. Sure, she borrowed a few ideas from him, ideas he'd long forgotten. If anything, she seemed to feel indebtedness. Combined with her newly acquired stature, her friendship would be more helpful to him than a TV series—if he could simply come up with a plot and write his novel. Proof of this came a few months later when Solstice, visiting her hometown, asked him to interview her for *World of Wisconsin* Magazine. Clay began by jokingly asking, "What was your favorite story in *Give Me a Second While I Execute the Dog?*" Solstice not only answered, but insisted the question appear in the printed interview.

She plugged his book on her Krumpf sponsored website. *If you read only one book this coming year, I'd have to suggest* Time As Measured in Cats. *But should you find time for two, I would also recommend Clay Turner's hilarious* Give Me a Second While I Execute the Dog.

In most every respect, life remained good. Banking on the TV series, Clay and Marta hired a contractor to finish the basement and purchased his beautiful silver Honda Gold Wing 1800. He rode that bike as often as possible, yielding to only the most serious winter snowstorms. Unfortunately, Duchaine was known for its winter snowstorms.

When spring finally returned, it brought news to offset the brightness and warmth. Representing Clay's first real setback, Comedy Cluster's parent company passed on making an offer. Per an email with no authorship attribution, Clay learned the project had "stalled in pre-pre-development," and worse, its sole champion, Vice Assistant Producer Brenda Vrotsos, had renounced capitalism and retired to an island off the coast of Greece.

Marta shared his disappointment over toaster-oven shrimp, but when she heard about his post on Facebook and Instagram, insisted he take it down.

"I'm surprised they let you use that headline." But they had, his *Comedy Cluster F****d* sneaking past their algorithmic censors. "But that's not what's *importante* here," she continued. "What do you have, 1200 followers at best? That's hardly a revolution. Giving out that email address is only going to make you *enemigos* in Hollywood."

Clay took it down the following afternoon, hoping his *1,246* followers had already taken to the virtual streets in protest.

Chapter 5
⌘

ZOO OUTING

Driving home from DU, Clay passed the entrance to Grandview Park—and wished he was meeting Solstice that evening. She would have commiserated about the day that wouldn't end, right up through it ending ignobly with Peckham cornering him in the faculty parking lot. "Turner, you need to ease up. I'm getting angry calls from parents. You know I don't like angry calls. I don't especially like parents. But they have a point. They're not paying us for C's."

Breathing heavily and stinkily, Argos watched with great interest as Clay huffed down the Double Sour Cream Baja Chicken Chalupa picked up at Senõr Seymour's Authentic Mexican. Taking a brief break to consciously chew, he texted Solstice, *I made it through classes with limited collateral damage. I'm looking forward to tomorrow. It's been too long.*

She replied quickly, or so he thought. The message turned out to be Marta's. She was pulling up at the Chamber for study group. *I'll miss you tonight. Were you able to get the laundry started?*

When he headed for his office, the dog stayed behind, his snout inches from the tabletop, causing Clay to return and properly dispose of the wrapper and bag, depriving Argos of a much anticipated snack. While there, he grabbed the folded newspaper he had rescued from the driveway.

Needing one last break before grading papers, all of which were likely getting C's, he allowed himself a quick look at the *Lamplighter*. Upon reaching the Business Section that took up most of page 9, he saw the name Randolph J. Simper. "As with any loss, this is a tragedy," Randolph had commented on the death of a former rival. "But Alex Derringer was neither an inventive man nor an honest man. I suspect that, outside of family and creditors, he will not be missed."

According to the article, Alex Aaron Derringer, developer of an app briefly marketed as Strippit, had declared bankruptcy after losing a patent infringement trial to Randolph's company, StripOff International, LLC. The court ordered that the app be recalled, a first for the industry. Telling friends he feared retaliation—he ranted about witness tampering and silent late night phone calls—Alex fled the country to live the life of an expat in London.

His face appeared with the caption, *Last days lived in fear.* In it, he was plump, bespectacled, and clearly nervous.

"A fortnight ago," according to London's Metropolitan Police, "a primate keeper came upon Mr. Derringer's nude, dead body in the London Zoo's Mandrill Enclosure." *Mandrills,* noted the *Lamplighter* article, *are those baboon-like creatures with flamboyant facial coloration.* After the coroner ruled the death "the result of extreme cocaine overdose," the Derringer family demanded a criminal investigation, contending that Alex had cared neither for cocaine or zoos. The investigation came to an abrupt halt, however, when Scotland Yard discovered a "large collection of mandrill porn" in Alex Derringer's private computer.

Still, the family wanted to know how Alex got into one very secure zoo in the middle of the night, and more so how he managed to scale the high glass walls of the Mandrill Enclosure while lethally high. "He took that cocaine at gunpoint," the mother contended. "It's the only explanation that makes sense to anyone who knew my boy. There were others involved, and my Alex was already dead by the time he came in contact with the mandrills… those horrible, shameless mandrills. They ought to be on trial, as well."

Clay truly did not know what to think. The death of this sad man with a strange fetish couldn't be construed as anything but a terrible, and terribly bizarre accident. At the same time, the patent infringement trial had clearly destroyed Alex Aaron Derringer well before the mandrills got to him.

There was no getting around the fact that Randolph J. Simper, the most powerful person Clay had ever met, held no reservations about unleashing that power on foes. Clay made a mental note to be honest and straightforward when dealing with Randolph. He would not abuse his new relationship with an old friend who was placing so much faith in him—and who clearly didn't suffer betrayal.

The first thing Clay did after logging in was to Google *Mandrill.* He suspected it was a popular search that morning among his fellow Duchainers, much like the search he resisted, the one for *Mandrill pornography.*

Chapter 6

⌘

THE GIFT OF THE MAGI

With the dryer humming down the hall, Clay assigned his last C-minus of the evening. "Sorry, Peckham," he whispered as he closed the Google document files, "but this is me being generous. How hard can it be to write a cogent essay based on a thought-provoking topic like *Explain Why the Bloated Entertainment Industry Favors the Crass and Banal over True Innovation?*"

In need of an emotional lift, he visited GoogleBooks.com, specifically opening an excerpt advertised still as an "authorized preview from Clay Turner's debut collection, *Give Me a Second While I Execute the Dog.*" This was "Dolly Parton," a short story that once inspired *The Dane County Free Shoppers Supplement* to proclaim, "Showing himself to be a talented weaver of tales, or should we say *tails,* Clay Turner can take an awkward situation and make it fun."

Argos was attacked by Dolly Parton.

I was following our lumbering Black Lab to Cleveland Park on April Fools Eve. The weather, true to the warnings my app had delivered, was seasonal, not a good thing in the upper Midwest. The air was cold and the sidewalks slippery with snow. Argos loved it. Stopping to further discolor a snow bank streaked with gray and black, drawn from a palette of pollution and road grit, he seemed to smile proudly.

Nearing our destination—the West Duchaine bluffs were coming into view—we met the most disagreeable schnauzer. Typical to his breed, the silver gray embodiment of untreated hyperactivity began barking the moment we came in sight. The owner, typical to her breed, seemed unconcerned; the only "Leave It" came from my mouth.

"Don't dignify his outburst with a response," I implored Argos, but of course he didn't listen. He bolted forward, yanking the leash from my hand. The schnauzer lunged forward as well, landing a solid bite to my dog's right ear. Argos crouched and got down on his stomach, surrender at its saddest.

"Get him away," the other human screeched, her loyalty as predictable as her pet's unhinged behavior. "Get that beast away from Dolly."

"I might consider that act of appeasement if Dolly didn't have her teeth embedded in his ear," I sputtered as we both reached the war zone.

When the Schnauzer finally relented, her owner picked it up and cradled it in her arms. *"Dolly, are you okay? Dolly Parton, girl, are you okay?"* This was when I noticed the cowboy boots poking out from under the woman's wide-cut jeans.

"By okay," I asked, *"do you mean, somehow cured of her anger issues? Or are you afraid she picked up ear poisoning from Argos here?"*

"That was pretty pathetic," said the middle-aged cowgirl, still holding the assailant. She turned to walk away.

Argos remained flat on the ground from head to tail, holding that submissive position until the woman and her creature vanished from sight. We both stayed quiet as we returned home, our tails tucked metaphorically between our legs.

The worst part of this unfortunate experience is that we're doomed to encounter the horrible twosome on future walks. Our small neighborhood offers few hiding places.

The good part, of course, is that I can do what I am doing right now. I can tell others, "Argos was attacked by Dolly Parton."

And... applause. At least that's what followed the last time Clay gave a reading.

So long ago. It seemed like a dream.

He turned off his PC before getting up to fetch a French vanilla yogurt pack, a small, unsatisfying sacrifice to his own Pavlovian lust for something sweet, substantial, and doughnut-like. It disappeared quickly, even with his thoroughly scraping the plastic clean. He placed his spoon in the dishwasher, took a seat on the couch to resume reading student papers, and promptly dozed off.

Darkness took hold well before he woke to let his barking dog out. The clock on the Blu-ray player read 11:45. He was tempted to call Marta to ask if everything was all right, his idea of *not all right* taking on several connotations, the first having to do with marital infidelity. He had never felt anything but anxiety over the makeup of her group: six men placing their immediate desires on hold in pursuit of uncertain future success; one hot, smart woman doing the same. Multiply y times six, add x, and you had way too much repressed sexuality, a topic he knew well. Cursing his affliction of being good at math, Clay twisted uneasily on the couch, unable to find a comfortable position, like a dog that needed to go out and pee one last time. It took him forever to fall back asleep.

He woke to the sound of a gunshot or firecracker—or as it turned out, the popping of a cork. Marta emerged from the kitchen holding the bottle and two crystal Champagne flutes. "I have news from my study group."

"What is it?" he asked drowsily.

"I told them about your lunch with Randolph."

"You did? Really?" He pulled in his legs to give her room on the couch. "What did they think?"

"They want in."

"They what?"

"Three of them want to form a consortium and invest. It would spread the pain if there are setbacks, though I would hope for the sake of my friends, there will be no setbacks. Randy can be part of it, of course; it *was* his idea. He can be the senior investor holding the most shares, each of which would cost $2,500. The two most successful *empresarios* in my study group are willing to purchase ten shares each. The other is up for a single share. They thought it sounded like a great adventure, and at the very least, a way to diversify their portfolios."

It bothered him greatly that the idea of investing in his book suddenly made sense when coming from the mouths of her MBA friends. On the other hand, something had changed for the better. She was virtually offering her own standing in the group as collateral. She was gambling on his ability to deliver.

He sat up in order to take the flute she was handing to him. "You should be flattered," she resumed. "Everyone in the group who can afford it wants in. For that matter, so do the younger guys who can barely afford their tuition. They're going to be sitting this out, but your three backers have money to throw around, and they're all grown men. They know about risk. Put their names on the *Agradecimiento* page. That and some modest return would make them happy."

"Really?"

"They were excited. Benedict Howell, the head of Bedrock Faith Based Publishing, seemed ready to pee his *pantalones*."

He took a good swig of Champagne. "What happened to your reservations?"

"I thought about our conversation from last night. It's clear you need both time and motivation. Talent alone isn't cutting it. Some pressure might be good for you."

"Yes, but—"

"Remember the story you told me," Marta said, "the one behind 'The Gift of the Magi'?"

"Sure," Clay said. "O Henry allegedly wrote it in a New York tavern while a courier waited to deliver it by hand to *The Atlantic*."

"Finished under pressure," Marta said. "O Henry needed that deadline."

Argos jumped onto the couch. With 95 pounds behind them, the dog's dull but prominent claws dug into Clay's leg. Petting Argos to calm him, Clay felt the presence of drool that had somehow spun its way all around the dog's head.

"I don't know about the pressure," he said, shaking his own head, "but we could use the money. And the freedom it would give me to write."

Marta smiled, and Clay thought he saw something that had faded from view around the time Comedy Cluster chose to pass on optioning his book. This was pride in her husband's talent, and it went well with Marta's natural beauty. He might even have detected a little faith.

This was the Marta he not only loved, but also the Marta who loved him back.

Taking a seat beside him on the couch, she said they could use some of the extra money to replace the carpets with wood floors. "If we're going to raise a *familia* in this house we ought to make it the perfect nest."

"That all sounds good to me," he said. "But with Randolph's investment, we hardly need their money for that."

"They *really* want in," she said. "For the same reasons Randolph does, to diversify their portfolios, to invest in something with a different kind of value."

Taking a seat beside him on the couch, she explained the "fine print" of the Consortium's tentative offer. Each $2,500 investment would be worth one half a percent of Clay's net profit from the book. This would apply to Randolph, too. If Clay made enough to pay back the Consortium's initial investment, he'd still do okay. "Plus," Marta added, "no one owns the rest of your books. You've got a foot in the door and the whole rest of your life to dominate the bestseller lists without sharing the profits."

Marta called their proposed arrangement The Business Plan. "Cute, huh? There's even a chance this will become our independent group project. The year after next, for our final grade. Two members were really pushing for it."

"You and who else?"

"More like, *who* and who else. I stayed out of it, too much self-interest. I let the others do the pushing tonight."

She yawned, checked her phone. "Oh *mierda*, look at the time. I'm headed upstairs."

One hour and three graded papers later, Clay found her sleeping. This prevented him from telling her a smoldering fire had raged back to life. This was his determination to come up with a brilliant plot and write a great novel.

As he had typed in an untitled document only moments before, *I am going to be the rare, valiant earthworm who, after setting out across the sidewalk on a cool rainy night, actually makes it to the other side before the pavement dries.*

Resting on his pillow, his eyelids feeling the weight of night, Clay realized he might not have come up with the most romantic image. Perhaps it was best Marta had not been awake to listen, preventing him from speaking it aloud.

But he was going to be that earthworm.

Chapter 7

⌘

FREE OF TIME AND SPACE

Clay stared out and down from the open air picnic pavilion, still waiting to see if Solstice would drive up or get dropped off, the latter prospect much more likely in regard to a woman who had never shown much enthusiasm toward cars and driving. She was already five minutes late, time enough for Clay to notice the tiny paint scratch on the back left fender of his nine-year-old Volvo, his hand me down from Marta. He really needed a new, more interesting car.

He looked around the pavilion with its rough-textured concrete floor and waist-high outer wall of limestone blocks, each the size of an antique steamer trunk, and saw how little it had changed. If the picnic tables had been repainted, and they probably had been many times, this had been achieved without discarding their familiar milk-chocolate brown. He almost expected to see Hound Dog Hummel drive by in his half-rusted-out Camaro convertible blasting heavy metal music recorded decades before.

At a quarter past eleven, Clay pulled out his phone to call Solstice, but was promptly distracted by a silent blur of white that turned into a sleek and magnificent Tesla Model X pulling off to the side of the road directly behind his car. Clay knew the make and model because it occupied a high position on the list of cars he would have preferred to his own. As he knew secondhand from his online research, the Model X accelerated like a sunning cat caught off guard by a feisty Black Lab out for a walk: zero to 60 in three seconds.

Three seconds.

"Clayton Elliot Turner, you worthless old English major!" Solstice chirped as she emerged from the low-lying vehicle with an ease and grace that impressed Clay.

"What's with the Tesla?" he asked, his eyes still fixed upon its shiny, seductive exterior. In his head, he whimpered like Argos when the dog had not been fed for thirty minutes. Why was *she* driving *his* car?

It was, he learned, a three-month lease, a gift from a publisher to a touring author who disliked flying more than she disliked driving. "The funny thing," she said, "is that I love driving the Tesla. It's comfortable, quiet, and more safety conscious than I am. And... it accelerates like a booster rocket. I do feel a bit guilty, though, thinking of all the writers who don't have money to buy a good meal, and here I am, getting expensive toys as gifts."

"It doesn't seem fair," he concurred.

She gave him a big hug, then led the way to the closest picnic table. They took seats side by side, facing outward in the direction of the one-way black-top road. "I got in the night before last," she resumed. "It felt good to sleep in my old bedroom. Aunt Ruthie hadn't changed a thing. I woke up feeling like I was in high school, ready to take on the world we knew then."

Taking in her words and smile and overall effervescence, Clay felt *he* could have been back in high school. This was a feeling he had only experienced with Solstice and brother Graham: sharing a bond that existed outside the standard space-time continuum, existing in a place where conversations picked up as if days and not years had intervened. Granted, he caught a hint of eyeshadow around her blue eyes and saw curls in her short black hair, choices that belonged more to her publisher than her. But while he couldn't remember her wearing makeup at all before the first professional headshots appeared on her website, she was still Solstice. She certainly had not changed from the neck down. Her body remained thin, short, and kid like, even when concealed by a light blue blouse and slacks that seemed dressy for hanging out in Grandview Park, a stark upgrade from the fraying jeans, plain gray T-shirts, and oversized plaid button-downs she had worn every day to Duchaine Senior.

"Clay?" she said. "You look like you're dying to tell me something."

"I do?" He wondered what she was seeing. "No, you're right. I do have some news."

"And?"

"It's a bit weird," he said. "I'm not very far into writing my next book, yet I've been offered a huge advance."

"That's wonderful! And, it goes without saying, very well deserved."

"I'd tell you more but there's some confidentiality involved. There's also the matter, as Marta might say, of jinxing the whole thing."

He hesitated. "It is six figures."

Solstice stood up and walked to the center of the pavilion. "Marta?" she said.

"She was adopted, you know. Honduras. She dropped the *h* to acknowledge that heritage."

"I can't believe this is happening to both of us at the same time," Solstice said with a huge smile. "I mean, it really is unbelievable, wouldn't you agree?" Her blue eyes sparkled as she revealed that Krumpf was negotiating film rights and foreign subsidiary rights, "all for a book that has yet to see its sixth printing!"

"It is something," was all Clay could offer.

"Maybe it's just me, but nothing in life is the way I imagined it. Like when I was on Oprah's new show. I don't know if you saw it." Of course, Clay had seen her. Everyone in Duchaine had seen her. "But what you couldn't see were the cameras surrounding me like monstrous alien robots ready to probe my darkest depths. My eyes burned. The lights made it worse. All I could think was how badly I wanted to rub my dry, itchy eyes. I felt about as comfortable as Emily Dickinson dragged out of her house for a public exhibition of her poetry."

Clay felt competitive and, in that moment, strangely determined. He wanted these things coming her way, he wanted them for himself, and now that he could finish his novel—his daring, addictive, commercial novel—he planned to get them. Starting with the car.

He was about to feel even more jealousy, whether or not he wanted to label it as such. Solstice had bigger news. As in, bigger than Oprah. Bigger than Tesla.

She and her partner were having a baby. After months of foot dragging by Solstice—"the usual suspects: art, career, freedom"—Cyndi had been artificially inseminated. The baby was due in October, right after a pending book tour wrapped up.

Clay didn't speak, his mind traveling instead to an alternate universe where he and Marta lived happily amongst their adorable, loving children. It was a universe in which getting published and acquiring advanced business degrees didn't carry the same heft.

A robin landed on a picnic table at the pavilion's far side. "So—" Solstice paused, seemingly aware of the cold front her news had precipitated. "You know, I've got an ulterior motive for being thrilled about your news. For months, I've been dying to talk with someone who's going through a similar experience. With books and success. I need to ask, do your nerves ever get the better of you? There are times I wake up in a hard, cold sweat, fresh from a nightmare in which all my good fortune suddenly deserted me. I'm reading before empty seats, or looking at a one-star rating on Amazon. Do you have such nightmares? Do you ever worry about your publisher taking back the advance, if you can't, say, meet a deadline?"

When Clay said he couldn't identify with that last worry it was true to the same extent as everything else he'd been telling her in that he couldn't imagine an actual *publisher* calling to demand its money back.

"Stupid me," she resumed. "I was asking the wrong person. You were always so full of confidence... and talent. You'll pull it off and, unlike me, without breaking a sweat."

Clay saw this is as an opportunity to get her thoughts on his own situation—without having to reveal the details of that situation. "No, no," he said, "I know exactly what you're talking about. All these lawyers, editors, and marketers... caring more about sales than substance... it's enough to make me yearn for the patronage system." He laughed ever so slightly.

"That's funny," she said. "But talk about trading an imperfect situation for a truly awful one. Who wants to be some rich person's pet?" She looked down at the compact red and white Igloo cooler sitting on the pavilion's concrete floor. "So, what did you bring?"

"Lunch," he exclaimed, happy for the change of subject. Solstice smiled, her blue eyes sparkling anew.

"Oh," she groaned as Clay pulled out the semi-squished Hey Howdy carton with a clear cellophane cover that revealed a selection of six glazed doughnuts.

"Sorry," he said, "they were out of the cream-filled long johns."

"It's not that. It's that I can name 200 reasons to not eat those."

"Like?"

"Gluten, sugar, fat." Solstice stared at him like a disappointed parent. "Clay—"

"I know, I know. I'm just a big kid. Marta's already pointed that out. But what puzzles me is this: Why is everyone else so intent on acting like grownups?"

"It is okay to eat like one."

"Sadly, for the most part, I do." Clay held up a doughnut and addressed it as if it were Yorick's skull. "To enjoy life or just fucking be."

Lowering the pastry, he said, "I felt like celebrating our successes today. In reality, I have become a boring disciplined person: a daily allowance of one small sweet on the order of double-dark chocolate gelato; a weekly stipend of one Hey Howdy pastry. It's like being in prison. But grading papers and walking behind a dog don't consume many calories. I own nice clothes. I want them to fit."

The smile returned to Solstice's face. "Oh, Clay, what the hell? What's a few thousand calories between friends? I'll have one of your death globs.

You choose one for me." The old Solstice had returned.

Once her mouth was full, she mumbled, "Mmm, there is something to be said for self-destruction."

Clay's doughnut delivered a respectable sugar jolt, making his fillings ache, if not as intently as would a cream-filled long john. He would need to eat more than one doughnut to get that full impact.

Solstice finished off her pastry and Clay glimpsed the sugary glaze on her lips as she got up to carry a napkin strangely free of creases and goop to the large green trash can inside the pavilion. "Look at that car," she said as she returned to stand near the end of the table. "I know you were surprised to see me pull up in it."

As if on cue, a pair of plump middle-aged women sauntered past wearing neon-bright track suits, pink and blue respectively, that brought to mind Easter eggs. Clay heard one say, "Tesla X, ooh... Must be nice."

Solstice continued, "Did you know I still use the vintage 1938 Royal typewriter I bought at an estate sale in Madison? Except when I'm blogging it's the best way to write. It makes me think first before committing a thought to paper. Some things were better before computers took over. That reminds me, have you been keeping up with our old classmate, Randy Simper? That article in the *Lamplighter* last night? He's a gangster... a very creepy cyber gangster.

"No offense, Clay—I know you got along with him all those years ago— but there was *always* something creepy about Randy. That Striptease thing only sealed it for me. It just can't be good, having that insane wealth to go with the insanity. How awkward would it be to have him show up at an L.A. book signing? Not that I'm going to worry about it since it's kind of hard to imagine Randy Simper scouring the *Los Angeles Times* Book Section."

"Randy was all right," Clay said, "in his own way. I suspect he never felt comfortable with the high-school concept of coexisting with all types of people, the very quality that made high school a great place for future writers. To be fair, Randy Simper is no different from all the other adults who elected, ultimately, to find more specialized tribes, like you did with the Writers Collective. I know for a fact he loves reading."

"As I recall it, I wasn't alone in applying for the Collective." Solstice glanced down at the sparkly watch on her wrist, another expensive present, perhaps, from that grateful New York publisher. "Wow, almost two-thirty. I probably should be going. I know we both have things to do." She started to turn and leave, but hesitated. "There was one more thing I meant to ask." Again facing Clay, she tried unsuccessfully to suppress a smile. "Want to drive the Tesla? I know you always liked boxes with wheels on them."

The internal dog-like whimpering stopped. Clay's inner self now drooled instead.

Holding out her keys, Solstice started down the twenty or so limestone steps that went to the road. Clay moved quickly and was only two steps behind her when a shadow crossed his face. He stopped, as did Solstice, who like Clay was now looking up to see a massive bald eagle less than a hundred feet overhead. "An omen," Solstice brightly volunteered.

"It is?"

"If not, it certainly should be." She started back down the rough-hewed steps. "Sometimes, I miss living here," Solstice resumed. "But for the past few weeks, I've been missing Cyndi and Arthur, our cat. All this traveling in circles—"

Clay felt the burn of acid reflux, an allergic reaction to irony. He, after all, would have given his right ear to bask in Minneapolis and San Francisco and Austin applause, and to drive his Tesla 130 miles per hour across wide empty spaces, and to sit in a plush hotel room eating all the snacks he wanted without being scrutinized by a whining, drooling dog. Marta would have called each night to tell him how much she missed him, and to apologize for under-appreciating his role in their house during the years he had slaved over his masterpiece. "Argos is driving me crazy," she would say. "I don't know how you ever put up with him."

Solstice and Clay had not quite reached the road when a recent-model, lime-green Volkswagen Bug jerked to a stop behind the Tesla without pulling completely out of the already narrow traffic lane. The passenger door flew open and a short, stout woman with gray hair and wide black sunglasses emerged.

"Ms. Jensen?" Clay and Solstice gasped in unison at the sight of their high school English teacher.

"Solstice Blume, I've been looking for you everywhere. I finally called your aunt. She told me to look here. Oh, hi, Clay. How's the novel?"

Jenni Jensen brought Solstice up to speed on her retirement from teaching and subsequent reinvention as a writer for the *Lamplighter*. "I still owe you for that first profile, don't you know. Right from that day, it's been magical. I have the freedom to work on my own schedule, and by that I mean whenever the mood hits me. And it hit me last night. Hearing you'd be in town a few days, I promised my editor a feature story on Solstice Blume's Incredible Writing Career told from the POV of her proud high school English teacher. Interested?"

Solstice gave Clay a sad look and shrugged. "Sure. When will you need me?"

"About an hour ago," said Jenni. "Coming?"

Solstice walked around the Bug's far side, lifted her hand for one last wave, and giving Clay a sincerely apologetic look, said, "Tell your publisher to buy you a Porsche. Sounds like they can afford it." Then she was in the VW.

"Good to see you, Clay," Jenni blurted while reclaiming her driver's seat in the VW. Her door closed and the car zoomed quietly away. He looked up; the eagle seemed to be following Jenni and Solstice.

"Not my omen apparently," he whispered.

"Or my car." He patted the Tesla's smooth, white fender.

Halfway home from Grandview Park, he thought back to one long ago summer afternoon. He and Solstice had been home from college, and he remembered the day for one detail only: her observation "As writers, it will be our job to shoulder the pain of the world." The notion held no appeal to Clay who then as now greatly preferred the prospect of shouldering the less cumbersome burdens of wealth and fame. So why was he the one driving home in a hand-me-down Volvo?

He quickly reassured himself that everything he ever wanted was in his reach: book tours and interviews; cars that went from zero to 90 in seconds; the family he and Marta no longer seemed to discuss. He had the talent to pull it off. All he needed was the gift of time—that and a plot—and Randolph J. Simper was about to provide the former.

Chapter 8
⌘

THE POWER LUNCH

Five minutes into meeting at Jacques D's, Randolph J. Simper seemed ready to withdraw his offer. "I don't see a need to bring others into this. Furthermore, I can't believe you invited them to join us. Here, today. I feel like I've been ambushed."

He and Clay shared Randolph's "usual table" close to the windows while separated from other diners by that moat of carpet. Randolph had just learned that a second, larger table was also reserved in their names. The plan was to move to the V.I.P. Room in 35 minutes at 12:45. But Randolph held veto power. If he said no, there would be no larger meeting.

Clay offered, "I don't know if this will make any difference, but this wasn't my idea. I was quite happy with your original proposal."

"Then why—"

"Marta talked with her MBA study group."

Randolph seemed more confused than angry. "Is she going to be here?"

Clay nodded, hoping this wouldn't irritate Randolph further.

"I guess I can't blame her for believing in your writing," Randolph said. "You are a great writer and I want to help you prove this. But I'm not going to pretend I don't resent being blindsided."

Clay, who had been looking forward to wearing his new jacket, tie, and shirt to lunch, now wanted to take off the jacket, remove the tie, and unbutton the shirt's collar that burned like bee stings. He had driven to Jacques D's basking in confidence and hope, looking forward to accepting Randolph's offer. But in the awkwardness that came with telling Randolph about the additional investors, his shirt had seemed to shrink a few sizes.

Clay was also beginning to question the idea of waiting for the entire party to assemble before ordering lunch. The aromas from other tables intruded into their conversation: warm peach cobbler, onion rings, fried catfish mingling with barbecued pork. His stomach grumbled its dissatisfaction at being left out. He took another drink of his Martini, trying to drown the hunger, but met no success. What was that new smell? Prime rib? Clay reminded himself that the ability to delay gratification was somewhat important to writing—something he'd been pretty good at up till that moment.

"I proposed investing $200,000 and that's what I would like to do, invest $200,000. That remains the offer." A thin dash of a smile appeared on Randolph's face. "I do like the idea of owning 40% of your potential profit. That's far more generous than anything I was proposing."

Marta appeared behind Randolph. When Clay got up from his seat to acknowledge her presence, Randolph turned his head and tried to say hi. Not much came out, and Clay could see that the multi-millionaire app creator was blushing. "*Hola*, Randy," Marta said. "Did Clay tell you my idea?"

Randolph was now standing. "It certainly caught me by surprise." Remembering the cloth napkin hanging from the front of his collar, he snatched it away.

"Surprised?"

"In a good way," said Randolph. "I was just telling your husband how utterly impressed I was by its brilliance and beauty."

Marta smiled like an MBA student learning she got an A on her test.

"Still, my original offer remains firm," Randolph continued. "I want to be able to say I had something to do with this novel. You tell your friends they're free to add to the pot and in any amount they so choose. But I'm still in for 200 G's."

"You can tell them yourself," said Marta. "They'll be here in a few minutes."

Randolph sat back down, his smile disappearing. "So I've been told." Marta's sunset red dress seemed snug as she took the seat to Clay's left—the seat that seemed to have appeared out of thin air courtesy of a staff that paid close attention to Randolph's table. A waiter hoisting a tray shot past, distracting Clay with the melding aromas of sweet potato fries and chicken Alfredo. Randolph spoke quietly. "H-how have you been, Martha?"

"I prefer to be known as Marta," she said, prefacing a story Clay knew by heart, word for bilingual word. Listening intently as she presented the story of how she embraced her proud Latino heritage, Randolph nodded when appropriate.

Once she had finished, Randolph asked the names of the new investors. She fulfilled his request, adding minor details about each study group member as she went. No sooner had she finished than Randolph excused himself from the table. He walked toward the restrooms but stopped short of the doors. Clay could see him making a call, cell phone in hand. A good ten minutes passed before he returned.

Smiling and wafer thin, a waitress walked behind him. She didn't let Randolph reclaim his seat. "Excuse me, Mr. Simper, sir, your group table is ready." Framed by long blond hair, the girl seemed barely out of her teens.

Randolph scowled.

Clay's stomach grumbled.

"We think you'll be pleased with the Vip Room," the waitress continued, prompting the question, was she trying to be cute, or did she simply not do well with initials? "It's just this way, through the doors."

The round table at the center of the room was set for seven. A man stood beside it. "Shaky Dick Breitbach," Randolph called to him. "Well, I'll be damned."

Built like a barrel without the solidity, Chamber President Dick Breitbach smiled uncomfortably as he approached. "Just Dick. Nobody calls me that other thing anymore."

Randolph nodded almost imperceptibly, providing a subtle "Understood."

It impressed Clay that Randolph had been able to recognize the Chamber President who had shed most of his once plentiful hair, leaving him with a dome as notable for its shininess as baldness. Breitbach wore an embroidered casual shirt, its tropical images—palm trees, hibiscus flowers, and brightly colored toucans—jumping out from a sky blue background. The bottom hem had been tailored to a straight edge, allowing him to leave the shirt untucked and take his labored casual look to its extreme.

"It's really great to see you after all this time," Breitbach said. "Everyone here is so happy for your success." Clay turned to take in the V.I.P. Dining Room, a location new to him with its south facing windows providing a fresh view of the winding river bordered by steep yellow bluffs and green wooded hills.

"Goodness gosh, Dick, to leave me behind?" Cessna Breitbach darted into the room, moving full speed until stopping abruptly, only inches from her husband, the closeness of which allowed her to tower over him. Already a good six feet to Dick's five and a quarter, she augmented her height with high black heels and puffed up blond hair that made her look, when contrasted with Dick, like she stood *eight* feet tall. She promptly introduced herself to Randolph, adding that she was one of the few Duchainers not placed there by accident of birth. She came from a well-to-do banking family in Moline, Illinois, and owned her own party-planning business. Part'e Hart'e did a lot of contract work for the Chamber.

Dick, for his part, came ready with Chamber hyperbole. "Have any of you guys checked out the new Panda Pickup at the mall? I've heard the food is spectacular."

Cessna was more interested in sharing the dream she held with husband Dick. "Once he has his MBA," she enthused, "we're going to start a travel agency and call it The World at a Discount. Our pitch will be, 'If there's one thing you can't risk, it's an expensive vacation gone awry.'" Clay assessed her voluminous hair, piled wavy and high. It actually didn't look bad on her, at least no more so than the multiple coats of makeup. "We'll offer incredible bargains to places no sensible person would even think of visiting," she continued. "We'll make danger the only real danger. If a fresh revolution breaks out in the Middle East—or better yet, some religious fanatics start crucifying American hostages—we'll arrange package vacations at cut-throat... sorry, poor choice of words... super low fares. *People are dropping... prices too!* Come heck or high water, plagues or drug violence, we'll be there, or rather our clients will."

Had this been a normal conversation with normal people who weren't offering to give him $253,000, Clay might have said, "I find that revolting on so many levels." He kept these words to himself.

Cessna gave Randolph an exaggerated smile, "It's something you might want to consider investing in, Mr. Simpler. At a later date, of course. Unless—" Clay heard the most strained laugh of all time. "Clay here makes us all billionaires."

"I liked the cut-throat angle," a new voice interjected with a clipped, urgent tone sternly accenting each staccato syllable. "It helps drive your concept home." Now standing between the two Breitbachs was an imposing, impeccably dressed man in his late fifties. This was Benedict Howell, the president of Bedrock Faith Based Publishing and the son-in-law of founder Magus Mullin. The oldest member of Marta's study group, his formidable presence contradicted Cessna Breitbach's claim that she was the only non-native represented at lunch that day. As everyone who read the *Duchaine Lamplighter* knew, Chicago native Benedict Howell had seized power at Bedrock in a very public battle with Mullin's actual son while the old man exhibited dementia and the cokehead son was creating his own. Rumors persisted that Benedict Howell had surreptitiously taken the role of Jerry Mullin's dealer, supplying more and more coke until Jerry could no more run a company than stop drooling or shaking. Jerry now resided in the same Gentle Acres Assisted Living suite his father had occupied right up to the night he smothered himself with a pillow.

Howell's angular face showed nothing in the way of cheerfulness, offset as it was by icy gray eyes and silver hair that seemed lacquered in place. This was Clay's first encounter with Benedict Howell but Marta had briefed him beforehand and he was dying to ask about Howell's family history, if only to watch Howell's expression and demeanor as he related it firsthand.

No sooner had Randolph and the others taken their seats than Clay turned to Howell to say, "I understand your family boasts an interesting past."

"Ah yes," replied Howell. "You want to hear the story of how my grand-papa changed the family name when he came to America."

"At Ellis Island?" asked Cessna Breitbach.

"Indeed, but hardly with the rabble swarms. Not Irish nor Eastern European. Grandpapa came in Nineteen Forty-Seven, leaving post-war Germany. As my father often recounted, our family name could have been more problematic, but only by two letters. And so we went from Himmler to Howell."

"Himmler?" said Randolph. "The S.S. commander?"

"He was not a close relative as much as my detractors wish it to be. Truth be told, my grandpapa rarely talked about time spent with his Uncle Heinrich."

Perhaps seeing the need for a new subject, Dick Breitbach nodded toward the empty chair. "We're missing someone."

"And that someone is about to miss lunch," Randolph said. "I cannot tolerate tardiness, especially in the context of a business setting."

Marta consulted her fitness wristband, tapping it twice to call up the time. The thin waitress slowly orbited the table, taking orders for food and drink. Clay chose fried catfish and, out of respect for his host, iced tea spiked with vodka.

A few minutes later, the waitress and a young male assistant delivered a wide variety of appetizers spread across two trays. "Thank you, Mr. Simper," said the waitress, "for sending your chef over yesterday. I think you will be very pleased with the ceviche. You've got to understand, you know, that as far as making something like this goes, there aren't a lot of Hispanics in Duchaine."

Marta cleared her throat, successfully snagging the attention of the waitress, and making her blush wildly.

"What I mean," the young woman nervously added, "is um we miss out on a lot of culture and good food here in Duchaine."

Everyone was watching Marta as she said, "It's true. I grew up in this town and I've never had ceviche. Thank you, Randolph. And thank your chef."

Two drinks and most of his meal later, Clay looked up from his nearly empty plate to see a heavy, unkempt man approaching. Taken together, his longish, uncombed hair and patchy beard brought to mind a bear coming out of hibernation. A rumpled yellow and green Packers jersey was tucked into his jeans in places, while hanging loose in others like covers dangling from an unmade bed. "Hey, group!" the man called out in a booming voice. "Artemis Cobb is in the house!"

Here, thought Clay, was a man who wasn't content to embarrass himself without including everyone around him. Clay immediately saw the flaw in his theory, however, as this particular ass clown had clearly never experienced personal embarrassment. This was the most disposable member of the group according to Marta, the one she could have gone without seeing for, well, a lifetime. Fortunately, Artemis skipped most of their study sessions, just as he did the actual classes.

Cobb turned to flag down a waitress—"Who do you have to fuck to get a drink around here?"—and Clay saw the back of his jersey. Instead of the clichéd name and number of a FAVRE (4) or RODGERS (12), Artemis Cobb's shirt was custom designed to blare, "COBB" and "1."

Clay heard no "Sorry, I'm late" as Cobb claimed the remaining empty seat. Ten years older than Marta and Clay, and a graduate of St. Gregory the Great Catholic High School, Cobb was new to Clay in physical presence only, his reputation well known in Duchaine. Clay had needed little briefing from Marta on the retired fourth-generation dairy farmer who had owned the land that became Duchaine Mall two decades before. Cobb sold the valuable parcel after managing it with unimpressive results for only two years, which corresponded with the time he called it his inheritance. Following the sale, Cobb became known as a connoisseur of wine, women, and drugs, if apparently not fine clothes. Clay was pleased to occupy a seat some distance from Cobb, thinking he might well smell musty.

Clay focused now on the turquoise designer glasses with lenses so thick they made Cobb's dark eyes look large and disconnected in their movements from the rest of the plump, darkly tanned face. Turning toward Randolph, the strange man smiled and loudly said, "Randolph J. Simper! This is a real fucking pleasure! I have your app!" The magnified eyes seemed to grow larger.

"*Que?*" said Marta.

"Sorry?" said Cobb.

"You're always taking photos during study group."

"Jesus Christ," Cobb said with an extremely forced laugh. "I got no reason to actually *use* Randolph's app. It's just… you know, Randolph here is such a local hero… it felt like it was my civic duty to download *StripOff*."

He returned his attention to Randolph. "I'm not shitting you, Rand, you got the best business model ever. It's like an addiction, all these apps you put out to go with the first one. Each more and more expensive. I've got 'em all, that's how it works. Difference between me and most of your customers is I can afford 'em." He scratched an itch on his stomach. "You and me have a lot to talk about, a couple of rich guys living life to the fullest, taking whatever we want, traveling the world, collecting old cars, hunting exotic animals. Rich guy stuff. Not like I have to tell you, Rand."

Randolph shifted in his seat, having already been on edge from the piped-in smooth jazz replications of songs from his teenage years which could barely be heard when sitting at his usual table in the main dining room. He wondered if he was the only one who even detected the noise pollution, and wondered even more strongly why anyone had ever listened to the original, pimply, mass-produced songs, let alone these less authentic incarnations.

Randolph nearly smiled to himself, thinking it odd he hated these particular songs more than the rest of music's vast recorded library when he truly disliked *all* music. Classical compositions offered too much variation to hold his valuable attention while rock, blues, and country suffered from too much repetition. The best he could concede was that music was a form of math, an art he otherwise enjoyed. But music made too much noise to be good math.

"I hope you're planning to make us all richer than shit," Cobb interrupted his thoughts. "I sure as hell don't want you to lose any of it. I worked too hard for my damn dollars."

"Didn't you inherit all your money?" Randolph asked. "The dairy farm? You sold your birthright."

"I seized the opportunity. Like my daddy used to say, when a cow stops giving milk you gotta sell the meat." Artemis Cobb ran one of his blocky caveman hands through the disheveled hair, likely the closest it came to getting brushed that week.

"The dairy farm was thriving when it became yours," Randolph differed, drawing from the research texted to him only minutes before by a team of private investigators when he was standing near the restroom doors. "And didn't your father also say he wanted you to preserve it for future generations? I was only in middle school, but I remember it all from KDUC."

"The big lies were all according to my Judas fake brother. Lucas Fucking Cobb. Conniving. Greedy. Adopted."

"I was adopted," Marta said.

"That's got nothing to do with it," Cobb bludgeoned along. "Like apples to orangutans. *You* weren't in court suing *me* and dragging *my* family name through the cow shit."

Clay didn't like seeing discomfort among his prospective benefactors, thinking they should save such bickering for after they wrote their checks. And so he said, "You almost missed a delicious meal, Mr. Cobb. I'm sure the waitress can take your order."

It mostly worked. "I think everyone here can agree the food here is spectacular," volunteered Dick Breitbach.

"I say we enjoy the food, view, and company," Clay resumed, "and discuss the classic American novel I'm going to finish with your help."

"I thought it was nearly complete," said Howell, "going on what Marta told us."

"I have been working on it for some time. There are just a few loose ends to tie up, but I have to get everything right if the Consortium is to get the return to which they're entitled."

"The timeline?" asked Cobb.

"I finish the book in two years, perhaps sooner, and make the following year a deadline for getting it published or at least under contract."

"And you've done this before?" asked Cessna.

"I'll be motivated."

Saying he spoke for the Consortium, Dick Breitbach presented the details. A $2500 investment in Clay's forthcoming first novel would be worth point-five-percent of the net profit. This would apply to book sales, movie rights, and public appearances related to the novel.

Benedict Howell added, "These terms apply to all of us, Mr. Simper included."

Randolph cleared his throat, sustaining the last sound to produce a subdued growl, a wolf ready to defend its territory.

Cessna presented a hefty stack of paper separated into several sections by brightly colored strips the size of bookmarks. "This is the contract. Twenty-eight pages total."

"That is one very thick contract," Randolph noted, to which Clay could have added, *Yes, much thicker than my manuscript.* "Did Mr. Howell add clauses for partitioning Poland?"

Mr. Howell did not seem amused.

"We didn't want to leave any *t*'s uncrossed," Cessna said. "This contract covers every eventuality from electronic publication to foreign translation rights."

"In great detail apparently." Randolph claimed the top copy. "My lawyers will need to review this."

"The same lawyers who brought down your rival, Strippit?" asked Breitbach.

"This will require my contract lawyers," Randolph said. "I see no need for copyright lawyers."

"Excellent," Howell said. "We welcome their review."

Dumplings and chicken arrived for Artemis Cobb as Dick Breitbach offered, "As an investor I am not altogether averse to risk. At times, in fact, I love it. Penny stocks, airlines."

Cessna looked at Marta and said, "Yet all he does is complain about his bad picks."

Dick responded testily. "I can afford to indulge myself. Invest in something I like."

Cessna laughed. "You mean this... a novel? Since when have you liked novels?"

"She's forgetting I own three first-edition Tom Clancy classics. Golden Age, wouldn't you agree? And besides—" He turned to face Cessna. "We both know I'm going to need a ghostwriter someday. *Lee Iacocca... Jack Welch... Dick Breitbach...*"

Clay's immediate reaction involved acid reflux, but a silver lining soon revealed itself in the guise of motivation. Clay would write the greatest novel of the 21st Century if only to avoid being contracted to produce *Taking Over the World at a Discount: The Dick Breitbach Story.*

"I have always been fascinated by artistic types," Benedict Howell interjected while Cessna distributed the contract copies. "It presents a significant contradiction in that some intelligence is required to create books, art, and music, yet pure idiocy is the main prerequisite for even vaguely considering one of these as a career choice. My father once said that Adolph Hitler did some regrettable things but the stupidest one was trying to be an artist."

Randolph cleared his throat, and said, "We will meet again. Same location one week from today. If my lawyers find no fault with this document, I will be ready to sign." He then called the waitress to discuss dessert—and getting rid of the piped-in music.

Chapter 9

⌘

EPIPHANY (OR, AT LEAST, A PLOT)

Standing outside the restaurant, Randolph shuffled nervously as Marta kissed Clay goodbye. Clay knew better than to make his main benefactor uncomfortable, of course, yet couldn't deny savoring the thought, *Here's one thing your money can't buy.*

He held the Volvo door open for her, and gave her another kiss. He then stood beside Randolph to watch her drive away.

"It still seems odd calling her Marta," Randolph said. "Martha is such a lovely name. I'm not sure I would have allowed that."

Clay almost stayed quiet out of respect for the $200,000 Randolph had not fully signed over, but owed his wife a response. "I can't deny it took some getting used to, but I like the name Marta. Even if I didn't, it's hardly my call. We don't really have a traditional Taliban marriage. We tried, but once they start driving it's a slippery slope."

Randolph shook his head. "I suppose it's like they say, you can't live with them and you can't live without them."

This time, Clay kept himself from saying, "I think *they* stopped saying that sometime in the last century."

Behind the wheel of his own Volvo, Clay took every route but the direct one home. Pushing 60 on a straight stretch of County Fair Road, he lowered the driver side window, took off his tie, and released it to the wind, the wind ripping it from his hand.

Back in town, still thoroughly lost in thought, Clay absorbed the cool, increasingly cloudy afternoon as he approached St. Gregory the Great Catholic High School. Directly ahead, he saw protesters blocking the road, then realized they were simply crossing the road to board three yellow school buses. They carried signs with images of either cute, happy babies or bloody, less fortunate fetuses, and Clay remembered the article from last night's *Lamp-*

lighter. This day marked the anniversary of the "abortion factory" opening on Lower Main nearly half a century before, and today, as in every past year, Duchaine's first and only family planning clinic was getting some visitors. Watching the protesters, who for the most part seemed cheerful at the prospect of leaving school early, Clay hit upon the plot for his novel. *Two outcasts find each other and fall in love. She is a full-time anti-abortion fanatic and he is an animal rights activist who finds PETA "dull and complacent." The two Midwestern-ers in their late twenties are brought together because they share the view that contemporary American society is the moral equivalent of Nazi Germany.* Here was an idea that had long intrigued Clay: that an individual could go through his or her entire life so far out of the mainstream as to be paddling non-stop to stay afloat in the festering backwaters of a slough.

The novel would address bigger questions, he thought now with a genuine smile, like the nature of reality and the fragility of shared truth. If everyone believed in "reality," it existed. But without that belief, it was no less a fantasy than the value of stocks on the New York exchange. *So long as we all pretend together.* Clay's characters were the nonbelievers, the heretics with their own fully fantasized alternate universe.

He told himself this would not be a political novel, because he wouldn't be a political writer. He would approach the topic as sociology, positing the theory that, in a crowded, thoroughly ordered civilization, politics offered the last refuge for unapologetic anger and hatred. As Clay saw it, one could take any supposedly clever political bumper sticker and paraphrase its message to read, "You, sir, in the car directly behind mine, are an absolute asshole." Politics, per Clay's supposition, had replaced public floggings and gladiatorial fights. In future years both distant and near, readers would thank Clay for pointing this out.

The two meet—his mind was racing now—*at the farmhouse of a mutual friend: a disgruntled soon-to-be-fired mall security guard who wants to start his own militia and overthrow the Jewish-American government, at least during the years there's a Democrat in the White House. Ironically, he is a genuine Nazi, a character flaw our two main characters are conveniently willing to overlook.*

But it doesn't take long for the two lovers to grow tired of driving to each other's "interminable protest marches" (his words). With the help of their mutual friend, they concoct a plan to blow something up, but can't agree on a single, specific target. He suggests a cosmetics testing lab outside of Milwaukee; she wants the closest abortion clinic. Over a few short months, tension builds to where they despise each other for their insensitivity to causes that are not their own. "I'm not going to prison for some fucking cats," the woman says, to which her partner responds, "And I'm not going to prison for some half-formed glob of cells."

Seemingly irreconcilable, these differences are destroying everything but their occasionally passionate rhythm-method sex life. Jared and Pita must find something in common to blow up together, a goal made even more difficult by their friend's obsessive wish to bomb the Clairmont Mall, his former and only place of employment.

A car honked behind Clay letting him know the protesters had successfully crossed the road. He raced home to begin his novel, envisioning it as a brilliant, quirky comedy. He couldn't wait to tell Marta he had his plot.

***

Comfortably seated in his dimly lit room, Randolph proceeded through the contract with great deliberation, listening carefully as his most trusted lawyer, Mason D. Barrell, read each line aloud. Now that he had become a "giant of industry," Randolph J. Simper did not use his own eyes for reading whether from paper or pad. He paid others to do this for him: a rich man's custom Audio Books service. This was how he had taken in Clay's *Give Me a Second While I Execute the Dog*—an exercise Randolph still remembered as marginally painful.

Mason D. Barrell was an ex-trial lawyer who got rich suing the Green Bay public school system after a classroom shooting. Officially retired when StripOff first contacted him, he was lured back into service as Randolph's personal lawyer at a hard-to-resist annual rate—and because he had blown most of his earlier winnings on five sprawling mansions in varied exotic locations and almost as many divorces. When he and Randolph first met in California, with the 56-year-old Barrell flown there at Randolph's expense, the lawyer said of the shooting, "It wasn't about the money."

Randolph had laughed, causing Barrell to glare. "I beg your pardon, sir, but our suit was *not* about the money. It was about improving school security."

Randolph laughed even harder. "'Wasn't about the money.' When a lawyer says that, he's talking *lots* of money. Wisconsin was lucky to have any schools at all after losing that suit. How many teachers' salaries do you think it takes to equal sixteen-million dollars?"

That was when Barrell conceded, "Well, maybe it was a *little* bit about the money." With those words, Barrell became a trusted business associate, placing him as close as one could come to being Randolph's friend. It was a distinction he retained seven years later.

Hunched over the hard-copy contract in the dim light of a single lamp and wearing tiny round glasses on a wide head that seemed supported by the bulbous double chin, Barrell looked like a toad in an illustrated children's book. "How curious," Randolph interrupted as Barrell delivered page nineteen of the proposed new contract. "Could you read that last clause again?"

The lawyer returned to the second paragraph's opening sentence: "'The CONSORTIUM holds the right to protect its investment by purchasing life insurance on the WRITER up to a value of eight million (8,000,000) dollars."

"Interesting, wouldn't you say?" Randolph interjected.

"Indeed. From everything you've told me about—" Mason D. Barrell held up his fingers to make air quotation marks. "—the *WRITER*, I'd say our Mr. Turner will be worth more to the Consortium dead than alive. You know what I'd call this? The ultimate termination clause."

"Do you think they're planning to let him write something first?" Randolph asked. "Give him the chance to surprise them?"

"That would seem the logical approach, as would the suggestion I'm about to make. Why not round it up to an even ten-million? It's a much tidier number. And if Mr. Turner is going to object to the life insurance clause, it won't necessarily have anything to do with the specific stated amount of potential remuneration."

Randolph stood up to stretch his legs. "I must say I'm surprised to find this language in the contract. I've been under the assumption I was working with a consortium of Hummer-driving mouth breathers. It made no sense for someone who has barely dented the top tax bracket to throw money away on a fifth-rate writer who may not even finish his book."

"From everything you told me, your lunch was no G7 Summit."

Irritated by a slight hint of chafing, Randolph adjusted the money garter on his thigh, and wondered if he shouldn't remove some of the hundred-dollar bills it held. Another crow cawed outside the shaded window, prompting Randolph to tense and Barrell to say, "You've got to love those birds picking the meat off bones even with traffic shooting right past them. They know what they want and they get it."

Randolph held off on summoning security. He was hearing the crow in a new way, admiring the shrillness of its cries. "I suppose so, Mason. It isn't an entirely unpleasant sound, provided one truly listens."

***

Ending his afternoon in a truly good mood, Clay surpassed his goal of writing ten pages in one sitting. Double-spaced and framed by one-inch margins on all sides, his rough first chapter showcased the number 28 at the bottom of its final page.

Clay was feeling so good—so confident, upbeat, and proud—that he prepared dinner at home, choosing to surprise Marta with his oven-broiled five-cheese nachos.

"Delicious," she sighed from across the glass kitchen table. "More jalapeños than usual?"

"This afternoon everything changed for the better," he said as she scooped up a generous portion of the refried beans and sour cream with a wide chip smothered in molten cheese. "The planets and stars—every last one—lined up in my favor. I now have my plot."

He shared his rough mental outline.

"Interesting," she said. "But are you sure it's a comedy?"

"A dark one, granted. It worked for Solstice."

"Then... well... great, honey. I am so *orgulloso*. I'd pull out that other bottle of Champagne if I didn't have study group tonight."

Clay wanted to ask what *orgulloso* meant. Proud? Amazed? But Marta spoke first: "Did you read the contract?"

"I guess if you're going to study group—though you could skip one night—I'll read it while you're out."

"Tonight's pretty important," she said. "Our first year finals are coming up."

After she departed, Clay kept his promise, for the most part. But the twenty-eight page document proved incredibly boring—WRITER this, CONSORTIUM that—and he ended up skimming a number of paragraphs as he sat at the kitchen table. Topics like international translation rights and print publication excerpts spanned dozens of single-spaced paragraphs when one short paragraph could have covered them all by simply stating, *The investors' return rate of one-half percent per share applies to all royalties received by the author in whatever format the work takes, including but not limited to the following...*

In between reading and enjoying a slug of white rum and Diet Coke, Clay paused to whisper, "Two-hundred and fifty-three thousand dollars. That's the number that matters here. I believe I'm finished with teaching and grading six-page papers that run six pages too long. Fare thee well, Douche U. Fare thee well."

Knowing Marta would have been very displeased with his inattention toward the contract, Clay promised himself to call an old high school classmate the following morning. He would offer to buy lunch for Moon McDermott, currently Duchaine's most notorious trial lawyer—and the only one with TV commercials, each loudly promising potential clients, "The Scrapper will get you everything you deserve... and more!"

Moon actually owed Clay a favor, even if Clay had been compensated for the ancient, original favor, helping to finish Moon's high school history paper on "Wisconsin's Earliest Settlers" the night before it was due. Having received only $35 for that ass-saving effort, Clay felt confident that Moon would review the Consortium's unreadable contract.

Leaving said document on the table, Clay retreated to his office to Google *BEST NEW SPORTS CARS*. There it was, the Tesla Model X. Zero to sixty in 2.8 seconds. He really wanted that toy, but per the cliché, first things came first. He typed up his notice for Duchaine University. *This is to inform you that, in two weeks, I will vacate my position at DU, thereby escaping the one circle of hell Dante failed to imagine.*

***

Six miles east of town, Randolph J. Simper leaned on the 24-karat gold rail of the open-air dining area that adjoined the other rooftop amenities that had yet to be used, among these a miniature golf course and Olympic size swimming pool. His 43,000 square-foot mansion crowned Mt. Pewauka, named for the Fox Indian Chief who found God in the form of Jacques Duchaine. Even if it was more hill than actual mountain, Pewauka towered as the area's highest summit, permitting Randolph to gaze upon the gently twinkling lights of the city, excluding those in the actual river valley. "Don't despair, my chosen one," he said, facing the general area of Cleveland Avenue where Clay and Marta Turner regrettably cohabitated. "Good fortune isn't planning to ignore you much longer."

Chapter 10
⌘

CALL NOW FOR YOUR FREE CONSULTATION

"This—" Moon McDermott paused for dramatic effect. "Is the definition of an ideal contract. They're essentially offering to pay you for simply promising to *try* to do something. It's insanely generous on their part. Foolishly so. You don't have to deliver a goddamn sentence to keep their cash."

Outside of Moon's many TV commercials, the last time Clay had seen Duchaine's most famous lawyer was as a skinny high-school senior with a complexion raw enough to be remembered years later—and with, per rumors at the time, a GPA that no longer supported even the early underpinnings of his plan to become a Supreme Court Justice. In the time between, Moon had become The Scrapper, looking exactly like he did in his TV commercials: wide Irish face with thinning brown hair offset by untrimmed shrubs of eyebrows and a wide, red broken-capillary nose, all of which conspired to make him look twenty years older than he was. One wooden plaque on his wall read, *IF YOU NEED AN AMBULANCE CHASER, HIRE THE ONE WHO KEEPS UP.*

Moon had been very gracious in setting up the "initial consultation" and surprisingly happy to read Clay's contract, noting how incredibly grateful he remained for the paper that saved his history grade. No payment required. No bottle of bourbon, no gift certificate for Jacques D's.

Clay thanked Moon for reviewing the contract. "To be honest, I didn't get far in my own attempt. All I could think was, I'm not a lawyer."

"Well, it's a fine contract in every respect. So—" Moon pulled a cigar from a dark hardwood box. It went no further than his hand. "How's your brother doing all these years later?"

"Colorado seems to fit him," Clay said. "He's still thankful for your help back in high school. Luckily, as you must remember, their lawyers lacked teeth. The lawsuit never happened."

Moon shook his head, waved his unlit cigar. "Ah shit, Clay. That was nothing compared to your writing that paper for me. I got a bit sidetracked my senior year, after Graham sent that Thank You package from Colorado. I'll say one thing, your brother knew his cannabis."

They caught up on fellow Senior alumni. Chuck Latham. Heather Pear. Barry Hendricks and Hound Dog Hummel, names that came up often in nostalgic conversations. "Hound's been a client of mine. Big surprise there, huh?" When Clay mentioned Randolph's return, Moon asked, "What the fuck for? To buy up Duchaine?"

Moon also showed trust in Clay by sharing "a proprietary idea still in its infancy. It does not leave this room." Moon was considering the addition of a financial planning service. "A practical one for these times. I match you with the right lawsuit for your retirement needs."

All the while, Clay had been taking in the office that spanned the considerable length of the ninth and top floor of The Duchaine Bank and Trust Building. The space boasted leather chairs, a fully stocked bar, and a full suite of kitchen appliances. It also boasted a framed poster on the wall behind Moon's barge-length desk that made Clay think he was one of the privileged few allowed into the sanctum. Reprising a theme from one of Moon's billboards, it wasn't something he'd want many to see. DRUNK DRIVERS DESTROY LIVES. This had been appended with BUT THEY HAVE BEEN VERY GOOD TO MINE.

The meeting ended with Moon telling Clay, "Don't waste one drop of sweat on this contract. It's packed with protections for you in every imaginable situation."

Clay felt pleased with himself, and pleased with his decision to consult an old friend. He was ready to sign the contract. The thoroughly reviewed contract.

Chapter 11

WORD COUNT

Time passes quickly when living outside it.

It sure passed quickly for a writer at work. Bringing characters to life and giving them things to do kept a novelist busy, blurring days together like cornfields glimpsed from a speeding Gold Wing.

Clay knew the seasons had changed, of course. He knew Christmas had passed, that trees stood naked as StripOff subjects, that snow was falling more often than not. But other than thinking it was probably January, conventional measures of time meant little to him. Days and weeks had been usurped. He tracked forward motion in paragraphs and pages.

Clay would have been quick to point out one big exception. He still recognized Saturday evenings. Even then, he owed his awareness entirely to Marta's interventions. When she came home to announce the end of her school week by popping a Champagne cork, his ears pricked up like a dog's. Staying in character, he shot toward the kitchen with the speed of a greyhound, sometimes passing the house's real dog. Did he drool in the process? He couldn't say.

With one cold sip of sparkling lightness, he felt himself transported to a sweetly scented oasis where candles replaced more conventional lighting and Marta slipped on her borderline negligee pajamas, then slipped them back off, then took Clay in her arms, squeezing and rubbing as if gently molding him, as if he were actual clay, then coaxed him on with calls of *"Más, más"* before finally shouting to the ceiling, *"¡Oh Dios! ¡Oh Dios!"*

He also found time for what Marta now called "The Month of Sundays." This was her winter break, four weeks total, all without school, two without work. She slept in while Clay wrote. He brought her venti vanilla lattes from The Grind, the new coffee place on Hill Street. Together, they did last minute shopping for her parents, bought themselves one very red couch, and after imbibing more Bailey's Irish Cream than intended one night, tested the sofa's durability.

And now, January, late in the month ... probably. Eager to finesse some dialogue that bothered him during his last visit to Chapter Six, he adjusted the blinds in his office, stepped over Argos, and got comfortable in his chair.

"Jesus," he whispered after bumping his mouse, causing the screen to come back to life. "February 10th. How did that happen?"

The answer, of course, was *Explosive Love*, all 168 pages of it. Protagonists Jared and Pita had recently celebrated nine chapters together. If yet to find a mutually acceptable site to destroy—giving *Explosive Love* the horizon point on which all lines would converge—the couple had gathered plenty of options. For this, they could thank their dedicated creator, Clayton Elliott Turner, steadfast borrower of library books, tireless reader of online articles, and nascent authority on clinic bombings, lab fires, and mink farm emancipations.

As for the myriad possibilities awaiting *Explosive Love*, it was all a matter of picking and choosing the best elements from each source. Toward that aim, Clay's mind never rested. Deep in its darkest recesses, ideas propagated and mutated, gained substance and strength, eventually to pour out like confused, newly freed mink, some stumbling and not getting far, others finding safe haven in Jared and Pita's story. These bursts of inspiration always caught Clay off-guard—the secret, of course, to any successful escape. He could be in the shower or picking up takeout. He always kept a notepad close.

One more activity tended to spring the locks. When Clay read fiction by others he was constantly interrupted by fugitive plot twists and runaway dialogue, and he had been doing plenty of reading. His stack of books no longer towered, having surrendered twelve novels, some so good he forgot to envy their makers.

"Thank you, Randolph," Clay whispered now, performing what had become a morning ritual. "Thank you for liberating me from alarm clocks and schedules, from grading papers and herding freshmen. Thank you for placing your faith in me."

Just before eleven, his computer froze up, a glitch he'd been dealing with more and more. He disconnected the power cord and crept back to the kitchen for an emergency tablespoon of double-dark chocolate gelato. The windows were bright: a formidable snowstorm. Marta would want him to shovel once nature settled down.

His afternoon went well, with much of it spent repaving that rough stretch of dialogue. Marta surprised him by calling to say she'd stay late at work and go straight to her study group. "You sure?" he had asked. "What about getting home in the snow?"

"How long have I been driving in Wisconsin?" she replied.

His computer refroze just after nine. This trip to the kitchen, he reheated two leftover pizza slices, spoils of a pre-storm supply run to Cortino's. Enjoying his snack, he stood facing the windows, borderline hypnotized by the bright, white sheets still tumbling down.

He decided to relax in front of the TV and wait for Marta's safe return. While entreating Argos to surrender a few more inches of couch space, he caught the last minutes of a Comedy Cluster pilot portraying a struggling abstract watercolorist and his rambunctious Great Dane. Clay closed his eyes to garbled thoughts of calling Moon McDermott in the morning to discuss intellectual property theft.

***

Sunshine returned the following day as did Clay's desire to write a great novel. But he didn't add a single word, having gone online to further research the LNL (Liberation Not Laboratories). Somehow, he had been sidetracked by a pair of nesting bald eagles.

He found it quite strange, in fact, the way his computer had redirected him to the DuchaineEagleWatch.org site without prompting.

But he kept watching.

Feeding the live action site, a camera snooped from only inches outside their nest, itself built high on a limestone bluff overlooking the river, location otherwise hidden from Internet stalkers. While the eagles slept, time stood still, leaving Clay determined to catch a trace of movement. But the raptors stood even stiller, creating the impression he was viewing nothing more than a photograph or that his PC had frozen up again. (*Don't even think about it, you metallic piece of shit.*) He literally jumped a few inches in his chair when the male took flight, lifting off more jerkily than gracefully. Clay looked at the time. Nearly 3:30. The eagles were addictive.

Soon after Clay resumed work on the novel, his PC froze up for the sixth time in half as many days, and seemed intent on staying that way. He retreated to his laptop, having wisely saved *Explosive Love* to it as backup. The laptop, too, refused to work.

He launched System Restore on both units and, knowing it would take eons to load, acquiesced to Marta's request he shovel the sidewalks. (Sure enough, she'd left a note on the kitchen counter.) The chore went surprisingly fast, absorbed as he was by the inescapable suspicion a hacker had taken up residence in his computers. Clay pictured a not altogether unsympathetic character: a 400-pound, unemployed tech wiz living in his divorced mother's basement admiring his newest sabotage efforts while chomping on white cream filled long johns. Competing theories involved Russian spies who looked like Jennifer Lawrence in *Red Sparrow* sharpening their skills between American elections and Geek Squad employees rustling up work on slow afternoons.

The following day, Clay was tinkering with a passage in Chapter 9 when the computer took over, replacing his window with the Internet eagle watch. This time, he refused to be abducted. But when he tried closing the new window, the computer ignored him.

Pulling the power cord from the back of the base unit, he caught one last flash of eagles. He walked to the kitchen, retrieved the gelato, and scraped clean the carton.

***

His PC cooperated the next morning, and he felt focused. So of course the phone rang. He immediately forgot the great line of dialogue he was planning to give Pita.

The Caller ID read, *Arthur C. Peckham.* Clay hesitated, having made the mistake of picking up months before to hear Peckham say, "I got the strangest letter from an East Coast attorney yesterday. An advertising agency accused me of stealing their copy. Knocked me back a loop. Luckily, once I figured out what the hell it was talking about, I was able to tell them the problem was fixed. *The perpetrator is no longer with us.*" Clay's old boss had waited a few seconds for emphasis. "In a way, I can't deny being impressed. Stealing from the pro's. For God's sake, Turner, I always liked your marketing copy. Never cared much for the writing in your book. That letter explained a lot."

This time, Peckham bore "exciting news. We landed your perfect replacement, a young poetry whiz out of Cleveland. We lured him on board by promising to publish his first collection through the Duchaine University Press. This is a big step forward for us. But man, he wrote the best brochure copy I've ever seen as part of his interview process."

"The Duchaine University Press?"

"Impressive, no?" Peckham responded. "This will be the celebrated inaugural publication."

"So, you could have done that for me?"

"It will be out in a year," Peckham ignored the question. "Publishing companies don't automatically materialize. Say, Clay, have you seen your book on Amazon? It's the talk of the faculty lounge this morning."

"What do you mean?"

"It's bad; you'll have to see for yourself. And to think, I briefly thought '346,922 in Books' meant you'd sold that many copies, not how far down it ranked in Amazon sales."

"What else did you see? What do you mean, it's bad?"

"Not that anyone ever thought your book was some kind of masterpiece; you're hardly the world's greatest writer. I mean, outside of the flyers you recycled. But even so—"

Clay heard anger in his own words: "What the hell are you looking at? I've got a five-star rating on Amazon."

Peckham waited a few seconds before responding. "You're sure about that, Mr. *Lazy Writer?*" He stretched out these last two words, achieving the clearly intended effect of making Clay very nervous about going online to see what had happened.

"You know, Clay, for as long as I've known you, you've had this annoying way of making it clear you—"

Clay placed his phone on the kitchen counter, leaving Peckham to wrap up his monologue in an otherwise empty theater.

"One star?" Clay whispered when the book came up on Amazon. "How in the hell?"

Seemingly out of nowhere, 848 "verified purchase" reviews had torpedoed *Give Me a Second While I Execute the Dog* with miserly one-star ratings, all but assuring the book would sink faster than a bestselling celebrity autobiography right after its 42-year-old former-child-star author is revealed by three dozen accusers to still be dating twelve year olds. As if this weren't suspicious enough in itself, the vast majority of Clay's single-star blows were accompanied by single words like *Garbage*, *Amateurish*, and *Sloppy*, each of which appeared over and over, firmly pointing toward an amateurish, sloppy conspiracy. Even the lengthier reviews employed these same choices: *Amateurish garbage that could have been typed up by the main character. Hardly a triumph when the main character's a dog. Lazy writing defined.*

The damage, Clay quickly learned, was not confined to Amazon. Like a malevolent hurricane, the storm had swept across three other Internet sites— Goodreads, Barnes and Noble, and Duchaine's own River Valley Book Store Online Catalog—leveling Clay's previous five-star ratings on each.

Shit, shit, shit. So much for getting randomly targeted by some hacker sitting in his mother's basement. Clay had an enemy, a serious one. But who could possibly hate him this much? On the list scrolling through his brain, Peckham's name came first—he had sure enjoyed sharing the Amazon news—followed by other jealous DU colleagues. How about a C-minus student and his parents? An army of the latter? But who among these suspects had what it took to be Clay's secret abhorrer? The ones with motives lacked means. The ones with means lacked motives.

He thought of contacting Randolph. *Someone's coming after me online. I can't imagine why anyone would want to sabotage our book by destroying my reputation and self-confidence, but it's hard to ignore the possibility.*

Caution prevailed, aided by paralysis. He couldn't have Randolph thinking he'd squandered $200,000 on a paranoid writer unable to handle pressure.

Clay's head reeled. It seethed with anger, pounded in pain. Tortured once more by its owner's math affliction, it tried calculating how many five-star reviews were needed on each site to undo the catastrophe.

A lot.

Or to be more precise, a whole fucking lot.

He felt almost glad to receive a second call, this one delivering a mysterious invitation. "I have something I need to discuss with you," Dick Breitbach explained. "Cortino's? Noon?"

***

Minutes later, Clay regretted jumping out of the shower to grab a third call. It wasn't Dick Breitbach rescheduling lunch. It wasn't Arthur Peckham calling back to apologize.

It was "Josh Bramlett here."

Clay did his best to wrap himself in a towel, an action that really required two phone-free hands. "Excuse me, who?"

"Oh, come on, you recognize my name. I'm in your novel."

Knee deep in confusion, Clay remembered a book he once read for extra credit in Jenni Jensen's class. A tips-for-writers guide produced by one very intense novelist, *On Moral Fiction* told of characters appearing in hallucinatory form whenever the author worked for days without breaks. They spoke to him, gave him direction with the plot.

"Is this supposed to be funny?" Clay asked.

"Seriously?" the man persisted, now with a hint of irritation. "Josh Bramlett? Winner of the silent auction?"

"I'm sorry, but—"

"I hope you're just messing with me, Mr. Turner. I won the auction for my name to appear in your novel. For the Duchaine University Construction Fund. Ever since, you've had me wondering if I'm ever going to see it. I haven't seen any construction either, for that matter."

"Oh yeah, *that* auction." The call now had roots outside of Clay's imagination, even if the caller's name had yet to resonate. "Who gave you this number?"

"What about *this* number? I paid $126 for the privilege of appearing in your book. I don't want to think I gave that money to a dishonest, lazy writer who doesn't honor his obligations."

"You didn't give me any money," Clay said.

"I told everyone at work my name was going to be in print. I told my kids. It's been forever. I keep going on Amazon to find a release date but don't see a thing. Is there a book?"

"Of course there's a book. I was working on it this morning, in fact, until you chose to distract me. If you won the auction, you'll be in my novel. It really only fetched $126? What did you say your name was again?"

Clay swore he heard a growl, followed by, "It can't be that hard to write a novel. I want to see something soon. Three months, four months top. Unless you want to see how difficult I can make things for you. You'll be sorry you ever messed with Josh Bramlett. Obligations are everything, Mr. Turner, and you have one to me. The world doesn't need to know you're a lying, cheating silent auction scammer."

"You got me there. Guilty on all counts. I set up an elaborate scam to steal your $126 for someone else's charity. That's really all it fetched?"

He heard three beeps: Josh Bramlett ending the call.

Clay pulled up Recent Calls and tapped Peckham's number. When the attempt went straight to voicemail, he left a message: "What were you thinking, giving some idiot auction winner my contact information? You had no right to do that."

With lunch less than an hour away, Clay pulled up an online version of the auction catalog for the Eighth Annual World Famous Chocolate and Cheese Lovers Festival, which took place only months after *Give Me a Second* made its public debut. There it was: *Item 17. See your name in Clay Turner's first novel.* Clay cringed at his own naiveté. Still in the grip of that first public acclaim, he had committed the closely related sins of pride and self-promotion. Not only had he offered to place a stranger's name in a novel he had not even started, but he had also given the proposition a full half-page in the auction catalog.

The winner of Item 17 will enjoy the unique privilege of seeing his or her name attached to a minor character in the much-anticipated debut novel by acclaimed Duchaine author Clay Turner. This is the prize that will cap your perfect night out by drawing the envy of all others gathered at the country club for this eminently worthy charitable event.

He Googled *Josh Bramlett Duchaine Wisconsin* to learn he was dealing with a divorced, 46-year-old loan officer at Duchaine Bank and Trust. Josh had two grown children, Linda and Randy. They lived in Chicago.

Here was a guy with time to post fake reviews online. Here was a guy who used the words "lazy writer" and exhibited more than enough unhingedness. But what of the requisite cyber expertise? If anything, Josh Bramlett seemed even less clue-ful than Arthur C. Peckham. Clay needed more information. He needed to conduct further online investigation.

He needed one more thing, something more immediate, and driving to lunch a few minutes later, he came up with the perfect way to honor his commitment to the silent auction winner.

***

Walking into the warm pocket of pizzaroma that made Cortino's one of Duchaine's most popular restaurants, Clay felt confused. Seated at the round table were Dick Breitbach and Benedict Howell ... and Artemis Cobb ... and a woman-child less than half Cobb's age who in a normal world would have been his daughter ... and Moon McDermott? What was going on here?

The lawyer better known as "The Scrapper" spoke first. "Hey, Clay, look who I ran into on my way out. I was just keeping your seat warm till you got here."

"You know each other?"

"This isn't New York," Moon said as he rose from his seat and leaned forward to pat Clay's shoulder. "Big town, small city. As I say at work, here in Duchaine, it's neighbor suing neighbor."

Moon excused himself and Clay took the seat that had indeed been warmed for him. "We already ordered," Breitbach said. "I hope that's not a problem."

"Quite the opposite," said Clay, noting the fragrance of pizza had intensified, made all the more potent by the lack of such on their table. Feeling almost as hungry as he was perplexed, he asked, "What's going on?"

"I talked with the city's head librarian." Breitbach wore a casual blue jacket that shouted Chamber of Commerce. "She liked an idea I had."

"Artemis and I invited ourselves along to make sure you were on board," Howell interjected, delivering each syllable like a quick, hard jab. With every inch of his gray suit tailored to absolute perfection, he was dressed for a day of top-level business meetings.

Cobb was not. Standing to locate a waitress and shout, "Is our grub coming anytime soon?" the lumbering lobotomy of a man still wore his rumpled Packers jersey, the very one he had worn to Jacques D's, the one he had probably been sleeping in. Regarding this last detail, Clay could tell which side Cobb had slumbered on: his left, the side with the matted down hair. The girl, her seat only inches from Cobb's, held a sartorial advantage over her date or client or whatever he was to her. Clay saw no wrinkles in her purple Cardi B Gangsta Bitch Tour t-shirt. Nipple protrusions, yes. Wrinkles, no.

"Well?" Breitbach said.

"Well what?" Clay asked.

Dick's expression showed the embarrassment of a man who had wanted to come by himself. "You're being asked to headline the First Annual Duchaine Lit Fest."

"It's the first ever," Cobb emphasized.

"First's always best," his companion added, her voice smoky and spacey.

"We're thinking June," Dick said. "That gives you four months to prepare."

Clay was taken aback. "Wait," he said, "a public reading? Is this your way of auditing your investment?"

"No, no, of course—" Dick stammered in synch with Howell's "Exactly."

"It would be good to know what you've been doing with our money," Cobb said.

"It sounds like a lot of pressure," Clay thought out loud, "trading near total isolation for the bright lights of public judgement." Privately, he considered how total that isolation had been. Sans feedback from Solstice. Sans the writers group he knew he should have formed months before. Sans even Marta. He definitely needed to share *Explosive Love* with her, the opening chapters at least.

"But—" Clay was distracted by Cobb's companion adjusting Cardi B in a manner that drew even more attention to the absence of a bra. He looked around for a waitress, thinking a glass of water would be helpful. His throat couldn't have been drier.

"But?" Dick pulled him back into the conversation.

"But maybe this would be good for me," Clay said as a family-sized pizza arrived and Cobb shoveled three slices onto his plate, showing he shared his companion's love of firsts. "Hell, I welcome the invitation. I'm writing a good novel. It might be fun to show it off."

Howell and the girl were also eating, the former with a fork. Dick handed Clay a mock announcement. He would be headlining the First Annual Duchaine Lit Fest. Sole headliner, in fact. This would be a major public appearance with Mr. Turner reading from his soon-to-be published novel. Benefiting the Duchaine Foundation for Playgrounds and the Arts, The First Annual Lit Fest would be held at the downtown library with plenty of seating for anyone willing to donate five dollars.

Clay reached to secure a piece of the disappearing pie but was stopped cold by the ding of his phone. Thinking it might be a text from Marta, his hand changed course. *Calm down, lazy writer*, Peckham had typed. *This is Duchaine for Christ's sake. If you want anonymity try New York City. Or gosh maybe you could turn on your Caller ID. See who's trying to call you. Sure works for me.*

Heading home an hour later, still hungry from talking while the others ate most of the pizza, Clay thought of grabbing fast food. Heading up Dodge, a swell of anxiety tried sweeping him away like those flood surges that follow a powerful storm, the ones that kill drivers in low-lying areas who never watch the news or simply assume warnings are meant for other people. Was it wise for Clay to share his months of labor with anyone willing to part with five tax-deductible dollars? What if the story was over their heads? Or they weren't the right audience? But he quickly talked himself to safety. He was writing an excellent novel, after all, and a deadline would motivate him to tidy up the first chapters.

He saw a package on his front stoop. UPS. Five-day delivery. The return address—Denver, Colorado—meant Graham had sent fresh contraband.

As the evening wore on, Clay held firm, refusing to open the package. It wasn't all that difficult. There was no way Clay would invite a major distraction into his home at such a critical time. Not only did he have a "much anticipated first novel" to finish writing, but he also had to prepare for an important first-ever event. He didn't need to be high.

Chapter 12
⌘

PRODIGAL BROTHER

Enjoying the medicine, bro? Graham's email began. *It's been too long. You need to come visit.*

It finished predictably with *Sorry I can't visit Duchaine but you know I got a good reason: I can't visit Duchaine.*

Clay responded, *I'll get out there when I can. There is so much going on right now. I am making serious progress on my novel and need to sustain the momentum.*

I miss you too.

For Clay, Graham Turner provided the only evidence of life before Solstice, writing, and Marta. He did this by providing the only memories from Clay's childhood that deserved to be called good ones. Like when Graham stood up to Archie and Vera. Or how Graham lowered expectations for his younger sibling from kindergarten through twelfth grade, making Clay look like some kind of homework-finishing, attention-paying marvel.

When Graham bolted Duchaine three weeks shy of his high school graduation, it ended a slow-building shit storm. As turbulences often do, this one first stirred on an otherwise flawless spring day. Graham, planning to get high over lunch hour, had witnessed a fatal accident in front of Duchaine Senior High. As the story went, and it went some distance before people got tired of sharing the details, a 42-year-old appliance repairman was "trolling" Beadle Drive—"eye-raping high school coeds," as a lawyer later put it—when his white van inadvertently plowed into freshman Noah Blazer.

It was Graham's account to police that assured no charges would be filed: no involuntary manslaughter, no driving too fast for existing conditions. Noah Blazer had walked into the van's path from between two parked cars, a good half block from the crosswalk and its traffic lights. "The kid was distracted by the phone in his hand," Graham had relayed. "No driver could have stopped that quickly."

That evening, Graham finally achieved his altered state, and while telling his stoner friends how painful it was to witness death, he made the mistake of adding the eulogy, "But I guess you could say Noah died the way he lived. Texting."

Graham's stoner friends found the joke funny and repeated it often in the halls of Duchaine Senior until it left the building, attained its own snowball momentum, and no longer needed their help. Three weeks later, the Blazer family threatened to sue for defamation. Clay arranged a meeting between Graham and Moon McDermott, a sophomore who shared several classes with Clay and was already planning to become a lawyer, federal judge, and ultimately, Supreme Court Justice.

Clay sat in to hear Moon explain, "Your so-called defamation falls under the legal umbrella of 'It's funny because it's true.' The driver was sober and heeding the legal posted limits for speed. The pedestrian was staring at his phone. There are lawyers who could win their case—I believe I could, were I older and lacked scruples—but you have little to fear. This is a frivolous lawsuit and will be dismissed as such."

Moon laughed. "It helps they're suing everyone else in the world, from the public school system to the street maintenance department. They're even going after the brake design team at Ford. The van's thirty years old!"

Archie Turner was less forgiving than the law. His seething, red-faced rage marked the first and last time Clay saw his father emotionally invested in the family. "Stop getting high! Keep your trap shut! No one's got time for this shit!"

The Duchaine School Board, seeing no room for tastelessness in the hallways of their non-charter schools and wanting to distance itself from frivolous lawsuits that bore any connection to the one they already faced, suspended Graham for two weeks in April. Graham responded by walking home, packing his few belongings, and emigrating to Colorado via Greyhound bus for its mountains, anonymity, and legalized medical marijuana.

***

"Colorado"

"I've got a great idea," my brother said after we finished a second joint. This, unfortunately, is no way to begin a story, especially a true one.

Dan lives in Colorado, and while visiting him last summer, he talked me into camping by a beautiful lake outside of Leadville, an old mining town high in the Rockies. "Isn't that magnificent?" Dan said of the mountains reflected in the water. He forgot to add, "when not obscured by rain and fog."

I was already tired before agreeing to the adventure. Argos and I had completed our first and sure to be only cross country trip. In fairness to the dog, he had traveled surprisingly well, meaning he whimpered no more than half the drive, escaped only twice at rest areas, and farted fewer than 300 times...

After two days of feeling damp, cramped, and constipated, not to mention disoriented from lack of oxygen and sleep, I was dying to see a bear in the wild, if only because it would have literally scared the crap out of me. The campers using our site shared only one outhouse, divided in two for differences in gender, and some of the men didn't treat our half with the respect it deserved. Even worse than the predictably wet seat, our "facilities" were ventilated by a wind-powered cylindrical fan on the wooden roof that drew its breath from the unsavory pool below the structure. I realized this because the strong winds outside had reversed the intended air flow direction. Each time I sat down for some serious business, I felt a frigid, smelly updraft. As a result, my business stayed unfinished, and I quickly learned that of the many things I can't abide in this life one is having cold air shoot up my ass.

Argos, the dog who was supposed to be protecting me from bears and mass killers, held firm to his position he would not leave the tent. I had to drag him outside to use the dog bathroom, synonymous of course with all of nature.

None of this bothered Dan, if only because nothing bothered Dan. Recreational marijuana was newly legalized in Colorado and he worked in a Denver dispensary, receiving fifteen-fifty an hour for his labor, along with—and this was the important part—a 60% employee's discount on all Bud Wiser purchases. Come rain or come fog while camping in the mountains, the brother who described himself as a professional stoner chose to sit under the tent's narrow awning and stare at the trees. From time to time, he enjoyed hot dogs fresh out of the plastic. He loved doughnuts, too, including the ones I had brought to meet my own nutritional needs. To strangers passing our campsite, Dan must have seemed my identical twin despite his being born a full two years before me and his weighing an additional thirty pounds, the result of Dan sharing my many weaknesses of the flesh and then topping them off with munchies...

It had been months since Clay last pulled out a copy of *Give Me a Second*, longer since reading "Colorado." Clay smiled at the memory of Chief Editor Leigh Cooley insisting he fabricate the detail of Argos making the trip with him, when in fact it had taken place the summer before Clay's sophomore year at DU, a full seven years before he experienced his first Argos fart.

He missed his brother. He thought about Graham often, same now for the unopened package in the garage. He wondered what goodies it concealed.

Chapter 13
⌘

FITS AND PIECES

Finishing her second glass of Chardonnay on a Saturday evening in April, two months before the inaugural Lit Fest, Marta seemed to be seeking a fight with the world.

Clay heard about the long, trying day of classes and the massive late-season snowstorm that slowed her drive home. "I'm so tired of everything, tired of *casi todo*," she said while reaching for the bottle. "The *idiota* professor kept staring at my *pechos* today. I might as well have been in my *grupo de studio*. What is it with men and an inability to support their heads in a fully upright position?"

Clay's hopes had been dashed. Gone was the friskiness that came with her first shimmering glass. Gone was the sweetly unfolding romance initially promised by the pristine snow accumulating outside their windows. The brie on her plate had not been touched. Neither had the strawberries, pineapple chunks, or water crackers.

"The weather may not admit it," he said, "but your summer break's not that far off. Three glorious months. No more teachers' dirty looks."

"Six more weeks." She broke into tears, which turned out to be an abrupt segue into telling Clay she had been questioning her decision to go after the MBA. "My study group's no better than Professor Plimpton. Clumsily hitting on me."

She wondered aloud if it wasn't too late to abandon her quest and turn her focus to starting the family they no longer discussed. "I want us to be happy," she said. "*Feliz.*"

Magnanimously... heroically... and most of all, foolishly, Clay talked his wife down, convincing her to keep her eye on her prize, "though you could give my prize a little more attention when you're through with your homework."

She excused herself and went to bed, making it there with only seconds to spare before she passed out. He tucked her in to the extent the covers she had landed on would allow, and kissed her on the forehead. Back in the kitchen, staring at the snow, he finished the bottle, wanting to believe he had just been a good husband by placing Marta's interests before his own. In truth, however, he suspected he'd been a thoroughly shitty husband by placing her interests before *their* own. He did not feel *feliz*.

***

Marta woke around three, couldn't fall back asleep.

Her thoughts were familiar, much too familiar. This didn't make them any easier to dodge. They came at her like headlights on a black, moonless night.

Being adopted wasn't easy.

Being different wasn't easy.

Being human wasn't easy.

Try all three at once. Hundreds of books examined that trifecta. Counselors devoted careers to it.

Marta had read none of these books. She had never once visited a therapist to discuss the complexities of her life. Living it had been plenty.

Her parents could not have been more supportive, but they could have been more understanding. Same for her husband. What she wouldn't have given for Clay to fully appreciate her need to learn Spanish. He didn't seem to see how this strengthened the connection, so long ignored, to her genetic and cultural heritage. He didn't seem to grasp how important this was. When she suggested a Honduran vacation as the reward for finishing her MBA studies, he could have said something more than, "That would be okay. I bet that would be interesting." He could have showed enthusiasm.

Growing up, she spent hours thinking, *If one more person tells my parents how lucky I am, that person is going to find him or herself very unlucky.*

Her mother always answered, "We're the lucky ones." Her own answer wouldn't have been so succinct.

From the outside looking in, others couldn't see the shipwreck survivor washed up on shore, existentially alone, bleeding inside.

Loved ones couldn't see the black hole at the center of her universe, absorbing all light, crushing any speck of evidence that might reveal the mysteries of its creation.

She felt herself smiling. *I didn't have a chip on my shoulder. I had the second largest country in Central America.* Maybe she could have used a therapist.

Nah, no way, pure *mierda*. She wasn't the one who needed enlightenment.

She wasn't the one too myopic to see past the straight-A student, loving daughter, excellent catch.

Lucky, lucky, lucky. So damned lucky.

Marta despised luck. She did not want to believe in it as concept or commodity. She preferred effort and ambition. She favored organization.

Luck could have left her in that Honduran orphanage.

Luck could have placed her in a very different home with a very different family.

Goddammit, Clay. Instead of talking about your twelve new paragraphs over whatever meal you've hastily thrown together, try telling me how great it would be to visit Honduras. Look up some of the words I've been learning. Why do you think I only use one or two at a time? Do you even listen? Don't think I'm here just because you got lucky.

***

Sunday limped past like a dog winged by a car. Marta slept until three that afternoon, by which time Clay, having become one with their couch, had flipped through every satellite channel a good forty times.

He thought about the package in his garage. But more often than that, he pondered running upstairs, gently peeling back the sheets, and declaring, "I love you more than anything. Let's start our family."

He didn't.

His final thought before dozing off was that he still needed to show her the novel's opening chapters. This required catching her in a better mood.

Looking out across the darkening river valley, he was getting high on the Bankston Quarry ridge with Solstice, Graham, Barack Obama, and that Irish actress from *Lady Bird* when Argos barked him awake. "He needs to go out," Marta shouted from upstairs. "Has he had a walk?"

Chapter 14

⌘

DRY RUN

Clay and Marta were driving to her parents' house late on a cloudless May morning with temperatures reaching for the low sixties and humidity stalled in the bearable range. Having done exactly the same on previous Sundays, this particular visit would have been unremarkable but for one bothersome detail. After an elaborate lunch, Clay was going to read the first two chapters of *Explosive Love* for Winnie and Will.

This had been Marta's suggestion, following her own lukewarm reaction to those two chapters and an additional three. "Maybe you should read it to Mom and Dad," she had offered. "They loved your first book."

Four days later, driving the car, Clay was nervous. He wanted to shut up but couldn't.

"You really didn't think it was funny?" he asked Marta while turning onto Eagle's Nest Drive, the two-lane road that ultimately connected to the north entrance of Eagle's Nest Park.

"I never said that."

"You asked if I was still sure it was meant to be a comedy."

"Again—" Her tone conveyed annoyance. She, too, wanted him to stop talking. "What I specifically said, honey, was that I saw the humor but didn't think everyone will. Really, Clay, abortion? Animal testing? Your hard-to-like characters? You knew you were taking *un riesgo*."

"You really didn't think it was funny?"

"Enough," she said. "This is supposed to be my one morning off. If we're going to talk, we're discussing something else."

This turned out to be Marta's father and how worried she was about him. Will and Winnie had been older adoptive parents when Marta was young, which meant that, now, they were simply old. He had just turned 75 and was telling family he had experienced a "mini-stroke" even if his speech and physical movement seemed unchanged and a barrage of medical tests failed to support his claim.

"He knows what it's like to have a stroke," Marta stated the obvious.

"Clearly," Clay said, saving her from repeating the story of the real stroke Will had survived the summer she turned thirteen, the very same summer Will and Winnie had taken her to France. Shortly after returning from that overseas vacation, Will had been driving his family to the Duchaine Mall for back-to-school shopping. Waiting for a stoplight, he declared it to be a perfect day. Only he didn't, with "Monkey scarecrow clock" coming out instead. He tried speaking again, but once again the words formed by his mouth did not match up with the ones his mind wanted to say. "Help" became "bird." "Stroke" became "flame." Yet, incredibly, he remained fully cognizant of the crisis, and managed to drive the car to Duchaine County Hospital where, two hours later, with help from a battery of drugs, he reclaimed control over his vocabulary. He was discharged two days later, officially diagnosed as "one very lucky man." Despite taking three direct hits to the language center of his brain, he showed no signs of physical or mental impairment.

"I know he thinks he had another stroke," Clay said now as they crested the hill and the river valley came into view. "But he is 75."

"So what are you saying? Shit happens?"

"I'm saying that older people can face setbacks without help from a stroke." Clay pointed out that Will still spoke with great clarity, a far cry from that long ago day when "I think I'm having a stroke" came out as "inkwell Millhouse coastal moose."

It was his turn to change subjects. "How about that story in the paper this morning?" There was no need to add, "The one about Randolph."

"Very strange," Marta said. "Even so, as hard as it is to like Randy's products, you've got to admire his business acumen."

Randolph J. Simper had appeared on page three of the *Lamplighter* that morning to proudly announce that StripOff International, LLC, was introducing "StripOffSceneStealer," an app that could take a video clip of an individual and "magically transform it into an incredibly lifelike nude movie." Although these video clips could last no more than ten seconds in duration, Randolph promised that future editions would accommodate much longer productions. He also revealed that his company was close to unveiling StripOffSquared, an add-on that created three-dimensional nude images from traditional 2D photos of fully clothed subjects.

"It still makes you wonder why he's back in Duchaine?" Clay said.

"True," Marta agreed. "Because he's still behaving like he's in California."

As they pulled onto the blacktop driveway, the Mississippi River filled the spaces between trees. Will and Winnie Jewell lived in a beautiful house in a beautiful location, their wide, white, three-gabled home overlooking the long, shimmering lake created by Lock and Dam #8 above Duchaine. Winnie answered the big green door, assuming a role usually performed by Will. "Marta," she sang before giving her daughter a double oven-mitted hug. Clay got one too. Stepping inside, he breathed in deeply to taste the aromas, some unique to this house, of squash soup, kale casserole, and beetloaf. His in-laws had been vegetarian for as long as he'd known them and he had grown to like the unusual dishes they served, beetloaf and a few others excluded, even if dinner at the Jewell house often meant stopping for additional sustenance on the drive home.

Clay also appreciated the fact that his weekly dinners with the Jewells helped undo the damage caused by other food choices. Kale might have been kale but was purported to be healthy.

"Where's Dad?" Marta asked and Winnie replied, "He's being a stubborn old jackass today."

"You okay, Mom?"

"I'm fine, sweetie. Really." But Clay saw more sadness than usual in Winnie's watery blue eyes. With her silver rimmed half-moon glasses and dark gray hair pulled tight to a small bun in the back, Winnie reminded Clay of a character from one of those ancient black and white movies people felt obligated to watch right before Christmas. Specifically, she could have played an older version of the "spinster librarian" from *It's a Wonderful Life* looking ever prim, efficient, and detached—a visual impression only slightly diluted by the liquescent eyes.

"Clay. Marta." Will emerged from his music room, moving slowly but moving nonetheless. "What's being said about me out here?"

The door to the music room stayed open and Clay saw its organized chaos. Cluttered with cassette tapes of every known configuration, vintage Pink Floyd albums missing their original covers, compact discs, electric guitars, bass guitars, amplifiers, and speakers, it was the dark subconscious of an otherwise bright and spacious house.

Music, such as it was, wafted from that room at a fairly low volume. Clay didn't recognize the band whose almost good players jammed to a basic blues progression while receiving disproportionate applause from some outdoor festival audience that had probably parted ways half a century before.

The music room was Will's private place, a portal to the 1970s as he had experienced them as a teenager in Duchaine. Although Marta's father no longer looked the part—his neatly trimmed gray hair, clean shaven face, and thick glasses in clunky brown frames wouldn't have seemed out of place on a retired Risk Management Manager—he had once been both hippie and rock band bassist, at least to the extent either was possible in a town Duchaine's size. All these years later, he still waxed enthusiastic about "progressive" bands with strange, nonsensical names like Winston Padlock and Suntanned Gravy formed in places like California and England. These bands, Clay knew from his weekly tutorials, once flared and collapsed like dying suns, existing now only in Wikipedia entries and Will's surprisingly precise memory when it came to his music. Like burned out cinders drifting through space, their fires had cooled an eternity ago.

"I'm needed in the kitchen," Winnie declared, making a swift exit. Marta followed, trying to catch up.

Will headed to the dining room at a much slower speed than Winnie had achieved. Clay followed, taking advantage of the pace to study the designs in the dark green wallpaper—wild turkeys, pies, cornucopia baskets—all much more intricate than he had previously noted.

Slender and tall—at six-two, Will had a good three inches on Clay—he modeled a fashion ensemble that not only made him look like a man in his seventies, but also a man *in the '70s*. He wore a dark gray sweater vest over a long-sleeved pastel blue shirt. His sharply creased pants brought back the gray tones, albeit here in a much lighter shade. It was an outfit worn by Will most every time Clay saw him, with shirt color the only variable.

Clay stopped at the granite top bar complete with liquor cabinet and sink to locate two tumblers and endow each with a shot of brandy. This was a tradition Will had started with Clay the year they became in-laws. The ritual had evolved only recently when Clay took over the pouring duties.

"Thank you, son." Will slowly took his seat—and tumbler. "Hennessy. Nothing finer."

Although Clay knew Winnie was glad to have him out here talking with his father-in-law, he still felt awkward taking his own seat at the unnecessarily long dining room table with its dark wood finish and four frilly white place-mats that brought to mind ice-capped islands in a vast northern sea.

Winnie spoke quietly in the kitchen, trying not to be overheard, but Clay was able to make out "I think he's using this stroke thing" and "it's inexcusable" and "he's hardly a kid." Clay searched his memory, trying to recall a single previous time he had heard Winnie angry. Will showed no reaction. Perhaps he couldn't hear.

Leaning forward, Clay straightened the silverware and placemats for a third time. Will watched without saying a word. "Almost ready," Marta said, coming out of the kitchen to join them at the table. Refusing all offers of help, Winnie made the first of several appearances, each time placing the fruits and vegetables of her labor before them.

"So, big day coming up," Winnie said after taking her seat next to Clay, the biscuit plate still in her hand.

"Three weeks."

He started to say something more about his Lit Fest reading when, from behind ornately embellished glass panes, the china in an elegant dark-wood cabinet rattled—a sound quickly drowned out by the flapping roar of a low-flying helicopter. "That's twice this week," said Winnie. "Why can't that Mr. Simper drive along the river like everyone else?"

"Robber barons make a point of proving they're not everyone else," Will said. "Where's the fun in having a helicopter if you can't show it off?"

"Did you see that vulgar clown in the paper this morning?" Winnie asked. "That, apparently, is what it takes to become wealthy these days."

"You're looking good, Dad," Marta said before pointing at the sweater vest she bought him the Christmas before. "Smartly dressed, too."

As Will said, "Thank you, sweetie," the entertainment system in the next room hummed to life. The CD—or record, or 8-track tape, Will owned them all—played an obscure album half a century old. Clay knew it well from his visits to the Jewell house.

Welcome to the garden with its beauty galore.
Here's everything you'd ever want, you don't need a store.
But there's always one last prize you think you need to seize,
That knocks you to the floor and puts you on your knees.

"*Poison Apple?*" asked Winnie, again peeking over the rims of her glasses. "Really, dear, for Sunday dinner?"

"This is a classic piece of music," Will offered a predictable defense. "I realize this makes me a lone voice in the wilderness these days but Seminal Pig's *Poison Apple* is one of the great musical statements of all time, certainly the most interesting album of the modern era. Don't get me wrong, I love the Beatles, they wrote the best songs. But I was a kid when they were together, and *Poison Apple* is, just, different. Critics decried the lyric as simplistic but it's good versus evil, light versus darkness. Someday they'll see it was misunderstood."

The young Will had written his own rock opera as Clay knew without having actually heard it. Few had, Will blaming its poor reception on incompetent band mates and an impatient mob. The first and only Duchaine Summer Riverside Music Festival, held in 1974, had not been the place to unveil an hour-long "Karma Train," especially with a lead guitarist more accustomed to performing simple three-minute ditties. Bum notes continued to sabotage the performance even after no audience members remained to hear them.

Holding his tumbler in his left hand, keeping it on standby as it were, Clay took a forkful of beetloaf. A small sip of brandy helped cover the taste.

"But there were greater forces at work," Will resumed. "Seminal Pig never recovered from this near universal drubbing. Their work went downhill, throwing off focus as their tumble gained momentum. Making things worse, much much worse, Liam Vermouth—the band's leader, singer, tambourinist, and songwriter—made up with his father, moving past years of resentment. This had been a key source of motivation up till that moment, his trying to get back at the parent who forced him to work summers in Torquay, England, at the family's Royal Splendor Memento Shop. 'A tambourine's all good and fine,' he often told Liam. 'But you're never going to make a living with it.'"

"The impossible-to-please parent," Clay interjected. "It's always explained my friend Solstice, writing to impress parents who can't be impressed."

"Right," said Will. "Like Lennon and McCartney, both writing for mothers who had died young. 'Julia.' 'The Long and Winding Road.' Or Mozart and Beethoven with their awful, pushy fathers."

"You don't think your parents fall into that category?" Marta asked Clay. "I know I never managed to impress them. It was hard getting any kind of reaction out of them."

"Enough about infuriating parents and rock's most underrated tambourinist," said Winnie, clearly taking a poke at Seminal Pig and her husband. "I want to hear more from the talented young person we're fortunate enough to know now." Facing Clay, she continued, "I understand we're in for a treat today."

Coughing ever so slightly from his brandy, Clay set down his crystal tumbler. The cabinet rattled again. Randolph J. Simper was completing his loop over the valley. Clay wondered if he was entertaining guests or, as Will had suggested, simply reminding everyone he had money and toys. He sure flew low over houses.

"I'll have to play one of Seminal Pig's earlier albums the next time you're over," Will shifted direction as was his wont. "There's some great stuff there."

Winnie shook her head.

***

Over Winnie's objections, Marta cleared the table. "You've got something better to do," she said to her mother.

That something better was adjourning to the front room, and taking her place in an uncomfortable armchair alongside Will and Clay.

"Mr. Turner, our distinguished guest," Winnie said. "Will you regale us with your novel?"

Clay leaned forward in his chair, tapped his stack of papers on his thigh to line up the edges. He cleared his throat and began.

All Jared and Pita wanted was to blow up something together. Married nearly three years in the eyes of God, if not in the eyes of the so-called law, Jared Purvis and Pita Wishart had assembled everything needed to create a bomb with the force of 5,000 tons of TNT.

Where others might keep a guest room or nursery, Jared and Pita had a storeroom crammed full of hefty plastic bags, each bearing the warning: DANGER, CONTENTS HIGHLY EXPLOSIVE. This was their cache of ammonium nitrate fertilizer, purchased on the black market, more commonly known as Craigslist. Pita's dog, a food-crazed ninety-pound Black Lab, was not allowed in that room.

Jared and Pita shared the $120 rent on a run-down, single-level, 800-square-foot house in New Stratford, Illinois, a quasi-ghost town forty minutes southwest of Chicago's outermost suburbs. They spent their afternoons and evenings staring at the unreliable widescreen TV in their front room illegally accessing cable to watch movies featuring only those actresses who didn't wear fur and whose names didn't appear in Pita's "Celebrity Baby Killers" pamphlet.

Jared and Pita ate microwaved meals on a card table in front of that TV and used their one-car garage for the manufacture of meth. The laboratory had been there when they moved in. The house they rented was still technically for sale—although there was little danger of someone buying it—and its owner saw the lab equipment as a definite selling point in rural Illinois. Having happily accepted this one piece of serendipity, Jared sold methamphetamines to supplement their food stamps and welfare.

Their three years together had been fraught with challenge. They argued often, usually about matters that had no impact on their actual lives. Pita would repeat something she'd heard on Fox News like "If the slaves had guns, there wouldn't have been slavery," which made it impossible for Jared to refrain from adding, "You know, if fetuses had guns, there would be no abortions. They are human beings, after all."

When Pita concurred, "Now that makes sense," Jared would berate her for not understanding sarcasm, or biology, or anything that required an IQ higher than 80.

As it turned out, procuring the explosives had not been enough to bring the couple happiness or even a sense of achievement because what Jared and Pita couldn't seem to buy at any price was an agreed upon target for an explosion equal to 5,000 tons of TNT. Neither could suggest a suitable demolition site the other deemed worthy of lifelong prison or death by injection. The impasse had sucked the last precious drops of romance out of the night they tried celebrating their third anniversary, which had quickly spiraled down-

ward from drinking Andres to staring at a shoplifted DVD of early Survivor episodes while Pita muttered, "This isn't working."

She didn't tell Jared about the tough week she had just experienced, much of it spent questioning her relationship with Jared after watching numerous news reports about the Idaho tax-protestor couple who, along with five FBI agents, died in a late afternoon firefight. Albert Owsley and Chloe Parker had shown no hesitation about setting the deadly ambush for the federal agents raiding an illegal pit bull mill that had failed to report its profits to the IRS. Seeing photos of the couple on TV, Pita couldn't help but contrast her own marriage to that of this normal loving couple. She admired the defiance in their expressions and envied a union made strong by shared ideals and practical, attainable goals.

And so Pita was saying, "If we're going to stay together, we need to make up our minds and fucking do something."

***

"Oh my," said Winnie once Clay concluded his two chapters. "You're taking on some serious subjects."

"It's funny, right?"

"It's certainly *different*," she offered. "I could see you put a lot of work into it."

"I liked that you put the Black Lab in there," said Will.

Clay waited for him to cite another favorable element. This didn't happen.

Winnie got up. "Does anyone need anything?" she asked. "We have cookies."

***

Clay's stomach churned, and he knew it wasn't so much the Brussel sprouts bisque as the questions he had.

You didn't think it was funny?

No one thought it was funny?

Sitting beside Marta on the hanging wooden swing that faced the wide valley above the dam—typically the ideal place for letting one's vegetarian meal settle—he tried refocusing his thoughts on the scene before him, a rare beautiful marriage between nature and human engineering. A lengthy freight train with dark green engines pulling boxcars of every color rolled north along the Iowa banks while a towboat slowly pushed sixteen barges in the opposite direction, dividing the lake into two mirrored patterns of moving, glistening ribbons.

Will and Winnie usually came out wearing a few extra layers of clothing to join the conversation and watch the world from a weathered pair of Adirondack chairs. On this afternoon, they stayed indoors. Worse, they were doing something they never did: arguing loudly enough for Clay to occasionally catch a word. He didn't like the ones he grasped: foolish, Marta, hopeless. The one full sentence he heard was shouted by Winnie who had probably only shouted a handful of times in her entire life: "What kind of investment is that?" Were they talking about his novel? They had to be talking about his novel.

His reflux burned.

Moving closer to the lock and dam, the barge disappeared behind a stand of great oaks lining the cliff edge of the bluff. "Oh shit," said Clay an instant before he was taken over by one of his sneezing fits. Roughly every eight seconds, he roared with great force, filling the spaces between with mumbled curses. For years this had been a cruel paradox: he loved the outdoors but found himself allergic to it. "Shit, shit, shit..." He sneezed into his sleeve.

Winnie chose that moment to reappear. She was holding out a tissue box. "Good Lord, Clay, are you all right?"

Clay shook his head to say, sorry, but no.

Marta asked, "Where's Dad?"

"He's back in his room, back in 1972." From behind a sad smile, she added, "He's not in the best frame of mind these days."

The barge's horn echoed through the valley, blaring with all the volume of Paul Bunyan's Babe. When quiet finally settled across the beautiful vista, Winnie said, "Can I talk with you inside for a moment, Clay?"

Marta looked puzzled though her expression couldn't have equaled Clay's in that respect. Inside the family room, Winnie switched off the sound system, silencing Will's *Poison Apple*. Apparently, he had started it again before making his retreat.

Welcome to the gold mine, home to all that glitters—

She took a seat at the kitchen table. Clay took the one opposite her.

"I hope you didn't read too much into our reaction earlier," she said. "It's just ... a very unusual story. We're proud of you and all you've accomplished. It's the good news I cling to when things get strange here."

She stared down at the table. "You know I'm right, you don't have to worry about what a couple of old people think. Your book is going to do well. You don't get a huge advance for something those big city publishers don't believe in. That makes it easier when I see all the bad investments Will's made through online investing. I love my husband, everyone knows I do, but he barely knows how to send email, let alone buy stock, and believe me, he's chosen some real doozies. Newspapers. Music stores. Those places that used to develop photos. I don't know if we'll be able hold onto our house, not without a miracle, or at the very least a reverse mortgage. We're going to be around for a while—despite what he says about his 'mini-strokes'—and we've always intended for Marta to have her childhood home when we're gone.

"Not to put more pressure on you but I have to believe your writing will make that possible with all the good reactions it gets. Maybe, now that you and Marta are both doing so well, I can look into one of those mortgages. If you two still want the house when Will and I reach the end of our travels, you and Marta should be able to make up the difference. It's not my first choice. You have to know that. You also have to know, son, we're rooting for you. You go finish your masterpiece."

Clay was speechless. Not that he or Marta ever thought about inheriting a dime, let alone a house. But to see Winnie struggling and placing such faith in him...

"Clay?" Winnie said. "Are you all right."

"Yes," he lied. "Sorry. My allergies. I thought I was going to have another sneezing fit."

Winnie leaned in to quietly add, "You don't need to tell Marta any of this. With everything looking up for both of you, there's absolutely no point in worrying her over her inheritance."

Half an hour later, walking to the car with Marta beside him, Clay could still feel the scratching claws of acid reflux, mixed with a dash of kale. Winnie made this worse with her cheerful goodbye: "We can't wait for the public premiere, Clay."

No sooner had Marta called out, "Let us know how Daddy's doing," than Will re-entered the real world, coming out the front door to catch up to his daughter and son-in-law. Holding a blue crescent-shaped tambourine, he soon stood before Clay.

"Liam Vermouth's," said Will. "He used this on *Poison Apple*. I got it on eBay and it wasn't cheap. But I saw it as a solid investment. You're going out there with your own *Poison Apple*, so to speak. Maybe this will bring you luck."

Chapter 15
⌘

OFF SPRING

Reading *Explosive Love* aloud at home, Clay recognized the significant debt owed to a theme that came up at Winnie and Will's, that of the unpleasable parent. This was because the main characters, Jared Purvis and Pita Wishart, took motivation from theirs. When Jared grew up in Cedar Lake, Iowa, his mother and father had been tepid vegetarians who weren't above eating the occasional defenseless sea creature. Starting when he was twelve, Jared had nightmares of tuna trapped in nets stripped of all purpose and hope. Then came the day he saw through his father, the man who sermonized endlessly about "the arrogance of man." Without realizing his son was coming down the basement stairs directly behind him, Greg Purvis stomped on a spider trying to cross the laundry room's linoleum floor. Worse, Dad's first clumsy attempt failed to fully eradicate the innocent victim, giving Jared time to move in closer and witness something truly awful, the arachnid pulling away in terror and desperation, much as a human would have done. When Jared shouted, "Dad, what are you doing?" his father stammered, "Well. It's. You know, just a spider."

One year younger than Jared, Pita grew up in a Milwaukee suburb. Her father had been a U.S. Congressman who advanced his career within the Republican Party by co-sponsoring a series of personhood bills he knew would never reach the floor of the evil, do-nothing Senate. (The Democrats controlled it then.) He was the keynote speaker at a national conference for Stop the Homosexual Agenda Movement. The NRA awarded him its highest honor, the OAS, Order of the Active Shooter.

Ultimately, Barnabus Wishart ran for Senate, at which time he took a surprisingly easy 180-degree turn. Abandoning his opposition to all forms of family planning, Candidate Wishart embraced the stand that the federal government should stay out of Americans' "private matters." This marked a fresh start for the self-proclaimed "grassroots politician" even if it lost much of its freshness when repeated 8,000 times in television commercials that showed him as the great defender of Social Security, Medicare, and worst of all, "personal choice."

Sickened by the hypocrisy each had known in their respective childhood homes, Jared and Pita had no place for it in their own lives. They vowed to reshape society "without compromise." Jared had just turned 27. She was 26. They were getting older; time would not wait.

Now only five days away, Duchaine's First Annual Lit Fest would provide the world with a second "first" since apart from Marta, Will, and Winnie, no one other than Clay himself had theretofore experienced *Explosive Love*. Reading the opening chapters again had done little to ease his trepidation. Not once had he encountered humor in lines that were supposedly brimming with said substance. Nor had he uncovered any likable traits in the unconventional, highly flawed characters he was trying, somewhat perversely, to paint as sympathetic. Instead, Clay heard each and every word through the ears of his wife and in-laws. Worse, he heard *Explosive Love* through the ears of the Consortium, whose members could easily wonder collectively, "Is this how we spent our $253,000?"

It also didn't help that his new tweed jacket, custom-fitted three weekends before in Madison, felt tight. To his surprise and disappointment, he had gained a few pounds since the test run at Winnie and Will's.

He cleared his throat in anticipation of Chapter Two. Standing directly in front of him, Clay's sole audience member poked his master in the crotch with his snout, the dog's way of asking, "Wouldn't it be more fun to go out back and play catch? You don't look like you're enjoying yourself."

Clay did his best to ignore the warm breath and scrotal discomfort. Argos, in turn, poked harder as if his snout were the finger of a very impatient person trying to summon an elevator and Clay's crotch had become the button for Down. "Leave it, Argos. Leave it." Opting for feeling foolish over reasoning with a dog, Clay climbed onto the couch, placing his private parts beyond the reach of nut-seeking snouts. His feet sank into the soft faux-leather.

Picking up where he'd left off, Clay read, *As it turned out, procuring the explosives had not been enough to bring the couple happiness...* But he didn't get much further before stopping with the intention of crossing out a paragraph he had recently inserted, thinking Marta might correctly see herself as inspiration for the line, "Even when you're home, you're not home." But this required getting a pen, and climbing down from the couch, and struggling to keep his balance while stepping around Argos. The dog, of course, moved at the last second, leaving Clay to check his fall on the couch. "Thanks for being so helpful, you utterly useless, wallowing walrus." Clay's mission forgotten, the paragraph stayed.

"Am I really going to read any of this at the library?"

He heard the desperation in his own words.

"What do I do?"

He retreated to the kitchen—Argos leapt to his paws to follow closely—and opened a bag of blue tortilla chips, escaping into a comfort zone he wouldn't be able to access from the library's main hall. When Argos started whimpering, Clay didn't bother to chide the dog on his lack of patience but instead dropped a handful of the snacks onto the hardwood floor. As always, Clay was impressed by how quickly these disappeared. "Good lord, Argos, I swear you're half goat."

Turning toward the front room to resume his self-torture, Clay grabbed a Fun Size candy bar out of the bowl that was a fairly new addition to the counter. The wrapper came off and Clay ingested the Three Musketeers bar as if he were Argos bypassing the steps of chewing and tasting. A Butterfinger took the same path but only made it halfway. It was stuck in his throat. Really stuck. He tried coughing, but this proved no less impossible than breathing. All that came out was a muffled air raid siren sound, probably too faint for even Argos to hear it.

Using a balled up fist, he whacked himself on the back of his neck. He tried this again, and again, five times, six, then fell to the floor to curl up like a fetus and presumably die. The siren grew fainter.

Soon, he had trouble seeing, or even keeping his eyes open. *No, goddammit*, he scolded himself, *you have to keep them open. Otherwise you're giving up.* His thoughts swam in many directions, frantically searching the roiling waters for some sign of hope.

Is this how it ends, watching my sensory world break up like a phone call with a bad signal while a dog takes turns between sniffing my face and crotch?

Clay once read that a dog will wait three days before nibbling on its dead human when left without freedom or food. Cats only made it a day.

He took little comfort from this knowledge, however, and only in part because he doubted Argos could hold off the full three days.

It was time for last thoughts: *A universe that is infinitely large makes everything, and every life, infinitely small. Each event is infinitely unimportant.*

But lying flat on his back, wishing he could do something as commonplace as take air into his lungs, Clay knew the moment mattered in a very big way. It had become, in fact, immeasurably large. The entire universe, or at least the facsimile constructed by his own gray matter, was riding on what happened next.

Whether from instinct or empathy, Argos barked three times. When Clay failed to respond, the dog jumped on top of him. Two hard hind legs dug deep into Clay's stomach. *Wake up, human servant! Wake up! I don't want to eat you in three days! I want you here, now, serving me food!*

Barely clinging to the slippery rim of consciousness, Clay felt movement in the sore stretched leather his throat lining had become. The candy bar popped loose. Clay was coughing, taking in air between each noisy seism.

He slowly rolled onto his side, while Argos deftly removed the mushy, mangled Butterfinger from his hair. Through wet, blurring eyes, Clay looked at his new best friend and knew he would never be dismissive about what had taken place, that he would never make jokes about how Argos had simply intended to salvage the candy bar. The instant Clay felt able to speak, he half-whispered a brittle "Good boy, Argos. Good boy."

Feeling lightheaded as he crawled to the front room and took a seat on the soft welcoming couch, Clay saw the world in a bold new light. And taking in that brilliance, he made a resolution. Simple, sincere, he would be a better person. No, he wasn't going to become a philanthropist with what was left of the Consortium's investment, but he was going to appreciate life more, seeking the good in each new day and in each person (and dog) who made up the core of that life. He would still produce a novel of worth but was going to do so because he liked writing and sometimes even loved the process. To prove the latter, he would finally take the steps he'd been putting off, like forming a writers group to let air fill the vacuum in which he'd been working.

Clay also promised to be better about chewing his food.

After fetching a large glass of water and drinking it slowly, he picked up the slim stack of paper that made up his excerpt for the reading. He coughed a few times, quietly and painfully, while focusing on the page that introduced Chapter Three. Silent this time, he read the first paragraph:

Most of Jared and Pita's neighbors in the small (population 2,000) town also lived off government assistance, which limited but didn't completely eliminate their meth-buying capacity. Other neighbors drove thirty miles each way to work in Clairmont's maximum-security prison. These neighbors made enough money to support meth habits but were disinclined to do so because they faced regular drug testing. For Jared and Pita, already competing with at least a half dozen other dealers, this meant funds were tight. They needed a new TV, laptop, and refrigerator but kept putting off these purchases.

This is a strong chapter, he told himself. He should have finished with it at Will and Winnie's. At the library, he would do just that. Despite their faults, Pita and Jared had their appeal. People were going to like this.

When Pita first met Jared at the house of a mutual friend, he had seemed larger than life. His dark hair and jutting, almost cartoonish chin matched his heroic desire to strike back at the oppressive regime that darkened every aspect of day-to-day life in the Jewnited States of AmeriKa. Pita shared his passion, along with his hatred for the thieving, taxing bureaucrats who kept everyone down. Jared and Pita were going to rise up. Together.

"I love your passion," he said on their first real date while driving to a protest vigil in Jared's vintage green 1970 panel truck.

"And I love your compassion," she said.

The vigil took place outside a mosque in Rockford where Pita, Jared, and two Christian Patriots who had Friended Pita on Facebook blocked off the main entrance, forcing worshippers of the Dark, Deceitful Prophet to squeeze past them and their "No Sharia Law Here" signs. Pita wore a makeshift burka, a flapping collection of sheets and an upside down American flag held together with staples, to help make her point. "Worthless, godless terrorists," she spat at one family.

When she took Jared to his first anti-abortion rally in the Chicago suburb of Oak Park, he somehow failed to notice just how much her speech about throwing doctors and sluts in prison resembled his notion of Sharia Law. He was much too in love to judge her. But the rally was, if he were to be fully honest with himself, a bit on the boring side. It wasn't half as exciting as his animal rights protests during which he got to disrupt fashion shows in Chicago and douse the catwalk models, some of whom were incredibly hot, with blood taken from actual death-chamber slaughterhouses.

Jared was taken aback on their first anniversary when, sitting on folding chairs in their weedy backyard, Pita suggested they strike back at the oppressor in a much larger way. "We need to destroy something that's more than symbolic. We need to blow up a death chamber." When he asked, "Wouldn't that make us terrorists?" she replied, "It would make us patriots. We would shine as Soldiers of the Cross." A slight breeze parted her always ruffled, strawberry blond bangs. She looked beautiful and childlike, two impressions at odds with her dangerous words.

"But you were outraged by the elementary school bombing last month," Jared reminded Pita of her reaction to the infamous act perpetrated by the Birmingham Butcher. The suicide bomber who blew up Faith Values Charter School had been duly reviled on cable news and social media ever since. Pita's Fox News displayed his photo constantly whether castigating immigrants from Egypt or El Salvador. This was how Jared knew the attack took place early one Tuesday before parents had time to drop off their children. The Butcher specifically targeted the teachers and administrators who had asked students to draw cartoons of Mohammed to show allegiance to the one true God.

"You're comparing me to those antichrist infidels?" Pita stormed back. "Of course, I was outraged, just like every other American. The Birmingham Butcher was a Moslem, a terrorist. From Pakistan or Syria or Belgium. One of those places."

Right, thought Jared, to be a terrorist you have to come from that part of the world that's not the United States. Never mind that the Birmingham Butcher had actually been a third-generation Irish-American loner who had pretty much lived on the Internet before and after he found Allah. Still, Jared pressed on: "But that's my point. How does blowing up a building with people in it make us any different?"

"I don't know," she answered sarcastically. "Maybe in the way the French Transistance was different from the Nazis."

Pita took hold of his hands and moved closer until her gorgeous but always intense green eyes simmered only inches from his. "Every day, Jared, we're surrounded by slaughter. Innocent babies by the millions. To do nothing is to take part. We need to not do nothing."

Eventually, Jared agreed. They were the French Resistance or Transistance or whatever Pita had called them. "But," he repeatedly appended, "we need an appropriate target, one we both can justify."

Their third anniversary dinner devolved into what had become the usual rancorous small talk. "Are we really doing the Madison protest this weekend?" Jared grumbled. "I am so tired of driving to your interminable marches."

"You think you're bored?" Pita retaliated. "You don't know what bored is until you stand in my blood-splattered shoes listening to you whine about stupid foxes who don't know better than to keep their paws out of steel traps. God gave man dominion over the animals. It's in the Bible."

Jared's response, "Then screw the Bible," had not gone over well. He slept in the meth-lab garage that night while Pita phoned their mutual friend, Josh, on the farm. Josh agreed to meet with them the following day, at which time he would help hammer out a compromise. "I'm sure we can find something for you and Jared to blow up together," said Josh. "I just know it in my heart."

But Josh's suggestion at that meeting simply added a third irreconcilable viewpoint. "Let's blow up the goddamn Clairmont Mall as a symbol of the oppressive Jewish Amerikan machine," he came close to shouting. "You wouldn't believe how shittily they treated me."

While Jared privately contemplated dumping Pita and going his own way, he and Pita compared their ideal targets. He suggested a cosmetics testing lab outside of Milwaukee; she the Clairmont abortion clinic. "I'm not going to prison for some fucking cats," Pita said, to which Jared responded, "And I'm not facing execution for some half-formed glob of cells."

While Josh slept on their beat-up couch, Jared and Pita yelled at each other in an unsuccessful attempt to conclusively prove which of them was the most Christlike and sensitive. When Jared slapped Pita, she punched him back. He grabbed her, planning to shove her against a wall.

"Now," she screeched, "take me." She threw her arms around his neck, and together, they fell to the floor. "I was hoping we'd have intercourse," she whispered. "Tonight works,

tonight's all right for it, and I'm sure in the mood."

Three minutes later, upon reaching what should have been ecstasy, Jared shouted uncontrollably, "You bitch, you bitch, you bitch."

"I hate you, too," she murmured, pushing him off of her.

Lying on his back, in the sweaty silence that followed, he felt more exhausted than satisfied.

"What are you thinking about?" she asked.

"I'm thinking why can't we use condoms like everyone else?" he said. "The rhythm method bites. Even our sex life is forged in the dull fire of compromise."

Rolling onto her side to face Jared, Pita felt the boney pain of hipbone pressed against hardwood, a less comfortable sensation, if possible, than having Jared on top of her, pounding away. She could also feel a disgusting trail of baby juice escaping and oozing down her skin. Using prophylactics, she explained yet again, was against her religion, even though she could never admit that the last thing she wanted in her own life was a baby. She didn't like them, almost as strongly as she disliked the slutty hoards that brought babies into the world because they couldn't practice abstinence or even the rhythm method. This self-admission was as painful to her as Jared's secret from her, that he, the great animal rights messiah to be, couldn't stand Pita's whimpering, slobbering Labrador retriever. The dog was named Wade, as in Roe v. Wade.

"All's well that ends well," Clay whispered to himself, "and Thursday is going to end well. One stressed out, overworked MBA student and two well-meaning in-laws aside, this is going to be a sophisticated audience. They will appreciate the dark humor of *Explosive Love* along with its flawed, complex characters."

He went to his desk and pulled up the file for his manuscript. Then, with surprisingly little effort, he added in very rough form the story of how Jared Purvis was saved from choking by Pita Wishart's dog. No writer refused a gift like that.

Chapter 16
⌘

PROGRESS REPORT

Early into his meeting with the two advisors that made up the Martha Jewell Reclamation Team, Randolph felt pleased with the reports he was hearing. Winston Barclay, one-time editor with Krumpf and Sons New York, restated his conviction that *Explosive Love* was and would always be unpublishable. No amount of editorial intervention, he maintained, could steer the manuscript from its current self-destructive track. The plot had taken some strange new twists, "never mind that it was much too strange to begin with, if you'll excuse my ending a sentence with a preposition, although I suppose I actually did not, having added these last clauses, and am still speaking even as I speak."

The three men sat in a large, dimly lit conference room, occupying positions 4, 8, and 12 o'clock on a broad round table edged with ivory recently smuggled out of Tanzania. With each separated by at least six feet from the other participants, they occupied small pools of light provided by three table lamps with stands crafted of 24K gold and capped with beige silk shades. In keeping with Randolph's distaste for brightness, the lamps were powered by 20-watt bulbs.

Barclay smiled. "As you can see, sir, your plan is working. The classic pride before a fall. Judged on the quality of Mr. Turner's writing, or rather, the lack thereof, the event at the library will rival history's greatest tragedies, the Titanic's maiden voyage, the Hindenburg's last flight, the fall of the Roman civilization. Our Mr. Turner is about to meet his iceberg, or his spark igniting oxygen, or his lead plumbing mixed with general malaise."

"We've already put some serious dents in his armor," added Ford Diesel, the sinisterly brilliant hacker Randolph had lured away from the National Security Agency. "Not to honk my own horn but I know I got under our target's skin with the Amazon review program. He didn't know what hit him.

Talk about rattling someone's confidence; that was a 9.0 on the Richter scale. I made him vulnerable to any kind of setback."

"You should have let me write those reviews," Barclay said. "With all due respect, the amateurism was a dead giveaway."

"The target wrote very little for weeks after that. I'd hardly call that a failure." Ford Diesel had a twitch, right eye and brow, and it was highly visible at that moment. The fasciculation fit with Diesel's overall resemblance to a ferret, both physically and intellectually—an observation Randolph had shared with himself in previous meetings. Barclay, with his dark features and small, dark, squinty eyes favored a mole. Randolph shuddered to think what animal he himself would be portrayed as to fill out the children's storybook scene. He settled on wily red fox. That, at least, would be accurate.

"I can verify the program's success," Diesel continued. "I keep tabs on everything he does."

"The Amazon reviews were a good start," Randolph assured him. "But only a start. What else are we doing to weaken his armor?"

"I mess with him all the time."

"How so?"

Diesel spoke with creepy joy of causing Clay's computer to freeze up at least twice each day. "It's something we did all the time at the NSA. People just assume computers do that on their own. But it was always us, having a little fun."

He held out his phone to share a photo. "And there's this. I got him hooked. He's wasting afternoons watching Duchaine Eagle Watch dot org. I've got to admit, it's hard not to become an addict. These eagles are really something."

"Back to my earlier question," Randolph interjected. "No one shares my concerns about the reading?"

"It is true we are dealing with rubes," Barclay said. "There's little we can do to prevent them from mistaking the literary equivalent of fast food for a gourmet feast. One factor works in our favor, however. Even these plebes are unlikely to gulp Mr. Turner's concoction down like chili-smothered cheese fries and carbonated corn syrup given the tastelessness he displays when discussing a societal issue central to their worldview."

"Why can't you just say abortion?" Diesel said, shaking his head. "We all know what minefield he's walking into."

"Why would I say abortion when everyone with an IQ over sixty, no offense to my colleague here, knows of that which I am speaking?"

"Let's stick with what's important," Randolph refereed. "Are we exploiting this vulnerability or do we need to look at it?"

"One of us is on top of it, sir," Diesel said. "I did a blast email to the faculty and students of St. Gregory the Great High School. *Join Us To Discuss A Serious Book About the Serious Topic of Abortion.*"

"Clever," said Randolph. "The last thing I want is to watch Clay Turner walk out of the library with a proud wife clinging to his arm."

"If he walks out at all," Barclay chuckled.

"If she's got any pride," Diesel said, "she'll be walking the other direction."

"Along with any hope for his future," Barclay added. "To borrow the vernacular of a sporting competition Midwesterners watch on Pay Per View cable, we have reason to anticipate a double knockdown. Having successfully infiltrated his computer, we know Mr. Turner is preparing to submit sample chapters to literary agents. Weeks will pass before he receives responses, but one can only imagine how damning these will be. This is Napoleon marching into Belgium, specifically the small, hitherto obscure municipality of Waterloo."

"Hey, I was supposed to present that report." Diesel's twitch picked up speed. "I'm the one who penetrated his cyber sphere. I'm the one who gathered that information."

"You didn't seem especially eager to share it," Barclay retaliated. "Freezing up his computer seems more prank than priority. Not everyone here has time for such follies."

"Without me, you wouldn't even know what's in his novel. You wouldn't know about the agents. Ford Diesel lurks inside every microchip our target trusts. In his car and bike. His phone and TV. I'm in his damn refrigerator for God's sake. I track his movements. I know when he's eating. I know what he's texting."

"We *both* monitor his movements."

"Tell me more about the submissions," Randolph said, lifting a hand. "*One* of you."

"He's preparing query emails," Diesel said. "He compiled a list of agents he plans to approach. He's starting with his top five."

Barclay spoke before Diesel had finished. "I know these agents. They will destroy Clay Turner."

"I was just about to say that."

"And you're the publishing expert *how?*" Barclay pressed.

"I'm the one who's set up shop inside our target's head."

Randolph's palm hit the table the way his father's once did in response to unwelcome suggestions like getting a dog or vacationing at Disneyland. Now as then, it did the trick. After taking a few seconds to savor the silence,

Randolph said, "Thank you, gentlemen. If I am to believe your reports, we are indeed making progress. The next few months should prove interesting."

Chapter 17
⌘

WINTER SOLSTICE

The mail came—always a welcome break for writers, just as it is for the elderly and America's prison population. Clay dutifully fetched, retrieving the day's haul from the box by the street while Argos lazily watched from the front door.

There was a bill from the University of Wisconsin-Duchaine Annex, a bill from Wisconsin Power, and a bill from Duchaine Water. But these couldn't compete with the white 9 x 12 envelope Solstice Blume had sent from Oregon.

Before he was even back in the house, Clay slit it open, using a car key that left a jagged crevice. *Break a leg, fellow writer,* she had written. *If there was any way I could be at your event, I would. Just please know I will be there in spirit.*

This turned out to be a cover letter because a six-page double-spaced story was also enclosed. *I found this the other day,* Solstice prepared him on a smaller sheet attached by paper clip, *and it brought back some wonderful memories. I wrote "Measurable Accumulation" my first semester in Madison. I know it's fashionable to eschew nostalgia but I get very nostalgic for times we shared. Remember the quarry? Remember riffing off each other? I still see ideas we came up with there in your writing just as I'm sure you see some in mine.*

Clay read the opening paragraphs and was promptly sucked in, mostly by his own familiarity with the story. But this time, he saw more than inspiration he had provided. Beginning in paragraph two, he saw himself. Marginally fictionalized at best, this was a non-fiction account of time spent together, and it very much brought back pleasant memories.

The snow didn't fall. It hammered. It hit. It slammed Duchaine to the mat like a sweaty 200-pound wrestler.

Craig was seventeen. Me, I'd just turned eighteen. Snow tumbled down in great phosphorescent clouds that briefly concealed the entire world while making the streets of

Duchaine close to unnavigable especially for a stoned high-school senior piloting those routes on the nearly bald tires of a very used Chevy Lumina. That was my friend Craig. The car belonged to Aunt Ruthie. She'd loaned it to me. Probably without knowing.

The roads were too slick to accommodate my own limited driving abilities. I had re-linquished the keys to Craig at the front door of the house he grew up in on Birch Street. Soon he and I were on our way to a party at the home of drama teacher Mercella Rosetta. English teacher Penni Penworth had invited me and Craig, insisting her "budding little Shakespeares" be part of the festivities. I urged Craig on. "Blizzard be damned. The party will be fun." As one of two calendar days that shared its name with me, December 22nd demanded celebration.

We spent upwards of an hour sliding around town while getting progressively higher. Craig cracked the windows a couple of inches, a precaution that probably made the car smell 5% less like a marijuana curing room.

"Your Aunt Ruthie doesn't notice the smell?" asked Craig.

"There are lots of things she doesn't notice."

"Same for my parents. Never give a flying shit. About anything. Their indifference comes naturally."

Two joints into our drive, we felt one with the universe and even more so with the Christmas lights rolling by in slow motion. "What's glowing?" Craig asked as we savored an especially bright block on Kipling Avenue. "Is it us or the lights?"

And then as if by magic we were parked in front of a driveway directly across the street from Marcella Rosetta's foursquare home. "It looks like it's in a snow globe," Craig said. "We're in a snow globe."

Laughing and effectively legless, we soon realized we no longer possessed the motivation or basic motor skills to dive out of the car to swim the shimmering white river that seemed to have trebled in width. We chose instead to smoke another spliff.

Silence created its own snow-like a blanket, a blanket torn in two when I heard myself blurt, "I'm a gay Jew who loves looking at Christmas tree lights."

"You forgot stoned*. That's a big part of the equation."*

"My parents are dead."

My words seemed to surprise Craig as much as they did me. Still, he had a response. "Could be worse. Mine are alive."

I was crying. He cried too. Once we were able to stop a brief eternity later, he said, "This is really good kush."

Two years earlier, I had come to Duchaine as an orphan. My mom disappeared before I even knew her. Said to be "a very kind soul," Kendra Boone was diagnosed with Stage 4 cancer, divorced, and cremated before I turned three. Howard Boone, my father in name only, died a frustrated crossword puzzle editor working on a "new collection that would revolutionize the medium." He pulled off the dying part the last week of my sophomore high school year by driving off in a blind rage after discovering proof of his third wife's infidelities.

> *This stuck me with Stepmom #2 Naomi Boone. If she had disliked me before losing Howard, this was nothing compared to how much she hated the prospect of sharing her new possessions with a confused, judging teen. It didn't take her long to find a solution. She Fed Ex'd me off to live with Aunt Ruthie, a long-widowed daytime TV aficionado who drank one glass of red wine for every hour watched. Come evening, Aunt Ruthie divided her time between searching for a lost cat that wouldn't have been lost if she hadn't been drinking and mournfully extolling "the very kind soul" of the dead sister who had deserved so much better from life and marriage.*
>
> *That cat turned out to be the first family member I ever felt close to, the first one who even tried to know me.*

This, as far as Clay knew, was the first time Solstice had exploited her cast of readymade characters in pursuit of her writing, and he almost felt jealous. He had nothing like this in the way of real-life material. In contrast, he could best describe his parents as *non-descript*, an adjective that rarely made its way into serious literature. Archie and Vera Turner were tiresome Methodists who did everything methodically whether having two sons two years apart or embracing Fox News as an alternative to thinking and conversing.

After Clay became the second and last son to move out, Archie and Vera followed suit. He transferred to a new office job, leaving Farm Haul Farm Machinery Duchaine for Farm Haul Farm Machinery Waterloo, some 99 miles east and south. Vera found a new bank to work in, and together they bought a condo with no guest rooms. Clay was left to drive there every fourth weekend and stay at cheap motels, a practice he discontinued after one year passed without Archie or Vera ever once, to his knowledge, returning to visit Duchaine.

He'd seen them only a handful of times since, thought about them less— or at least made this his goal. Their unwavering indifference eventually stopped keeping him up in the early morning hours. It stopped exerting even a negligible influence on the writing career they had once discouraged. (Archie Turner on a sixteen-year-old's first self-conscious attempts at poetry: "Jesus Christ, am I raising a girl in my house?")

Archie and Vera lost something too, depriving themselves of chances to further disparage Clay's wife, their first slight meant to be secret but caught on video by a camera still running after Clay and Marta's wedding ceremony had commenced. In the video's coda, which Marta had never seen and never would see, Vera said loudly, "I wonder if it will last." Archie followed this with "With God as my witness, I didn't know there were any Mexicans here in Duchaine. Not till he brought one home to meet us."

Returning his attention to "Measurable Accumulation," Clay shook off that memory, permitting his return to a happier time. *Craig and I discussed our options another few minutes before reaching a bold decision. We would exit the Lumina, cross Fremont Avenue, and enter Ms. Rosetta's house to join the party in progress. We talked about the mega-hot "drama queens" who waited beyond that front door. Nina Poser, Lexi "Cooter" Rhodes, and the junior with the name that intrigued us both—Kate Wunderlick.*

We never took those last snowy steps to impress female drama students with an endless barrage of witty jokes. We chose instead to continue reviewing our plan. We sat there ten minutes. We sat there for twenty. We sat until our ambitious scheme, like so many others concocted on nights identical to this one, disappeared quite literally in a cloud of smoke. His eyes wet from a coughing fit, Craig abruptly determined it was time to go. The car slipped free of the snow fort rising around it. We set out to explore new arrangements of holiday lights.

Craig completely ignored the stop sign where Bryant met Mt. Vernon. We plowed through an intersection no one else was using. It soon became clear a cop had witnessed the infraction because Craig was using his rearview mirror to take in a new configuration of colored lights: stark, eye-singeing blasts of red and blue. I didn't need to be told to hide the stash. But I must have been too attached to it to toss it outside into a happily complicit snow bank of which there was no shortage of choices.

"Ditch it," he exhorted. "Now."

We turned onto Rush Street. We planned to surrender. But on an impulse, Craig killed the car's lights and took another quick right into the parking lot of Bryant Elementary. Our hearts pounded like snowplow blades scraping concrete. The puffy explosions of red and blue shot past in the rearview mirrors from right to left. "Incredible," said Craig, "I lost him."

He followed this boast with a heartfelt "Shit." The unplowed lot had impounded Aunt Ruthie's Lumina. The car refused to budge. The harder he pressed down on the gas pedal, the angrier it became. It howled like a wolf from the friction of tires gnawing at ice. It quaked like a bull taunted by waving red flags.

Craig called his dad. He didn't get an answer, not even voicemail.

He tried calling the one guy he knew with a winch on his pickup. Mad Dog Maddox told Craig he'd be right there. "That's if you were one of my fucking friends."

We walked to Aunt Ruthie's through the uncaring storm. Icy winds whipped our faces. Snow spilled over the collars of our boots. Snot froze in the deepest catacombs of our sinuses. Yet we rarely stopped laughing. "Who needs a stinking drama department?" I asked as we cut across Taco John's parking lot. "We create our own drama."

I waited patiently beside the Walmart loading decks after he announced, "Do I need to pee? Indood I dee."

"I wish I could do that," I called in his direction. "If you're a guy, the whole world is a restroom."

Craig improvised a parody of a poem we had studied at school: "Whose woods these are I think I know. His house is in the village though. And so his eyes shall never see, a piss taken upon his tree."

I woke up in my own bed the next morning, my cheeks chafed red, my brain dried out like leaves in a pile an instant before the bonfire gets them. But I was otherwise intact. Craig talked with Aunt Ruthie in the other room while an English muffin and three tall iced teas got my heart beating again. Aunt Ruthie had already fed Craig.

"Nonsense," he told her, "the couch was really comfortable. I can see why you like it so much."

The frigid air outside jumpstarted my brain. We each carried a snow shovel over our right shoulders as if these were soldier's rifles and aptly marched to the Bryant School parking lot. Erroll Eddington, Craig's dad in theory if not practice, had refused to drive over and help us.

We shoveled furiously like chain gang prisoners under the watch of vicious guards. "Back before high school, I did this on snow days," Craig said once we had finished digging and panting. "One lady in our neighborhood used to give me forty dollars and there wasn't much to her sidewalk or driveway."

We climbed into the car and lit up a joint. I let him drive.

"Cute," Clay said aloud, "and based in Duchaine. Duchainers like seeing Duchaine in their art." He wished he had something like this to open his reading.

Standing in his front room—Clay wasn't sure why—he read "Measurable Accumulation" aloud. Even less explicable, he made a few edits in his head, making it sound like something he had written. He could have given it life after all. It was his memoir as well as hers. Curling up at Clay's feet, Argos seemed to like what he heard.

Upon reaching the end, Clay chastised himself, "You need to get back on the chain gang." Minutes later, he was sitting at his desk, making changes to the *Explosive Love* chapters he was planning to read at the library. Once he was satisfied with these, he clicked Print and leaned back in his chair.

From behind him, the printer jerked to life, beginning its wheezing, horror flick chant. *Help. Me. Help. Me. Help. Me.* When it got tired of repeating this, a window appeared on Clay's screen. OUT OF PAPER. Unfortunately, he knew the ever needy machine wasn't just speaking for itself. *He* was out of paper. Rolling his chair to the room's far side, he learned he was only six sheets shy of finishing his printout. "Of course," he muttered.

Feeling no great desire to drive to Staples all the way out by the mall, he printed the remaining pages of his selection on the back of Solstice's "Measurable Accumulation" piece. "She'd understand," he explained to Argos, now sprawled out next to his chair legs. "She wouldn't expect me to hold onto this. I've never been a sentimentalist." *As people will discover*, he added in his head, *when they hear me read from Explosive Love*.

Eating a non-candy-bar snack—the Ben & Jerry's Americone Dream brought icy relief to his scratched, bruised throat—while flipping the channels on the family room TV, Clay stopped on a History Channel documentary about Amelia Earhart. To his surprise, she had embarked on her famous last trip with a navigator, and had not died alone.

Clay imagined a novel, *Amelia Earhart's Navigator*. It opened with an epic fight: "You're the worst navigator ever." "Well, you're the worst pilot ever." But as the television documentary continued its process of edification, Clay was disappointed to learn the navigator was male, and that Fred Noonan had not been entirely obscured by history even if his legacy was greatly overshadowed by that of his boss. Watching his fantasy of writing a steamy lesbian romance novel—a *commercial* steamy lesbian romance novel—disappear beneath the Pacific's choppy waves, Clay switched channels.

He landed, unfortunately, on Comedy Cluster where a rambunctious Great Dane was running into walls with its head stuck inside the wastebasket it tried raiding. Clay groaned and switched off the TV. Finishing the last spoonful of Ben and Jerry's, he wondered how he ever got by on chocolate gelato.

Chapter 18

⌘

THE READING

From its very first mention, Clay had imagined his reading taking place in the downtown library's main hall, shutting down in the process all other library business. *Freeze there, middle grade maggot! No one's here to check out J.K. Rowling! This night belongs to Clay Elliot Turner!*

His disappointment in learning he would be speaking on the third floor subsided only when he stepped into Angler Auditorium and saw it ran the length of the stately stone building. The glass panes of the great skylight directly above the slightly raised stage showed off the same intricate metal lattice design that distinguished the arching stone-framed windows that broke up three of the room's four walls. The high walls themselves were simple, but were also adorned, directly behind the stage, with brand-new posters of Duchaine's successful homegrown authors: Clay himself, from a photo that originally appeared with a *Lamplighter* profile; the made-over Solstice Blume; and Fillmore Banks, whose portrait was remarkable in itself in that the author had seemingly combed his hair.

Clay's jacket felt even tighter against his arms, shoulders, and chest as he waited for Duchaine's mayor, the Honorable Jeb Moberly, to stop thanking everyone who had ever stepped inside a library for "their proud place in preserving the literary arts and making nights like this possible." The portly mayor—in high school they called him Moby—then painted Duchaine as the Milky Way's indisputable center of enlightenment. These observations used up four of the five minutes allotted to the mayor's prepared remarks, leaving a scant sixty seconds for him to introduce the author shuffling impatiently Stage Right. "It is my privilege to introduce a hometown author, ready and eager to regale that hometown with a passage from his first, forthcoming novel. Library patrons…" He waited an extra two beats. "Clay Turner."

Clay stepped forward, cleared his throat, and waited for the applause to dissipate: 200 people, probably more, from high school students to elderly women, every one respecting him, respecting his talent. Joy and relief washed over him in waves. He wanted to dive headfirst into the roaring sea of appreciation and stay immersed forever. More practically, he wanted to finish his novel so he could make additional public appearances.

When silence returned, he said, "I would like to read from my novel in progress. I hope you will appreciate the work and passion I have placed before its altar. And so I give you, *Explosive Love*...

"*All Jared and Pita wanted*," he continued, "*was to blow up something together. Married nearly three years in the eyes of God if not in the eyes of the so-called law, Jared Purvis and Pita Wishart had assembled everything needed to create a bomb with the force of 5,000 tons of TNT.*"

At the end of paragraph nine, he paused to take a drink from the water bottle on a small table adjoining the chair he had chosen not to use. Scanning the faces spread out before him, he thought the admission-paying literary enthusiasts seemed restless. There had certainly been no laughter or even knowing smiles. Will and Winnie, Row 2 center, looked every bit as troubled as they had weeks earlier, and worse, so did the daughter sitting beside them. The look in Marta's eyes made clear: this isn't working, you're losing your audience.

As he flipped to page four, a middle-aged couple got up and moved toward the closest side entrance, picking up speed as they neared the actual door as if that might cloak them prematurely in invisibility. Three more admission-paying attendees followed suit. Clay had not previously noticed these nuns in the back of the room. But now they stood out in full nun regalia, white habits and hoods with accents of black. Duchaine's nuns were said to be liberal in their politics, but this must have stopped at abortion, forcing them to walk out in protest, their habits turned to burkas.

Had it just been the nuns, Clay might have consoled himself with the assurance, controversy sells. By the end of page six, he felt sweat building not only under his armpits, but everywhere. He saw a wet spot on the paper where his thumb had just been gripping it. Upon reaching the first section break, he stopped abruptly, took a sip of water, and feeling unable to read another word, asked, "Any questions?"

The audience, clearly caught off guard, sat silent for most of a minute, which would have been preferable to what followed. Getting up from his chair in row three to be seen, a slovenly man in a *Confederacy of Dunces* hunting cap wanted to know how one went about finding an agent who charged only 5%. Also, how feasible was it to land a million-dollar advance on a first novel? His, he continued, was entitled *War*. "Like *War and Peace*, but just

War."

"I think those questions are best left for agents and editors," Clay said. "Or perhaps an online search."

"Then here's a question for a writer," said an elderly woman Clay recognized as a neighbor from down the street, one who may have waved once while she was doing yard work and he was passing on his Gold Wing. "Is what you read supposed to be funny? Because it didn't seem to be."

"Abortion is no joke," a high school coed offered without bothering to stand first.

"Neither is animal abuse," said a man near the back.

Clay had come ready with a prepared answer: "Agreed, but *Explosive Love* is about neither. It's about extremes, not the particular social movements hijacked by extremists like Jared and Pita."

"Could have fooled me," said a woman a few rows back. "Pro-lifers base their actions on strong moral foundations."

"Really?" a young woman responded. "And the rest of us don't?"

"No one *hijacked* the pro-life movement," an older woman spoke up. "It started as a coalition of white conservatives fighting to keep religious schools segregated. I liked your parody there. But the animal rights stuff is just insulting."

"*You* are insulting," a pro-lifer shouted.

"Look up Bob Jones University. Green v. Kennedy."

"People, people," a man called out from the middle of the audience. "I think we can all agree on one thing. His book sucks. It insults *everyone* here."

Silence returned, settling like frost on a cold winter's night. "Really?" Clay muttered. "Now you're in agreement? This is what it takes to heal a divided nation?" He felt the fire moving across his face, and wondered just how red he was.

"Come on," he took up the volume, "these comments would only be valid were *Explosive Love* about abortion and animal abuse. It's not."

"Don't insult our intelligence," a woman fired back. "Sorry, I forgot. That's your thing."

Clay reached for the water bottle, managing only to knock it from the table and watch it roll slowly away. "Look," he said, "I don't know if there's a First Rule of Reading Fiction in Public. I'm guessing if there is, it's Don't Argue with Your Audience. But you've got to understand, my novel is about extremists and extremism. It's about radicalization, about people on the fringe, each viewing the world through his own misshapen prism."

Three young women—Clay recognized one as a former student, Pat Dixon, or Hickson—were doing the same invisibility dance he had witnessed earlier, crouching as they moved toward the hall's rear exit. From a seat near the front, Dick Breitbach caught his attention. Dick's lips moved slowly, forming the words, *What are you doing?*

"I have been reading from an early draft," Clay surprised himself by saying, feeling how Will must have felt when his stroke placed unintended words in his mouth. "That was a chapter well into the book," he built on the lie. "Perhaps it wasn't the best introduction to *Explosive Love.*" The unplanned words kept coming out. "Let me read from the opening chapter. I think you might enjoy this."

Knowing how wrong he was to do so, not to mention stupid and shameless and disloyal and reckless, Clay flipped over the stack of papers.

"Winter break had come, and with it winter,*"* he offered his own slightly modified version of Solstice Blume's story, effectively rebooting the evening. "Jared was seventeen. His friend Pita had just turned eighteen." Idiot! Idiot! Make a clean break! Stop this now! No, no, no, it doesn't matter that she appropriated some of your ideas in her sci-fi. "Snow tumbled down in great phosphorescent clouds that briefly concealed the entire world while making the streets of Duchaine close to unnavigable especially for a stoned high-school senior piloting those routes on the nearly bald tires of a very used Chevy Lumina. The car belonged to Pita's Aunt Callie. She had loaned it to her niece. Probably without knowing."

The only defense Clay could mount was that his actions weren't premeditated. This was only Second Degree Plagiarism. "Conceding the roads were much too slick to accommodate her own limited driving abilities, Pita had relinquished the keys after meeting Jared at the front door of the house he grew up in on Birch Street—"

The audience seemed to relax. But while flipping pages, Clay glanced up to see Jenni Jensen seated front and center, eye level with his crotch, much as Argos had been when Clay practiced at home. Jenni seemed to be scrutinizing him—harshly. Had Solstice sent their old teacher "Measurable Accumulation" when she mailed Clay his copy? Was he about to be publicly exposed, caught in the act of literary theft? He felt the dampness spreading beneath his clothes, felt his once smooth shirt turn scratchy and hard. What the hell had he done... what the hell was he *doing?* There was no defense. As he reached the final page, he felt his flesh burning and freezing at the same time. "They took turns shoveling, then climbed into the car and lit up a joint," he concentrated to the best of his abilities on the text before him. "Pita let him drive."

The big applause was back even if Clay was unable to enjoy its return. "Questions?" he said.

"This represents quite a leap in your growth as a writer," came a comment from a woman in the second row whose short brown hair with silver highlights glistened as if she'd just walked in from a downpour. "It's so much gentler... sweeter. I liked your first book for the most part, but this... this is like sunshine at the end of a long winter. You proved yourself with this one, Clay Turner. You proved yourself."

"I have a question." The bloated man in the hunting cap was back on his feet. "Why does your first chapter take place in Duchaine if the novel takes place in a fictional Illinois town? And the main characters? They knew each other as teens? I sort of felt snookered, the way you started with one premise and switched to another."

"It's complicated," Clay said. "But there is a connection."

"I'm glad to hear this," the man resumed, "because the sections seem fairly disconnected as they now stand."

He saw the three young women who had snuck out earlier standing close to a back entrance. Had they been lured back by "Measurable Accumulation" or the applause that followed?

Seated in the second row, the main library's acquisitions manager stopped chewing suggestively on the tip of her pencil to raise her hand and acclaim, "I too loved the opening. You should be very proud to have written it. I loved every word. My flesh is still tingling."

"I'm glad you enjoyed it. Do you have a question?"

"Oh yes. How is that lovable scamp, the irrepressible Argos?"

"The dog and I are getting along better than ever," Clay happily volunteered. "Argos has not only grown larger, but he has also truly grown on me. You'll be pleased to know I've found room for an equally spirited Black Lab in the new novel."

"Oh, for cute," the acquisitions manager chirped. "I'd love to discuss this more with you sometime."

"I have a question." A short, skinny guy stood to show off a black suit that seemed more suited to a funeral. Clay recognized Josh Bramlett from the "Prime Suspect" dossier he had compiled on his hacker. "Good evening, everyone," said the middle-aged silent-auction winner and graduate, per Clay's research, of an eight-week cybersecurity course required by his employer. "I'm Josh Bramlett. Some of you might recognize me from Duchaine Bank and Trust. I probably made it possible for you to own homes. My name is supposed to be in Mr. Turner's novel. I won that dubious honor at a silent auction, paid good money. So why didn't I hear it tonight? I deal in obligations. Most people take obligations seriously. My question for Mr. Turner is, Why don't you?"

Clay glared in the direction of the man's thick, black eyeglass frames while struggling to find a more suitable response than "You're fucking kidding me" or "You've got a lot of gall showing up here." The loan officer stared back with equal intensity.

Clay said, "Believe me, Mr. Bramlett, your name appears in the novel. I'd go so far as to say you're getting a lot more exposure than you paid for. I did your name justice."

"Excuse me?" a familiar voice called as Duchaine University President Arthur C. Peckham rose to his feet in a distant row. "Do you think this new book will dig you out of your one-star rut on Amazon?"

"Amazon's fixing that. That was cyber sabotage. Read those reviews, you'll see, they all sound the same." Clay's eccrine glands had come back to life; he felt sweat in new places. "I mean, no, don't go online. Ignore those reviews. They were generated by someone who doesn't like me, someone trying to slow my momentum." He looked again in the direction of Josh Bramlett. "I have my suspicions. But check Amazon again in a few weeks. You'll see five-star reviews. For God's sake, does anyone have a real question?"

The audience shifted uneasily in their seats, clearly ready to call it an evening. But as if to make sure Clay wouldn't walk away from his appearance any less tense than Peckham's question had already left him, Jenni Jensen raised her hand. "The opening chapter you just shared with us… it represents, as noted, a significant departure from your previous output. Wherever did you get your ideas?"

Forced to come up with an answer more original than "the mail," Clay related his own wonderful memories of that winter night from high school, all of which quite fortunately overlapped with those of Solstice Blume. "It just seemed like a good way to start a novel," he added. "Writing about something I knew and loved."

The rest of the audience seemed pleased with his answer. But Jenni murmured, "Uh huh," while cross-examining Clay with a look she had honed to perfection working as a high school teacher. *Did you really write this paper?*

Whatever price would ultimately be exacted for his unplanned act of piracy, the applause that followed Clay's final "Thank you for coming" produced more noise inside the downtown library than all the disruptions of the previous twenty years combined. Beaming with pride, Mayor Moberly bowed alongside the author, and in fact took three full dips to Clay's deliberately modest one. Clay watched Jenni get up and walk to a side door. When he left the stage to join his well-wishers, he whispered to himself, "What I have done?"

The Consortium was almost unanimously delighted. Dick Breitbach led the chorus, gushing, "Bravo, Clay, bravo. Rough start, but that last chapter was the best thing you've written by miles, and I'm counting all that cute crud you used to come up with in high school."

Marta nodded enthusiastically, whispering, "*Sí, sí,*" a reaction Clay found disconcerting. Surely, she had enjoyed *Give Me a Second While I Execute the Dog* more.

"A true comeback," echoed Benedict Howell. "It gave me some much needed confidence in the strength of our investment."

Artemis Cobb, again wearing his Packers jersey, said it almost made him want to read. "I really liked your mentioning the mall. I felt proud, knowing my own family's pivotal place in the proud history of Duchaine Mall."

Providing the one exception, Randolph J. Simper continued to sit quietly amidst a modest entourage much as he had done before and during the reading. The single time he and Clay had locked eyes, four pages into the stolen piece, Clay thought he detected suspicion. But why?

Marta saved Clay from dwelling on the question by kissing him square on the lips for over three seconds. It was an affectionate move that seemed to make Randolph J. Simper extremely uncomfortable. The romantic display also seemed to bother the main library's acquisitions manager, now giving Clay a look of *I may have lost another battle, but this war is not over.*

Marta made love to Clay that night, releasing all the pent-up energy of the wall of water that would escape were Lock and Dam #8 ever to burst above Duchaine. The raging, heavily concentrated surge swept him along like a piece of debris, letting him know there was no point in resisting a superior force of nature.

Later, lying in bed while Marta slept, Clay considered changing Jared and Pita's terrorist target. In placing an entire city at its mercy, a dam would provide much more drama than Clay's previous choice: an indoor water park resort in southern Minnesota that had once refused to let Jared and Pita check in with a stolen credit card.

Clay woke early the next morning and promptly went online to get a first peek at that day's *Duchaine Lamplighter.* A wave of relief swept over him when he saw Arts and Literature Critic Jenni Jensen recounting how local literary lion Clay Turner had delighted patrons of the arts by bouncing back from a first, poorly chosen selection. Clay's greatest fear from the night before, that Solstice might have mailed a copy of "Measurable Accumulation" to their old high school English teacher, was carried away on the backwash. To his further relief, the editors of the *Duchaine Lamplighter* knew better than to print selections from a copyrighted novel in progress. He saw no excerpts from "Measurable Accumulation."

Feeling as if he'd received a stay of execution—which in many respects, he had—Clay crumpled his printout into a lumpy cantaloupe-size ball, deposited it in the grocery bag he had selected for disposing of backyard dog feces, and vowed to return to his earlier plan of becoming a better person.

No more stealing from friends.

He put on his work shoes—basically a pair of once dressy slip-ons—and walked outside to reap another bumper crop of prime Argosian excrement. The dog watched with great interest, stopping at one point to contribute a generous helping of fresh bag fill. "Showing off your special talent, boy?"

No sooner was he back inside than his phone dinged, incoming text.

Your reading, Graham wanted to know, *how did it go?*

Clay replied, *Too many valleys, not enough peaks. The audience had problems with my novel.*

After a pause, Graham responded, *The novel you sent me was edgy cool. Sounds like the sticks aren't ready for it.*

Clay clicked on his brother's number.

"A real call?" Graham answered. "What is this, 1998?"

"It's good to hear your voice too," Clay said. "It's been too long. For the record, Duchaine's not the sticks."

"Whatever you say, bro."

After spending ten minutes on high-school highs and lows, Graham said, "I loved the shit you sent. I love all your writing."

"Apparently, not everyone has the same taste in shit," Clay said. "I had been planning to submit sample chapters today. To agents in New York. No way now. My masochism's wearing thin."

"Bro, come on. Forget this paranoia shit. You've got to keep plugging away. It's not like wealth and fame are going to come looking for you."

"I don't know."

"I do know," said Graham. "Send the stupid queries."

"I'll think about it. Maybe. When my ego's in remission."

"Jesus, bro, I'm the one in this family who runs away. What have you got to lose? It's like the old saying, when you hit a low, there's nothing else to do but get high."

"That's an old saying?"

"Fuck yeah. It's our state motto. You really need to talk Marta into moving out here."

Argos barked. Walk time.

"Guess I'm off to Cleveland Park," Clay excused himself. "I'll have to tell you how Argos saved my life some other time."

Forty minutes later, Argos lapped at the reheated lasagna still in its original microwave container. But he wasn't the only one getting a reward. Using a 10" chef's knife, Clay sliced four Fun Size candy bars into thirds. He carried these to his office on a paper plate where he ate each chocolatey nugget with great deliberation.

Be here now. Remember to chew each bite at least twenty times.

A nudge of his mouse revived the window for *Craigslist > western Wisconsin > community > groups.* Pleased with the classified he had written, he tried to click *Post.*

The PC had other ideas. A single letter of the alphabet appeared in the screen's top left corner, north and west of the Craigslist template.

R

Almost instantly an *e* joined the R. Clay watched baffled as a *g*, an *a*, and another *r* quickly materialized without input from Clay, the keyboard, or mouse.

Leaning back in his chair, he watched the message slowly type itself.

Regarding your appearance at the Lit Fest I don't know what that was you read that last fifteen minutes...

Shit.

...but we both know you didn't write it.

A layer of sweat cooled Clay's arms and neck. If Josh Bramlett was his secret abhorrer—and all evidence indicated he was—how could he know "Measurable Accumulation" had been misappropriated? How could anyone know?

Clay typed, *Whoever you are, you are incorrect. I don't always use the computer when writing. The chapter I shared at the library was one of many composed on an old-fashioned typewriter. For the purity of it. Using a typewriter makes me think first, before committing my words to paper. Although this new chapter admittedly began life as something separate from my book, I have been adapting it in regard to location and time. This will give the novel with which you claim familiarity a gentler, more reflective opening.*

Now, please, for the sake of art and creative liberty, get out of my computer and leave me alone. I have done everything I'm supposed to. I am finishing the novel. I have honored my commitments to readers and silent auction winners.

He closed Google docs, ran a Norton safety check, clicked the prompts for System Restore, then let the program run while heading to the kitchen to microwave a frozen cheese pizza that failed to live up to the promise of the packaging photo. Twenty minutes later, wishing he had gone with the frozen enchiladas, he unplugged the computer to complete the reboot. A sticky note covered the camera's lens. In case Josh Bramlett had accessed it.

I am not your Duchaine Eagle Watch dot org.

When he fired his PC back up another ten minutes later, time enough to microwave and enjoy the enchiladas, he whispered to the invisible hacker, "I'm sure you found that whole process amusing. I know you're still here."

Sure enough, a new line appeared on the screen.

You are fooling no one.

Chapter 19

⌘

RAINBOWS AND LEPRECHAUNS

Three weeks after the reading, Clay still couldn't believe what he had done—or how badly he'd been shaken by the reaction to the real, unplagiarized *Explosive Love*.

Standing in the garage, in the space meant for a third car, the space Clay and Marta used for storage, he held out the blue, crescent-shaped tambourine that had been hanging from a nail on the wall. It was the one given to him by father-in-law Will—the only thing ever given to him for good luck. He gave it a rattle.

But Clay had not come for the tambourine. After digging under a tower of rarely used luggage, he retrieved the package from brother Graham and ripped it open one layer at a time. RAINBOW GOLD, read the label inside. THE WORLD'S MOST EDIBLE EDIBLES. A PRODUCT OF BOULDER, COLORADO.

I shit you not, added Graham's handwritten message, *this is a magical concoction made out of rainbows by Leprechauns.*

An hour later, Clay whispered to himself, "I've got to stop eating these things. I can't get too wasted." But instead of adding, "I need to get back to my novel," he said, "I have to be at Hey Howdy first thing tomorrow."

He fell asleep picturing a leprechaun rainbow harvest.

***

Clay's computer froze up for a third time the next morning. It didn't help that he was already in a sour mood, having slept too long to hit the window for Hey Howdy long johns. Whispering, "Wonderful," he clicked Randolph's number.

Not expecting his call to be answered, Clay had his message ready. "I hate to bother you with meddlesome problems," he said, "but you know technology better than anyone else in Duchaine. I seem to have an enemy—an enemy who attended the library reading. For reasons I'll never figure out, he declared cyber warfare on me and, by extension, you. I have been working non-stop to deliver a quality novel. This person does not want to see that happen. He hacked my computer and caused all kinds of problems. You could say he's screwing with your investment."

Clay was surprised to hear Randolph pick up. "I'm so sorry to hear this, my friend. Worry not. I have the resources to sort things out. You called the right person. I've got things under control."

***

That afternoon, Clay threw the box of edibles into his kitchen trash can. Five minutes later, he rescued it, telling himself the edibles would inspire him, or at the very least inhibit his inhibitions. Writers and drugs went hand in hand, pipe in mouth, needle in arm. If nothing else, he was placing himself in hallowed company.

"I think you let these broil too long," Marta said over dinner of five-cheese nachos. "Did you use the timer?" She looked into his eyes. "Clay, honey, are you high?"

"Just tired," he said, looking away, feeling like he'd been pulled over by a cop, and lying accordingly. "I got a lot done on my book today. I think everyone will be surprised the next time they see it."

Marta was chewing. "That's *bueno*," she said at last. "You know, these really aren't bad if you bury them in sour cream."

He couldn't disagree. They tasted great. But then, he *was* higher than shit.

She finished eating, apologized for not helping clean up. "At least *no hay mucho que hacer* with your nachos." She gave him a kiss and headed off to study. Stopping halfway up the stairs, she turned to add, "You shouldn't worry so much about your novel. Everyone loved that last part you read at the library."

***

For two fuzzy weeks, Clay made no progress on *Explosive Love*. He did eat a lot of Hey Howdy pastries, if hardly any long johns, his restraint in regard to the latter owed only to his inability to rise before ten. Each evening, he passed out more than fell asleep, only to wake after midnight with worries crowding his skull. The biggest of these: did he lack the talent to salvage his novel?

Which left him a wreck.

Which led him back to the Colorado box.

One afternoon, Clay finished off a second Rocky Mountain High Turtle Nut Brownie while watching the reality show that had become his newest addiction. This was "My Favorite Amendment," a show "by and about gun aficionados." He felt productive when watching because "MFA" had the potential to provide ideas and even dialogue for his characters.

Profiling four families in different regions of the United States, the show followed its subjects to gun shows. It followed them to shooting practice. It followed them to child custody hearings, arraignments for violating child custody arrangements, and even one Klan gathering. Clay learned the strongest reasons for keeping an arsenal: immigrants, "urban dwellers," creditors, Jews, and the Feds. He learned the Klansman's Top Five illegally obtained prescriptive drugs: OxyContin, Lorcet, Norco, Hydrocodone, and Kadian. ("Rush Limbaugh took 'em," offered the older, toothless man wearing a MAGA hat. "You can't ask for a higher endorsement than that.") Finally, Clay learned how much of their public assistance two subjects spent on firearms. "Pretty much the whole shitload."

Two hours into raiding his DV-R cache, Clay's cannabis pitched him a paranoid curveball. *What if it's true Randolph is gay?* he pondered while trying to focus on a fight at the Klansman's one-bedroom house. "Go ahead and shoot me, you bag of bleached out horseshit," the man's drunken wife was shouting. "You don't have the fucking guts."

What if Randolph moved back to Duchaine not out of respect for my writing, but out of an obsessive plan to steal the object of his lust, namely me? What if he thinks he's buying me? What if he's pulling me in over my head, thinking I'll swim to him for help? Crazy, sure, but so were most things, from religion to sleeping to eating other life forms, when you thought about them high. *And how else to explain Randolph's moving back to Duchaine? The Business Plan came right after that. It seemed pretty important to him.*

The next morning, Clay couldn't believe how badly he'd let suspicion get the better of him. It sure seemed ridiculous now, the thought of a massively successful app pioneer moving back to the Midwest for the primary purpose of pursuing a married man he first desired as a closeted gay high school student.

Stranger still, Clay vaguely remembered letting this crisply-baked brain curd segue into a recipe for spicing up *Explosive Love*. He felt fairly sure he typed in the changes—and somewhat sure he deleted them soon after.

Waiting for his PC to fire up, studying his own dark reflection in the slowly stirring screen, Clay vowed to swear off the Colorado confections, a pledge he kept until two that afternoon.

***

Early Monday afternoon, Solstice called to breathlessly share news of—yes, he knew it was coming—her sophomore novel. She caught him watching "My Favorite Amendment." One of the show's stars, who happened to be Florida's Lieutenant Governor, was teaching her eight-year-old to shoot. He had already killed a neighbor's cat.

The show went to one of Moon McDermott's commercials. "The Scrapper will get you everything you deserve... and more!" Clay scrambled to find the remote.

"Sorry," he said as he paused the recording, "I couldn't get to my radio to turn down NPR. They're profiling a bluegrass musician who apparently has some anger issues."

He tried to stay positive when Solstice resumed, "I'll have to send you page proofs, if I can stop myself from marking them up until they look like highly redacted intelligence reports. It's all so insane. I'm still reeling from dealing with foreign translations and foreign audio books for *Time As Measured in Cats*. Can you believe Warner is casting the movie right now, even as we speak? Hugh Jackman. Keira Knightly. A week hasn't passed since they secured the rights. I know, I know. No sane writer would regard these as problems. They'd tell me to shut my damn mouth."

He heard her take a deep breath. "I'm so glad I've got you to talk with," she resumed. "It's good to have company in the fast lane."

***

Setting a new record for warmth, the last Friday in August burned like a fever. Being high didn't help. Taking up the heat, DuchPubLibrary.org chose that day to post audio from the First Annual Duchaine Lit Fest. Visually accompanied by slides of the event, the podcast greatly took up the odds that Solstice would discover his already too public plagiarism.

Others had no problem finding the podcast—or trashing the real opening chapter to *Explosive Love* via the Comments forum.

This sucks with a capitol S.
Abortions no joke. Its murder.
Animal testing is cruelty and so's listening to this.

Clay's symptoms now included shortness of breath and crushing depression. Was this how it ended? Embarrassed, exposed? At least he couldn't blame his hacker, whose writing, incredibly, seemed sophisticated in comparison.

Two things that ought to be illegal this writer and abortion.

"The outraged competing to out-rage one another," Clay noted. "My students could have written this dreck."

I know he's not real but I wanted to rescue the dog out of this novel.

It got worse. The comments about abortion and animal cruelty paled before a recurring theme that was truly disconcerting, most compellingly presented as *Someone ott to blow something up in your honor to show you just what funny ain't not.*

***

September made sure no one would ever mistake it for August. Temperatures dropped. Skies stayed gray. Twilight came early.

Clay spent days without pulling up his latest draft, staring instead at the first fallen leaves outside his windows, and worse, social media. His breaks for "My Favorite Amendment" took up entire afternoons, lasting so long he needed breaks from his breaks. He doubled his midday pastry consumption and let the rising, falling buzz of the cricket death knell outside hypnotize him each evening. Winter was coming, it warned, and not everyone would be sticking around to enjoy it.

He ignored most phone calls. If anyone genuinely needed him, they could leave a message.

For the most part, he ignored his Voicemail, too.

On the first day of October, he regretted playing one back. At first anyway, because ironically, Clay's reaction—*Just what I need, another Arthur C. Peckham voicemail*— turned out to be correct.

"Those are some nasty comments on the Lit Fest post," Peckham had noted. "You going to have someone clean those up for you, too? Or try anyway? What are you on Amazon now? Three stars? Oh, sorry, two-point-five."

The message made Clay angry, the closest he'd felt to alive in some time.

"I am a writer, goddammit," he whispered to himself. "My first book did well. I can save *Explosive Love.*"

Within two hours of hearing Peckham's voice, Clay made a belated return to Craigslist for Western Wisconsin to post his ad for "Successful Author Seeks to Form Writers Group for Purpose of Critiquing." Assuming a decent response, his novel would finally get feedback from qualified readers.

He might even find a group he could brainstorm with, bringing an end to his self-imposed exile.

Chapter 20

⌘

CLASS PROJECT

Clay felt threatened, confused, unable to process what Marta was telling him, and it wasn't just that he was high. "Picked up from work in a silver stretch limo?" he said. "A two-hour lunch at Jacques D's? You never even told me you were seeing Randolph today?"

"You're kidding, right? I mentioned it several times. You knew last weekend."

If this was true, he did not remember.

"Randy and I have been talking about an MBA project for months," she added.

This, too, was news to Clay.

"Ever since we talked at the library. Right after your reading."

Clay had not seen them together that night.

"He's *muy* excited about doing this. He's ready to share everything he knows about business."

"When does this start?" he asked, but Marta had turned her focus to the details of lunch.

"It was a thrill," she said, "seeing the Maître D waiting for us at the curb. He took my hand as I stepped from the car."

Jacques D's dining room had been nearly empty, save for Randolph and his guest, a watchful staff, and a string quartet on loan from the Chicago Symphony Orchestra. "Randolph just loves classical music."

Two crystal Champagne flutes had appeared on the small round table while Marta savored the fifth course, a dessert of tiramisu, made to the specifications of Randolph's chief Italian chef. The young waiter eagerly filled both vessels with "King Brut, Vintage 1988" and Randolph made a toast: "To getting all that you deserve." The glasses clinked loudly—Randolph didn't seem concerned this might chip the clearly delicate flutes—and

Marta's study group had their group project: to document the rise and further rise of Randolph J. Simper's StripOff empire.

Barely glancing at the dried out fried chicken Clay had picked up from the Hey Howdy deli, Marta gushed over Randolph's willingness to meet with the study group for however long was needed, during which time he would generously share his history, genius, and hopefully, business secrets. This would all start the following spring. Ultimately, the study group members would fly on one of Randolph's private jets to his California-based headquarters.

"It's so *emocionante*," she enthused to Clay after pushing away her plate of barely touched chicken. "I can't wait to talk about it *más* at group tonight. Speaking of which, I'd better get moving."

She went upstairs to freshen up; he nearly called after her: "You didn't say a single word about *my* big night." But in truth, even he had not been thinking about his writers group scheduled to meet for the first time ever at half past seven. Marta's account of lunch had blindsided him with all the force of a stretch limo running a red light and taking out a Gold Wing motorcycle.

Still, Clay remained hopeful about his critique group's inaugural meeting. One of the Craigslist respondents about to show up had apparently been present at the library for Clay's reading. Of greater importance, Mr. Damon Debbitts had preferred Clay's first selection—the one Clay had actually written—over the second. *Like chocolate, I enjoy my comedy dark, and despite a few very real flaws, which I would be happy to discuss face to face, I found* Explosive Love *to be ripe with promise.*

Clay had purchased cheese and crackers for the meeting. He knew the group would total at least three, and felt hopeful a fourth writer would show. Sitting in his office, he revisited an email that had been weighing on him like a camping trip backpack. In it, brother Graham had made the confession: *I keep toying with the idea of visiting Duchaine & keep talking myself out of it.* Clay still felt the shock, suspecting that, outside of work and fetching fast food, Graham rarely left his Denver apartment.

Hilary wants to see me.

Clay was still working on a response to this disclosure, with "Don't be an idiot" ranking as the top contender. Hilary Mallory had been Graham's high school girlfriend, and quite possibly his only girlfriend ever. That ended when Graham fled Duchaine and Hilary swore off unreliable stoner boyfriends in favor of a real man who would never leave her—or let her go. This was Tim "Skull" McCracken, the most psychotic psychotic Clay had ever personally encountered.

Two months ago she struck up an online conversation with me, Graham's email had explained. *I was smitten or re-smitten or whatever the right word would be.*

Clay finally typed the reply he had been considering for hours. *You and Hilary want to see each other. I understand that, but must also point out that coming here for that purpose could well be the most stupid, not to mention last, thing you ever do. You, my brother, are ignoring the larger truth.* Hilary Mallory remains married to a *barrel-shaped auto mechanic once jailed for beating a disgruntled client with a used muffler.*

Graham, it turned out, was online at that moment. *Woah, bro, don't turn into Dad. Hilary and I chat every day. Sometimes for hours. Facebook friends. Capital F.*

Clay replied: *VIRTUAL friends.*

A few minutes later, Graham responded, *She misses me.*

She's married, Clay typed with more passion than before. *Five kids. Not three, not four. Five. I'm done for now. Phone me when you're able to think freely.*

Clay had lied, feeling anything but done with the matter. He felt responsible for this rekindling of communication between Graham and Hilary. During the spring, he had run into Hilary at Hey Howdy directly in front of the pastry shelves. "Well, Clay! You've put on a little weight," she had started their conversation. "Keep it up and you're going to look *exactly* like Graham. You're—"

She stopped abruptly, cleared her throat. "How?" Her eyes grew misty. "Is he?"

Now, thinking back on that question, Clay regretted giving an honest answer of "Same as ever" as opposed to something on the order of, "You didn't hear? It was tragic. The dispensary Graham worked at went up in flames. People were high for miles around." Clay could have saved Graham from both danger and self-deception, either of which was enough in itself to undo the progress Graham had made of late. Not that he'd evolved much in practical terms, but he'd at least stopped calling Clay to float half-baked dreams about quitting his job as a Stoned Pathways Sherpa, the lofty title Bud Wiser conferred upon lowly cashiers, to open Cottonmouth Joe's Munchie Stop adjacent to a dispensary. "It would be a place where cannabis enthusiasts could sit and dine on their favorite snacks. We'd serve Cheetos, Hostess Cupcakes, Twizzlers too. If someone could loan me the money, bro, I'd pay it back the next day. You should see the Taco Bell next to our dispensary. I shit you not, there's always a line. A lot of our clients are already high when they come in to replenish their stock. They see my snack shack on their way out, they're gonna have trouble looking away." Graham would always pause at this point, waiting no doubt for Clay to say, "Maybe Marta and I could look at our savings." But what Graham heard instead was, "There's no such thing as a Twinkees fast food establishment." To which Graham would reply, "Well, there ought to be. I've even got a slogan. You don't have to be high to eat here, but it helps."

Argos farted from his place near the door, returning Clay's focus to the email he now composed for Graham. *Think hard before you open that door to your past. I still see Skull McCracken from time to time. He's still plenty scary. Think about your dreams of starting your own business. Think about breathing and walking and other small luxuries Skull would be interested in taking from you.*

He was distracted when Marta appeared suddenly like a silent Ninja warrior. She had changed clothes for her weekly study group session. Bright and airy, to the point she now risked an overly plunging neckline, she looked ready to hit a dance club. Worse, she seemed almost giddy as she leaned in to say goodbye, thrilled by the prospect of sharing her news about the class project.

Please don't lean over like that at study group, Clay thought as she straightened back up. *Thank God you're wearing a bra.*

She clutched a small stack of papers separate from the bright-red, shoulder-strapped computer case she always took to study group. A title jumped out from the outermost sheet. Black and bold, at least 30 point. **The Business Plan**.

"The Business Plan?"

"The title for our project with Randy. Perfect, wouldn't you agree?"

He reminded her it was already in use. The Consortium? Their investment in his novel?

Marta smiled. "Oh yes," she said, "that was *broma*. But seriously, honey. A $200,000 loan versus building an empire. You tell me which one's an actual business plan."

He sighed as she vanished, again displaying her Ninja speed, and vowed to look up the word, *broma*. Did it mean funny? Cute? Clever or stupid? This time he needed to know. Back at his desk, he dispatched his email to Graham and pulled up Google Translate.

***

For the sixth time that evening, Clay advised Damon Debbitts to be patient and wait, giving the others a chance to show. At fifty-three past seven, Damon was the only other writers group member present in the flesh, although the flesh he did bring was enough to mold an additional member. Fortyish, Damon Debbitts smelled like ham and cigarettes. He also seemed on edge, an admittedly understandable state for a stranger waiting inside a stranger's house for other strangers to arrive almost an hour after they should have arrived. Thousands of horror movies, thought Clay, were routinely constructed around much weaker premises.

Clay had been thinking about horror movies ever since he first opened his front door to see the man who, wearing the same *Confederacy of Dunces* hunting cap he wore now, had stood up at the library to ask Clay questions about big advances and agents who worked for nothing. Tonight, to complete his writerly fashion scheme, Damon had added a dark green military surplus jacket. Like the hat, it stayed on indoors. Clay could not deny taking some pleasure from his guest's disorderliness, a trait that made Clay, in his new black jeans and long-sleeved dress shirt, appear quite neat and organized.

Clay glanced at his phone. *7:55*. "I had four replies to my initial Craigslist invitation," he explained without adding that the lone female respondent now seemed a likely no-show based upon the email she sent after receiving the first three chapters that made up *Explosive Love*. "Sixty pages? For a writers group that hasn't met even once? As Hemingway once said to Fitzgerald, you've got to be fucking kidding."

At 8:02, Damon asked again, "Could we begin?"

This time, Clay shrugged. "Sure, why not?"

A bead of sweat rolled down Damon's forehead. It was warm in the family room; Clay had mischievously set the thermostat to 75 degrees to see what it would take to make Damon remove his hat and jacket. Apparently, it took more than 75 degrees.

"You have created an outstanding novel." Damon leaned forward in the love seat that seemed much smaller than usual. "I liked so much about it. Who's your agent? How much is her cut?"

Clay explained that he was looking at the top tier of literary representatives—"the ones you can't find online"—to sell *Explosive Love*. "I have yet to make my final selection."

"Oh, sure," said Damon, "that's the obvious strategy. And it gives you time to do several rewrites. Maybe replace your characters with more appealing—and believable ones. Get rid of the lame comedic trappings and all the pretenses that this is any kind of literary work. Let *Explosive Love* be the suspense novel it's struggling to become, turn it into one of those lightweight trifles a narrowly educated investment advisor might buy in an airport bookstore."

Leaving no room for Clay to insert a defense, Damon extended his critique to include weaknesses in structure, word choice, and character motivation. At 8:26, Damon pulled a Camel cigarette pack out of a jacket pocket and, completely ignoring the look of censure Clay was most certainly giving him, flicked a red plastic lighter to fire one up. Within seconds, Clay's home smelled like a Colorado campfire that had recently been used for grilling ham. "And the main characters' attraction to one another, I simply could not suspend my disbelief, and believe me, I have witnessed my share of strange behavior."

Clay resisted his impulse to ask, "In mirrors perhaps?"

At 9:32, Damon seemed to wrap up his critique, even if he didn't actually stop talking. "You know Solstice Blume, right? I saw a lot of connections between the two of you on Google. Thought she might be here tonight. Is she going to be part of the group? That would be truly outstanding."

"Solstice and I share works with each other all the time." Clay almost smiled at the unintended irony. "That's more important to me than a writers group made up of strangers with no actual publishing experience."

"Are you okay?" Damon asked. "Are your clothes too tight? You've been squirming since we sat down. No offense, I'm not being critical. I hate dressing up like this, too. I prefer a good pair of sweatpants. My work clothes. The comfort lets me focus more fully on my writing. I'll send you a link to an article regarding the medical and psychological benefits."

"I'm not sure what you're talking about," Clay said. "These pants fit perfectly."

"It's your discomfort." With that, Damon took up the "crisis of punctuation." Flipping page by individual page through his copy of *Explosive Love* a second time, he assailed errors and repeatedly shared his own preferences, such as "The fewer commas the fewer comatose readers." Damon got very excited on page 52. Looking up from the paper, he came close to shouting, "You used an exclamation point for Christ's sake! What is this, eighth grade?"

Clay could have defended the lonely exclamation point but responded in the same manner he had to Damon's previous criticisms by glancing at his phone to check the time. Compounding Clay's frustration, the device seemed in no greater hurry than Damon to put this battered, limping evening out of its misery. It was only 9:16.

Nine!

Sixteen!

It took Clay a moment to realize that Damon had pummeled his last "superfluous, amateurish comma" and was done dismantling *Explosive Love*. Strangely enough, Damon was asking, "Would you mind telling me how it ends? I thought the plot was outstanding."

And so, beginning at 9:19 on a smoky Wednesday evening, Damon Debbitts became the first person to hear Clay's outline for the final chapters of *Explosive Love*.

Damon seemed to approve of all he was hearing. Clay couldn't decide if this was a good or bad sign.

***

For Pita Wishart, bottoming out came with waking on the couch from a night of chugging shoplifted MD 20/20. Josh Bramlett, the unkempt mall security guard friend and co-conspirator, had fallen asleep between Pita and Jared, his hand between her legs. Worse, *her* hand had landed high on Josh's left thigh in disgustingly close proximity to his crotch. Much, much worse, Josh's other hand rested on Jared's thigh, just as Jared's hand had found its place for the night on Josh's right thigh. Pita felt certain nothing beyond what she was witnessing had transpired, but then, she had no memory whatsoever of a mutual groping session. *Yeewwwwhhh*, she squealed, startling both Jared and Josh as she launched herself forward from her place on the couch.

"This isn't my life," she said to herself. Something had to change, something big. Fortunately for Pita, outside forces were about to bring about that change.

Four days later, United States Senator Barnabus Wishart sought reconciliation with his daughter by asking her to travel to Paris with him. "Like we did when you were little, and just like then, no one will know me there." This last detail probably had less to do with nostalgia than with current online rumors about a pregnant Congressional page who may or may not have had an abortion. But who could say no to Paris?

Jared took it poorly. Standing in the narrow doorway to their grungy cluttered kitchen, he said, "Your father is buying you back now that he knows the price. How do you think you can travel to Sodom and not turn yourself to stone? You've already mastered the coldness part."

"You don't know anything," she said from her place on the futon recently purchased from Goodwill. (Following the night with Josh, Pita no longer used the couch.) "I am not going to abandon a single belief. I just need a break. And besides, Lot's wife was turned to salt, not stone. You really don't know the true word of God."

"I don't know anything?" Jared exploded. "Who's been posting revolutionary slogans on Facebook accompanied by photos of our explosives? You don't think Homeland Security has Internet access? Maybe you should have finished college, took a few courses in Thinking 101, Miss *I Was An Honors Student In High School.*" This—Jared's sense of superiority at having finished four years of college—was a weapon he almost always kept sheathed, having learned to bring up the fact in only the most heated of arguments. He had, in fact, acquired this restraint because he couldn't stand Pita's hurtful petty rejoinder: "Yeah, as a C student." But on this day, he was way beyond that fear. "You have no right to call anyone stupid," he angrily sputtered.

Pita retaliated by stomping on a spider that made the mistake of crawling out from under the couch.

"You monster."

"It figures you'd care more about an insect than me," she spat. "You and that bug have lots in common. Like that bug, you don't have a soul."

Jared could have pointed out that spiders weren't insects but instead drilled straight to the core of his anger. "I don't suppose you've ever noticed there are too many people on this planet. We're like a prairie dog colony with no natural predators hell bent on devouring every last strand of grass." Jared loudly crushed his empty Mr. Pepper can—the generic pop from Gas 'n' Go—in his right fist. "Eight billion people... about seven billion too many... yet you can't stop singing, 'Every Sperm Is Sacred.'"

Pita was on her feet. "Right, but you can never have too many spiders."

Jared's face burned with rage. "Maybe your prairie dogs need to practice some population control," he said, "*before* the plague does it for them. Maybe they need a prairie dog abortion clinic."

Scratching, slapping, and screeching, Pita lunged toward him, target: face. "Who's the cold-hearted bitch?" she shouted. "Who's the murderer here?"

When she left for Paris seven days later, she had no intention of returning to Jared. Ever. For all she cared, he could keep his hands on Josh Bramlett's thigh.

The first night in the City of Light, Barnabus Wishart insisted on celebrating hard-won freedoms, "specifically my own." Over dinner and Champagne in an upscale shopping district near the Eiffel Tower, he told his daughter he was getting divorced and leaving the Senate for a lucrative lobbying contract. "This is hush, hush, of course. Lobbying firms aren't supposed to approach elected officials until after they leave office."

Wanting Pita back in his life, he had transferred two million dollars to a trust fund established in her name "where your greedy, thieving mother can't touch it. A lot of work went into this, a lot of lawyerly skill. But you need to be kind to your father. While I'm alive, I manage the trust."

The following morning, armed with only a phone and her father's English-to-French translation book, she ventured out from their luxurious, three-story townhouse that looked like all the other yellow-gray buildings fronted with Lutetian limestone. Two blocks south, she entered the building she needed, a *pharmacie*.

She scoured the shelves of the small, cozy room for OTC drugs that physically resembled the pills in her father's Jumbo Monthly Organizer. Consulting the photos in her phone, and translating signs and labels as she went, she found three varieties of cold relief not recommended for patients with high blood pressure. (It went without saying these were not meant as replacements for the Rosavustatin and Lisinopril and Metformin her diabetic father had been taking since his second stroke.) Walking back to the townhouse, she purchased a selection of pretty treats from a pastry shop to give herself an alibi for going out.

On her sixth morning in Paris, Pita took charge of the sightseeing schedule. She and her father hired taxies, walked along Rue Mozart near the Seine's concrete banks, checked out the Notre-Dame cathedral's shell, and climbed a steep hill to admire the majestic Sacré Cœur church.

Looking out across the wide river valley with its many iconic sights, her father asked, "Are we planning to visit any attractions with elevators, say, the Arc de Triomphe?"

"Just one more thing I want to see," she said, adding the "Daddy" that seemed to disable his threat sensors.

Forty minutes later, they were exploring Pére Lachaise Cemetery, which itself occupied the side of a hill. "We couldn't have started at the top?" her father gasped between long, open-mouth breaths.

Other comments included, "Why are we here? Jim Morrison, Oscar Wilde—you don't give a shit about these degenerates," and, "I'm not feeling well."

"It's just the heat," she said in response to the latter. "We'll find something to eat after this. A little Champagne will cure your ills."

The sidewalks and pathways became more crowded. The Honorable Barnabus Wishart bumped into the bustling, self-consciously fashionable Euro-masses. He tripped on cobblestones. He sweated like a Frenchman. Finally, while facing the tomb of Isadora Duncan, he suffered the stroke that disabled his language center.

Trying to ask for help in his own native tongue, the Senator's brain substituted random words for the ones he was trying to use, turning "I think I'm having a stroke" into "Soup, Formica, choo-choo." To his own amazement, he was fully cognizant of the sounds he was making, as well as the ones he meant to produce. But this brought no comfort or hope of rescue, not with his daughter's lack of concern. She had to know he was trying to say *ambulance* and *1-1-2*. Yet all she could manage was to pull him out of the teeming procession.

"You'll be fine, Daddy. Just rest for a minute."

Looking into her frigid green eyes, he realized the danger he had placed himself in. He called out to strangers, "Rubber, Trump, sediment." This prompted only brief glances from these French socialist ingrates who wouldn't even have a country of their own had it not been for the United

States, causing him to wonder how many spoke English as a second or third language but simply assumed the tourist's word soup was beyond their level of fluency.

Americans shuffled past as well. (Not everyone was impeccably attired.) Their faces said it all by nervously looking away. "Sorry, but we came here to get away from crazy homeless people."

Pita surprised him by calling out in what sounded like immaculate French. Not that he could check her for accuracy. He didn't understand a word.

It was immaculate French. For five days, Pita had thoroughly rehearsed lines like *"Désolé, mon papa gêteaux avait trop bu"* (sorry, my sugar daddy had too much to drink) and *"Il êtra amende en quelques minutes"* (he'll be fine in a few minutes). Her audience reacted as expected by picking up speed as they shuffled past.

The Senator chose to stress the urgency of his crisis by faking a fall. Or had he really fallen? Either way, he was on the ground, and had hit a corner on Duncan's tombstone much harder than he would have preferred while pretending to fall. His world seemed to be getting progressively darker—and more confusing. Words like "Voters!" and "Immigrants!" came less frequently.

"Désolé, mon papa gêteaux avait trop bu" and *"Il êtra amende en quelques minutes,"* his daughter repeated. What was she saying?

He tried looking up toward her face; she was still standing, couldn't even bother to kneel. His eyes remained focused on the expensive beige dress shoes he had purchased for her the afternoon before.

"You heartless bitch." Somehow he was able to pull out these words.

"You raised me well," she quietly replied.

The passersby stopped to form a semi-circle.

"Mon pauvre père," Pita cried, each word trembling with emotion. *"Il s'est évanoui,"* (My poor father. He fainted.)

Finally, she got on her knees and leaned in close. "Did you know Isadora Duncan choked on her scarf?" she whispered. "It got caught in her own car wheel."

Minutes passed before she heard the familiar French sirens straight out of some libtard movie about the fake Holocaust. By the time paramedics arrived, her father was well beyond saving. Years too late, in her opinion.

Back in the States, she purchased a mansion in suburban Rockford, an hour outside of Chicago. Jared was invited to occupy a guest bedroom and make love to Pita on Tuesdays, Thursdays, and Saturdays—she used birth control now—and walk and feed her Labrador Retriever all through the week. These were among the duties listed in the "non-nuptial agreement" her lawyer drew up. She gave money to anti-abortion groups. She purchased billboards that shrieked from cornfields to drivers passing on highways: *All children are precious, no matter how small or unborn.*

Josh Bramlett inherited the rental property, at least to the extent he moved in; no further rent was paid on his behalf. Come Christmas, the Clairmont Mall went up in flames following several explosions. Soon afterward, Bramlett's New Stratford residence exploded in a flash that could have been seen from Pluto. The FBI ruled this an accident: just desserts for a meth addict and supplier running his lab alongside a cache of explosive materials. Despite whispers during her campaign to become Illinois' Congresswoman for the 16th District, Pita's alleged ties to the dead ex-security guard never became an issue. As she made clear in her first national Fox News appearance, "What else would you expect from the liberal media? Of course, they're going after a candidate running on the platform: *Liberal Media, Give Us Some Truth.*"

"And that's pretty much it," Clay told Damon Debbitts.

"Pretty perverse," said Damon, shifting his weight on Clay and Marta's couch. "Letting money solve her problems. Much like real life."

"It's funny how a big idea can blossom from a small observation. Only a few weeks ago, I was stuck behind a Ford Ram pickup with that slogan on a bumper sticker. *Liberal media, give us some truth.* I knew it belonged in my novel."

"Interesting," said Damon. "But what was the big idea?"

Clay's phone rang. Looking at the Caller ID, he picked up to say, "Hey, Solstice."

Damon loudly interrupted, "Can I talk with her?"

Clay told Solstice he would have to call her back in the morning. He glanced at his phone as he clicked End Call. *9:46.*

Damon, likewise, consulted his watch. "This is unfortunate. I have missed the last bus."

And so Clay's evening took another strange turn, several in fact, as he navigated the dark hilly terrain east and south of his city. Damon lived on Ram's Head Ridge overlooking a Ford dealership, the loading docks of Wal-Mart, and winding tree-lined Crayfish Creek. The brick houses Clay passed were small, three rooms at most. The other houses were trailers.

Clay asked Damon if he had to work in the morning.

"Writing *is* my work. Toiling for others simply means you have to render up taxes and make payments on student loans. I also devote several hours a day to reading. One cannot write without reading. At present I am revisiting the complete works of Joseph Conrad. I hardly need to tell you, of course. I am sure you read relentlessly."

Feeling no need to confess how little fiction he had read the past months, or how the act drained him of energy and hopefulness, replacing these precious fluids with jealousy and self-doubt, Clay said only, "Are we getting close?"

"Up here on the right," said Damon Debbitts.

The headlights of the Volvo hit what looked like a small salvage yard where old American automobiles that could no longer fetch $100 on Craigslist went to be stripped of parts. When Clay asked Damon if he collected cars, he learned that Damon oversaw collections of both automobiles *and houses*, if not by design. The man now lighting a cigarette in Clay's Volvo had inherited the compact brick house made even grungier by the headlights' glare. It was one of five he owned and "the only one not in a flood plain." Put them together, Damon suggested, and his family would have had one good residence. As it was, he had grown up in houses with eight electrical outlets for every one that actually worked.

As for the ghostlike cars in the yard—Clay counted ten, among them a white Chevy Impala on cinder blocks and a blue El Camino with a jagged glass frame where the windshield had been—these too were part of Damon Debbitt's dubious birthright. All were missing a part of significance, whether a passenger door or hood or grill.

Damon's father had been an engineer at Farm Haul in its glory days when the tractor manufacturing plant employed half the men of Duchaine. He made good money. His wife never worked. But instead of buying one car that looked good and ran well, he bought dozens that didn't set standards for performance.

"Are you picking up a theme?" Damon asked Clay. "It's why I stopped driving. I got sick of cars."

Clay saw movement in the yard: something darting behind an Oldsmobile Torino that was missing its front fender assembly. A dog... only it wasn't a dog. More like a fox or coyote.

"You should read my book," said Damon. "You'll find my family the source of great interest."

Clay's phone buzzed. He pried it from his pocket, an act that required considerable effort. Ever since Damon had asked about discomfort, the jeans had felt incredibly tight; he couldn't wait to get them off later. The Caller ID showed *Marta*. She was probably home from study group. "Hey, honey," he answered. "I'll be home in a few minutes. I had to take someone home after writers group."

Seconds later, he said, "Yes, that was tonight."

Turning his attention back to Damon, Clay said, "I hate to bear bad news,

149

but there will be no writers group in the foreseeable future. Solstice Blume wants me to read her new manuscript. With my own writing deadlines, that leaves little time for your *Peace*."

"*War*." Damon dispatched an angry cloud of smoke in the direction of Clay's mouth and nose. "You know this isn't fair. Not after I invested hours reading your chaotic first chapters. Besides, I absolutely believe you would find *War* a fascinating tale."

Clay pressed the car's Unlock button, twice, each time producing a loud car-wide click to make sure his passenger understood it was time to get out.

"It's not really about war in the traditional sense," Damon continued. "More the battlefield of everyday life. *War* is the story of an app inventor who steals his ideas from others and destroys anyone who gets in his way. I probably shouldn't tell you this but it's based on my cousin."

Clay no longer stared at his phone.

"You've probably heard of him. Everyone has. That's right, you've got it. Randy Simper is my first cousin, and he's also a vile, nefarious thief."

"That does sound promising, Damon. Very promising. Despite my important commitments, I would like to read it."

Damon offered to find the extra copy he had and bring it by Clay's house.

As Clay drove away, he wondered if *War* really told damaging secrets about Randolph or if it would amount to nothing more than an airing of imagined slights by a man who found himself in his cousin's shadow.

"On the other hand," Clay smiled as he whispered to himself, "Damon owns *five* houses. Randolph, to the best of my knowledge, owns two."

Chapter 21

⌘

ALL AT ONCE

Reading through the marked up *Explosive Love* chapters, Clay found Damon's comments either helpful or overwhelming. At least it proved easy to make small choices. The exclamation point, for example, had been removed, though Clay resisted the demand to purge all commas after reaching the conclusion Debbitts was commaphobic.

As November settled in, Clay felt dissatisfied with the little progress he had made. He was tinkering, not writing. Then came the flu, a wily flu outsmarting the shot he got weeks before at Heitzman Drug. Aches and chills pummeled his frame, kept him pinned to the couch. Naps offered refuge if not without throwing in increasingly strange dreams. Clay raced his Gold Wing across the surface of a lake, understanding that to slow was to sink. He stood on a bookstore stage before an audience of empty chairs. Three hungry Kodiak Bears roared at his window, which fuzzily transformed, as he opened his eyes, into Argos protesting the illness-imposed walk moratorium.

Marta stayed healthy. She did this by practicing social distancing. Each evening after work, she stopped maybe ten feet from the couch, asked Clay if he needed anything, then hurried upstairs with that day's choice of carry-out.

Day Four dumped on him like a cement mixer's chute. He felt the weight, felt the gooey wetness hardening fast. But then, suddenly, come afternoon, the fever lifted and with it the pressure. He felt himself swimming in a pool of lucidity as vast as it was soothing and cool. His thoughts, in kind, became fluid, and in them, he found everything needed to raise *Explosive Love* from the depths. Immersed in ideas for serious structural changes, infusions of conflict, and overall plot reinforcement, it was as if the walls in his brain had been washed away, opening his conscious mind to joyful inspiration. All at once, there they were, just waiting to be typed: the solutions his subconscious had been privately pursuing since Damon Debbitts first alerted him to the problems.

Clay got up quickly, tripping over Argos, and headed for his computer.

By the time the flu lifted completely, Clay could measure his progress in 61 fresh double-spaced pages and numerous significant revisions to the chapters Damon had critiqued. It may have been the fastest he had ever worked.

Having a new appreciation for the only other member of his writers' group, Clay thought again of the worn cardboard box Damon had left inside his screen door after learning that Clay had the flu. The box was thick, enough to keep a screen door from closing. *War* may not have been *War and Peace*, as Damon had noted, but it looked about as long, and this had deterred Clay from taking it out of the box in his weakened state.

He now retrieved the first few hundred pages, and was pleased to find a steady march of a story that, unsurprisingly, never slowed for punctuation. The author's minimalistic approach extended to humor, invention, and playfulness, yet Damon had created a tale as riveting as it was revealing. The main character, Andrew J. Kelp, waged war on his foes like a corrupt Third World general whose cunning and desire were never impaired by ethics or morality. He ruled over a universe with himself at the center, encircled by infinite greed and controlled chaos from which no reader could look away, let alone one familiar with the character's genesis. Little of the storytelling seemed to qualify as fiction, more like wartime biography under the thinnest of veils. If Clay felt regret every third or fourth page about having been lured onto Randolph's battlefield, he reminded himself he stood on the outermost ring—and not with the unfortunate souls who found themselves on the wrong side of *War*.

Josh Bramlett, for example. Clay could only hope Randolph had gone relatively easy on the silent auction winner. Sure, Bramlett deserved some bad Karma, and he had been more than deserving of Clay's angry texts, like *Get a hobby, Leave me the fuck alone,* and *Fictional Josh Bramlett is considerably more interesting than Real Life Josh Bramlett.*

But while Clay had been more than happy to see the cyber sabotage end, he now wondered if Bramlett had surrendered after hearing reasonable entreaties—or being terrorized into a submissive stupor? Worse, had he done more than disappear from Clay's screens by disappearing altogether? Clay had seen nothing in the paper or on TV, but there was no forgetting the old question, *If a tree falls in the forest and nobody cares, does it make the 9 O'clock news?* Josh Bramlett had not seemed like the kind of person anyone would miss.

Working in favor of the loan officer's continued existence, Randolph's retaliatory measures rarely went unnoticed. (Damon barely disguised his source materials, making it easy for Clay to find the original accounts online.) Take the story of M.K. Kelgard, the "once heralded game designer" responsible for the failed Strip Offtimum console, who perished "in pursuit of game design realism," puréed by a homemade, 10-foot-tall robot wielding a spiky, skull-topped club that shot flames.

Or Wallace Scrivener, the actual inventor of StripOff, bought out for a pittance—and found dead four months later of truly mysterious causes. Although the Monterey Bay Aquarium curator swore their display tanks were inaccessible to the public, visitors had watched in horror while Scrivener pounded on the two-foot thick Plexiglas until he was overwhelmed by the sharks devouring him.

And what of Erika Donne, the App reviewer for *Fidgety Digits* Magazine? She took artillery fire from every direction after crashing through the fence of Area 51 in a massive, speeding semi with banners shouting from both sides of its trailer, *FREE THE ALIENS.*

If none of this made Clay exactly happy to have Randolph consider him a friend, it was again, highly preferable to foe. As AlienTruth.com lamented, *Truth seeker Donne's body looked like a sponge with all the bullet holes.* The Monterey Bay Aquarium website promised, *Measures have been taken to ensure we never see another freak accident of this nature.*

This was as much as Clay could dwell on the matter. Worrisome as these stories were, he had done nothing to incur Randolph's wrath, at least so far. His focus was required elsewhere, on finishing *Explosive Love*, on keeping Randolph and the rest of the Consortium happy.

For the first time in months, his outlook bordered on optimistic. The Tuesday after Thanksgiving, he finally submitted five sample chapters to as many carefully selected agents. *Needless to say, I hope you enjoy your first brush with Explosive Love and ask to see more. Thank you for your consideration. I look forward to hearing from you.*

He was sincere in ending each query with *Sincerely Yours.* Clay *was* looking forward to hearing from these knowledgeable professionals, just as he looked forward to seeing Damon's suggestions for the balance of *Explosive Love.*

In the meantime, he kept his front wheel straight and kept up the speed.

Chapter 22

⌘

CHILI DOG SALAD

Duchaine's Second Annual Lit Fest followed the first by only nine months. Giving Clay a fresh taste of acid reflux each time he saw a KDUC news story, newspaper ad, or mailed announcement, Fillmore Banks, third-rate author and fourth-rate mentor, was being feted at the downtown library. The timing of the event coincided with the "world premiere of the legendary lost novel, *Cruel Comedown*, available now in hardcover, paperback, and electronic editions." This was how Small Packages Press described the release in their flyer promoting the appearance. Also promised: "A brand new novel will follow, bringing the Fillmore Banks legacy up to the present day."

Jenni Jensen gave her *Lamplighter* article the insulting, utterly incorrect heading: "Small Packages Bags Its First Major Author!" A full-page ad for the Lit Fest continued the misinformation campaign by quoting *Publishers Weekly*: "*Cruel Comedown* from Fillmore Banks stands as the first important title from the late-blooming Small Packages Press."

As such, Banks was swimming a thoroughly undeserved victory lap in Duchaine's small pond. Mayor Moberly personally promoted the event on KDUC's nine o'clock news, calling it "the biggest night yet for Duchaine's Annual Lit Fest." Fillmore's appearance, he added, would take place on the library's main floor, closing down regular traffic for the entire evening.

By the time that evening arrived, Clay had found something else to do and was missing the event. Feeling confident Jenni Jensen would be in attendance, Clay was using the opportunity to break into her house.

For the record, he preferred the term "sneaking in." After all, he planned only to remove one small, low-value item. It was an article no one would miss, at least not immediately.

A call from Solstice had necessitated the sneak in, forcing Clay to again place on hold his plan to become a better person. As she had explained on the phone a week earlier, their old teacher had pulled out every last Solstice Blume creative writing assignment from high school English—and wanted to see her short pieces from college to trace her transformation into a brilliant sci-fi writer. Were publishers to ever desire a Solstice Blume anthology, Jensen would have it ready for them. "She's going to separate the barely salvageable from the recyclable," Solstice had explained to Clay. "Personally, I find it a bit difficult to believe anyone would be interested in pieces I wrote as a student. Like any other serious writer, I'd like to think I've improved a hundredfold since then."

Unfortunately, in promising to share her work with Jensen, Solstice had made it very likely the retired teacher would encounter a third category of "Early Solstice Blume Writings" beyond *Salvageable* and *Recyclable*: that which Clay had deemed *Plagiarizable*.

"Measurable Accumulation" would surely be part of the collection, and once Jensen came across the short piece Clay had read aloud during his own Lit Fest triumph at the library, she would be strongly tempted, if not morally obliged, to destroy him. She would appear on KDUC, leading off the evening news with a gripping tale of theft and betrayal, ironically robbing Clay of his reputation, marital security, and any other reasons he might have for climbing out of bed each day. There was also the matter of the Consortium's investment. Randolph J. Simper and Marta's classmates would surely demand their funds be returned, spent portion included.

Clay stood on the damp asphalt-shingled roof, still warm from the afternoon sun, of Jensen's screened-in back porch. The day had been pleasant for February in Wisconsin, the temperature hitting 43. The nine-day old snow was nearly melted.

His clothes were torn, his flesh bleeding in several highly sensitive locations, all victims of the razor-thorned rosebushes lining the shaky lattice panel he had made his ladder. His stomach churned from nervousness. When he tried catching his breath, his attempts were complicated by the flimsy, pinching Spiderman mask with the too-short elastic strap purchased at a Madison Walgreens. Clay had traveled to Madison to avoid the possible complications of having to explain the acquisition to anyone he knew—or make any kind of impression on a local Walgreens cashier. Minus this precaution, either risk would have risen to the level of downfall were Jensen to own video surveillance equipment. Clay had imagined a dark, grainy security-camera clip airing on the nine o'clock news, followed by a Walgreens employee revealing, "I remember selling that mask to some nervous looking dude. There's a camera right over my register if anyone wants to see what he looked like. I think about it every time I need to pick my nose. You don't have to show that on the news, you know. Or me saying that." The news anchor would have then concluded the story by imploring, "Anyone knowing the identity of this man who looks a lot like Duchaine's own Clay Turner is encouraged to contact local police."

One development had already worked in his favor. Marta's Wednesday had gone long, sending her straight to study group from work. Getting ready proved easy. There was no feeling rushed as he filled his backpack with necessary supplies, like the chisel he now held in his right hand.

He pressed an old dish towel against the bathroom's casement window to muffle the shattering. He had no such remedies for burglar alarms, and when none wailed in response, he experienced a feeling as close to relief as he possibly could under the circumstances.

What he did hear was a gray Schnauzer barking at him from the bathroom's tastefully tiled floor, also gray in dusk's fading light. The neighbors most likely heard this barking, just as they most likely ignored it. Schnauzers, Clay knew from the online research he and Marta had completed before rescuing Argos, barked at any hint of provocation, whether a UPS truck bouncing past or a dandelion tuft blowing across a neighbor's lawn three doors down. No one inside or outside the houses Schnauzers pathetically claimed to guard took these dogs seriously.

Even so, Clay took one last cautious look around the periphery. Small jungles of trees and shrubs hid the Clemens Street houses on either side, but he could see the house behind Jensen's, the one on Glass Street with the backyard abutting hers. Were the residents of that house to look out, wondering why the damn Schnauzer was barking again, they would see the world's least convincing Spiderman impersonator crouching on a porch roof.

Clay checked the time on his phone—7:30—and couldn't believe he had not thought to charge it earlier, its power at 28%. He figured he had two hours in which to safely maneuver as measured in segments of Mayor Moberly's bloated introduction, time for Banks' reading, and time for the Q and A. But Clay was taking no chances. He planned to exit the crime scene by eight... eight-fifteen at the latest.

Reaching through the broken pane and turning the metal crank lever, he opened the outward swinging casement as wide as he could. The next step, squeezing his body feet-first through the opening, proved more of a challenge. He got stuck halfway like a medium-sized package jammed into a small mailbox. His stomach bore all the weight, wedged as it was against an inch-wide wooden ridge that felt like it had been sharpened. A minute passed, then another. He moved ever so slightly, and just as he accepted this was how he'd be discovered by Jensen, the police, and viewers of KDUC, his body tipped downward. A shoe made contact with the bathroom floor.

There was more good news in that Clay felt no teeth gripping his foot or ankle. Jensen's Schnauzer showed much more interest in barking. "Calm, boy, calm," said Clay, slowly placing his weight on the ceramic tiles. "Everything's okay."

Once on his feet, he tried petting the dog. It kept barking. Out of the backpack came a Milk Bone made for a much larger beast. The Schnauzer seemed intrigued. With little trepidation, it accepted the bone, the transporting of which to another room required its full Schnauzer strength and concentration. With the dog gone, Clay placed the Frisbee he had appropriated from the pile of toys Argos had never shown any interest in on Jensen's bathroom floor. This, he hoped, would explain the broken window when she discovered it later that night.

With his flashlight app's beam crawling up and down the damask papered walls, he entered the bedroom. Issuing a thunderous fart, he cursed himself for having prepared and devoured a chili dog salad for dinner with its combination of onions, pickles, tomatoes, mustard, ketchup, and canned Hormel chili. He felt a second stirring, and hoped the magma would stay in its chamber, saving any actual eruptions for when he got home.

Shining his light on the tile floor, he saw blood, big drops of it, along with a few small puddles. Sliced by the window's broken pane, his arm was bleeding. Concerned more for the tile than with passing out, he yanked tissue after tissue from a festive, decorative box on the sink counter, even as he used his other arm to open drawers in search of large bandages. *Ah, thank God, bottom drawer. Steady. Got one.* The clumps of soggy bloody tissue went into the backpack, so as not to leave evidence. More followed after he wiped the window's serrated edge and the tiles and even a few places on the bedroom's wooden floor.

Still on his knees, he felt the stab of a glass shard. He shone the light on his pants, didn't see any fresh blood, even with all the punctures and tears that had not existed an hour ago. Luckily, he had paid only $6 for the sweatpants at a Madison thrift store, a real bargain given how good these pants both felt and fit. They were also pitch black in color, same as the matching $5 sweatshirt, making the outfit a perfect fashion choice, blending comfort with camouflage.

He smiled, inwardly acknowledging the Damon Debbitts influence. Clay had greatly appreciated the link sent by his writers group colleague. *NEEDS BEFORE NORMS*, the article was titled. *Wearing the Right Clothes for a Wrinkle Free Life.* If only it had convinced Marta. Her review of the printout left on her placemat stopped at six words: "I hope this is a joke."

Finally satisfied with his cleaning efforts, Clay got back to the task at hand, his phone's beam bobbing wildly again. Whereas a certain oversized Black Lab would have chased the light, barking loudly the whole time, Jensen's Schnauzer followed only with its eyes, quiet as a cat, likely stuffed from eating that Argos-portioned Milk Bone. Clay advanced on a faux-antique roll-top desk, its top board supporting dozens of books in lopsided columns, which didn't make it much different from the rest of Jensen's furniture as her dresser and jewelry armoire held similar stacks. He saw no TV.

He ran his light up and down the spines of the books on the desk, scanning for authors' names, thinking he might find his own. He did not, although he recognized many other titles and names, including *Time As Measured in Cats*. Examining a thoroughly used paperback edition of *Catch-22*, he wisely admonished himself: Keep your eyes on the prize. But then he saw a hardbound copy of Fillmore Banks' first novel, *Big Fish*. Screw the prize; Clay found himself browsing the spines of the books on the dresser. If his old teacher had books by Fillmore Banks, she had to have his.

Stop, stop, stop, he scolded himself. Jensen had only acquired *Big Fish* for purposes of research, ordering a used copy for one cent plus shipping from Amazon to help her prepare the questions that would bring Banks to his knees in an unexpectedly humiliating question and answer session. Her review in tomorrow's paper would read more like an obituary, all under the headline, "Talentless Fraud Exposed in Library Debacle." It was the headline Clay had feared seeing the day after his act of plagiarism.

He checked the time. Holy Christ, 8:17. Almost as bad, the phone's battery was at 18%. Under no circumstance would he allow himself to be distracted again. Eyes on the prize goddammit. The desk supported other paper products besides books, and among the scribblings and typings and *Lamplighter* clippings he located a manuscript-size mailing container with a dozen colorful stamps making up the postage. Better yet was the familiar, careful handwriting. *Solstice Blume, 2850 Brookwood Parkway, Hillsboro, Oregon.* Delighted and relieved, he clutched the box to his chest.

A door closed downstairs. He heard other noises: two people talking? A light came on, its dusky glow barely reaching the upstairs bedroom, muted, like the conversation he was now hearing. The Schnauzer raced out the main bedroom door, presumably headed for stairs.

Jensen must have left early or—Clay's phone now showed 8:33—*relatively* early. She must have realized how pompous and untalented Fillmore Banks was and chosen to skip the Q and A.

"I can't believe you ended your question and answer session so abruptly," the retired English teacher said as Clay moved closer to the top of the stairs to better eavesdrop. "Two questions! You told them you were through after two freakin' questions!"

Who was she talking to?... it couldn't be... no, it absolutely could not be Fillmore Banks. But his was the voice that Clay heard next: "It's always good to leave them wanting more."

Jensen said, "That lady from the library surely wanted more."

"Indeed, the acquisitions manager," Fillmore said. "She seemed more accessible than an ATM."

Clay shifted his weight. A floorboard squeaked, effectively stopping the downstairs conversation along with Clay's breathing and heartbeat.

"When I write my article for the *Lamplighter*," Jensen finally resumed, "I'll report you had double the attendance of the first Lit Fest when Clay Turner read from his new novel."

"Clay Turner? Is he a local author? I'm having trouble placing the name."

"He was one of my students the same year I got to work with the incredible Solstice Blume. He surprised me with the quality of the piece he read at the library. It showed a thousand-percent improvement over his usual substance and style. He also took a lot more questions that you did. I mean, seriously, Fillmore, you didn't even acknowledge the third one when that woman asked why so much time had elapsed between your first and second books."

"It seemed a good time to excuse myself," Fillmore said.

"With twelve other hands raised in waiting?"

"You were there," he said, "and you heard me tell them I had an important interview with a writer for the *Lamplighter*."

"You were afraid you'd miss the liquor store closing," noted Jensen.

"Well, that too. Thanks again for stopping."

Tired of spying and angered by Fillmore Banks' inability to even recognize his name, Clay shuffled quietly to a second bedroom near the front of the house. Sitting on the edge of a twin-sized guest bed, he peeled off his sweaty, sticky mask and used his phone's flashlight to examine the individual contents of the mailing container. First one, not it. Second one, intriguing title: "My Fake Internet Feud." But for Christ's sake, stop reading the damn thing. You're here for a reason. Find what you came for, then get the hell out.

So why was he reading the single-spaced, single-page composition with a handwritten note for a header? *This is the first piece that made me think of myself as a writer. I was in sixth grade when I wrote "The Boy Who Purred."*

It began: *Michael loved his cat.*

Baxter loved to purr.

One day when they were playing together, Aaron started to purr. "Oh my," cried his mother. "Oh my," cried his father.

Michael's mom and dad rushed him to the doctor to find out what was wrong. Dr. Sara took a few notes and listened to him purr. "Can you tell me what's wrong?" she asked the boy.

"Nothing is wrong," he replied. "It feels good. It feels like a smile happy and warm only deep down inside."

Dr. Sara asked Michael if it would be okay to listen using her shiny silver stethoscope.

"Sure," he said, the purr getting louder. She leaned in close and a funny thing happened. She too began to purr.

Dr. Sara held out the stethoscope. "Listen to this," she said to Michael's mom and dad. The grownups took turns listening.

"Purring feels good," Michael told them. "It feels like a smile happy and warm only deep down inside."

His mom and dad were puzzled, especially when they heard themselves starting to purr. Dad wanted to say how good it felt but there was no need. His purr said it all.

Michael went on TV. He told everyone how he came to be the little boy who purred. "It feels like a smile," he began.

People everywhere listened to Michael's story. When the boy started purring they scratched their heads and listened some more. Then a funny thing happened. They began to purr all over the world. Grocers and mayors. Firemen and astronauts. Teachers and movie stars.

It was just like Michael said. It felt like a smile happy and warm only deep down inside.

Cute? Silly? Was she really that good with spelling (stethoscope?) in sixth grade? All Clay knew for sure was it surpassed anything he'd written in grade school or middle school, if not high school, college, and beyond. Here again was proof that Solstice was the real writer. And that cats were better for writers than dogs.

Someone coughed downstairs.

Idiot, Clay scolded himself. *I presume you're done now. Eyes on the prize!*

There it was: "Measurable Accumulation by Solstice Blume." Clean crisp sheets. A staple in the upper left corner neatly binding them in place.

He pressed to turn off the flashlight app, but the phone did it for him, its battery drained. Rising to his feet, he stole "Measurable Accumulation" for a second time, this time in a very real, physical sense. He folded the manuscript into fourths and squeezed it into a pocket. Then, re-disguised as Spiderman, he tiptoed back to the desk to replace the borrowed container.

But no sooner had he completed this task than he heard footsteps on the stairs. Fillmore and Jensen were on the move.

Clay's stomach churned anew. More gas escaped.

The footsteps grew louder. He slipped into a small sitting room where three windowless walls framed a love seat. Son of a bitch, he'd walked into a trap. The bedroom provided the only exit.

"I don't go home with men I don't know," Jensen said with a girlish giggle that would have been embarrassing were she still the eighteen-year-old college freshman she was trying to affect. "I'm not that kind of girl."

"You are now," Banks said. "I guess that makes me the mysterious dashing stranger."

"In reality, I know you better than any other man I've ever been with. Through your beautiful writing, you have peered into my very soul and shaken my very foundation. Your words give me goose bumps."

"I'm pleased to hear that," he said. "Say, where did I set my Scotch?"

Without any semblance of foreplay, the two were on the bed, making love, or at least making the grunting and moaning noises that were sometimes associated with the act. *Like a bad porno soundtrack*, thought Clay, before amending this to *a parody of a bad porno soundtrack*. He closed his eyes, wishing he could do the same with his ears.

"You know, Fillie," Jensen cooed, "we didn't really have to leave early to stop at the liquor store."

"We didn't *what?*"

"I stocked up for tonight. I was feeling lucky."

"You've certainly done your homework, dirty girl."

Clay cringed for what had to be the thousandth time that evening. Jenni Jensen? Dirty girl?

"Yes," she said. "I certainly did my homework. But you do mention Scotch Whiskey about every sixth page in your novels."

"You caught me there, Jamie. Now, enough with the talking. Bring it on home for Fillmore, you dirty, dirty girl."

Clay's stomach growled again. He could no longer deny the fact he would soon need a bathroom and, after that, a vomitorium.

Fillmore interrupted his thoughts by asking, "Err, um, Jamie, why did you shave?"

"I wanted you to see what you were getting into."

"Okay, I guess... it's an interesting choice... for someone your age."

"Hush," said Jensen in a not so hushed tone. "I want to make love to this recording."

"Music?" Fillmore whispered.

"To *my* ears," she said. "It's your reading from earlier tonight. From my phone."

Had there been a God, and had it revealed itself in that sitting room, at that moment, Clay would have asked for only one thing: a swift and merciful death.

Fortunately, at least to some small degree, the recording was lo-fi, the words barely bubbling through the thick heavy mud of a riverbed. It still sounded like Fillmore Banks, granted, more so in fact than the grunting and panting he was producing for his present audience of two—three counting the Schnauzer—but most of the words were unintelligible.

"Good choice," Fillmore said now. "I thought your little recording might cost me my concentration, but I've never been so hard."

Clay tasted vomit.

"So, so hard," Jensen concurred.

The dog was back, jumping at Clay's leg, wanting to enjoy a little intimacy of its own. Clay pushed it away and went back to trying to ignore how badly he needed that bathroom.

"Ouch," Fillmore grumbled. "Ooh, ooh, ouch." And then it was over, with the death-match chase between a cougar and an emaciated, alcoholic mountain goat giving way to heavy, catch-up breathing on the old goat's part. Heavy silence followed. And lingered.

After a good twenty minutes, Clay felt sure the two must have fallen asleep, and was just about to sneak through the bedroom when Fillmore said, "So, you were Solstice Blume's teacher?" This was the cue for the still wakeful Jensen to boast about her current project. "Yes indeed. Better than that, her early writings are sitting on my desk. What an honor to be able to read through and organize her early works. It's a fortunate English teacher gets to have one great writer like that in her class—and take some modest credit for her evolution."

Silence returned, soon punctuated by snoring. Testing out the love seat, Clay made himself comfortable, but not too comfortable, conceding that, as loud as Fillmore's snoring was, it wasn't powerful enough to mask his own snoring were he to fall asleep. Of greater importance, he needed to escape. Twenty minutes tops.

That chapter in time passed with painful slowness. Occasionally glancing at the phone on his lap, as if he thought it might resurrect, Clay's eyes grew heavy. Sleep seemed inevitable until Fillmore and Jensen jointly abandoned the pursuit. In place of the snoring, Clay heard shuffling and jangling.

"Where... are you going?" Jensen asked. "What the hell are you doing with my car keys?"

"Jamie baby," Fillmore replied, "I was just borrowing them. I planned to return them, along with the car, of course."

Like a wounded wild animal—the cougar taking a bullet in its leg—Jensen snarled, "I don't believe this. I do not fucking believe this. You, Fillmore Banks, are not the man in your books, apart perhaps from the excessive drinking. You're not even a man. Get the hell out of my house. Now. Without the keys."

"But, Jamie."

"It's *Jenni*, asshole."

Clay heard the gentle tapping of bare feet on hardwood—a sound losing volume. Fillmore and Jensen were leaving the bedroom and going downstairs. Clay wasted no time. He darted back into that same room, took a quick left to the bathroom. Several minutes later, he had squeezed back out the window, tearing the butt seam in his sweats as he did so. But when his feet made contact with the porch's shingle roof, they refused to stay in place. He was sliding on ice, moving quickly toward the lattice. Needless to say, he hoped to find it sturdy enough to counter his momentum.

It wasn't, and soon he and the lattice were slowly tipping sideways and down, gaining speed as they went. A forest of prickly rose bushes, barren in February, broke his descent, an experience made even less pleasant by the Spiderman mask. That and shitting himself. Once able to disentangle, he found the closest thing he could to a hiding place, a bulging lilac bush also stripped of growth for the winter. In discomfort he would have called unimaginable only hours before, he waited a good half hour to avoid risking an encounter with Fillmore Banks who was standing in Clemens Street, shouting at the house, "My words gave you goosebumps, goddammit. I penetrated your soul." Such a meeting, Clay knew, would result in nothing but catastrophe, including but not limited to criminal charges, public humiliation, and disqualification from all future literary endeavors.

Clay spent at least some of his time wisely by concocting a story for Marta so that he would be ready if asked to explain where he had been all night. In this story, he dutifully attended the Second Annual Lit Fest event. Afterward, on the library's main floor, he reconciled with Fillmore Banks. Later, the pair celebrated their renewed writers' bond. Clay drank too much Scotch, and slept on a musty sofa.

Getting home just before midnight, his was the only car in the garage. Standing next to it on the cold concrete, he took off his clothes and threw them away. Backpack, too. It was one more action that would never reach Marta's attention. Lucky for Clay, she had never shown much interest in what went inside their garbage cans.

He felt so rank he took a shower. A long one. He had just turned off the water when he heard Marta say, "Since when do you take showers in the middle of the night? I hope you don't think you're getting lucky at 12:30 on a study group night. One of us has work in the morning."

She was asleep by the time he dried off, flossed, and brushed.

Rest didn't come so readily to Clay. For three hours, he twisted and turned. When it finally hit, it hit hard. The next time he opened his eyes, his wife was long gone, as was the morning.

When Marta got home from work that evening, she didn't ask why he was grilling on the back deck in a coat, hat, and gloves. She didn't even ask about the scratch on his cheek. Perhaps she felt overwhelmed by the smoky magnificence of buffalo burgers topped with melted bleu cheese. "This is a nice surprise," she said when he served her on the formal dining room table he'd set. "Weren't you freezing?"

"I wanted to surprise you."

He did have one thing to show for his most recent criminal effort: the scattering of ash that had once been "Measurable Accumulation," now lining the bowels of his charcoal grill.

He could taste his friend's writing in his buffalo burger, a little extra kick, reassuringly flavorful. Indeed, he found it so pleasant he felt compelled to enjoy a second burger.

Chapter 23

⌘

REJECTING THE REJECTIONS

Winston Barclay expressed surprise that Clay's submissions to New York were generating encouraging responses. "These are serious literary agents, cream of the cream," he noted from his place at the table in the dimly lit conference room, where he, Randolph J. Simper, and Ford Diesel had convened for the March meeting of the Martha Jewell Reclamation Team. "Apparently, to borrow a common expression, street slang if you wish, they are losing their edge. Two of the five editors queried by Mr. Turner want to see more of the novel."

"He's receiving good news?" Randolph said. "Why weren't we prepared for such an outcome?"

"He won't, and we were," Diesel assured him. "We intercepted the replies. He doesn't see them."

"What is he seeing?"

"Red," said Barclay with a smile that seemed designed to frighten young children. "Considering the email responses we sent in place of the originals, he can only be seeing red."

***

Blindsided. There was no better word to describe how Clay felt. The first five responses he had received from New York agents not only abandoned, but assaulted a long-standing literary tradition. Like timid boyfriends breaking off relationships with "It's not you, it's me," agents were expected to feign neutrality. They were supposed to offer non-judgmental apologies on the order of "I'm sorry we cannot provide a more personal response, but we receive hundreds of queries each week" and "Your story, unfortunately, failed to move me enough to consider representation. Nevertheless, publishing is a very subjective world. I encourage you to keep submitting. Best wishes with your continued endeavors." The reason agents did this, Clay had always assumed, was to avoid angering dangerous loners or giving the next big writer a letter to wave during *Stephen Colbert*'s final segment while snarling, "Those assholes were so wrong."

Going by what came up on his screen when he opened the first rejection email, agents no longer adhered to tradition. Now they went straight for the jugular. *Unless it was your goal to elicit repulsion on the part of your readers you did not succeed in prompting a satisfying emotional or intellectual response.*

The second note metaphorically knee-capped Clay with shotgun blasts of *Perhaps you should stick with writing cover letters. This at least showed competency. Your manuscript on the other hand is a bit of a train wreck, and in this difficult market.*

The third rejection was equally cruel, but Clay almost felt nostalgic for it when reading #4. *While it's understood that publishing is very subjective, I had no difficulty seeing the absolute implausibility of finding even a single sympathetic reader for such a shoddy, shallow effort.*

Five hard passes. Five direct hits to Clay's momentum, motivation, and possibly foothold on reality. Unfortunately, these rejections didn't make up the only negative waste piling up in Clay's world. Wherever he looked, he saw an unfinished chore: a loose doorknob wanting to be tightened; a chip in the paint that needed retouching; an unpaid credit card bill. There were also the items he had simply not put away, the ones turning his once tidy office into a storeroom cluttered with magazines, books, and receipts for his personal taxes, along with all the stupid shit he had printed out: new menus from restaurants, articles about cars he wanted to own.

His eyes singled out a newspaper he should have thrown away, the one with Jenni Jensen's scathing review of Fillmore Banks' Lit Fest reading and new book. *Fill More Banks?* her headline had clumsily scoffed. *No Thanks, This One's Overflowing with All the Wrong Stuff.* The paper had proved interesting for one more item connected to "*Lamplighter* journalist and arts critic Jenni Jensen." A police report documented vandalism to her house in the form of broken glass and destroyed latticework perpetrated by a scorned lover and alleged attempted car thief who now had a restraining order against him.

Cluttered space, cluttered mind, Leonardo da Vinci once noted, and Clay thought this a true enough observation. The disorder in his office certainly conspired with the rejection notes to drive him into a very dark place, taking the bleak and somehow making it bleaker.

He felt adrift on a dark choppy sea, totally unmoored. He didn't know where to turn or who to trust. He sure didn't know what to do next, apart from carefully selecting the excerpts Marta would hear. "Difficult market."

"Publishing is very subjective." Was it time to simply quit? Was it worth starting over? Was that even possible?

Briefly, he considered a third option: washing down a bottle of expensive Champagne, staggering to Cleveland Park, and leaping off the limestone overlook into oblivion.

***

"I saved the best development for last," Barclay said with a gleam in his black mole eyes. "We are witnessing the final destabilization of the 'author.'" The scathing tone in his voice added more sarcastic emphasis on this last word than his air quotes ever could. "Mr. Turner is sending his own rejection letters. Back to the agents. Rejecting their rejections."

"Hey, *my* report." The twitch in Diesel's right eye and brow was more visible than ever. "I spent two days assembling that information."

"And I, making sense of it."

"Tell me more," Randolph said, lifting a hand. "*One* of you."

"Starting only a few days ago," Diesel said, "our Mr. Turner has been typing increasingly angry letters to the agents who passed on his novel."

"Again, these are not the actual agents," Barclay reminded the others. "I have been quite prolific of late." The pride in his words could not be missed. "Each time we intercepted an encouraging reply, I replaced it with a message employing the most scathing terms. This is something I quite enjoy and dare say have mastered."

"But," Randolph addressed the original point, "you say he's rejecting these rejections?"

"It is a phenomenon I have never witnessed before," Barclay noted. "In my business we rarely receive additional communication once a rejection note has been dispatched. The exceptions to this rule tend to entail heartfelt, generally over-the-top pleas that argue for a second chance. But these sarcastic, angry letters, this is something entirely new." Barclay smiled, his thin lips parting just enough to reveal a crowded collection of tiny yellow teeth. "As I have stated previously, I believe the 'author' is losing the battle on several fronts."

"He completed two so far," Diesel chipped in. "I think he was exhausted. He put a lot of work into them."

"He also sent out one more query," Barclay added. "One that seemed important to him."

"Anything on the state of his marriage?" said Randolph.

"I was hoping you would ask, sir," Diesel replied. "We have reason to believe he cheated on Marta."

"We do?" Barclay asked. "Why was this not mentioned in our pre-briefing briefing?"

"Last week he drove to Madison, binged on long johns at a Krispy Kreme, and shopped at a Walgreens drug store. He then spent an entire night at the house of his 64-year-old retired English teacher from high school. We were unable to get crisp video captures from the Walgreens stop, but it makes sense he was buying condoms. He also purchased a kinky mask of some sort—the surveillance video left a lot to the imagination—presumably for role play in the boudoir."

"All of which showed up on his credit card?" Randolph said.

"He used cash."

"Fascinating," said Randolph, truly caught off guard by the information. All along, he had been expecting to hear reports of cheating *on*, but not *by* Clay. That Marta remained relatively chaste he found strangely reassuring.

"Sick," said Barclay.

"I am sure this information will prove quite valuable," Randolph added. "Quite, quite valuable."

Diesel then shared his latest report on the piece Clay presented at the library for his own Lit Fest appearance. "Still a mystery, sir," the hacker said. "As you know, we transcribed your recording from that night. We subsequently cross-referenced the text against most everything written since the Alexandria Library fire. We found no matches on Kindle or Facebook, or for that matter in every email and attachment kept on file by my former employers at NSA. As far as we can ascertain, Clay Turner wrote the piece he read that night. It was an original composition."

"But," Randolph looked up from his folded hands, "it was good."

With a dry chuckle, Winston Barclay interjected, "Mr. Simper, there is *some* competent writing buried in the *Explosive Love* mix. The book is not entirely dreadful. Would you like me to read from one of the new chapters?"

"God no," Randolph said, shaking his head. "The sample you shared two meetings ago gave me all the information I needed."

Chapter 24

⌘

PROBLEMATIC

The winter got in a last few hits: frigid blasts, snow days for schools, dogs demanding walks on slippery sidewalks. Clay's depression deepened like the snow in his yard. The most he had accomplished was dispatching one last e-query. Other than that, he watched TV and drank himself to sleep each night while imagining himself on *Stephen Colbert* holding five rejections over his head and snarling, "Those assholes were so wrong."

On one March evening slightly worse than most others, Marta sat in silence, simply staring at Clay's specialty nachos. Not that this surprised him. Months had passed since she last asked how his writing was going. Still, that night's nachos were among his best, artfully combining blue chips, canned black beans and kernels of corn, chopped onion, sour cream, guacamole from the Hey Howdy deli, one fresh Jalapeño pepper, and five varieties of newly shredded cheese.

A compliment wouldn't have seemed out of place.

He briefly considered asking, "How was your day?" but already knew the answer. It had been hard; work was hard, school was hard, marriage was hard. For both Clay and Marta, bad days had gained a significant numerical superiority.

Even so, the nachos were more than delicious. *Muy sobrosa? Gracias?*

It wasn't until he got up to gather the plates that she finally spoke. "Sweatpants? Again?"

"I keep telling you, they're surprisingly comfortable. Perfect for a long day of writing." He stopped before adding, if I ever get back to it.

"You could still change for dinner." She got up to return the sour cream to the fridge. Opening the door, she asked, "You bought an entire box of those disgusting long johns?"

"You realize that, however well you take care of yourself, the sun will still expand and destroy all the planets."

"Jesus, Clay, what is going on in there? You've got all the time in the world to write. Your reading went well. But looking at you, you'd think civilization had crumbled. You wear clothes you wouldn't have been caught dead in a year ago. You eat like a teenager whose parents are gone for the weekend. *La depresión es contagiosa.*"

After reclaiming her place at the kitchen table, she buried her head in her hands. "Maybe it's time to *disponer* your sweats and go back to taking pride in your appearance. If nothing else to show your wife you still care. You didn't write your first book in sweats, or covered in dog hair."

He leaned over to hug her. She pulled away. "Sorry." This was her last word before standing and going upstairs.

Clay shambled to his office.

✳✳✳

That same night, he logged in to discover a new screen saver, a photo straight out of a psychology textbook. In it, a lab rat the size and firmness of a throw pillow had been lowered upon a basic metal kitchen scale. Its bulging abdomen drooped down both sides of the silver platform. Its face cried pure misery. A caption revealed that scientists had cut the critter's vagus nerve, the one that sent messages from stomach to brain, essentially silencing the plea, "Enough with the food! I'm stuffed already!"

Clay felt one with the luckless rodent. "Is this what I suffer from?" he whispered to himself. "SRN. Severed Rat Nerve?"

At least he had something planned for the evening. A few weeks had passed since he sent his first emails to agents rejecting their rejections. Wrapping these up sounded like the perfect therapy.

He took a sip from his Chivas and Coke, sighed, and pulled up the email he had started during that first rush of indignant rage. *Dear Ms. Thrombone,* it began. *I regret to inform you I must pass on your recent rejection note as I receive several each day with most exhibiting much greater creativity and technical skill, and with most coming from agents distinguished by a far more impressive body of work. That said, I was disappointed to learn that you "could never love characters so shallow and improbable." If I may suggest, your reaction may be symptomatic of a much deeper psychological failing, this being your inability to fully love anything, including children and pets. As such, I, unlike the other unfortunates who have previously entered and exited your sphere, will try not to take it personally.*

Feeling inspired, he began a second rejection note: *Please forgive the impersonal nature of our response but we receive so many of these banal, unimaginative messages.*

It was clear little time was spent on my submission. Perhaps if you took the time to read my chapters again, this time without your head up your ass.

Clay's Secret Abhorrer chose that moment to return.

What's with the slowdown of late? asked the hacker who wasn't Real Life Josh Bramlett or Arthur C. Peckham or a beautiful Russian spy. Clay now regretted pouring so much naiveté into those suspicions. Not when the correct answer had been so obvious.

It's going on two years. Others are getting impatient.

Prime Suspect Randolph J. Simper was back to rattle Clay, break his spirit, and drive him insane wondering why. What was the game here? What constituted victory? All Clay knew with certainty anymore was that, whatever Randolph's motive, there was little chance the multi-millionaire would back down. Having read Damon Debbitt's *War* manuscript twice in its entirety despite its 892-page length, Clay knew just how capable Randolph J. Simper was at achieving his goals. Clay's old classmate played to win. By rigging the game. By making the rules. By planting Mandrill porn in his enemy's computers.

While reading *War* the first time, right after his bout with the flu, Clay had called Randolph to verify his suspicions. Leaving a voicemail, Clay masked his motives with the message, "Thank you for freeing me from the hacker. He was definitely slowing me down."

As with the earlier phone call, Randolph picked up. "I'm so glad you called, my friend. I had been meaning to give you an update. It took a while to clean out your systems because I had to make sure I had the right culprit. It wasn't who you thought by any stretch."

Pausing, Randolph seemed hesitant to continue. "Forgive me for being the source of bad news, but—I really hate to tell you this—there seems to be something between your wife and one of her study group friends. The man is pretty powerful, if only by Duchaine standards. He's got a motive for seeing you fail."

"And this is?"

"I'm not ready to divulge that at present."

"You really won't tell me who's trying to steal the woman I love?"

"*Trying...* sorry, friend. That's generous of you."

Clay's sigh had to be audible on Randolph's end.

"What matters here," the software titan continued, "is it's under control. The hacker's been hacked and is about to reexamine his very existence. At the very least, he won't be dropping in unannounced. I can't have my prized 'investment,' as you say, watching eagles nest all day."

When Clay said, "Watching eagles, what do you mean?" Randolph's nervousness was palpable.

"How did you know about the nesting eagles?" Clay repeated.

The call ended abruptly.

Clay repeated his question to the dark phone. "How did you know I was watching eagles?"

But he already knew the answer, and it could be summed up with "Duh." Only one person in Duchaine possessed the resources and tech savvy to completely infiltrate Clay's world.

Now, weeks later, with the new intrusion still on his screen, Clay typed, *I'm the one getting impatient. Find someone else to torment. I have important work to do.*

He thought back to his first lunch meeting with Randolph, specifically to that terrible, riveting sight of an eagle plucking a rabbit from its quiet, nervous, grass-eating existence. The rabbit, in hindsight, had given its life to foreshadowing, falling from the sky to warn Clay he was clearly not the eagle in this story.

"You keep picking me up and dropping me," he muttered now in the direction of his screen. "If you won't stop, at least tell me why. Are you torturing me for pleasure or killing me methodically? Or is this just some rich person thing? Because you can."

The most obvious theory had Randolph destabilizing a marriage, destroying it one half at a time. But to what end? To walk away with Marta as his prize? To purchase Clay? Champagne and a string quartet argued for the former. But either theory spawned more theories. Each motive required an underlying motive.

Here, Damon Debbitts had offered no help. Even with 892 pages to tell his story, he came up short on explanations, offering instead words like *inscrutable, unknowable.*

He wrote, *Andrew J. Kelp did not deal in conventional human currency.*

He did not love. He didn't love people. He didn't love life.

When Clay gave Damon his comments on *War*, he shared a theory: *Perhaps your Andrew J. Kelp is more hologram than human. There's no breaching the depthless, illusory projection for one simple reason. There's nothing inside.*

Clay also recommended inserting a semi-colon. *He didn't love people; he didn't love life.* Just to irritate Damon.

To gain the world but lose your soul—Randolph J. Simper had pulled this off. Whatever material once constituted his inner being, it was gone, sacrificed to his virtual empire. Clay's theory took this one step further, with Randolph returning to Duchaine in search of whatever it was that first filled the void.

Walking to the kitchen where the windows now glowed brighter than a white monitor screen waiting for Clay to type something, he noticed how much faster the snow was coming down. He stared as if hypnotized—four minutes, five—before remembering his original plan to zap himself another small plate of nachos, maybe six-cheese this time. Pulling out the ingredients, it only made sense to simultaneously prepare a second plate for Argos. True, the dog was getting fat, 112 pounds at his last vet weigh-in, but Clay couldn't stop thanking his loyal, food-loving friend for saving his life. It was why Clay always ordered an extra calzone or bowl of orange chicken when in the mood for carry out.

Needing a break, Clay stretched out on the couch and located an installment of "My Favorite Amendment" on DV-R. Florida's Lieutenant Governor was railing, "They're throwing the Second Amendment in the dumpster." Her son had been reprimanded for bringing a Glock .45 caliber G.A.P. to his third grade classroom. "They act shocked it was loaded. What good's a gun that's not loaded?"

Ten minutes in, Clay forgot to fast forward through a string of commercials. A celebrity voiceover told him he needed a new car—a fact that couldn't be challenged. Others suggested vocational training "to start your new life" and warned of erections lasting over four hours. Finally, Clay's old classmate, Duchaine's own litigious TV lawyer Moon McDermott, stood before him in a suit much cheaper than he could afford, selected no doubt to put potential clients at ease. "Have you ever been mistreated by a literary agent or editor? Have you ever felt betrayed by a multi-millionaire app inventor who hides his ulterior motives behind six-figure gifts? If your pride has been injured, your dreams of success maimed, The Scrapper will give you everything you deserve… and more."

Clay jerked himself awake, in the process spilling the bowl of M&Ms on his sweatpantsed lap. *Which was worse?* he asked himself. *The nightmare? Or that I'm dreaming about TV?*

When Clay returned to his desk, the message on the upper left corner of his screen sent him into a tailspin, plummeting to Earth like a 747, his thoughts slamming about like luggage torn free of the overhead bins.

We know what you were doing at Jenni Jensen's. Does Marta?

Fuck.

Clay sat motionless, fixed on these words, oblivious to the whimpering of dogs, oblivious to a humming furnace that rarely rested, oblivious to the dull chattering of snow pelting glass on a windy winter night. His vision blurry from staring too intently, his migraine raging, it hit him just how exhausted he was. He imagined himself a climber whose luck ran out a few hundred feet shy of Mt. Everest's summit. Another fucking blizzard... well, isn't that a surprise?

Chapter 25

⌘

THE WET SEASON

The rain was unrelenting, as dense and consistent as the gloom it brought with it. All across the Midwest that April, a "historic deluge" flooded basements and fields, sent streams to record levels. Living on a hill didn't help at all. The sense of doom seeped into Clay's psyche with a steady drip, drip, pooling on floors, weakening walls, submerging what remained of his ego.

Tuesday had started badly in that it started without him. Lulled by the rhythm on his rooftop, he slept through the dog's usual "Good morning already, feed me and let me out" whimpering, which meant Marta had fed the dog and let him outside, which meant Marta had been five minutes late leaving, which meant Marta would not be smiling the next time Clay saw her.

Eating toaster-oven pizza for breakfast at noon, he assured himself the day couldn't dump anything worse on him, but this represented a serious failure of imagination. Two hours later—"Shit, shit, shit"—all incarnations of *Explosive Love* vanished from his hard-drive. Various back-up drafts saved throughout the writing process as attachments to self-addressed emails disappeared, too.

It was over. All of it. *Explosive Love*. His long-suffering fantasies of becoming a successful writer. His lowered expectations of simply having a complete manuscript to show his investors. So what if Damon Debbitts had the version he'd sent out for critiquing? Clay had written many new pages, made many more changes. Of all the things a writer could have in common with Ernest Hemingway and Margaret Atwood, both of whom lost entire manuscripts early in their quests for greatness, this was not one Clay wanted. He didn't see himself bouncing back as they did, writing dozens of classics to offset that first loss.

After more than an hour of panic and search, Clay came across one extant *Explosive Love* file, one he swore wasn't there before that moment. It turned out to be one he revised while high and paranoid—one he thought he'd deleted right after writing it. Was this coincidence, he wondered now, or had that specific draft appeared for a reason? Was Randolph telling Clay this was the only version worth saving? Pita had not fared well after Clay inserted a gratuitous intra-sexual affair as a possible gift to Randolph, thinking that, had Randolph returned to Duchaine in pursuit of Clay's affection, it couldn't hurt to toss him a little false hope.

After Pita caught Jared and Josh making passionate homosexual love in the garage, she flew into a red-coal rage. "You worthless Christ stabber. That's what you are—a Christ stabber. You stabbed Him in the back. But that's how you like it, isn't it? In the back. God is going to kill you with AIDs, that's what he thinks of your unholy union. I can't believe you can be so stupid."

"I'm the fucking idiot here?" Jared exploded as Josh Bramlett cowered in a corner, showing limited success at covering himself with his clothes. "Who's been posting revolutionary slogans on Facebook accompanied by photos of our explosives? You don't think Homeland Security has Internet access?"

The argument that followed mirrored the one in Clay's other drafts. Jared called Pita stupid. She stepped on a spider. He went after her faith.

Scratching, slapping, and screeching, Pita lunged toward him, target: face. "Who's the cold hearted bitch?" she shouted as Josh, still naked, slipped out the side door. "Who's the murderer here?"

Giving Jared's pretty boy features a reprieve, Pita turned to punch the automatic garage door opener.

"Jesus, Pita, you know better than that." Jared felt blood dripping down his cheek. "The garage door stays closed. No one needs to see what's in here."

Like a tornado changing course, Pita turned and stormed outside. Jared followed as best he could, ducking to get past the closing door, having punched the opener's pad a second time.

Using the front door this time, Pita shot into the house. Jared turned to follow her, but made it no further before the garage door hummed, rising back up. He reached that door just in time for Pita to surge back out, pushing him aside. She was dragging a bag of ammonium nitrate.

"And where are you going with that?" he demanded.

"That's for me to know and you to see on TV."

Josh, peeking around the garage's far corner, suddenly found his voice. "Pita, Jared, we're all friends here. Brothers in arms."

"That," she said coldly in his direction, "is the tiniest penis I've ever seen."

"You've seen lots of penises?" Jared asked.

Ignoring him, Pita lugged the bag toward his vintage green 1970 Chevy panel truck.

"You're not taking my classic C-10," he shouted. But as much as Jared wanted to run

to her, grab her, and make her stop, he felt like he was in a bizarre nightmare, frozen in place, feeling doomed, and wanting more than anything to wake up.

Pita charged in and out of the house, each time returning with a hefty new bag. Once she'd built up a sizable mound, she heaved the bags into the back of the truck, one at a time, even after it appeared she'd run out of space. Somehow, between ramming the bags with her shoulder and kicking them with a cowboy boot, she forced two more into the passenger seat. Turning to face Jared with a look more crazed than usual, she shouted, "This is our moment of glory. And you, bug lover, are going to miss it."

Pita ripped open the driver's side door, lobbed herself down on the seat, started the truck, and without looking back even once, set off for a target she had found online. This was a Planned Parenthood office adjoining a non-profit animal shelter. It was in Bolingbrook on the outside ring of Chicago's suburbs.

On a two-lane highway just south of Ottawa, Pita showed off her new mastery of the stick shift by roaring past a rusting El Camino with a bumper sticker that offered hope. LIBERAL MEDIA, GIVE US SOME TRUTH. This reminded Pita she had public support and that she would soon be properly embraced as the hero she was by the patriotic Christian majority still angry that the one president who toiled to make his country great again had suffered such malicious attacks from vote-faking traitors who loved Mexicans more than Americans.

These were her last thoughts as an ancient red Farm Haul tractor pulled onto the road directly in her path. The explosion that resulted shook the ground with the force of a minor earthquake, even causing Jared, some thirty miles away, to wonder what it was he felt beneath his feet. Ironically, the farmer who caused the collision had just departed a fallow cornfield, having helped plant a billboard that proclaimed to the world as it drove by on County Road 17, "All children are precious, no matter how small or unborn."

Depending upon which cable news network one watched, Pita achieved either fame as a glorious crusader for God and the Constitution or infamy as America's stupidest terrorist. The FBI questioned Jared extensively but he held firm, painting himself as the innocent victim of a zealot who posted threats on Facebook. "I was lucky to get out of our house before it blew up," he said to each new law enforcement official who interviewed him. "She must have started the fire right before she took off on her insane mission... her insane secret mission."

The FBI ultimately bought Jared's defense, and didn't even notice how the explosion caused by the fire at home had occurred a good hour after Pita's collision. Former security officer Josh Bramlett, the couple's "longtime mutual friend," had backed up Jared's claims with eyewitness accounts of terrible fights and desperate pleas—from Jared—for help.

Before he set fire to the house and garage, Josh had helped move the meth-lab equipment to his two-room hovel of an apartment. Jared moved in as well, allowing the two Christ stabbers to live happily enough ever after, supporting themselves through the manufacture and sale of methamphetamines. Pita's Labrador Retriever Wade lived out the rest of its *newly shortened life in an animal shelter, abandoned there by Jared. Fortunately for Jared, this necessary action did not interfere with his continued zeal for animal rights.*

Apart from letting Jared take down the Confederate flag that had made up the entirety of his wall art, Josh Bramlett also held firm to his passions. On the night of his First Anniversary with Jared, the Clairmont Mall mysteriously burned to the ground. He and Jared were nowhere near, vacationing as they were at an indoor water park in southern Minnesota, courtesy of three credit card applications that had disappeared from mailboxes in various Chicago suburbs.

Initially, Clay had questioned one detail in this prospective ending: would fertilizer explode on its own upon impact? Or would it need some kind of catalyst? But Google had proved these concerns unfounded. A simple spark, prevalent enough during a high speed collision, would provide the requisite jumpstart.

A message appeared in the usual spot, the screen's upper left corner. *How's the novel looking? You didn't lose it, did you? Perhaps you left it at your girlfriend's? Or have you already lost her, the way you're losing your wife? It's pathetic enough being a lazy writer. You can't be a careless one as well.*

Clay typed. *Give me back my novel. It's not yours to play with. I'm not yours to play with.*

***

The Hungry Wong was closed when Clay pulled up in its parking lot. *Home in Taiwan. Back one month.* He did not find this information helpful since the sign's author had failed to supply a starting date. One month from when?

Over "tasty chicken" from the mall's food court, Clay told Marta the most recent version of *Explosive Love* had been deleted and that he suspected Randolph of breaking into the computer and that he wondered if he was romantically interested in him. "He knew about the eagle watch website." A glistening nugget rolled off Clay's plate, bounced once on the table's edge, and landed on his new slacks. Argos took over from there.

Trying to ignore this, Clay asked, "How could Randolph know about the eagle website?"

"The eagle website?"

"He diverts me to it. He's been pulling the strings all along. He kills people, you know."

"Well," she said. "That's a lot to take in."

"It's definitely a lot to deal with."

She placed her plastic chopsticks on her paper plate's rim.

"Honey—" She hesitated. "Have you ever thought about counseling?"

"For us?" he said. "I suppose it could be beneficial. It might help us get back to our priorities."

He swore she laughed ever so slightly before crushing him with "For us? No, for you."

***

Clay was carrying a bottle of Dalwhinnie 15-Year Scotch when he knocked on the front door of Fillmore Banks' house the following day. It was a pleasant morning, the sun high, the air fresh and cool, neither of which would penetrate Fillmore's heavy window coverings.

"Cal? *Ms. Whinnie?* My oh my. This is a surprise."

The front room of Fillmore's house seemed danker, darker, and mustier than before, although the initial shots of Scotch tempered that harsh appraisal. Seated on a couch hidden by a throw cut from a fabric that looked identical to the dark, heavy window coverings, Fillmore ran a hand through disheveled hair. The hand pulled back in defeat, leaving Fillmore's hair to keep resembling a small animal that had crawled onto his head and curled up to die.

"So, tell me, sir," Clay asked from his hard scratchy armchair, "how do you handle rejection and harsh criticism?"

"Ah," Fillmore said, a reaction which turned out to be aimed at his Scotch. "A very fine burn indeed." He held up the glass as if admiring its contents. "Listen to me, Cal. Rejection and harsh criticism I can handle. It's indifference does me in. I did not write *Cruel Comedown* for it to be caged in a drawer and kept from the world."

"You waited decades."

"And only to be proved right. Decent sales, good reviews, excepting that crazy bitch in the local paper. She doesn't understand the special needs of an artistic being. She doesn't know what it's like to spend one's day nailed to a cross, looking out and down upon the unenlightened masses dashing past in blithe ignorance." Fillmore Banks twisted his body sideways to stretch out lengthwise on the couch, his legs hanging over one armrest.

Clay got to the reason for his visit: "I'm writing a novel that's dark and unconventional. I sent it to Small Packages. It's been two months. I thought they'd get back to me much sooner."

Fillmore Banks did not respond.

"If you could put in a word for me, that might sweep away any reservations they're having. Could you at least get them to share the file I sent? All the versions I had were erased."

Fillmore Banks was snoring now.

Clay left the third-full bottle on a cluttered kitchen counter, partly out of respect and partly out of concern for getting pulled over on his Gold Wing 1800 three times over the legal limit while transporting an open bottle of liquor.

"Thank you, Fillmore," he called out while pulling open the front door. "I'll leave you to your cross now."

Chapter 26
⌘

VISITATION RITES

The doorbell rang, yanking Clay from an unplanned nap. His long john slipped from lap to floor—what was he thinking, trying to eat two?—but he had time to retrieve it. Argos had already taken up defense of the front door. "Who made that sound?" the barking demanded. "Who dares approach this house? Prepare to tie, infidel scum!"

Clay lurched forward out of the chair.

"Leave it, Argos, leave it," he shouted as he reached the foyer. He opened the door and the barking stopped, but only because Argos now needed his energy for shoving his snout into the crotch of the visitor's sexy nurse costume.

"How delightful," cooed the downtown library's acquisitions manager. "Is this... Argos?"

Her eyes hidden behind black sunglasses, she bent forward to pet the dog, causing the low-cut uniform to reveal the little cleavage she possessed. A long, chestnut-brown shock of hair, held together at the base with a white scrunchie, tumbled forward over a shoulder.

"Your owner did a good job of portraying you. I feel like I'm meeting an old friend."

Clay's first question was for himself. "Am I still asleep?" In genuine shock, he stared past the acquisitions manager toward the black 2019 Jaguar XJ R parked at the curb. An insignificant distraction, but still, why did everyone have a cooler car than he did?

"May I help you?" he asked tentatively.

She laughed. "I hear there's been an unidentified viral outbreak. We'll have to quarantine your bedroom."

"Sorry?"

"Don't tease me, Clay. Not after sending a text telling me to meet you here." She slipped off the glasses and came closer. "It's two o'clock on a Thursday afternoon. You tell me, why am I here?" She moved closer, placing her wide, dark eyes only a foot or so away from his.

"I... didn't text you."

"You want to see it?"

"This... this... it's not what you're thinking. Someone's been messing with me."

She looked as confused as he was.

"I have an enemy. Someone's trying to sabotage my writing." He added an "Oh shit." Marta's Volvo was coming down the street.

It pulled into the driveway, stopped a car length short of the garage door. Emerging in a blur, Marta didn't bother with being confused. She had gone straight to livid. "What the hell is this?"

He offered the same explanation. He had an enemy. He'd been set up.

"He texted me," the acquisitions manager offered unhelpfully. "He told me to come over."

"Is this what goes on when I'm not here?"

"No, no, no. Believe me, I'm as surprised as you are."

"Believe you? That's *broma*." She looked Clay up and down, did the same for his guest. "I believe you should leave. I believe you should go with your visiting *cuidadora*."

"You need to believe me. She just showed up. I never contacted her. Ever."

The acquisitions manager interrupted: "It doesn't matter. You get to keep him. I don't need paranoiac drivel and sweat pants at 2 in the afternoon. I don't even want to know what that white cream is, eeuugghhh, with dog fur. I'm gone."

The visitor trotted to her car, her mane waving in time to the movement. Marta stared at her husband, coldly, as if examining a bag of trash that had blown onto her front porch. "This is unbelievable," she said at last. "I came home because I heard something *muy inquietante* at work. I heard you'd been seeing our old English teacher. It sounded *loco* to me but now I'm not so sure."

"What people? When?"

"This isn't a big city. People have seen you together."

"Jesus, Marta. Jenni Jensen was at my reading like everyone else. So was the crazy library nurse. That's the last place I saw either of them. Before just now anyway. I'm not seeing anyone behind your back."

"I had lunch with someone from my study group. You were at her house."

"Who from your study group?"

"Why would that matter? You were at her house."

"Jesus Christ, honey. You've got to believe me. Someone is out to get me, out to drive me crazy. Someone's in my computer and now, the librarian's phone. Is it your *friend* from study group? What aren't *you* telling me? Who did you see at lunch today?"

"You're not turning this around. I went to lunch with a concerned friend. I didn't sleep with a retired teacher in her sixties."

"Nor did I. That was Fillmore Banks. I was just there."

Tears formed. "For the love of God, Clay. This isn't *gracioso*. This is our *vida*. I can't take much more of your *pamplina*. You need to get professional help. *Pronto*."

"This is all some strange, twisted attempt at sabotage."

She reeled in her emotions, the wife of Lot turned to salt. "Save it for your therapist." She walked away, holding her car keys. "It's that or your new landlord."

After watching her drive away, he opened Messages on his phone. Sure enough, there was a text, sent to a number he didn't recognize. *This is Clay Turner. The author. I'm home and alone and feeling blue. I need a good nurse. Wear something appropriate.*

Clay had never felt more confused. Or angry. He would never have written *feeling blue*.

Chapter 27
⌘

LIFE BETWEEN STROKES

Early one foggy Saturday morning, Marta left town with her study group. Randolph's private AW101 helicopter flew them to Madison where, outside his hangar, they switched to his Airbus A319. They planned to stay in California six days.

Clay saw neither helicopter nor airbus. A limousine stole her from him, taking her and the rest of her study group to Randolph's local manor and its rooftop helipad. The black Mercedes-Maybach S 650 Pullman had been close to invisible through the thick, swirling fog that transformed their parting scene into an old black and white movie.

She had not kissed him. As for parting words, she said only, "Tell me how it goes with the therapist."

She called that night to say she was "very excited to be staying in Randy's elegant guest quarters. This place is bigger than all the houses on our street combined."

Clay got only texts the next three evenings, each more disheartening than the last. *Having best time*, read Tuesday's missive. *Learning so much. Wish I could stay 2nd week. Wish I had more vacation time.*

He could make no similar claims about having a best time. At breakfast each morning around 11, the long johns he had stocked up on made his teeth ache as they always did, but without providing the compensation of overwhelming sweetness. His nightly Crown and Cokes, mixed to be strong, seemed useless and weak. His bed no longer cradled him with smooth, spongey softness; it felt more like stone sprinkled with sand. Worst of all, his phone failed to alert him to incoming texts or calls from California, no matter how close he kept his head to it while staring at the bedroom ceiling at three in the morning.

On Friday, he took his first-ever selfie, a major concession from a writer who had devoted an essay in his first book to ridiculing the fad that forgot to go away like normal fads. Intended to show Marta he still changed out of his sweats for dinner even when she wasn't there, he attached it to a text that was every bit as degrading. *And look who's wearing his good clothes to dinner*, he typed as if describing a clever six year old. *I do this out of respect for our marriage. I do this out of love for you.* She did not reply.

That text had almost included a lie. The therapist seems okay. First session went well.

He had deleted this because the therapist did not seem okay and the session had not gone well.

Dr. Thurber was stern, older. She wore oval Benjamin Franklin glasses that gave her more than a slight resemblance to the legendary statesman and inventor, though Clay imagined him with a more cheerful disposition. They also gave Thurber her one superpower: the narrow lenses compacting her disapproval into a damning, laser-sharp glare. It was a power she used often.

Thurber shared Marta's skepticism. Clay knew this because, minutes into their first session in her strip mall office, she said, "Now, now, Mr. Turner, let's not abuse my trust." She said other things therapists were probably not supposed to say, like "You can't blame everything on screwed up parents. Otherwise, none of us would get anything done." The worst had to be "I've always held the theory some people hide behind mumbo jumbo textbook theory to make up for the simple fact they're assholes. It's one of those things we can't fix."

She made him feel defensive, combative—not the results his wife presumably sought. When Thurber asked, "How common are these episodes of paranoia?" he nearly responded, "Are you working for Randolph? Did he get to you, too?"

If time moved slowly, it lost even more velocity after Marta announced her group was spending a second week. *HR told me I could borrow against next year's vacation.* At least it was only a week, he tried comforting himself, having determined time would stop altogether sometime mid-May if it continued in its current trajectory.

Everything went to hell Week Three, starting with the twelve hours spent at Duchaine County Hospital. A mild stroke had knocked father-in-law Will to the floor of his bedroom early Monday morning leaving him partially paralyzed, unable to use his left arm and leg, until the ICU staff pumped him full of blood thinner. Even while discharging him Wednesday morning, the nurses warned of aftershocks, "some as severe as the initial quake." The language center in Will's brain, at least, seemed only slightly scathed—he occasionally slurred his speech while tutoring Clay from a hospital bed about his glory days with his band Bloated Treasure—and Winnie insisted the "upset" not interfere with Marta's trip. "This is so important to her. She keeps emailing to say she's having the very best time. With Will safe at home, there's no need to worry her. We'll tell her here face to face on Sunday when she can see for herself just what her father's been up to."

The vet called Wednesday afternoon to ask Clay where the hell Argos was, adding, "You were supposed to be here 20 minutes ago and we've already rescheduled his annual checkup twice." Clay and the dog raced there by Volvo, only to learn Argos now weighed a "hefty" 118.

"You're killing this dog," said a moon-pale long-haired boy of a man who probably weighed less than Argos. "He needs to lose weight. Now." The young tech paused to examine Clay from head to toe. "I've heard about your book and how you don't like dogs. Everybody here has. You're not killing him on purpose are you?"

The tech handed Clay a DVD-R as he waited for his receipt. "You need to watch this." Stored in a simple Ziploc baggie, the disc had no label.

"Argos, no," Clay said as his dog seized the moment to water a potted Yucca plant. "Sorry. I'll watch the video."

A distraction arrived by email right after he got home. Unfortunately, it took the form of the one rejection letter he knew he wouldn't be able to handle, the one he wouldn't metabolize. Leigh Cooley, Chief Editor for Small Packages Press, had written, *At first we wondered if this had really come from you. One intern floated the theory it was some sort of parody of a submission meant to confound and intrigue us in the final weeks before you delivered your actual manuscript. If this was your intent, then congratulations, you sure got everyone talking here. We look forward to seeing your novel. The real one.*

If this was not your intent, then where am I to begin?

Sadly, she easily found that starting point—*ludicrous plot*—which segued into *unlikable characters, sloppy prose,* and *confusing structure.* Adding irony to injury, Ms. Cooley had not even cared for the passages inspired by Argos, the "lovable, larger than life Lab" who once helped inspire Small Packages to publish Clay's first book. *The scene in which Wade rescues the choking Jared, your emotionally dwarfed animal rights obsessive, did worse than fail to suspend disbelief; it spawned disdain for a novelist who would stoop to such a forced emotional trick to grovel before an audience he had been losing steadily from page one.*

If nothing else, <u>Explosive Love</u> had me questioning how it was we ever liked that first effort of yours.

It was almost as if the editor Clay remembered for her passion, professionalism, and humor had become a different person. He briefly considered calling her, but, hell, where to start?

In closing, I suppose I am obligated to "thank you for thinking of us." If I am to be honest, however, Mr. Turner, I look forward to not hearing from you again.
Walking to the kitchen in search of relief, he got a text from Marta. *Things going great. Glad I stayed.*

No *Missing you.* No *Now that I've had some time away, I see what a special bond we share.* No *I really appreciate that you changed out of your sweats for dinner these past months. I love that you're seeing a therapist.* Making her message all the more puzzling, it was identical to her text from the night before.

He typed, *Being away from you makes me realize even more how much I need you, and how few things I truly need. I don't need expensive cars. I don't need to sit at a computer and write "papers" for others to grade. I don't need sweets that hurt my teeth. I need you. I also need to see you happy and to see you succeed. We have traveled too far together to abandon the journey. Let's reclaim the adventure and passion. Let's discover new lands. I stand ready to help you solve those impossible math equations at 11 pm. I stand ready to learn Spanish and help you dig into your heritage. I stand ready to do whatever is needed. I miss you. I need you. I love you. I need to hear your voice. I need to see a real message.*
He attached photos as he had been doing since she left: July Third fireworks; Argos playing in snow; their much underutilized bed.

He received no reply, not then, not twenty minutes later, not forty minutes later.

At five o'clock, he was facing the street from his open garage door. Feeling a change in the air, he wasn't surprised to see the dark, churning clouds rolling back in from the west. He called her number. *This is Marta.* Only it wasn't Marta. It was the same goddamn recorded answer he'd been hearing for days. *Sorry I couldn't grab the phone but I am either working or studying. Leave a mensaje.*

Needing a diversion, he popped the DVD into his player. As it turned out, the veterinary tech had handed him a PETA production that graphically documented the horrors of factory farming and mass slaughter. Clay was sickened, so much so he couldn't imagine eating another buffalo burger or drumstick. Or continuing as a member of the human species. Or worse, watching the DVD to its gory conclusion. Had he been wrong to sardonically bring Jared Purvis to life? Had Jared been right all this time?

He got on his Gold Wing and drove. It was pouring now, and the high curved windshield diverted the artificial gale away from his face and straight toward his hair, which in turn whipped his skull to express its displeasure. He regretted tossing his helmet onto the garage's concrete floor, but only because it could have helped shield him from the storm. Safe and alive, not so important.

He pointed his bike toward Iowa, sticking to the Interstate if not the posted speed. Leaving Wisconsin, in this case, meant crossing the river on I-90 just below Lock and Dam #8. This took him across the New Bridge as Duchainers still called it, even if the arching gray structure had been in use a good five decades, here in a place where nicknames held firm. He changed roads at Exit 42, doing his best to shake off the cold as he sped north toward Minnesota where the rain finally stopped, then came back down the Great River Road.

A series of self-congratulatory signs advertised *America's Most Scenic By-way*. But the night was too dark and his speed too great for anything to be scenic. He couldn't even make out Lake Pepin as he passed it. A rare natural lake, no dam required, it ranked as the largest on the river and claimed the additional honor of being *The Birthplace of Water Skiing*.

He plowed through a second wet, churning storm just south of that lake. Thunder. Lightning. Sulfur-white flashes. Not a good night for water skiing. Or being on a motorcycle. Even after the deluge let up, its moisture lingered in the sponge-like air. Clay could still taste it, feel it, and smell it.

Eighteen miles from home on Old Monastery Road, Clay took up the speed. At 110 miles per hour, dark telephone poles zipped in and out of the white oval oasis created by his headlight. Like thoughts through his brain. Flitting. Fleeing. As the needle hit *119*—the fastest he'd taken his Gold Wing—he realized he would sell the bike, self-publish the novel, and give back whatever money was left to the Consortium even if he was technically under no obligation to do so. He would enroll in a two-year vocational college and undergo retraining. (The welders in a commercial for Duchaine Community College looked so happy.) A life without writing. Possibly no reading. Away with words, away with those damned strings of symbols that caused humanity more trouble than an apple in the Garden of Eden by allowing and forcing a species of unwitting idiots to store information and share ideas that caused envy, depression, confusion.

When and if Marta finally left California, he would drive to Madison and bluster his way to StripOff International's private hangar and heliport at Dane County Regional Airport. He would be wearing the long-sleeved crimson-red shirt she had given him at Christmas, complemented by the gently pleated charcoal-gray slacks from that same morning. He would be holding an expensive flower arrangement from Hey Howdy's floral department. "No helicopter ride today," he would say. "Your poor husband couldn't wait that long."

On the ride home, he would tell her, "I'm going to study welding. I'll fix things in a world without ambiguity or subjectivity. Where you get something right or get something wrong. No in-betweens. No mixed reviews.

"I will shed my ego," he would continue. "Hell, I've already shed it, along with my lust for expensive cars and other toys. I will leave writing to the professionals. Like Solstice."

Near the iron gate to Swiss Valley Park, now locked with chain and padlock, the Gold Wing ran out of gas. Worse than ignoring the gauge dropping into the red zone, he'd done the same when his low fuel light came on, thinking he could easily make it to the Hey Howdy station on Dodge where he got a discount. His evening ended with a quarter-mile walk—one quarter of a mile farther than he had walked at any one time in months—to the Gas 'n' Go on Nine Mile Road. The pimple-fighting high-school flunkout behind the counter made him purchase the plastic gas can as well. "Sorry, dude. We don't loan those out. Never, no expections."

Walking back to his bike, he stopped twice to fully take in the ozone: the pleasant aftertaste of a spring rainstorm. He didn't enjoy the feel so much; the humidity was heavy and ill-mannered, refusing to move out of his way and let him pass. His body reacted in kind, producing a layer of shirt-sticking sweat to serve as a lubricant. The plastic, two-gallon container added its own kind of weight; he switched it often from hand to hand.

After refueling the bike, he held onto the gas can, thinking he might include it "free with the gently used Honda Gold Wing 1800" when he posted his listing on Craigslist. Or maybe not. "Does it run out of gas often?" potential buyers might ask, impelling Clay to lose the sale by replying, "Only if you travel too far into the wasteland of your mind."

It was midnight and chilly when he reached home. The air no longer smelled fresh, at least from where Clay stood on the driveway, its redolence replaced by the dead-fish decay of earthworms whose misfortune had exceeded their ambitions.

Argos urinated on a hapless lilac bush. Sixteen seconds and still going strong. His phone buzzed. He had a text. *Things going great. Glad I stayed.* Jesus, Marta, really? He tried calling, got her voicemail.

According to the screen, he had a message of his own to retrieve. At 11:37, Brother Graham had called to say, "That visit home I talked about earlier. It's happening. I'm in my car." He went on to explain the trip's sudden urgency: a need to physically escape a career setback that involved the discontinuation of employee discounts at the recreational marijuana dispensary following a federal bust of three Bud Wiser coworkers, each alleged to have sold his or her own employee purchases outside of Colorado.

"Argos, get back here," Clay called across the street to the dog who had taken advantage of the distraction. Argos gave himself up without a fight, running straight into the open garage. Looking down by his feet, Clay saw something surprising: an earthworm still writhing in a small puddle of water, fully halfway across the pavement's expanse. He gently rolled the worm with one hand to place it on the palm of the other. He then carried it the rest of the way across his driveway—or hoped he was doing so, given that it was impossible to tell which way an earthworm had been traveling—and laid it gently on the sheltering grass. "You made it, friend. You made it across."

He wished a big hand would reach down and do the same for him.

***

After driving all night to reach Duchaine, Graham Turner headed for the state-run dog track where Hilary Mallory, the girlfriend from high school, worked as a cashier. Or he tried, because at 10:15 he was idling at a railroad crossing as a Burlington-Northern freight approached from the south. *Ka-koom.* His car absorbed a hard bump from behind. "Dick wad," Graham mumbled. "We're not in Denver." The vehicle behind his—a big ass GMC Yukon—rammed harder.

At the very least, Graham had been thinking his respite from Denver would get him away from people who drove like, well, they were in Denver, with half of them staring at phones when stopped for red lights while the other half honked at the cars in front of them the second the lights changed just in case those other drivers were looking at their phones. Graham had been wrong... worse than wrong. No Denverite had ever been impatient enough to deliberately slam the back of his car at a railroad crossing.

He felt his car lifting, from the rear, hoisted by the silver-gray Yukon. "Jesus," he muttered. "The crossing. He's pushing me onto the crossing." Graham was ready to concede that Clay had been right about Tim "Skull" McCracken and that Hilary's scary-as-shit husband had somehow anticipated his visit and was now planning to watch the douchebag stealing his unfaithful whore bitch wife get crushed by a 36-ton locomotive. But Graham didn't see Skull in the rearview mirror. He had checked out Skull's photos on Facebook, and as impossible as it seemed, this guy was bigger and uglier.

After nervously jerking the gear selector into Reverse, Graham pressed his gas pedal all the way to the floorboard. His tires squealed and burned and did little to stop his forward movement. Shifting back into Drive, he took a sharp left onto the tracks, making the ties his pavement. His very bumpy pavement. The green engine's whistle blared, louder than any sound ever before produced on planet Earth. Its headlight and wallboard rails were all Graham could see in his rearview mirrors. Looking frantically for the next crossing, thinking that's where he would make his exit turn when the rails no longer held his poor, abused tires in place, he took up the speed, pulled ahead of the train... all at the last possible second.

"It was bumpy as shit," Graham told Clay on the phone from somewhere near Des Moines, his car now facing decisively west, full retreat, Colorado bound. "I shit you not. I'm sure it knocked a few things loose. Some inside me. Neck's really hurting. Good thing I've got a suitcase of edibles."

"Speaking of which," Clay had asked, "just how stoned were you? Are you sure he was trying to push you on to the tracks?"

"I'm insulted, bro. My mental state was only marginally altered, business as usual, nice sheen on the world. That's what I like, a pleasant glow, while keeping my paranoia levels in check. I didn't imagine this, no more than I'm imagining the two missing taillights on my CR-V."

After a few seconds of silence, Graham said, "You were right about Hilary and fucking with Skull. This was no accident, unless someone accidentally got me while looking for you. I was missing a rear plate—it's something I'll have to get fixed, along now with the taillights—so the driver wouldn't have known I was from Colorado. He could have thought it was you. We do look kind of alike. Shit, bro, does anyone want you dead?"

Needless to say, when Clay opened his garage door early that afternoon to get his mail from the box and saw the "big ass" Yukon blocking his driveway at the curb, he couldn't help but remember Graham's question.

But where was the driver? The car looked empty. Clay hurried back into the garage, pressed the button to close its door. He sprinted to his office, yanked his phone from the charger cord, and called 9-1-1.

A busy signal? Really?

He tried again, got the same signal. He called Marta, got her voicemail, called Graham, got *his* voicemail. "This is Graham. I'd love to talk but can't get up from the floor right now."

What could he do? Run? Hide? Piss his sweatpants and faint? He had to think of something fast. A stranger lurked outside his house—a stranger who tried to push Graham in front of a moving train. Clay's phone and wallet went into front pockets.

In the kitchen, Clay tore through cabinets and drawers looking for weapons: rolling pin, chef's knife, barbecue fork. Argos tried helping, but mostly got in the way.

In the living room, Clay froze in place. A mountain of a man sat dead center on the red couch. He wore only dark colors, from his black boots and gloves to his dark gray trench coat. His face was scarred, its expression a scowl.

"Mr. Turner—" The man stood, took one step forward. "I've been looking forward to this meeting." Draped by the coat, his wide, solid body looked like an evil voting booth: Election Day for the dead. He was holding a black truncheon. Clay didn't see a gun.

Argos lurched forward. The truncheon went up. But before the man could strike, the dog wagged its tail in a show of trust. His snout slipped between the man's thighs.

"Woah. Hey, boy."

These words could have been directed at Clay, who had darted through the kitchen and into the garage. With a quick slap to the door opener, light poured in from the driveway. He then did something he would never have guessed to be in his repertoire. He dove at the opening and rolled out onto the driveway. As bad as this hurt, there was no time to care. Pushing himself to his feet, he pressed the bottom key on the outside keypad. The door's motor hummed back into action.

He was halfway across his neighbor's lawn when the garage door again switched course. Clay didn't look back. All that mattered was holding onto his lead, which might not be so hard. The intruder did not move quickly. Clay had been right to gamble on this.

Argos caught up on his right. "Thank God he didn't hurt you, boy." The dog didn't stay to socialize. Instead, he turned right, darting between two houses. *Sorry, man, just escaped. Got to make the most of it.*

Clay kept running like never before. Thinking the stranger must have a gun, he zigged and zagged, praying that something he'd read years ago was true—that it was hard to shoot a racing, retreating body. If he could just make it to Cleveland Park, one short block away, he could slip into the woods, and then, without slowing his pace, figure out what the hell to do next.

Chapter 28
⌘

WAR

After squeezing around the last chain-link fence post that helped mark the official boundary between park and wildness, Clay half ran, half stumbled down the steep, rocky bank thick with spring growth. The weedy fragrance filled his nose and made him sneeze. With his balance regained at the head of Trail 3, the name he and his explorer friends gave it as kids, he shot past the weathered rock steps that connected with the limestone overlook known for taking the breath from strangers overcome by the river valley's magnificence. It was a place Clay had visited several times as an adult, taking Marta there to view the July Third fireworks. This time, he didn't stop.

From the valley below came sirens, lots of sirens, howling like an energized wolf pack. Some close, some distant, they all seemed to move in the same direction toward the east side of town. They weren't coming to rescue him.

Passing the Indian burial mound for the first time in years, he almost smiled, thinking how blindly he and his friends once accepted that this long, lumpy ridge could be nothing else, without once going online to verify their belief.

Clay slipped on patches of mud and water. A branch snagged his shirt; twigs snapped. He heard the muffled thunder of a boulder tumbling downhill somewhere behind him and heard swearing from the same direction. The assassin was catching up, a hunter determined to bring down his deer. Clay stopped at the junction with Trail 5, the hard, dirt descent more chute than path that ended abruptly at the Bluff Street Extension, a long-abandoned street that once connected his neighborhood to downtown Duchaine. *What choice do I have?* he asked himself, right before a "Got you now" decisively answered the question. Looking down Trail 5, he positioned his feet, leaned backwards like a snowboarder, and downward fled, more skiing than walking. An outgrowth of tree roots soon lifted his feet, knocking him onto his ass, which instantly became his sled. Rocks punched and poked as he continued downward, gathering speed. Prickly shrubs got in a few jabs.

"You can't get away," came the gravelly voice from above. "You'll never escape." But Clay suspected he had. The voice was losing volume.

This break didn't prevent him from running once he was on the Bluff Street Extension, headed downtown, or for the bridge, or... Clay cursed his options and how limited they were. Feeling a draft on his right thigh, he looked down to see the wide, flapping tear in his sweatpants and blood from the gash beneath it. As Dodge Street came into view, a fresh choice emerged: a city bus pulling over to pick up a passenger. Breathing heavily with sweat to match, Clay took his place behind the uniformed McDonald's employee who had been waiting at the stop. As the accordion doors closed behind him, he watched the young woman drop a handful of coins into the fare box, slowly, one at a time.

The bus pulled back into traffic. "Fare, please."

The driver looked vaguely familiar: Charlie Hood, one-time star shooter for the Duchaine Dambuilders, the year Clay's classmates watched with much more interest than he had as their basketball team made it to State and valiantly fought to almost win one of their final match-ups. Charlie Hood was heavier now, having clearly outgrown the snug fascist-brown uniform required by his job. He was balder too, a curly ring of hair circling his shiny dome like the outer wall of a robin's nest.

"How much?" Clay asked him.

"You don't have a pass?"

"I don't have a pass."

"Everyone has a pass."

"She didn't have a pass."

"Two dollars. Exact change."

Knowing he carried no change, having rarely carried any his adult life, Clay struggled to pull out his wallet. "Are you able to break a twenty? I don't have any singles."

"Sorry, sir, exact change only."

"What if I just gave you the twenty? And you kept the change?"

"That would violate my professional oath."

"I don't have exact change," Clay said. "I have a twenty."

"You're giving me no choice but to pull over and throw you off the court... I mean, place you on the curb."

The McDonald's employee got up from her seat. "I'll pay his fare." Clay's eyes focused on the slim gold badge that showed her to be an Assistant Manager. "I can't sit back while some ragged drunk begs for a free ride. Just call me the Good Samaritan."

She handed Clay two wrinkled dollar bills. When he repaid her with a twenty, she did not refuse. A familiar voice called from the back of the bus. "Clay? Turner?" Damon Debbitts was looking up from a paperback book.

Charlie Hood fairly shouted, "Now, please take a seat."

Staggering toward the rear of the moving bus, Clay brushed against a fourth passenger: a tiny, older woman who seemed uninterested in all that was transpiring. She didn't look up as Clay apologized in the direction of her silver blue hair and continued on his shaky path.

"Mingling with the peasants?" Damon said as Clay took the sideways two-person seat in front of Damon's bus-wide bench straddling the vehicle's motor. He picked up the scent of ham and cigarettes. "Thanks again for your comments on the manuscript."

Clay shifted and squirmed, unable to ignore the muddy discomfort soaking through the seat of his pants. He nearly asked Damon, "You don't see anything strange here?" but let him continue. It wasn't like Damon could help.

"I still can't believe you felt the need to point out you didn't find any typos. It should go without saying that real writers don't make typos. But that's neither here nor there."

Squinting his eyes, Damon carefully studied the other few passengers as if what he were about to share was a classified government secret. "There's a bidding war in progress."

"Seriously, Damon? That's great."

"It's somewhat unilateral as bidding wars go." Damon closed his paperback, placed it on the seat to his right, and leaned forward toward Clay. "Cousin Randy is offering two-million dollars on the condition I destroy all copies, paper and electronic, of the manuscript."

"Two million dollars?"

"I'm holding out for five." Damon smiled a creepy I've-got-teenagers-chained-in-my-basement smile. "*War* is a great book, a certain classic. I don't think Joseph Conrad would have burned *Heart of Darkness* for the Nineteenth Century equivalent of two million dollars."

Damon laughed, just barely; it had the sound of incompletely suppressed flatulence. "Seriously. Imagine that. Cousin Randy paying five million dollars for something he hates. He once told me the only thing more stupid than reading a novel was writing one. That was the day I decided to write about him."

"He hates writing?"

"Writers. He hates writers."

Damon's face hardened with anger. "Would you believe his lawyers offered me a paltry $300,000 upfront? To Cousin Randy, $300,000 is like spitting in the ocean. Even the five mill, that's bus fare to him."

His expression changed. "What the hell happened to you?"

"Nice of you to notice. I just slid down a steep trail with branches sticking out. Someone's trying to kill me."

"By sliding you down a steep trail?"

"There's no way it's your cousin?"

"What? No. Does he know you read my manuscript?"

"It's a long story. I knew Randolph in high school. He took an interest in my writing, but ended up trying to sabotage me."

"I'm confused. Since you missed it the first time, he hates writing. He hates all art, music, painting, everything."

"But having me killed, it makes no sense."

"Nothing you're saying makes sense," Damon said. "Be that as it may, you got away. That in itself does not sound like my cousin."

"I don't know. He kills people and I'm pretty sure the guy chasing me plans to kill me."

"The *guy*? Randy sent one operative *and* you got away?"

Clay pulled out his phone to retry 9-1-1, jumped when it reacted with three sharp siren blasts. An Emergency Text Warning hijacked his screen. *MAYORAL ALERT FOR DUCHAINE EAST OF KENNEDY AVENUE. BEE INFESTATION. VANDALS SHOT UP SIX COMMERCIAL HIVES. ALL SCHOOLS ON LOCKDOWN UNTIL FURTHER NOTICE.*

"Look at this," Clay said. "You've got to admit it's something Randolph would do. Throw the cops a distraction. Tie up 9-1-1. Come to think of it, isn't that where the Emergency Call Center is located? The new county complex?"

"Your phone's almost dead. Twenty-four percent."

"The message?"

"Clever, but hardly Cousin Randy clever. Were he involved, you would be waking in that cloud of angry bees. You would be naked, too, and coated in bee attractant." Damon leaned forward. "What about the post of your reading at the library? *That* stirred up some angry wasps. Those sanctimonious human suppositories got pretty upset. You don't see unbridled anger like that every day. Well, except everywhere else online."

Clay couldn't believe he had not considered these virtual vigilantes earlier. "There were some vicious comments. But killing me? I don't think anyone really wanted me dead."

"Yes, they did. They said so. Repeatedly."

"But what about this?" Clay said. "My assassin didn't even attempt to shoot me. He had a truncheon."

"Now that sounds like Randy. It's hard to make a shooting look like an accident. But smack someone on the head, you've opened the door to all kinds of scenarios—mandrills, sharks, killer robots. Depositing you in the middle of a bee infestation? No problem."

This was punctuated by a thud.

"What the hell?" Clay grabbed the metal bar framing his seat back.

"Some moron just hit the rear of my bus," Charlie Hood loudly answered the question just as an ugly, scarred bald head appeared outside Clay's window. "Everybody stay in their seats," the bus driver shouted. The Yukon seemed only inches away.

The car pulled ahead to reach the bus driver's window. The stranger was shouting but could not be heard. Hood pushed open his window, trebling the volume of Yukon roar.

"FBI!" The stranger's gravelly voice competed with his vehicle's growl, matching it in volume and tone. "You are harboring a fugitive! Pull over at once!"

"My cousin has been known to employ law enforcement impersonation," Damon conceded. "If it is him, he'll be thrilled to get a two-for-one special." He turned his attention toward the front of the bus. "Driver! That man is a killer! Do not pull over!"

"Everyone, stay calm," Charlie Hood commanded. "I'm a member of the Nation of Iowa Homegrown Sons of Liberty militia. I got a conceal and carry, though you can bet yourself ten dead Muslims I ain't got no candyass permit." He reached for something in his jacket. "I, goddammit, am the NRA!"

"Pull over immediately!" The assassin produced a large automatic rifle. "This is your last warning!"

The gun fired, or rather, *a* gun fired.

"Son of a bitch!" the bus driver screamed. "I shot myself in the goddamn leg."

"Pull over and abandon your vehicle! My beef is not with you!"

"Do not listen to him!" Damon shouted at Charlie Hood. "Do not pull over!"

The bus driver pulled over. Even with the limp of a man who had just shot himself in the thigh with a gun, Charlie Hood was out the door in less time than it took Clay to mutter, "Shit."

The next surprise may well have been the greatest as heavy, slothful Damon Debbitts lunged forward to secure the front of the bus. Seconds later, his girth spilled over the driver's seat. The bus jerked forward, and Clay, who had almost made it to Damon's side before he felt himself falling backwards, grabbed hold of a shiny silver pole with all the strength of a stripper in an earthquake.

Damon, he could see, was not prepared to die. After slamming the bus against the Yukon, Damon took up the speed. Considerably. The Yukon fell back to reassume its original place to the rear.

"I didn't think you drove," said Clay.

"It has been a while, but then, it's hardly brain surgery."

Damon calmly added, "I suggest you find a seat."

"I'm good," Clay said.

Not so for the McDonald's manager who had previously offered to pay Clay's fare and was now trying to extract the please-let-me-off cord from its casings. *Ding, ding, ding, ding.* The elderly woman showed no reaction, prompting Clay to wonder if she were actually alive.

Clay pulled out his phone, pressed 9-1-1, only to get the incredibly hard-to-believe busy signal. He kept trying the number, kept getting the same.

Soon, the bus was on Jones Street, heading west toward the dog track and River Bank Industrial Park. Clay saw the flashing red lights of a railroad crossing sign and heard the blaring horn of an approaching train.

"I know this works in movies," said Damon as he accelerated yet again and bounced the bus across the tracks, taking his new vehicle directly in front of the monstrous green locomotive now ready to do the assassin's work for him.

"Jesus, Jesus, Jesus," the McManager sobbed as the train loudly scraped the bus's tail end, knocking it a few feet left with an almighty thud, while effectively cutting off the pursuing Yukon.

"I need to hide," Damon said, adding to himself, "I should have taken the two mil."

Clay pointed out that the police station was only eight blocks away.

"You've read *War*. The cops are probably in on this, at least to the extent they look the other way."

"I went to school with some of those cops," Clay pleaded. "Go to the police station."

"You went to school with Cousin Randy, too. You can't trust anyone." Damon seemed to be thinking. "I know where we can go. Cousin Randy knows my five houses, but there's a sixth one he's never seen. It's not as finished as the other five in that it lacks plumbing. And heating. And drywall. It's a few blocks off Asbury near the communications tower."

"That's an upscale neighborhood," Clay noted. "How do you get away with leaving your house unfinished?"

"It was originally a detached two-car garage. The owner of the actual house worked at Farm Haul alongside my old man. He needed to pay off a gambling debt. My father wasn't one to pass up a piece of low-priced property."

When Clay's phone delivered another round of busy signals, he nearly tossed it out a window. Taking a deep breath, he turned off the device to make it untraceable—and leave him the option of trying again later.

Damon used Palmer Street to get back across the tracks and out of the flats. After crossing Main by the Old Town Clock, Damon pulled the bus over to release its other two paying passengers. The McManager, no longer seeking divine intervention, bolted out the door. The elderly woman, now at least breathing, required assistance from both Damon and Clay, after which Damon returned to the driver's seat and lit up a cigarette.

East Third got them up the hill. The sky churned black behind them now: a summer storm approaching. The Yukon had not reappeared.

They ditched the bus between two semi-trailers at the Kohl's store loading dock. If not completely hidden there, it was hardly in plain sight.

"Quick, this way," Damon said. Clay saw the communications tower, a few blocks distant, now trying to pierce the deepening cloud cover.

"We shouldn't be walking down Asbury," Clay argued. "We should be using an alley, a side street at worst." The passing windows of boutique shops, unique to this part of Duchaine, mirrored their images, letting Clay see the bedraggled homeless guy the McManager had made him out to be. At Bonnie's Bridal, the spreading crimson circle on his tattered slacks stood out against an array of ivory-white dresses.

The sidewalks were empty in response to the building storm. Constantly changing its composition, the sky had become a wide, damp canvas where grim watercolors swirled and bled into one another.

Panting like Argos, Damon announced, "I'm not going to make it." They were at the corner of Flora and Asbury. "I'm not used to this level of physical exertion."

"We walked *two* blocks."

"It's over," Damon said. "Acceptance. It follows denial."

"But—" Damon Debbitts was gone, having disappeared into Colleen's Homemade Candies.

A woman came out of that same store, eyes fixed on her phone. She jumped back a few inches upon noticing Clay, before clumsily digging into her purse and handing him a dollar. Before he could return it, she hurried away.

In the distance ahead, a few blocks down Asbury, Clay glimpsed the Yukon, coming his way. He ducked into Bedtime Boudoir, earning a few screams for his bloody wound, and watched from behind two shapely mannequins dressed in skimpy black lingerie while the Yukon drove past... then, *son of a bitch, how did he find me,* jerked back into view, its tires squealing in reverse. Clay didn't bother asking if the store had a back door; he was already using it.

The sky chose that moment to unload, giving Clay some cover by limiting visibility. On Evans Drive at the end of the alley, he was running again, passing the communications tower. A bulge in the chain-link fence, where kids had probably pried it back to crawl under, invited him to seek higher ground at a place no outsider would know existed or find on GPS. The tower would give Clay a hiding place in the sky, along with a vantage point over his mysterious enemy.

Up he went, stopping every twenty metal rungs to take a deep chilling breath, shake the water from his hair, and scan the perimeter, or what he could see of it, for the roof of the black SUV.

Reaching the iron-grid platform close to the top, his body hunched over, hands on his knees, he heard his own panting. He pulled out his phone, turned it back on, waited and waited some more, and tried calling 9-1-1. He couldn't hear a ring, never mind that he was on top of a fucking cell phone tower. He had no bars. He put it back to sleep.

Clay felt a sneeze coming on, tried holding it back. But his nose seemed determined to give away his hiding place. He felt tears mingling with the rain on his cheeks, and only then realized just how much his leg hurt. He gripped the platform's metal rail tightly and whispered, "1 Mississippi, 2 Mississippi, 3 Mississippi..." waiting for the pain to return to its previously intolerable level. At "42," he let go of the rail, tore a sleeve from his shirt, and wrapped it around his pant leg to contain the bleeding.

The rain picked up; the ground disappeared. Clay heard thunder in the distance, detected a slight taste of Sulphur. The tower groaned: an eerie metallic screech. This was followed by a loud, sharp clank. Metal on metal? Gun hitting step? Clay's eyes were still teared up, making everything blurry as he turned to keep watch on the square opening at the top of the narrow ladder casing, thinking that—ugly and wide, hard and scarred—his killer's face would be the last thing he saw.

I will kick his hands, Clay promised himself. *I will kick his scarred ugly head.* But where he wanted to add, *He's going to be sorry when he's bouncing all the way down the ladder on his scarred ugly face,* the thought was usurped by, *I am going to die. I am a fat, unfocused fraud of a writer and I am going to die.*

Another clank, louder, closer, had Clay wishing he believed in God. Having already composed a prayer in his head, he lacked a place to send it.

Chapter 29
⌘

EVERYTHING ENDS BADLY

Ten minutes later, high atop the communications tower, the assassin was no longer asking politely. "Give it up, Turner," he insisted instead. "It is fucking time for you to fucking end this." He wanted Clay to tumble down the stairs and wasn't planning to say it again.

The rain had finally let up. But the air felt even colder on Clay's tight, wet shirt. "One last wish. I call my wife."

"You held onto your phone? You know they can be tracked?"

"Is that how you found me?"

The killer mimed zipping his own mouth shut.

"The person who hired you—someone did hire you—he's been tracking my movements. Am I right? That's how you found me."

Getting no answer, Clay continued, "But you were sloppy executing your execution. Racing buses in public? Letting me run down neighborhood streets?"

"I strongly resent that," the assassin said. "We're done speaking now. This isn't one of those old *Superman* movies where I tell you everything, thinking you'll be dead at the end, only to be surprised when the man of steel brings in the cops to take my ready-made confession."

"In other words, that *is* how you found me?"

"You don't shut up, do you? I followed the goddamn police monitor. That's how. Runaway buses. Homeless people bleeding on mannequins. You left a trail like a fucking tornado."

Clay turned around, stared out into the void. Barely reaching the volume of whisper, he asked, "What if I just jumped? Wouldn't that make it easier for everyone?"

"I'd have to stop you."

"Right. It's supposed to look like an accident." He turned back around to face his killer. "Why? Why didn't you just shoot me back at the house?"

Clay took a few seconds to breathe. "Oh, yeah... idiot writer dies in bizarre accident. Distraught widow comforted by app tycoon."

"I'm sorry, but did I already whack you in the head? I don't remember doing it, but you're making me question my memory."

"It's him, isn't it? The guy who hired you, he likes bizarre accidents. It wasn't just some stranger riled up over abortion or animal abuse."

"What... guy? What animal abortions? Him, who, what? What the fuck are you talking about?"

Clay thought he heard clanking from below and wondered if it was even remotely possible that a third person was coming up the ladder. But who would that be? Was Randolph J. Simper about to appear, having just sped here in a limousine from the airport? Would he witness Clay's unwilling suicide, taking delight as he helped thin, if ever so slightly, the world's artistic population? Would he instruct the killer to shoot Clay "nice and clean, in the chest" for the purpose of mounting his head on the wall of a subterranean trophy room maintained for the exclusive benefit of sick rich bastards? There was also the possibility Randolph would let Clay beg to be spared, after which Randolph would keep him as a pet, locked away where no one would see it.

Under better circumstances, Clay might have smiled, accepting that this last possibility did not represent all that huge a departure from the past several months. Randolph's pet. Stay, boy, stay.

The assassin reached under his coat.

One last attempt at stalling his murder: "Why does everything on this planet end badly? You could argue it negates any good that preceded it."

"What if it's a beginning?"

"You? Seriously? An afterlife?"

"Reincarnation, in point of fact."

"And yet you kill people for money? That wouldn't impact your karma?"

"I like to think I'm moving the process along."

Clay saw the truncheon, saw the big block fingers holding its handle just as the universe turned bright and tingly.

Everything vibrated.

"What the fuck?" shouted the assassin, reacting to both the lightning strike and being tackled by a smaller, weaker man. A writer, no less.

A lightning rod must have grounded the tower. Clay's body had not been burned by the jolt.

But something burned now ... the Taser ... activated on contact when its owner hit the wet metal grid. Clay rolled away quickly, and within seconds was descending the steps, which were every bit as cold and slippery. He bounced, he gripped, he occasionally slid. Risking death to escape death.

"Jesus," came a voice from the vicinity of his feet as those feet collided with a larger, harder object. "My head."

"Dick? Breitbach?"

"Clay, good, you're alive," the Chamber president said quietly. "I have a plan. It wouldn't have worked with you dead."

Dick tugged at Clay's pant leg, then dropped back down the ladder's rungs, before ducking off to the side on what turned out to be another metal platform. Clay followed. "Shh," whispered Dick, now standing right next to the ladder. He held what looked like a strange toy gun, too long for a pistol, too short for a rifle.

"You should have ended this when you had the chance!" The rock-hard words rolled down from above like an avalanche, accompanied by angry, hollow stomps: the cut-short killer in pursuit. "You're going to wish you settled for dead."

The stomping grew louder, stopping with another "What the fuck?" The assassin leaned sideways, then forward toward Dick. His eyes widened. His hands gripped Dick's collar, then loosened, then slid down the jacket front.

Dick pulled the limp mountain a few feet more onto the platform, keeping it from sliding down the ladder. "Tranquilizer dart," said Dick as he threw a white cloth over the edge of the platform and pulled out a pair of handcuffs. "Probably not quite enough to kill him, but you never know. The guy's kind of in a risky business. Accidents can happen."

"I thought those took ten or fifteen minutes. Except in movies."

"You know your tranquilizer darts. They take forever to kick in, unless you hit an artery."

"You think you hit an artery?"

"I think the ether did what it was supposed to do."

"That's why you tossed a rag over the edge?"

"He's going to be asleep for a while. When he wakes up, he won't be happy."

"Impressive," Clay stammered. "But where did you—"

"Our vet's getting a free Chamber membership this year."

A slim beam of sunlight poking out from under the cloud shelf painted a bright stripe the length of the assassin's horizontal body. Clay pulled out his phone.

"You held onto your phone?"

"I know, they can be tracked."

"You at least turned it off?"

"I did. I just want to try Marta."

"Keep it off. You can call her before you get in my car. The phone stays off after that."

At the bottom of the tower, he turned on the phone, hit Recent Calls, and promptly pressed Marta. She answered almost as quickly, only it wasn't her. "Clay, we've been wondering where you disappeared to," came the voice of Randolph J. Simper. "We wanted to make sure you got Marta's message. Hope you don't mind my keeping her here."

"Where's Marta? I need to speak with Marta?"

The phone beeped three times. Call Ended.

"Something's wrong," Clay said.

"You're just figuring that out?" Dick motioned to a car on the street. "We need to move."

Chapter 30
⌘

ETERNITY ON A BUDGET

Still wet from the rain, the blue hood of Dick's refurbished 1970 240Z gleamed like it had been laminated. Clay glanced around the leather interior. Had he not known cars, he might have thought this one was new, fresh off the lot. Not a blemish to be seen, and more intriguingly, the car *smelled* of newness, delivering that strangely pleasing nasal jolt. Perhaps it really was new, a collector's kit imitation 240Z, which would still have been cool. Dick was probably long past noticing the smell, and even if he wasn't, could not possibly have discerned it at that moment through the stench of leg-bleeding, tower-climbing, chased-through-woods Clay.

Dick confirmed this last suspicion by saying, "You know, Clay, you really look like dog doo. Smell like it too."

Clay looked down at his silenced phone. "It was Randolph before. When I tried calling Marta. He answered her phone."

"That's strange."

"Try terrifying."

They were headed downtown descending the steep hill that was East Third. Clay looked out upon his river valley town. The church spires and town clock glistened, still wet from the rain. Strangely peaceful, the scene had to be reassuring to all the other drivers headed that direction. *Take your time, pick up some groceries, head home from work. You're lucky to live in this beautiful place where nothing bad happens.*

"Aren't you supposed to be in California?" Clay asked. "With *him?*"

"I had stuff I needed to do at work. Howell and Cobb—and Marta—didn't seem to have that problem."

"But why are you here?" Clay asked. "How did you find me? What's your connection to Randolph's plan?"

Dick smirked, shook his head. "Randolph's plan? Jeez, Clay. You don't think if Randolph Simper wanted you dead, you'd be a lot less talkative now?"

"Then who?" Clay whispered as the truth hit like a punch to the gut. He turned to face Dick. "You're part of this?"

"No, I am not."

"You're part of the Consortium."

"I'm not part of *this*." Dick stared straight ahead, quietly cleared his throat. "I was—and then with objections. I fought against The Business Plan right from the start. It was Benedict Howell who came up with it; he really is a Nazi at heart. In my defense, I'm hardly the first person in history who went along with one of those guys because he was scared. All that matters now is I'm here. Risking my rump to save yours. And you'd better believe I'm risking my rump."

"They called *this* The Business Plan?" Clay muttered before asking the real question. "Why?" He stared at the side of the driver's head. "Why have me killed?"

"Duh. The insurance clause in your contract? You never thought that could come back to get you?"

Clay's response—"The insurance clause?"—seemed to leave Dick incredulous. Clay could see his exasperation as he asked, "You didn't read the contract you signed?"

"Most of it," Clay said. "It went on forever without saying much."

Clay then learned two things: Why one should always read contracts before signing them; and what exactly he'd signed. "Benedict Howell had pushed for the lengthy document," Dick elaborated. "He said it would lull you into not paying attention. I feel kind of stupid now, having argued you were much too smart to be duped so easily."

"But," Clay said, "that's not completely true. I had a lawyer read it for me. Moon McDermott. He didn't say a thing."

"The Scrapper?" Dick delivered a fresh incredulous stare. "He *wrote* your bleeping contract. That bloated ambulance chaser does work for Benedict all the time, ever since they settled that lawsuit from an elderly man who slipped on ice in the Bedrock lot. The old man never saw any money, of course, not after Bedrock—read: Benedict Howell—paid off Moon. That's the kind of settlement The Scrapper gets his so-called clients. *Everything you deserve... and more.*" Dick was shaking his head. "Jeez, Clay. That sleaze pouch does commercials. On TV. What were you expecting?"

After spending a few seconds in silence, Clay asked, "But killing me. It seems an extreme... and extremely risky way to make some money."

"Benedict," said Dick. "He ran Bedrock into the bedrock. Leveraged massive debt against the company."

"Even so, how did he get anyone else to go along?"

"Artemis Cobb's in the same straits," Dick said. "People who've never had money don't realize how easy it is to blow 12-million dollars. Artemis Cobb managed his inheritance like a lottery winner. A debauched lottery winner."

Clay asked, "Randolph? He must have played some role."

"He didn't want to know. Not the details anyway. He found such information too close to complicity. As I understand it, he simply told Artemis Cobb, 'You people do what you need to do. It has nothing to do with me. My fingerprints stay on my fingers.' On the other hand—"

"The other hand?"

"I guess he said something about liking the timing. With having everyone, including Marta, in California."

Clay hesitated before continuing, "What about—?"

"No, no, don't even think it. Marta was in the dark. She would never."

"How about you?" Clay asked. "How did you end up in the middle of this?"

"It sure wasn't the insurance clause, anything but. Truth be told, that didn't really set off any bells. Like you said, there was so much in that contract to digest. As for wanting in on the original investment, I thought it would be fun to put some money in art. I knew you from high school. I always liked your writing okay. It's not Tom Clancy but you seemed to have something. Besides, Cessna's richer than crud. Born with a silver nipple in her mouth. And I married into it, talk about a good investment."

"One more thing," Clay asked with a sigh. "Was Marta seeing someone in the group?"

"You mean like, *seeing* seeing?" Dick said.

"Randolph said something."

"That at least makes sense—Randolph trying to stir things up. It was pretty obvious to everyone at that first meeting, and at the Lit Fest reading, that Randolph wanted to sleep with your wife. I mean, so did half the study group, but Randolph had that strange intensity he always has."

Clay whispered to himself, "I am a myopic, self-absorbed fraud."

"Don't get me wrong, Clay, I wasn't in that half that wanted to sleep with Marta. I mean, sure, you have a very beautiful wife. But so do I. Cessna's all the woman I could ever need or want, and did I mention, she's richer than sin?"

Dick waited a few beats before saying, "Your leg? Hurts?"

"Legs, head, arms, chest. I've had better days."

Dick reached over and into the glove compartment. Retrieving a small pill bottle, he said, "Take two of these. OxyContin. Dulls the pain."

"You take these?"

"Hey, I know we're in the Midwest," Dick said, "but that doesn't mean we're all meth heads like Artemis Cobb. Apologies if meth's your drug of choice."

"Artemis Cobb is on meth?"

"Duh," said Dick. "You're shocked because he's always so proper and graceful?"

Clay placed the unopened bottle back in the glove compartment. "I'm still confused about Randolph. Unless I'm missing something—which apparently is something I do—he had nothing to do with the insurance clause. He didn't really think he could win Marta over with his money and power?"

"She's there isn't she?"

"He gave the money to me, not her."

"He showed he could buy you. And for what? A rich person's chump change? That couldn't have impressed her. That is to say, you sure didn't impress her. Randolph must have."

"But she was never interested in him. Never was. Never could be. She went out with him and some friends a few times in high school but turned down his offer for a real date."

Dick smirked again as he said, "Turning Randolph down. That could explain his obsession. Rejection doesn't sit well with him. And there's always been that matter of the graduation speech."

"The speech?"

"And all the controversy."

"The controversy?"

"It was a pretty big deal. You were probably too busy dating your future wife to notice. Randolph was supposed to be valedictorian. But there was this rumor he'd blackmailed his teachers to give him straight A's. Apparently, he'd hacked their servers and found their secret pleasures. As student council president, I had no choice but to launch an investigation. It ended up being real frustrating, I can tell you that. Only the P.E. teacher, Coach Anslaugh, seemed ready to talk, and then he had that weird accident."

This Clay remembered. Mr. Anslaugh had died bungee jumping from the bridge late after midnight using hundreds of tiny bungee cords loosely linked together. "Didn't he hit a barge?" Clay said. "They're hardly invisible with their spotlights."

"Yeah, I mean, who does that? From what we were able to learn, the last thing Mr. A did was to use his phone to login and change Randolph's grade to an F, knocking him out of the game. Pretty big coincidence, wouldn't you say? Your friend Solstice got the gig. She used her valedictorian speech to help school Randolph, saying something to the effect that science without liberal arts is a cold and dangerous thing, and that you couldn't be a fully rounded human without art and music and literature. You couldn't be a grownup. I always remembered those words. They had a part in my wanting to put money into your book."

"And now you think he's back for revenge? For something that happened fourteen years ago?"

"Maybe. But he's not the one who hired a hit man. I think he just wants Marta. She was on student council, too, you know. In his mind, maybe she rejected him twice."

They were turning onto Gifford Avenue.

"Guess she's where he wants her now," Dick said.

"Well," Clay muttered to himself, staring out the passenger window. "I guess he wasn't gay."

Dick chuckled. "Who thought he was gay? I've heard Randolph called a lot of things but gay was never one of them."

They were north of downtown heading toward Eagle's Nest Park and Lock and Dam #8. "Randolph does have a boatload of money," Dick said. "People are attracted to that. That's not why I married Cessna, of course. Well, hardly the main reason. And it's not why Marta would leave you for Randolph, I don't think. She's just fascinated by his world. Exotic. So different. You guys, you know, you've been together a long time. Acres of greener grass out there."

"I need to get her back."

"What you and I *need* is to stay alive. None of this other stuff matters right now. The crud in the contract. Your troubles with Marta. What matters is that Benedict and Artemis can't afford for either of us to be breathing and able to speak. They need to hush this up. Send us off on the trip of a lifetime, the one that wraps it up. Like something my travel agency would offer: *Eternity on a Budget.*"

"It's time to turn our phones back on," Dick said. "If anyone's tracking us, we're going to fool them. If you need to check your messages, now's the time."

"Do you think Randolph's tracking me?"

"You think?"

Clay pulled up his Voicemail, tapped the first one, *Caller ID: UNKNOWN.* A man's raspy voice sent a chill up his spine. "We have your dog."

"Your house—" The phone beeped three times, then shut itself down to protect the battery.

Clay whacked his phone on the dashboard twice, then stared at its screen, trying to will it back to life. "Someone's got my dog," he said.

"Shoot."

"We need to rescue him—"

"Have you been listening to me?" Dick said. "We need to get out of Dodge."

"And Marta."

"What did they say?"

"*Your house.* Then my phone died. Do you think they're actually in my house? Are they watching it? Not that it matters, we need to free Argos. He saved my life once. It's my turn to save his."

"First things first. We need to get rid of our phones. And we need to get rid of this car. Trade it for something they won't be looking for. Maybe get you cleaned up in the process."

Clay finally had something to offer: "I know where we can get a car."

Dick told Clay to use his charger. "Yeah, I know, it seems counterintuitive. There's a reason for waking that phone from its coma."

Minutes later, Clay and Dick were leaning over the rail of the Gifford Avenue Overpass, looking down on I-90, standing on the narrow curb directly in front of the 240Z with its orange emergency lights flashing. They were waiting for an open-top semi-trailer. One headed east. Toward Chicago or Milwaukee.

"Perfect," Dick shouted when one emerged. They tossed three phones— theirs and the assassin's—outward to create an arc that would intersect with a trailer's trajectory.

"We did it," Clay shouted as the phones crash-landed on a load of huge jagged rocks. "If anyone's tracking us, we're headed east."

"Let's hope the heck they think so," Dick said. The truck disappeared over the hilltop.

Chapter 31
⌘

THE GETAWAY VOLVO

"Good Lord, Clay, you look like Satan himself just dragged you through hell." Winnie Jewell stared at him with eyes that would have been plenty wide without further magnification by her librarian glasses.

"Close," said Clay. "I need to wash up, borrow some clothes. Car, too. The Devil's not done with me yet. Or with your daughter. You and Will can't tell a soul you've seen me. You can't get sucked in."

"You need the car?"

"For our escape. And Marta's rescue."

The eyes had opened even wider. Clay gave Winnie the highly abridged version. He sanitized it too, scrubbing away any names and information that could place Winnie at risk for knowing too much. As his story took them up the cold metal tower, she took a seat, the closest chair.

"My, oh my," she said once he had finished. "Help yourself to anything in Will's dresser or closet. My keys are on the kitchen counter."

"Thanks, Mom." He headed first for the bathroom where he washed his face, hair, and leg with a washcloth, then looked for the biggest bandage he could find. Next, he was standing in the bedroom, comparing his choices for clothes, none of which held much promise. In Will's dresser drawers, he found items that didn't belong: unlabeled cassette tapes amidst socks; a home blood-pressure kit partially buried under crisp white handkerchiefs; an empty binocular case made of old leather, its brownness fading. When Clay walked back into the front room, Dick laughed. "You look very—what's the word I'm looking for?—fashionable."

"My father-in-law is taller than I am."

"So those are supposed to be what… pajama shorts? They almost cover your shins."

Clay ignored him in favor of Winnie. "So where's Will?" he asked. "The door to his music room's open, but I didn't see him in there."

His mother-in-law teared up, shook her head slightly. "He's—" Trying to hold in the tears, she sniffled. "I wasn't going to tell you. It's clear you've already got more than enough to deal with."

"Tell me what?"

"He's in the woods."

"He's what?"

"I'm not sure. He disappeared into the woods. Because he was confused. Or something. He's done it before—I never wanted to worry you or Marta—but he always returned an hour later. One-fifteen tops. This time it's been three."

"We're talking the woods behind this house?"

Clay's question was important because the woods behind the Jewell house were basically trees on slopes overlooking a plunging bluff eager to deposit careless trespassers onto the Burlington-Northern railroad tracks several hundred feet below.

"I'm confused," Dick said. "Why is your father-in-law wandering the bluffs?"

Clay brought Dick up to speed on Will's stroke and possible dementia, how he'd always been a great guy, a true eccentric, but no longer exercised full control of his actions.

"We'd better find him," said Dick. "What's one more person to save?"

Behind the house, Clay and Dick advanced to the woods, choosing an opening in an oak tree wall that turned into a path, before turning into a much less easily defined path, before turning into a dusty rocky rut carved down a slope that dropped thirty feet to where the real cliff began. Making that descent, Clay grabbed at shrubs and roots to keep from going too fast or losing his balance, either of which would have counted as the last thing he ever did. A few plants fought back, stabbing him with sharp sticks and snagging the sweater vest.

"Crap on a cracker," Dick muttered from above, "it's a thousand feet down right there. Are we trying to do the assassin's work for him?"

Clay hit a narrow ledge at the same time his face collided with a swarm of gnats. "Of course," he muttered without bothering to swat them away, his attention more focused on the immensity of nature spread out before him—and just how far down this nature was.

"Look out!" He felt Dick Breitbach bump into his back, pushing him perilously forward, but soon felt two hands on his shoulders, steadying his stand. His shoe had dislodged a good-sized rock. It bounced three times, boom, bang, boom, with plenty of space between each thud. Going straight down. Way, way down.

"What is it with dangerous heights and this day?" he asked Dick. "Everywhere you turn, another Dick Breitbach vacation package."

"I like the way you think positive. You missed your calling doing P.R. for the Chamber."

Off to their right, the path regained definition, snaking north along a limestone shelf that couldn't have been more than three feet wide. Spitting out the last few stubborn gnats, Clay took the lead. When he looked out to his left, which he immediately vowed to not do a second time, the wide river lake went from a bland silt brown to a rich blue hue that outdid the sky's. A breeze rolled down the valley, cooling his face and arms and again reminding him that nature made the rules in this contest. He didn't need the wind picking up. Not here.

A few minutes later, the path disappeared around a corner into a deep indentation in the bluff wall that created a gap perhaps fifty feet across. Making the turn, he kicked another large stone loose with his shoe. This one produced two loud thuds in rapid succession while building the momentum it would need to crush an innocent cliff-dwelling critter or bang up a train car. Whispering, "Sorry below," he saw a much wider ledge on the hollow's far side.

He also saw Will.

Clay picked up his pace and was soon looking down at his father-in-law who seemed strangely serene. The lanky older man in a sweater vest similar to the ones Clay had just seen in a drawer sat cross-legged on a ledge wide enough to accommodate six or seven more visitors.

"Ah," said Will, "the eagle has landed."

"It's worse than I thought," Clay whispered to Dick.

"No, look." Dick pointed above the path they had just traveled on the opening's other side.

It took Clay a moment to recognize what he was seeing: the white security camera seemed so out of place as to be surreal. But then he realized just how familiar that camera was if in a Sphinx riddle kind of way. *Even if you have never seen it, you have seen through it.* The camera belonged to *DuchaineEagleWatch. org*, and it pointed at a great male eagle regurgitating food for five or six very appreciative baby eagles. Clay caught a glimpse of light gray fur.

"Minced rabbit anyone?" Will asked while handing Clay an old pair of binoculars.

Magnified through powerful lenses, the eagle eyed Clay distrustfully, even threateningly. Sure enough, a tuft of fur seemed snagged by the hook of its beak like lettuce caught between teeth. "I am not going to let that happen to me," Clay quietly announced.

"Now what are you talking about?" asked Dick.

"I am going to be one tough motherfucking rabbit. The eagle can kiss my ass."

"Right." Dick leaned close to what was now Clay's one good ear. "You know, I always wondered where they put that eagle camera. Now we know."

***

The front door of Clay's house stood wide open, a detail impossible to miss with what had to be every light turned on inside. For the sake of stealth, he parked his mother-in-law's Volvo wagon across the street and one house down. "Careful for traps," Dick whispered as he and Clay crossed the front lawn and opened the gate to the back. "It's pretty obvious someone's been here. Might still be. The perimeter's been compromised."

"Is that what you learned from reading Tom Clancy?" They were in the backyard, staying close to the house.

"Great, right?" Dick replied. "You should use more language like that in your books. That's if you live to write any more."

"I suppose it couldn't hurt."

"Crap," Dick said. "I mean, literally, crap. Have you ever heard of cleaning up after your dog?"

"Sorry about that. But he's the one with the strange habit of pooping outdoors. I've tried talking with him about personal responsibility."

Standing side by side, they leaned close to the glass of a kitchen window. "I feel like a prowler," Dick whispered.

"You are a prowler. This is prowling."

"Okay, English major. I feel like a burglar—that's the word I should have used—about to break into a house."

"I wouldn't know," Clay said, marveling at his own disingenuous.

"I'm sure you heard about Jenni Jensen and that other writer," Dick said quietly. "After we sponsored the second Lit Fest, I guess he went home with our old English teacher for a social drink. From what I heard at the Chamber, she politely asked him to leave, and he did, but only to come back and try breaking into her house. Climbed up the lattice, even broke a window. Maybe you can tell me, Clay, what is it with writers?"

Clay barely heard, mesmerized as he was by what he saw in his own house. The TVs were on, the refrigerator door open.

"How strange is that? They've got everything turned on."

"Maybe they're trying to lure you in, hoping those things would bother you."

"How so?"

"Power bill, environment. The instant you close that refrigerator door, house explodes. Raging inferno."

Clay smiled to himself. "I thought of a way to secure the perimeter."

"Nice," said Dick. "*Secure the perimeter.*"

It took a good minute to locate the circuit breaker box in the dark, a few seconds more to pry open its heavy steel cover. "Shit," Clay muttered, "I wish I had my phone."

"Who are you going to call? An electrician?"

"Now it's my turn to say Duh. I was thinking more along the lines of Flashlight App." But even as Clay said this, he found the two main switches and cut all power to the house. He couldn't see much in the darkness that ensued, not the outline of his hands, not Dick tripping over Marta's potted plants as they fumbled back toward the kitchen window vantage point.

"I don't see anything," Dick noted.

"I'm blind too," Clay commiserated.

"Not what I meant. If someone's inside they aren't using their phones or flashlights to find their way, and as far as I can tell, no doors to the outside have opened."

Clay waited a full ten minutes before turning the power back on. He then walked to the back door. "I'm going in," he said. "Want to stand watch out front?"

"If you hear an owl hoot three times, it's me," Dick said. "It means someone's coming. Be careful in there. Could still be traps."

Apart from all the blazing lights, which Clay turned off one switch plate at a time, mostly sure no one would set traps that intricate or small, he saw nothing to make him suspect there was anyone else in the house.

It seemed empty. Felt empty. No Marta. No Argos.

Is this my future? he wondered, looking around the family room before killing its lights. *Is this me period? Empty and big, pretty much useless, a waste of space? If I fail to get Marta, will I end up wishing the assassin had taken me out at the start?*

Clay changed clothes in the fully lit bedroom, matching the other shirt Marta got him at Christmas to decent black slacks. He grabbed three pairs of underwear and his favorite charcoal-gray sweats for backup. These he stuffed in a pillowcase.

The furnace hummed to life and Clay noticed how warm it was inside. The intruders had cranked the thermostat up, probably as high as it went. This he couldn't let go, booby-traps or no. In the front hallway, he set it back to SCHEDULE, and did so without exploding. This left him more confident about taking on the open refrigerator door. He proceeded to that appliance, and looking inside, saw nothing out of place. A six pack of Orange Crush, a Hey Howdy bakery cheesecake, two containers of generic imitation Cool Whip. Ever so gently, he pushed the door closed.

Scanning his kitchen counters, he found nothing in the way of kidnapper's notes, or for that matter, clues of any kind. He grabbed a bag of dog treats, passing on the snickerdoodles he and Argos would no longer be eating. Now that they were going to be healthy.

Walking out the front door, Clay found there was one more thing he could not find. Dick Breitbach seemed to have vanished completely—Clay looked right and left, even up into the hulking, old oak tree—until Dick called from across the street, "Clay. You need to come over here."

Dick stood next to Clay's elderly neighbor, Mr. Collister. (Clay wasn't sure of the first name, Kurt? Kirk?) They huddled in a shaft of yellow radiance straight out of a Michelangelo painting but more directly attributable to the porch's overhead light. The two looked frozen in place, like martyrs trapped in one of those paintings. Why so stiff? Clay wondered. Was someone hiding just inside the door, holding them hostage with a pointed gun?

Clay walked that direction. Stepping off the curb, he fingered the pistol in his own pocket—the pistol he had quietly removed from the assassin's pocket. He felt the trigger guard with his forefinger, located the actual trigger, and asked himself, "Do I have the courage to use this? Do I have the control? It might help if I'd ever used one before. I know you're supposed to breathe in when pulling the trigger, no out, it was definitely out."

A dog barked inside the house. The sound was loud and crazed and unmistakable. The son of a bitch, whoever it was lurking just out of sight, had Argos.

Clay was getting close. The gun pointed forward, pressed against the cloth of his pants.

Mr. Collister chose that moment to speak. "We have your dog."

How was it that Clay had never noticed the dry, cracked-leather tone of his neighbor's voice?

"I left you a message. I told you someone had left your front door open, and that the dog must'a got out. Ellen found him digging up the garden."

Clay let go of the gun, his hands still shaking.

"You can blame my phone," he said in an excited tone he could not control, his adrenalin still pumping like marching band drums in a parade. "The battery died." He felt, too, the presence of relief, thankful he had not fired the gun.

Argos bounded out the door. Ellen Collister—it was the first time Clay recalled knowing her full name—must have opened it for him. Argos, for his part, ran straight to Clay and shoved his nose into the bag in his master's left hand. Clay pulled it away, lifted it to shoulder height, and removed two bone-shaped biscuits. "Sometimes I think the whole point of evolution was to create a species that could prepare food for dogs," he noted.

Argos seemed appreciative, no look of, "We're out of snickerdoodles?"

Watching the dog wag his tail as if there weren't a problem in the world, Clay felt something new for that day: the barest presence of optimism. Perhaps luck would prevail with the remaining rescues. Mr. Collister promptly quashed this thought, however, asking, "What's with your wife, Turner? She called here. Left the strangest message."

Clay asked if he could hear it.

"You could just call her yourself."

"No phone," said Clay. "Remember?"

"Honey, could you pull up that message from Martha Jewell again?" said Mr. Collister to the screen door. Without stepping outside, Ellen pushed the door just open enough to hold out an early model iPhone in a black rubber case. Its speaker was on, letting Clay hear:

"This is Marta Jewell from across the street. *Anfitrión*. I am traveling for my school work. *Comporta*. I will return late Friday. *De forma*. I'm trying to reach my husband. *Extraña*. He doesn't pick up. *Preocupa*. Could you let him know I really need to talk with him? *Poco*. Thank you. I really appreciate it. *Asustado*."

"Are those... Mexican words?" Mr. Collister asked. "We always wondered where that wife of yours was from."

"I believe Clay's wife was born in Honduras," Dick impressed Clay by saying. "They don't speak Mexican there."

Back in the Volvo with Argos and Dick, Clay said, "Damn, I knew something was wrong in California. We need to rescue my wife. The Spanish was code. She said, 'Something or someone—I didn't understand the first word—*behaving strangely*. *Concerned* or *afraid*—I think that's *preocupa*. Then, *little frightened*.'"

"Wow, I barely remember my French from high school. *Merci. Bonjour.*"

Clay didn't explain the newness of his skill. Starting only the week before, right after his sophomore therapy session, he had immersed himself in on-line Spanish lessons.

During that meeting, he had achieved what counselors call a breakthrough. Once he had grudgingly accepted he had no choice but to return to Dr. Thurber's office, he decided to put his hour to good use. He vowed to come out understanding his wife more.

He started by lying to the therapist: "I'm adopted."

Instantly, almost magically, Dr. Thurber took his side, the sternness melting like butter in a microwave. "That explains so much. Adoption never goes away. It's a scar that never heals; it's a cataract, blurring your worldview." She talked about fight versus flight—the wizard brain versus the lizard brain amygdala. She stressed the fear of abandonment, the need for constant assurance. "You're carrying so much on your shoulders."

After letting the session go long a full twenty minutes, she ended by saying, "So what do you think? Is that the problem here? The need for more consistency?"

"Precisely," he replied. "I needed to give Marta more consistency. If there was even the slightest hope she'd give me one more chance."

"Sorry, I'm confused," said Dr. Thurber.

"That's okay. Great session. I'll see you next week."

Just as Dick turned the Volvo's key, a car came down Cleveland, bathing them in light as it got close. The bronze Mercedes slowed as it passed.

"Holy crapster. I don't believe this," Dick whispered as the car sped back up and disappeared. "I hope he was looking at your house and not over here."

"That *who* wasn't looking over here?"

"That was Benedict Howell's Mercedes." Realizing he could stop whispering, Dick cleared his throat and continued, "It wasn't him, of course, unless I'm wrong about his still being in California. Had to be his lackey."

"His lackey?"

"Personal assistant, a.k.a. butler, secretary, shopper, you name it. Clown used to sit in for Benedict in Saturday class. Good thing we went back in to turn on lights."

"A CLS550 Coupe," Clay noted. "Impressive."

"German, of course," Dick added.

Starting the Volvo, Clay said, "I might have an idea."

Chapter 32

⌘

BE THERE SHORTLY

"Where are we going?" Will asked for a third time from the Volvo wagon's second-row seat.

For a third time, Clay answered, "We're going to California by way of Colorado. We're picking up my brother to go rescue Marta."

To which Dick again countered: "We are not going to California. We are going to Colorado to lay low and figure things out."

Will said, "One more question—"

"His name is Damon. He's a writer like me."

Damon Debbitts had been surprisingly easy to find, hiding as he was in the one garage facing the alley between Evans and Roth that smelled of fresh cigarette smoke. He had opened the door holding a table lamp at shoulder level to defend himself against the assassin.

"And we're going to where?" Will asked.

In Denver, they would do more than lay low and contemplate their options. They would test Clay's strategy for toppling Cobb and Howell. It required his brother's help. Damon's too.

Dick was okay with this part of the plan. Phase 2 gave him pause, however. As he now reminded Clay, "We are not going to California till the other thing's fixed, not till we hide out for a while. We need to save ourselves before we save anyone else. Put your own oxygen mask on first."

Will was there because he wanted to be there, having shoved his way into the car and refusing to budge. "I can help, son. I know I can." He was there, too, because Clay had grown tired of arguing with him to get back out. Winnie had merely sighed, but she at least stayed behind, promising to give Argos the very best of care.

"And there's this," Dick added now, handing Will the iPad that belonged to the Duchaine Chamber of Commerce. On its screen were the names of

American cities and dates from April and May. "Clay's friend," said Dick. "Solstice Blume's at a bookstore. The Creased Page, Denver. She's doing a reading there. They say it's a real city landmark, kind of like our own River Valley Bookstore."

Clay started to ask how he had known, but Dick didn't let him finish the question. "Tour schedule," Dick resumed. "Her agent sent it after rejecting the invitation to do the Third Annual Duchaine Lit Fest. A lot of folks here felt betrayed by that. In her defense, I doubt Solstice ever saw the actual invitation. She probably gets a million requests."

"Funny thinking back on how the Lit Fest took off," Dick continued. "That first one was only to check up on you. I thought it might be good to see where you were on the book."

A road sign read, *Waterloo 30*, leaving it for Clay to extrapolate the mileage to Denver: *A long fucking way still*. Dick took up the speed, and Clay felt glad to not be driving. "This isn't a bad car," said Dick. "Not something I'd collect but—"

"You collect cars?"

"Provided they're sporty and fast."

Clay's sigh did little to hide his envy, yet he couldn't deny his prevailing thought. Perhaps it was simple familiarity, but he felt comfortable in the Volvo's passenger seat, not cramped like he had in Dick's Z car. Screw the assassin, and screw his own past obsessions. Dick could keep his pricey cars. Volvos were perfectly decent automobiles taking their value more from comfort than vanity and speed. If Marta liked Volvos, they were good enough for him.

From the seat directly behind Clay's, Will schooled Damon on the intricacies of old people medical stuff. "Not too long ago, I did one of those Cologuard tests at home. Talk about a crappy day. They say collecting a sample, packing it up, and shipping it out beats a colonoscopy. If that's true, it's not by much. It's faster, sure. Gives you more *quality* of degradation than *quantity* of degradation. That's to say, it's still pretty gross. I won't disgust you with details."

Will, of course, provided the particulars, every last one, from the mildly repulsive to the sewage-gushing-from-the-toilet-in-that-one-scene-from-*Parasite* repulsive. The story should have ended with his placing the box out front for pickup. Hours later, however, a frustrated UPS driver woke him from a nap by ringing the doorbell incessantly.

"I was dispatched to pick up a package," the man blurted before Will could open the door wide enough to see the brown uniform. "There is no package."

"There was," Will assured him. "I placed it out here myself. Right there, by the column. My stool sample. For a laboratory test."

The driver quickly shut Will down. "I get it, I get it." He typed a short message into a handheld device the shape of a parking meter head. "Guess this hasn't been a great day for porch pirates."

"It's called a DIAD," interjected Dick Breitbach. "The thing he typed on. It's a Delivery Information Acquisition Device. UPS sails one super tight ship; it's hard to not be impressed. One of their drivers scratches his armpit, management knows it."

Will followed his tale with a brief survey of the pills he had with him, courtesy of Winnie's remembering to collect them at the last minute. Clay knew these medications. He knew their efficacy, he knew the frequency with which his father-in-law took them, having enlisted Will's expertise to help Pita Wishart murder her father. These were the pills denied Senator Wishart in Paris.

Dick asked Will what strokes felt like, and Will began a story Clay knew well. A beautiful Duchaine morning. Innocent trip to the mall. The next time Clay caught himself paying attention, several minutes in, it was to hear Will say, "From everything I've read, my strokes could have been a lot worse. There are many strange after effects. Like involuntary masturbation."

So much for feeling comfortable. Even with all the bizarre contributions Clay had heard his father-in-law make to conversations over the years, he did not need to hear this.

"Can you imagine?" Will continued. "That would certainly leave one open to the old joke, 'Are you happy to see me or are you masturbating involuntarily because you had a stroke?'"

Clay leaned into the door and pressed his eyes closed while using the palm of his right hand as a pillow. He tried narrowing his focus to the constant numbing vibration: the kiss between tires and pavement that managed to be both fleeting and continuous. But no matter how hard he wished it, sleep would not come. Like debris in a dust devil, too many thoughts swirled in his mind. He could forget any hope he had for rest. Not a fucking chance.

He woke up in Denver just after noon.

***

Clay, Dick, Damon, and Will waited in the musty hallway outside Graham's apartment in Aspen Towers. Damon smoked a Camel. The rundown building had always seemed perfect for Graham if only because skunk-sharp smoke rolled out continuously beneath several doors. At present, no marijuana fog came from Unit 57, leading Clay to assume his brother wasn't home. Or passed out on his floor. Either way, there was no choice but to wait.

To reach the fifth floor, they had come up an elevator designed more for freight than passengers. Moving pads protected two sides while the back metal wall looked dented and scratched. In the half hour since, no one else had stepped out. Leaning back against the wall, the three Duchainers sat on a thin, worn carpet that had probably never been cleaned, Graham's slumlord preferring inadequate lighting to hiring cleaners. Dick played games on the iPad. Will asked, "Where are we again?" then closed his eyes and quietly snored.

At ten past four, the elevator door opened with a ding and out stepped Graham Turner. Upon seeing Clay, he dropped his 7-11 Slurpee. "Jesus, bro." As Clay, Dick, Damon, and Will rose to their feet, Graham bent down to rescue the large plastic cup, leaving a bright red igloo he didn't seem to notice. "You scared the shit out of me. You don't do that to cannabis enthusiasts."

"Mr. Jewell?" he said now, followed by "And ... am I supposed to know the rest of you?"

"Dick Breitbart," said Dick, extending his hand. "President. Duchaine Chamber of Commerce."

"Damon. Damon Debbitts."

Ignoring his brother's confusion, Clay said, "We've got a crisis. I met that monster who tried pushing you onto the railroad tracks."

"You're shitting me, bro."

"He *was* looking for me. Mistook one brother for the other. Yesterday, when he found the right one, he came very close to killing me. I'm hardly out of danger now. Think you could make a call for me?"

Graham nodded and took a slug from what was left of his Slurpee.

"Shit," Clay added upon realizing the only place he had Randolph's number was a phone he'd tossed into the back of an open-top semi. "No, wait. I know where I can find it." Seconds later, he was sitting before Graham's PC on a soft but lumpy office chair. Scrolling past old emails, Clay found the number in a Sent Message to Marta from the summer before.

"You gave her his number?" Dick asked from over his shoulder.

"Stupid, right? But it didn't really matter. He called her first before she had her chance."

Clay coached Graham on the call he was about to make, then relinquished the chair to his brother. "Ready?" he asked before dialing the number.

Interestingly, Randolph answered on the third ring.

Clay heard only Graham's half of the exchange that followed. "This is Graham Turner, Clay's brother, and anyway, my brother just called from a payphone in Milwaukee... No, no, I didn't know they still existed either. He said someone was trying to kill him but the attempt was a no-go. I guess Artemis Cobb and someone named Ben Dick Howell were behind it. They're planning to put it all at your feet... No, really... I *am* serious as shit... You got it, setting you up... The assassin's already talking... Oh sure, you're welcome... If he calls again?... Sure, I'll let you know." Graham ended the call.

"Great job," said Clay. "I'll bet that takes care of one problem. Randolph J. Simper does not simply neutralize his enemies."

"Nice," Dick quietly inserted. "*Neutralize.*"

"What do you mean," asked Will who'd been standing quietly in the doorway to Graham's small kitchen, "*he doesn't just neutralize his enemies?*"

Damon answered, "He *negativizes* them."

"Say what?" said Graham.

"Taking their lives is only the first step," Clay said. "Randolph J. Simper murders their reputations, too. As long as you're sitting there, you should Google *ALEX DERRINGER MANDRILL PORN.*"

While Graham did this, Clay asked Dick how long they had before the Solstice reading.

"Day after tomorrow," Dick said. "Tonight, we rest up, order some food. Tomorrow, hiding and resting." Calling after Graham, he asked, "Any chance you know where we can get some cannabis?"

***

It was the most crowded reading Clay had ever attended. Unable to endure the claustrophobia of the Main Events Hall, he and Will had retreated to the floor of the Young Readers room leaving Dick, Damon, and Graham to fend for themselves, stretching and squeezing to land a glimpse of Duchaine's most successful literary export. Having come to appreciate the value of anonymity, Clay felt grateful for the wall that supported his back at the end of a hallway created by towering shelves of vampire romance novels.

According to the flyers he saw everywhere, Solstice was reading from her "newly published national bestseller *A Few Timely Repairs.*" This marked his introduction to her second novel. She had not sent him a manuscript, and he had not reminded her of that promise, or pre-ordered a copy of the actual book online, or gone to River Valley to simply take a look inside it. "Josie Heard kept a journal," Solstice was reading, her words shrunken down, compressed to squeeze their way out of speakers mounted in ceiling panels. "Within its pages existed the world's only mention of the Third Reich, the assassination of Trotsky, the Oklahoma City bombing—"

Clay opened the hardcover copy he had grabbed by the main counter. He read the description on the inside flap. *In this wondrous new book, Solstice Blume takes a classic sci-fi theme and makes it her own. Imagine being the daughter of an eccentric ridiculed for insisting she had been abducted by cat-like aliens two months before her daughter was born. Lorna Heard swore she had viewed magnificent wonders all over the universe, a claim dismissed as impossible. She never backed down, insisting instead, "They know how to crash the barriers of time."*

Imagine standing alone in the knowledge you have somehow inherited this "magical" power. You are standing in the shoes of Josie Heard, a young woman who has no problem squandering her gift on youthful curiosity. She makes day trips in time, a tourist admiring construction sites for Stonehenge and the Egyptian pyramids. She sees woolly mammoths and stegosaurs, attends Oscar Wilde premieres, hears Beethoven improvise on piano.

Now, imagine yourself as an adult, wanting to save a partner riddled with cancer. You wonder if you could turn your gift into a bona fide superpower. If time is no object, do you set off in search of the answers you need?

But don't stop there. Imagine dedicating your power to greater challenges. You wonder if you could "fix history" by stopping its most infamous monsters ... peacefully. What if you were able to get Hitler into art school or land Charles Manson a recording contract? What if you could give Kim Jong-un a haircut that made women like him for who he was and not his abusive power. You understand, of course, such travels come at great risk. Indeed, you could write yourself out of the story by triggering the butterfly effect. Research is required and great care demanded if you are to become history's greatest revisionist.

Perhaps it would be safer to focus on salvaging the future you have already visited. Could you reign in the greed that feeds the "global cancer" eradicating species? Could you find ways to keep the deserts we have now from escaping their borders...

Clay's guess was yes, Josie Heard would accomplish these things and more, just as Solstice probably could if she put her mind to it. He couldn't deny being impressed, and was fairly certain he had not contributed to the premise. The closest memory he could dredge up came from high school. Following their exposure to Birth of a Nation in history class, he remembered her asking, "Too bad someone couldn't have talked D.W. Griffith into choosing a different topic."

The book's dedication was unusually long: *Like many others in high school, I was lucky to have a teacher make a lasting impression on me. One warm spring day, a pair of wasps interrupted Mr. Mathieson's sociology class. They hovered near the ceiling. We stared and cowered. We twisted our bodies as if we could somehow achieve wasp invisibility.*

"Does anyone here not know the meaning of paranoia?" Mr. Mathieson asked. "Because that's exactly what this is. Not only are neither of these wasps going to single you out and swoop down to punish you, but no one in here will be stung at all." Ten minutes

later, he was dead, contorted and swollen on the linoleum floor, the victim of anaphylaxis, extreme bee sting allergy.

Fiction, Clay noted. There had been no Mr. Mathieson.

This is not the teacher I wish to single out, though thanks to Mr. Mathieson, I still harbor an inordinate fear of bees and wasps and pretty much anything with wings. No, this collection is dedicated to the world's greatest English teacher, Ms. Jenni Jensen...

Solstice made it to the end of Chapter Two before stopping, thanking everyone for the thunderous applause, and asking, "Does anyone have a question?"

An audience member supplied an unintelligible one.

Solstice gave it the required amplification: "Why did I become a writer?" She waited a few beats. "On the surface, it's pretty simple. I loved books. I loved getting lost in a story. I loved the idea of writing one. Our teachers made it sound like fun, like it was something anyone could do. Even then, I knew this wasn't true. I knew it took special skills and passion.

"But if I am to be completely honest, I also became a writer for the same pathetic reason everyone else does. As an insecure teenager with no point of reference, I was easily impressed by my own drive and cleverness. It seemed obvious I was the smartest person in the world, and I thought it unfair to withhold this information from others. I needed to prove there really were two kinds of people in the world: me and everyone else. Years later, when I saw how far from the truth this actually was, and how tragic it would have been for the human race had I turned out to be the greatest mind it ever produced, it was too late. I had a writing addiction. I craved it as a habit. I craved it as a quest. I savored how I felt when all the pieces fell into place, creating this incredible, three-dimensional puzzle merging feeling, insight, and beauty. Like a wealthy thrill junkie paying to climb Mount Everest, I had found my summit, and it was as breathtaking in its thinness of atmosphere as it was blinding in its brilliance. I knew I had been granted the most privileged of all privileges. Very few others would ever reach such a place."

"You're saying it's good to be successful?" a muffled female voice asked.

"Yes and no. No, if we're talking in terms of selling books. Yes, if we're talking about writing. That's the success I crave, having a good day at my typewriter."

Clay had never become a writing addict. Although he too enjoyed the occasional rush of watching the pieces fall into place, the past months had revealed him to be nothing more than a circus monkey who knew a few tricks and craved approval. Solstice was the writer here. He was the groveling fraud.

One hour and fifteen minutes later, he first glimpsed her from his place in line, its long, winding train finally down to a few dozen freight cars. Damon stood several feet behind Solstice, clutching his signed copy of *A Few Timely Repairs*.

"I didn't know readings could be that much fun," said Dick, who with Graham, Will, and Clay made up the caboose. Solstice squealed when she saw Clay, then apologized to the fan whose book she was supposed to be signing. "Sorry, *To Marian and Helen*? Is that right? Once I mess up, it's there forever."

The line advanced slowly, its sluggishness exacerbated by fans wanting to share their own heartfelt tales.

"My Aunt Sue went to school in Madison. Could you sign this copy for her?"

"I like that you have a cat in the story. I have one, too. Mitt's his name. They sure get up to some mischief at times. Like the time Mitt unrolled a whole roll of toilet paper. You can use that in your next book if you want."

Once the last hangers on stopped hanging on and The Creased Page handlers had repeatedly thanked Solstice, she suggested to Clay they retreat to a nearby bar. Not too surprisingly, the Banger Grill turned out to be noisy— muddled music and boisterous talk—this to Clay's preference. He didn't need eavesdropping strangers.

No one seemed to recognize Solstice. "This is what I love about being an author," she said. "I'm not even slightly famous. I meet the people I want to meet and everyone else leaves me alone. The Creased Page counted between 400 and 450 listeners tonight. Sounds impressive till you look at the math. What's the football team here in Denver? The Broncos? What if they sold a total of 450 tickets to one of their games? Would anyone consider that a success? And admittance tonight didn't cost a dime."

Dick and Will started their own conversation. Damon went to the bathroom. Solstice leaned in close to Clay's good ear. "I know what happened at your reading."

"You do? How?"

"YouTube. Facebook."

"Oh right. The podcast."

"I felt bad for you. Sounded like you got stuck in a hole and panicked."

"You mean, plagiarized."

"Well, yes, that too. But how? You couldn't have memorized 'Measurable Accumulation.'"

"I had run out of paper at home before the reading and so printed my excerpt on the back of the copy you'd sent. But I never, never, never intended to read from it."

"It sounded like it went over well. I was pleased with that. It was strange Jenni never mentioned it; I sent her a copy."

"We both know the real reason I ended up reading your piece," Clay said. "It's that I'm the shittier writer. My novel was not going over well."

"You're a *different* writer than I am. Your crowd was not listening well."

"No. They were listening."

When Solstice asked, "Why are you here?" she got a more interesting answer than she could possibly have expected.

"A professional hit man?" she said. "Not everyone gets that kind of attention."

Clay told her they were headed to California to rescue Marta.

Solstice said she was traveling the opposite direction but would do anything to help. Her next reading was 20 hours and 600 miles away. Kansas City.

"Perfect," Clay said. If someone would take a picture of the two of them together at the Banger, she could post it on her blog with the caption, *Look who surprised me at my K.C. reading.* Were the Consortium and Randolph using every means at their disposal to try and track Clay's movements, and they most likely were, this could give him some cover.

Dick walked away from the table, disappearing into the crowded main area while looking at his phone. When he returned it was to say, "Regarding California—"

"Listen, Dick, this is my wife we're talking about. If you're afraid to go, I'll get there alone."

"I thought writers were supposed to be good at listening," Dick said, shaking his head. "We *are* going to California." With his head still in motion, he explained that Cessna had called to say they just might be safe. "My former investment partners are all over the news in Duchaine."

As Cessna had learned from KDUC's nine o'clock news team of one, Artemis Cobb and Benedict Howell had indeed been negativized. The MBA classmates were returning to Wisconsin on one of Randolph's private jets when, suddenly, they declared their desire to start new lives in the western wilderness. As if paying homage to D.B. Cooper, they donned parachutes and exited the plane. The pilot claimed that by the time he figured out what was transpiring, it wasn't safe to leave his post.

According to FBI agents investigating the deaths, Cobb and Howell had set their phones to show slides of black-on-white male sex, as well as StripOff photos of Adolph Hitler, Donald Trump, and Vladimir Putin. This would have been strange enough, the agents noted, even had the pair not chosen to deplane over Idaho's most notorious white supremacist compound.

"Perhaps Howell and Cobb thought the nude shots would help them," Clay suggested. "After all, what you just described has got to be every white supremacist's secret homoerotic fantasy."

"All the more reason to kill them," Dick said before surprising Clay with some genuine insight: "The way I've always seen it, we crush in others what we can't control in ourselves."

The prospects worsened for Howell and Cobb when the Sons of White America searched their fanny packs to find copies of the Koran, vintage *I'm With Her* bumper stickers, and a complete *Tales from the City* collection from Armistead Maupin. "What happened next," according to federal agents, "wasn't pretty."

"You've got to give Randolph credit for one thing," Clay marveled. "He doesn't dick around."

"Your solution worked," Dick said. "We should be safe now."

"From them anyway," Clay said.

Three young women, uniformly thin and attractive with their hair in various Day-Glo colors, approached the table. "Excuse our intrusion, Solstice, but we just loved your reading tonight. Could we get a photo with you?"

Dick took the photo, then used Solstice's phone to get one of her with Clay. "I'm driving the Tesla again," she told Clay as Dick approved the results. "I've come to realize it's my editor's tax write-off. Her authors drive it a few months each year, rest of the time it's hers. It's parked at my hotel just down Colfax. Want to see how fast it goes?"

The words Clay heard coming out of his own mouth sounded both strange and strangely true. "I'm over cars."

"You love cars."

"I have graduated from re-education camp and am no longer a covetous materialist. What I want now is Marta, my dog, and our home. Kids would be great as well. I'd have no problem hearing, 'He's a third-rate writer but a first-rate dad.' Hell, it can go on my tombstone."

"You've got your priorities straight," Solstice said. "But I can't lie. As much as I miss Cyndi and Arthur and our beautiful Alden, it's hard being a new parent. It's good to have an occasional break, good to be reminded there's life out here."

She handed him her phone to show off Alden. "You know me, Clay. I've never wished you anything but the best. You find Marta and make things right. And try not to get assassinated. You need to hold out for that tombstone."

At that instant, the building shook, accompanied by a tornadic roar that was quickly replaced by desperate screams. Violently parting the doors, a woman burst through the front entrance. At least Clay thought it was a woman; she was coated in dust as if she'd been power sanding drywall. A second ash-gray person entered. "They…" The man coughed three times. "They blew up the flipping bookstore!"

"We've got to get out of here," Dick said, placing his hand on Clay's shoulder.

Damon handed Solstice a business card. "I'll get Clay to share your email. Send you that book I was telling you about back at the store."

Solstice seemed to give Clay a look of, *So this guy really is with you?*

"You take care, Clay Turner," she whispered before kissing him on the forehead.

"Post that photo," he told her. "But place it here. Location: Denver. Add some tag like, *My author friend Clay Turner, possibly the last time anyone saw him, minutes before the deadly Creased Page inferno. I sure hope he's okay.* I know you'll come up with better wording."

Outside Banger Grill, the soot-covered world seemed divided between people who gawked at scenes of destruction and people who darted in randomly chosen directions like spiders escaping shoes. Staring past them, Clay noticed something very strange, something at odds with the tall stranger shouting, "They used drones! The fucking terrorists used drones!" He saw a Chevy panel truck, circa 1970, parked in a bus stop. From inside its cab, a young woman and man seemed to be assessing the chaos.

Pita and Jared—the way Clay had imagined them. Feeling an Arctic blast cut right through his bone, Clay asked his brother, "What businesses adjoined The Creased Page?"

That's when everything went black.

Chapter 33
⌘

THE TRAPPINGS OF WEALTH

Marta had been told she could leave anytime. A limo would whisk her from Randolph's "Desert Paradise" to the Los Angeles airport or any destination of her choosing. She had only to ask.

"Bullshit," she muttered to herself while pacing her palatial bedroom cell. She was a prisoner, the prisoner of a very strange prince in a very strange castle, holding her captive through some twisted spell. That and a lot of locked doors. When she had called Randolph's bluff by asking to leave, she was told arrangements would be made "after you have a few days to rationally review your options." When she asked again, she got more excuses. It was a situation requiring a brave knight, one who would soar across the moat on the back of a mighty steed and ambush guards to rescue a distressed maiden. So where was Clay? Where was the husband who once loved her enough to risk everything and now couldn't be bothered to answer his phone?

She wondered if she still loved him. The answer had to be yes: the changes, as prolific as they were, had come too recently to completely redefine him. But there was no denying the depth of Clay's fall—and why it so depressed her. Marta understood her need to be surrounded by ambitious people. She understood why she had married one, and understood the need to be ambitious herself. It had all come from living with a wonderful, loving father who was admirable in every respect except for his inability to wake himself from a decades-old dream he had never properly pursued when he had the chance.

Her husband couldn't have been more irresistible, more attractive, more *sexualmente*, than when he first got serious about finishing his novel. God, how she wanted him then. How she'd taken pride in being his partner. In the months following, these feelings faded at the same speed her focused, determined dreamer shape-shifted into an overweight thrift store shopper looking for slip-on shoes to match his sweats.

How far underneath was the husband she loved?

She tried calling him again, got *Clay here, sorry to miss your call, you know the rest, wait for the beep*. Why didn't he answer? But maybe the question to ask was why *no one* felt inclined to answer their phones. She was getting three bars of service. Her texts received answers, at least from her parents. But try to phone out and she got only recorded messages. Still, still, still… there was simply no way Randy's technology could be sophisticated enough to create the illusion her own phone was working while keeping her, in reality, incommunicado. *Por supuesto que no.* No fucking way. Or was there?

Was a certain software pioneer monitoring her every attempt and making sure she received only voicemail responses—amazingly authentic voicemail responses that could well be fake—for her efforts? And then there was the weird incident that involved finding a landline phone in a large, empty room. Unable to reach Clay, she'd left a message for their neighbor, inserting a plea for help in Spanish—the best code she could devise under stress. She had barely finished when that strange, mole-like man appeared in the doorway. "Do we have a problem here, Martha?" Jesus, why couldn't anyone here call her Marta? "This room really isn't fit for company. Perhaps I should escort you back to your wing."

"*Mierda*," she now whispered to herself. "My marriage needed a reboot. If nothing else, Randy sure provided that. Now where the hell is my husband?"

***

Randolph loved his California mansion, and now, with Marta under its impressively high ceilings, it had become a true home. She seemed so happy, so different here. If she seemed a bit restless from time to time, who doesn't when starting a new life?

Even so, he already knew there would never come a time she fully wanted to leave. Sure, they might visit Duchaine years into the future; she, after all, had family there and he still maintained a duplicate mansion. But at the moment, there seemed no point. Only fools walked away from paradise, even for short vacations. Just wait till she discovered the three Olympic-size pools, two inside and one on the roof. Just wait till she found herself winning every game in her own full-size bowling alley, competing against, unknown to her, professional bowlers paid to play well but not too well. Just wait till she discovered the techno-magic of their palatial bedroom suite. He had already retired Virtual Martha in anticipation of that evening. Three's a crowd—wasn't that the cliché?

Had Randolph believed in fate over his own unparalleled ability to manipulate circumstance, he might have shared some of the credit for the way events had transpired. What were the odds of Clay Turner attending Solstice's reading in Denver that night? Or that misguided domestic terrorists straight out of Clay's novel would set siege to the bookstore while he was in it? Perhaps *Explosive Love* had not been so ridiculous after all.

He turned on the wall-sized screen and watched Marta pace her suite like a contented zoo animal. This was home. This was family. This was good.

***

As luck would have it, Clay had chosen the perfect place to pass out from stress and exhaustion. The stretch of East Colfax that fronted The Creased Page and Banger Grill had temporarily become the hub of Denver's paramedic community. Mistaken as a victim of the blast, he received prompt, thorough attention. The medics gently revived him, poured him full of bottled water, and got him to the car. "You're gonna be alright, son," one assured him. "Any other time, we'd take you to ER but we got others needing it more."

Clay still wondered if he had hallucinated the Jaredmobile, his confusion not helped by the knowledge Graham shared with him in the Volvo. In addition to the stoner landmark Wax 'n' Wane Record Store, the Creased Page blast had leveled a family planning clinic and an "exotic pet store" that had been protested of late for selling puppies to medical labs.

Had two of the lunatics overreacting to his Lit Fest podcast been, to borrow something his useless father used to say, completers and not just complainers, a pair of copycat killers determined to take fiction and make it real? Had Jared and Pita come to life and, freed from the restraints of Clay's plot development, found something to blow up together?

Chapter 34
⌘

THE SIEGE

The Concert to Save Marta began promptly at 10:00 AM Pacific Daylight Time. With the bass guitar and portable amp Cessna Breitbach had brought with her on her flight, Will Jewell was performing "Karma Train" for the second time ever in public. It also marked the first time the one-hour piece was performed solo on bass and vocal, a possible first for any rock opera.

The song began slowly, tentatively. *"There is no question that love is the answer."*

Listening on a digital walkie-talkie supplied by Dick, Clay recognized the melody from *Poison Apple*, the Seminal Pig album so admired—and apparently copied—by Will. But no sooner had Clay thought this than the rhythm picked up and the stolen melody gave way to one much simpler, one that lacked, among other distinguishing characteristics, melody:

You might want off but you'll remain.
No one leaves the Karma Train.
Even stops in old Duchaine.

Clay did concede his father-in-law possessed a fairly decent singing voice even if this discovery achieved the effect of adding yet one more misplaced brushstroke to confuse the overall picture. He also couldn't help but note that Will knew a lot of words that rhymed with train.

You'll come to know its stark refrain:
Pleasure for pleasure and pain for pain.
We all ride the Karma Train.

"Is that music?" Randolph J. Simper mumbled to himself. Leaning on the 24K gold rail near the edge of his one-acre roof, he was thoroughly focused on the elderly man playing an oddly shaped guitar in the middle of his private road. The strange man stood close to Randolph's security gate, also crafted of genuine gold. Had he chosen a spot any closer, he'd be feeling the burn of the Total Lockdown Acid Spray that had already taken care of countless desert creatures who, in lacking a basic understanding of property rights, had made that very mistake.

The air was hot, the sky overhead both crisp and blue. Because he looked east, sunshine blanketed Randolph's face. "I'm so sorry, sir," Mason D. Barrell said while handing him a pair of binoculars. "We know how much you despise the presence of music. The local sheriffs have promised a swift response. They also apologized profusely for letting such a travesty occur in the first place. I think they're worried about the future of their salary enhancements." Barrell now held Randolph's wide silk umbrella by its hand-sculpted ivory handle, tilting it at the precise angle required to fully shield Randolph's face and arms from the sun.

"I meant my question in a literal sense," clarified Randolph. "Is? That? Music?" He held the binoculars to his eyes to closer inspect the lanky quasi-musician in the thrift-store sweater vest. The man matched Randolph's image of an aging drug addict, the kind who'd buy meth from the awful characters in Clay Turner's awful novel.

"Whatever it is," Barrell concurred, "it's not very musical."

"Could I borrow those?" asked Marta as she appeared beside Randolph. She was escorted by Ford Diesel who might as well have been handcuffed to her the way he maintained closeness.

"Diesel," Randolph snapped, "what is going on here? I don't recall inviting our guest outside."

Turning toward Marta, "I warned you to stay inside. My Chinese software competitors are attempting a raid. They commenced with some form of auditory torture."

"*Papá!*" shouted Marta, catching Randolph completely off guard by the scope of the revelation. He felt it necessary to remind himself that his choice of genetic conduit for maintaining the Simper line had been adopted at birth. There would be none of that strange singing hippie in future generations.

"That," he said, "is your father?"

"*Sí!* And here he is to take me home!"

"As I once alerted the Green Bay Board of Education after receiving an insulting settlement offer, we will see about that," said Mason D. Barrell.

"Indeed," said Randolph. "Mr. Diesel, could you please escort our guest back to her quarters?"

"Papá! I'm here!"

"You really would be much safer inside," Randolph told her. "These confrontations can get very dangerous."

Marta didn't budge. "Papá! Papá!"

Like the lion shakes his mane
An old man shakes his cane
But he's shaking it in vain
'Cuz no one can detain
The train that's gone insane,
The train that pulls the chain
From Mexico to Maine.

Randolph had no sooner ordered, "Get me a bullhorn," than he was greeted by a fresh unpleasant sight, that of Clay Turner pulling up on a motorcycle. The kickstand went down. The author dismounted, a bit clumsily for someone who'd been riding a motorcycle for years, and took his place standing to the right of the "Karma Train" engineer.

Seconds later, Randolph felt the bullhorn's handgrip slipping into his fingers. "Your electronic megaphone, sir," said the sycophant lawyer to make sure he got credit.

Randolph promptly raised it to his mouth and squeezed the power trigger. "Could you please stop that intolerable racket?" he commanded Marta's eccentric, possibly certifiable father. "Real music would be insufferable enough, but this!"

He was ignored. The rail-pounding "Karma Train" kept chugging along, thundering through the canyons and tunnels of his brain.

You may think that you'll abstain
But, dear sir, I must explain
Black ain't white and sun ain't rain,
And we all ride the Karma Train.

A lengthy instrumental passage followed. It consisted entirely of two bass notes alternating in a slow see-saw pattern.

"Clay!" Marta shouted. "I'm up here! *Aquí!*"

Randolph tried reclaiming his focus. "Give it up, Clay," he suggested via bullhorn. "You lost this war before you even realized it was being fought."

"The war has just started," Clay shot back.

"You need to let her go."

"*You* need to let her go."

The idiot author waited a few beats before adding, "You know, Randy, there is one more thing you might find of interest. I'm not Clay. I'm Graham."

The roof shook beneath Randolph's feet. Had someone penetrated the fortress? How? His security was foolproof. What in the name of sanity was happening here?

"My brother's over there." Graham pointed left, the opposite direction from the actual breach. Even from this distance outside the front security gate, Graham could see Randolph and his entourage looking about in confusion. Then came the spray of fireworks: Cessna Breitbach's colorful contribution to the Siege of Simper Manor. This was followed by an earth-rattling explosion. Graham saw smoke, then flame. The weird Chamber of Commerce dude had done as he'd promised, calling in favors garnered from serving on Chamber outreach committees and "breaching the perimeter."

"War's over my ass," Graham whispered to himself.

***

"We're in!" shouted Dick. "This dog hunts!"

There had been no alarm or acid spray or drone attack. Damon Debbitts had taken care of that for Clay. One day before, he drove deep into the desert to find a man he had interviewed by phone for *War*. This was Randolph's original Head of Security, the man who made Randolph's products and homes impenetrable. Fired three years ago, he had since outsmarted a series of creative murder attempts—and told Damon everything he knew. Late last night, while he and Damon shared Camel cigarettes and Jack Daniels shots, Bucky Buckminster Gates had deactivated Cousin Randy's Safe Zone.

Clay still had trouble believing the highly sophisticated armed assault vehicle he rode in belonged to Palm Springs' police department. Dick had called it an MRAP or Mine-Resistant Ambush-Protected Truck. Painted black and boasting mechanical battering rams that apparently worked quite well, it had been built at a price of $500,000 for the second Iraq War and looked like something out of a grim future—or a dystopian film about that future. "Courtesy of Homeland Security," Dick had explained. "They give cops all kinds of crapola. Even back home. The Duchaine P.D. could invade a small country."

"Or just do battle with the neighboring police states."

"It was nice of them to loan it to us. Same for supplying the Gold Wing—probably confiscated from some suspected drug dealer. Guilty verdict not required. As for it all winding up in our hands, connections are always a good thing to have. Now cover your ears."

Dick fired off an earsplitting round. "You've got to admit this is kind of fun." Clay sat directly behind the Chamber president, leaning left to see out the slim strip of a windshield. Not that he saw much beyond dust and smoke.

He climbed out first in a room the size of Duchaine's snowplow garage. Through the lingering veil of smoke, he saw debris amidst treasures that included Egyptian sarcophagi, fully intact brontosaur skeletons, and an incredibly detailed reproduction of the "Mona Lisa." But there was no time to wonder if Randolph had somehow acquired the original without the world knowing. Having heard from Graham that Randolph and Marta were on top of the building, Clay led Dick out of the room and up the first set of stairs they found. Six flights later, he emerged on the roof to see fireworks, additional smoke, and the amazing woman who, if there was any good left in his life, still wanted to be married to him.

"Honey," he shouted, "cavalry's here!"

"But no one ordered it," Randolph's bullhorn declared from the center of a large, bright circle that must have been the helipad but now looked more like a target. "You're not wanted here."

"Am I, Marta? Am I wanted here?"

She spoke but Randolph drowned her out: "I think you should focus on the fact that she *is here*. This to me would seem the most important detail. What is it you lawyers say, Mason?"

"Possession is nine-tenths of the law," said a man with the face of an overweight toad.

"Hardly an alibi for keeping someone against their will, unable to use their phone to reach the outside world," Clay said. "And you should definitely come up with something stronger for the serial murders."

"What the hell is that?" Randolph asked him. "It doesn't look like much of a weapon."

"This?" Clay smiled. "It's my lucky tambourine, of course. A treasured gift from my father-in-law, once played by the Twentieth Century's premier tambourinist."

A string of police cars, augmented by armored vehicles even more freakishly futuristic than the MRAP, now squealed up the road. Technically outside their jurisdiction, and more used to Coachella drifters, the Palm Springs and Indio police departments had come to demonstrate the strength of Dick Breitbach's connections.

Brother Graham now appeared on the mansion's sprawling rooftop, emerging from the smoldering chaos accompanied by two Hispanic women with long dark hair strangely similar to Marta's.

"Traitors," shrieked Randolph. "Which of you opened the gate? Your parents signed agreements with me. I own you."

"*Libertad!*" spat one while her companion declared, "*Hemos estado esperando el día en que la policia meustran aqui arriba,*" which Clay impressively understood to mean "We've been waiting for the day the police show up here." The middle fingers pointing upward as they turned toward the stairs demanded less in the way of translation skills.

"Sir!" shouted the toad-faced man approaching Randolph. He held a pistol over his head, erratically waving it the whole time. "It's not too late, sir! I can get you to safety!"

A fireball flew straight at Randolph like a thunderbolt from Zeus. It hit the side of his head and knocked him down screaming. Cessna had somehow managed to aim a powerful bottle rocket directly at a target, a feat Clay would have thought impossible, not to mention incredibly risky. What if she'd hit him or Marta or Dick?

Cops poured onto the roof. Several soon hovered over Randolph, competing to see who would handcuff the writhing, sobbing software titan. Others questioned Randolph's associates. Marta and Clay ran toward each other. Just as they met and embraced, causing the tambourine to jingle excitedly, a cop in full body armor dangled a gun by their heads, asking, "Somebody lose this?"

Clay gestured toward the man-toad, now doing his best to slink away.

It couldn't be more plain
That with each loss and gain
We must ascertain
Again and again
We all ride the Karma Train.

Clay could hear Will playing a crescendo, all on one string of the bass. Then *bomp, bomp, bomp, bomp, bommmmmmmmmmmmmmmmmmmm*. The "Karma Train" had come to a stop.

Chapter 35
⌘

EN LA CENA DESEADA
(DESIRED AT DINNER)

From his comfortably padded seat, Clay could see the river valley stretching north to Lock and Dam #8. He saw the bridges and the harbor, the marina and City Island dog track. He was dining at the table once reserved for Randolph J. Simper, "the use of which in perpetuity" had been one tiny part of the legal settlement against StripOff International. In the aftermath of a disastrous criminal trial on sixteen counts of murder and kidnapping, Randolph had agreed to very generous terms in the civil suit, much as the Howell and Cobb estates had shown little resistance to paying a hefty price for "a failed assassination attempt on Duchaine writer and one time classmate of Solstice Blume, Clay Turner."

The families of Randolph's assassination targets owned what remained of StripOff International. To receive compensation, they had divided and drained the company's assets, stripping these off, so to speak. To compensate the rest of humanity, the business ceased all marketing and development efforts. It became an empty shell, existing only to legally block others from creating similar products.

Marta didn't mind letting Clay enjoy the best seat at Jacques D's. Her new office on Mt. Carmel Road from which she managed their assets and charities looked out upon that same gorgeous valley. She enjoyed her responsibilities and took pride in the fact these fully required an MBA. It gave her pleasure to know that she and Clay had more security than either could once have imagined and that the same held true for Winnie and Will. She also derived a great deal of satisfaction from managing the William Jewell Don't Ignore Your Dreams Foundation. The generosity of the non-profit's Deserving Artists Grants in Literature and Music attracted many hundreds of applications. These were advances with no hidden clauses.

On some Sundays, Clay and Marta were joined at Jacques D's by friends Dick and Cessna. The Breitbach's World at a Discount Travel Agency was thriving, a distinction verified by a recent full-page profile by Jenni Jensen in the *Lamplighter*. Dick no longer worked for the Chamber.

On other Sundays, Clay and Marta brought her parents with them to brunch. Only the weekend before, over a veritable five-star vegan feast, Will had announced he was working on his first new rock opera in decades. "Think *Tommy* with zoo animals." He surprised Clay even more by saying, "Duchaine is a small town in many ways. Did I ever tell you I knew Fillmore Banks in high school? I've sometimes wondered if I inspired that musician in *Big Fish*. Even though I never left and returned home, there are lots of similarities, some way too big to be coincidental. I'll probably never know, of course. I couldn't get past page five of that book."

On this bright May morning, Clay and Marta had the table to themselves. She, as he had learned only days before, was pregnant with their second child—Winnie was watching Daniela for them—and was every inch the glowing cliché. No mimosa's this morning, only chai tea and a protein rich Thai omelet.

Inspired by her choice, Clay had selected Vegetarian Pad Thai, despite the appeal of the restaurant's Meat Free N'awleans Jambalaya. If anyone could find a complaint with Jacques D's these days apart from the long wait times inspired by the artificially low prices subsidized by Clay and Marta, it was the difficulty of choosing from the amazing selection of gourmet vegetarian splendors that owed their existence to the permanent hiring of Randolph J. Simper's ex-chefs. Randolph had beseeched the court to let him employ them at country club prison but, per Mason D. Barrell's press briefing at the trial's end, "The state has cruelly deprived my client of the standard of nourishment to which he is both entitled and accustomed."

In a private conference, per Clay's sources, the judge had declared this a moot point. "Who the fuck said you were going to a minimum security prison?" he asked Randolph in front of his supersized legal team. "The jury just found you guilty on eight counts of murder."

Jacques D's owed its vegetarian bent to a vet tech as much as it did Winnie Jewell. Watching the first eight minutes of the world's most intense DVD-R had been enough to persuade Clay to surrender his niche in the food chain. Now, restaurant critics for the *Chicago Tribune* raved about the Midwest's Best Meat Free Menu, though they were less than passionate about beetloaf. They also questioned the presence of long johns on the menu. Indeed, they questioned the very *nature* of long johns, inadvertently showing their true ignorance when it came to genuinely world-class cuisine.

Marta noted with a smile that Clay could have been graduating from Duchaine Community College that very day as a welder had he initially hung in more than two weeks.

"For the millionth time," he admitted freely, "I was wrong about embracing a pursuit free of subjectivity. I, Clay Elliot Turner, am consigned to an ambiguous universe where black and white sometimes blend to form gray. Worse, I am a full-blown writing addict."

Since acquiescing to that self-knowledge, he had written every day, breaking up the drudgery by walking a much thinner version of Argos. His agent waited on revisions, while perfecting a bona fide strategy for getting *Explosive Love* the best deal possible. Her advice had been to make the book *more* controversial, drawing more on recent, real world incidents. She had secured an introduction from a prominent Connecticut Bishop who believed extremism in the defense of most any cause was probably just an excuse for bad behavior. Not really the message of *Explosive Love*, but Clay would take all the cover he could get.

A second collection of essays and stories was already on the fall schedule for Small Packages Press. Better yet, Marta had declared herself a fan, telling him over and over how much she loved each new invention.

One of these she liked so much she made everyone they knew read it. This was the cute piece, the embarrassingly cute piece editor Leigh Cooley (the real Leigh Cooley, not some Randolph J. Simper toady) kept calling "the closer." Argos claimed authorship for "Reflections," having culled its two dozen short paragraphs from the journal he had apparently kept forever. *My favorite time is when I go for a walk and all the world is bright and clean and strangers smile as they pass and I take a big dump on the church lawn and watch Mr. I Make All the Rules Human Being bend over to bag it up like he's some freaking Untouchable.*

Damon Debbitts was more guarded in his praise for *Travels with Argos*, especially in regard to the "gratuitous scatological humor of 'Reflections' and 'A Bad Day for Porch Pirates,'" but was helpful nonetheless. Damon had also asked, "Apart from changing his name to Walt, did you change *anything* in your father-in-law's story?"

He and Clay regularly swapped pages in their writers group. Clay took pride in his contributions to *War*, now scheduled for publication by Krumpf and Sons, winners of a real, multi-party bidding contest. No longer a novel, the book had become a "hard biting exposé." It had shed its "working title" as well, the publisher rebranding it *Exposed: Randolph J. Simper and the StripOff Debacle*. As Clay often quipped to Damon, "Your cousin should have given you the five-million you wanted."

One exceptional evening, Solstice sat in with the writers group, boosting its membership a full 50%. The meeting, of course, had been timed around her visit—and a chance to preview chapters from her "next one." This time, Clay couldn't recall contributing to the premise, which had gravity mysteriously disappearing and Americans calling on their collective strength to outlast The Dropdown. They ate incessantly, "maintaining" to counter each new loss of gravity with a gain in personal bulk.

Clay suggested a plot tweak she called "helpful." Damon advised she cut back on commas.

Her visit also gave Marta and Clay the chance to meet Cyndi and beautiful three-year-old son Alden, while providing Solstice an opportunity to lavish thoughtful gifts upon Marta and Daniela. Damon, looking quite comfortable in his expensive designer sweats, witnessed the first minutes of this from a red couch shared with a sleeping Black Lab. Damon excused himself when his chauffeur arrived.

"Your long john, sir," a waiter interrupted Clay's thoughts.

"Go ahead, honey, *disfruta*," said Marta of her husband's one remaining indulgence (not counting the occasional package from Colorado). "I've watched you lose 27 pounds, and you get plenty of exercise, not all of it from walking the dog."

"Last night." He nodded. "It was amazing. I woke this morning wondering if I'd dreamed it."

"Life's good," she said, her smile providing further corroboration.

"*La vida no es algo que damos por sentado*," he agreed. "It's not something to take for granted."

Clay knew she was grateful he had translated this now that *she* was the one trying to keep up with *his* Spanish. He also knew she was pleased to be reminded he still took his twice-weekly Spanish class at Duchaine University seriously. Their visit to Honduras had turned into a second honeymoon, more than giving her the graduation present she wanted. "First time," he liked to remind her. "We're going back when the kids are older. Your birthplace is Central America's second largest country. We barely scratched the *superficie*."

She often made it clear she loved this husband of hers who stuck with goals and beliefs. As well she should have. Appreciative of life's smaller blessings, Clay Turner was a man who could live without fine clothes, rare Scotch, and expensive cars, and indeed showed restraint in material self-gratification. It was Marta, in fact, who had surprised him with the birthday Tesla parked in their new four-car garage alongside the aged Volvo and Gold Wing that still got plenty of use.

Watching a rabbit chew grass outside the window, clearly oblivious to the danger that always lurks just out of sight, Clay recalled a conversation that had taken place atop a communications tower some two years before. "We all make mistakes," said the hit man now serving nineteen consecutive life sentences for his own collection of blunders.

Fortunately, Clay now understood, we sometimes make the right ones.

ACKNOWLEDGEMENTS

Once again it pays to have smart friends. Thank you, Mark Kjeldgaard, Bill Jones, and Erika Ericksen, for suggestions both excellent and essential. Thanks, too, to Timothy Hillmer, Robert McBrearty, Mark Lamprey, Lucia Lamprey, Bob Ebisch, Marian Hoffman-Ting, and the selfless volunteers of the Duchaine Historical Society.

CPSIA information can be obtained
at www.ICGtesting.com
Printed in the USA
LVHW020601061220
673432LV00006B/1277

9 781952 085031